"Only a fool averts their eyes in the face of the enemy."
The Broken Second Valkyrie
Rusalka Evereska
A second-generation Valkyrie at Hamburg base.
An outstanding Valkyrie, a skilled soldier, and a
beauty who can be rather inflexible.

A proud third-generation
Valkyrie
Natalie Chase
The mastermind behind
the Miracle at Lamia
Alejandro Ostley

Rusalka's friend and
second-in-command
Xenia Stingl
The free-spirited and
innocent First Valkyrie
Amy

"—To comrades."
"—To comrades."
Rusalka reluctantly joined Alejandro's
toast. If it was to comrades, to the dead,
then she had no reason to turn it down.

The sisters who hold the key to defeating the pillars
Claudia Brafford
Has been living a life on the run with her younger sister after the pillars destroyed their homeland.
Shirin Brafford
Claudia's reliable younger sister. Are her sudden fainting spells a portent of fate?
She kept singing as their flight continued—across the green earth, through a world being drained of life, beneath a sky dominated by light. Running on and on and on until the end of the world arrived.
—Never knowing whether their flight or the world would end first.

A cool and collected new blood
Leili Haltija
The offbeat big hitter
Alma Conturo
The fiery tip of the spear
Lisbeth Crown

The glue of the squadron
Natalie Chase
The Broken Second Valkyrie
Rusalka Evereska

"—Claudia Brafford, reporting for duty."
Wearing the IPO uniform, Claudia saluted Rusalka. It was a proper air force salute, proof of the pride she had for her father's and grandfather's service records.

Tappei Nagatsuki

Illustration by

Takuya Fujima

New York

Warlords of Sigrdrifa Rusalka

Tappei Nagatsuki

Translation by Dale DeLucia
Cover art by Takuya Fujima

Yen On
150 West 30th Street, 19th Floor
New York, NY 10001

Visit us at yenpress.com
facebook.com/yenpress
twitter.com/yenpress
yenpress.tumblr.com
instagram.com/yenpress

First Yen On Edition: April 2022

Library of Congress Cataloging-in-Publication Data
Names: Nagatsuki, Tappei, 1987- author. | Fujima, Takuya, illustrator. | DeLucia, Dale, translator.
Title: Warlords of Sigrdrifa Rusalka / Tappei Nagatsuki ; illustration by Takuya Fujima ; translation by Dale DeLucia.
Other titles: Senyoku no Sigrdrifa. English
Description: First Yen On edition. | New York, NY : Yen On, 2022.
Identifiers: LCCN 2021060086 | ISBN 9781975335137 (hardcover)
Subjects: LCGFT: Fantasy fiction. | Light novels.
Classification: LCC PL873.5.A256 S4613 2022 | DDC 895.63/6—dc23/eng/20211220
LC record available at https://lccn.loc.gov/2021060086

ISBNs: 978-1-9753-3513-7 (hardcover)
978-1-9753-3514-4 (ebook)

10 9 8 7 6 5 4 3 2 1

LSC-C

Printed in the United States of America

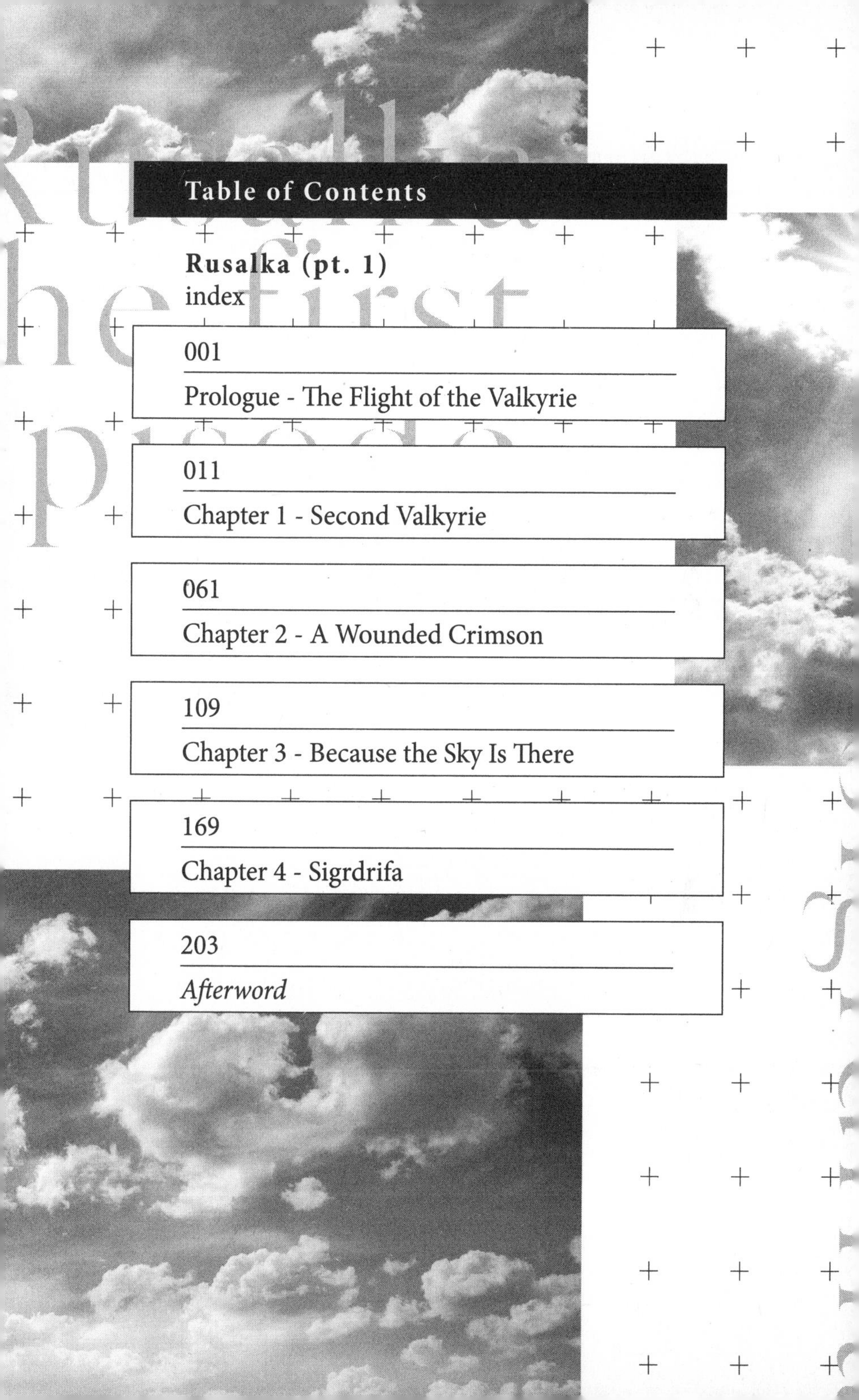

Table of Contents

Rusalka (pt. 1)
index

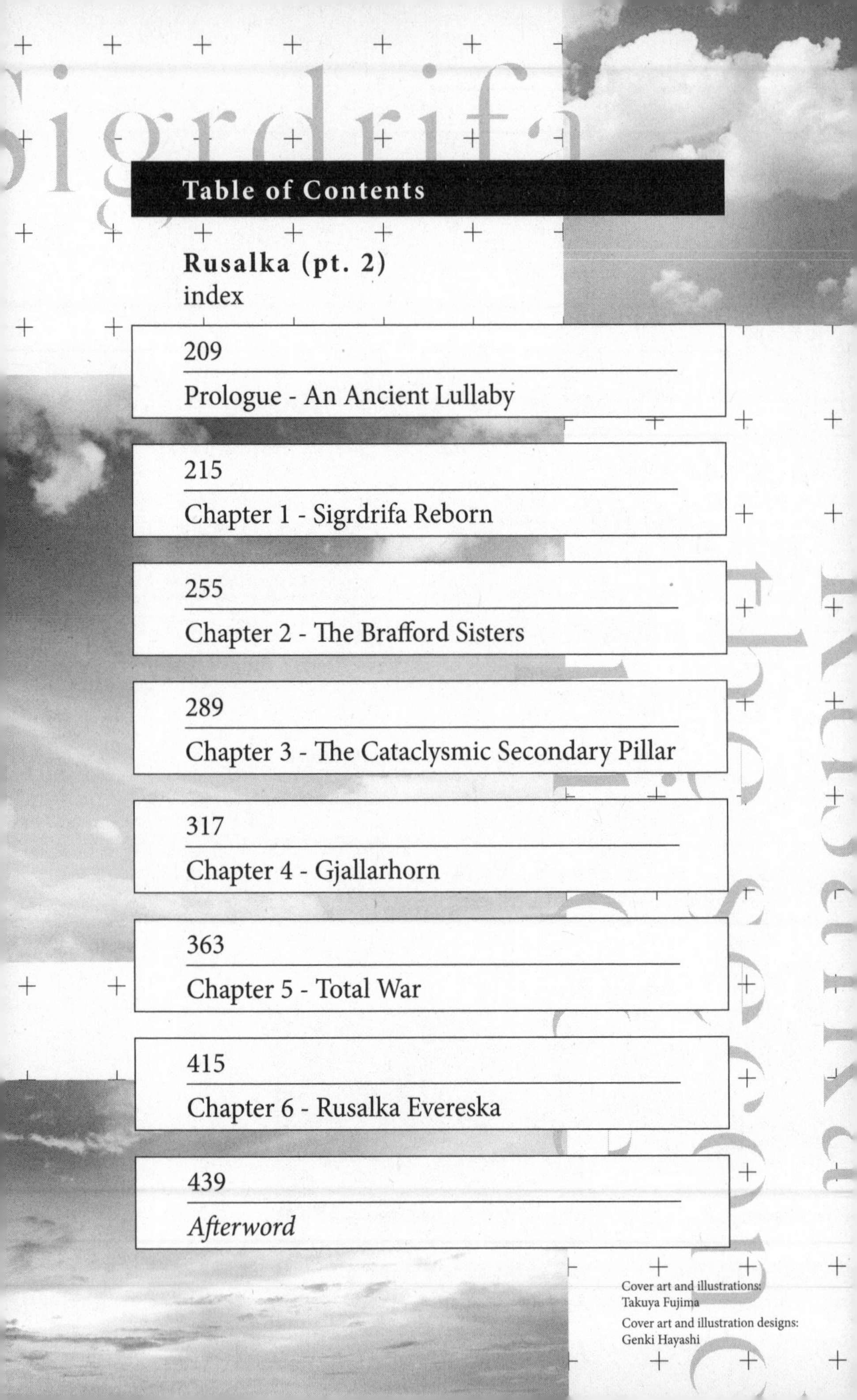

Table of Contents

Rusalka (pt. 2)
index

Cover art and illustrations:
Takuya Fujima
Cover art and illustration designs:
Genki Hayashi

Rusalka (pt. 1)

Prologue
The Flight of the Valkyrie

1

—There was a rumor being whispered around the army.

"Have you heard? Word is the brass has some new secret weapon they're bringing to the front."

"______"

"You mean the rumor about them having some kind of ammo that will actually work on those monsters?"

"______"

"Yeah, apparently there's some new groundbreaking shit that's supposed to turn the whole war around."

"______"

"Is it true there's some crazy ace who took down one of those massive pillars of light?!"

"______"

"Come on—don't leave us hanging here, Rusalka."

Rusalka blinked as her colleague leaned in front of her, looking into her almond-shaped eyes.

"...Hmm? Me?"

She suddenly noticed that all her squadmates sitting at the same table in the mess hall were staring at her. Under their collective gaze, she reviewed everything she had heard so far.

If I recall correctly, it was—

"Let's see. Am I understanding correctly that you're asking what I think about your starry-eyed pipe dreams?"

"Damn! You're not wrong! And I get why you'd call it that, but still!"

"Well, yes, it would certainly be a dream come true. In the end, they're just dreams, though."

"Absolutely no mercy, this woman!"

She had actually been trying to be considerate in her own way, but their reactions were not quite what she'd hoped for.

There seems to be a morass of misunderstanding that is difficult to overcome between men and women. However, I cannot give up on trying to establish mutual understanding. My comrades in arms deserve nothing less.

"I will continue my attempts to mingle with everyone."

"And what's with that condescending tone...? Who died and made you God?"

"Gettin' all full of yourself just 'cause you're good-lookin'...!"

"And what's this 'attempt to mingle' crap? I sure as hell didn't hear you while we were shooting the shit just now."

"My apologies. It didn't appear to be a conversation worth pursuing, so I focused on eating instead," Rusalka said simply.

"Why, you little...!"

Her squadmates looked taken aback by the biting sarcasm. But her expression softened as she shook her head.

"That was a joke."

"Oh... Wait. What part of that was supposed to be funny?"

"If some new exotic weapon were actually developed, it would undoubtedly be wonderful. I wouldn't mind if it were new ammunition that worked against the enemy, some groundbreaking equipment that will change everything, or even an ace pilot."

Counting on her fingers, she listed off all their examples of wishful thinking in a quiet voice.

There was nothing wrong with giving voice to dreams. They were the manifestations of goals or wishes that people wanted to come true.

"———"

Listening to Rusalka's lyrical recitation, her colleagues fell silent as they grimaced. The silence wasn't unpleasant. It was simply that everyone around the table was feeling the same thing.

Their dream was shared by everyone who stood on the battlefield—even all the command staff and generals staring up at the skies hoped for the same thing.

Whether it was a new secret weapon, some fruit of human wisdom that actually worked against their enemies, a devious strategy that could turn the whole war around, or some unbeatable ace pilot who had no need for trivial tactics—

"______"

——Because without a miracle, the fight against the pillars of light would have to go on.

2

In the year 2019, humanity confirmed the sudden appearance of inexplicable pillars of light, and they were forced into war against the mysterious hostile entities.

Despite its beautiful, illusory appearance, the first pillar appeared on a mountain range in northern Europe and devastated the entire region. It absorbed the very life force of the land, an effect that came to be called "draining," transforming the area into a barren wasteland in a gradually expanding radius centered around the pillar.

Faced with an unknown presence that was scarring the mountain range and causing all nearby plant and animal life to wither away, humanity did not immediately respond.

There was an initial delay in grasping what exactly was happening, and an overly optimistic view of the situation allowed the desolation to continue spreading freely until, finally, the team that had been dispatched to investigate the pillar became the first human casualties. That was when people began to recognize the real danger.

And once humanity took decisive action to eliminate the pillar, the situation changed dramatically again.

When the pillar of light came under attack, countless creatures poured out of it.

This wave of hostility crashed into the advance force that had assembled to destroy the pillar of light, and they were annihilated instead, forcing humanity to rethink how they would deal with this new enemy that had appeared on their doorstep.

However, after that flash point, the pillar of light's sphere of influence began to grow faster and faster, accelerating dramatically. Before long, the draining effects encroached upon parts of northern Europe where many people lived, forcing the residents to either leave or perish.

And then, as if mocking the refugees who had no choice but to flee their homes and abandon their homelands, more pillars started to appear all around the world, ravaging the lands wherever they emerged. Even when whole armies were deployed to stop the relentless advance, the hordes of monsters spawned by the pillars would easily crush whatever forces the humans had arrayed against them.

Eventually, these hostile alien entities were collectively termed "pillars," and it became common knowledge that the eponymous monoliths themselves were cloaked in some unknown energy field that was completely unaffected by all conventional ordinance, making them the ultimate enemy for humanity, which had focused much of their war-fighting capability around explosives and physical projectiles.

Countless lives were thrown away as more and more land was contested and then ultimately ceded in a hopelessly lost cause that could barely be called a fight. Before long, more than half of the world's standing armies were destroyed, and increasingly younger recruits were being sent to the front lines.

—Humanity was unmistakably wending their way down the path to extinction.

"—Please respond. Someone. Anyone."

She called out over the radio, but all she got in return was a crackling noise.

The annoying, unending chatter that normally came from the rest of the squadron was gone. Their lame jokes and crude humor and the hints of concern for her had been swallowed up in a sandstorm of static, almost as if they had all just vanished into thin air.

"——"

Sky-blue eyes scanned the battlefield from the cockpit.

Here and there in the dark, overcast sky, she could see flashes of red—proof that some were still fighting. Proof that survivors were still trying to take down the heartless enemies filling the air even though their weapons didn't work.

It was also a display of futile resistance that would only end in more deaths.

"—Ngh."

She bit her lip, the taste of blood quickly filling her mouth.

The people she had shared meals with in the mess hall, people who had waved to say *See you on the other side*, people she trusted with her life and who had trusted her to watch their backs in the air...were nowhere to be found.

Rusalka was flying all alone in an empty sky.

Not a single word of regret or sympathy came out of her mouth. She was certain that crying out their names in grief now would only insult the memories of her brothers in arms.

Paying no heed to what was crashing through Rusalka's heart, her instrument panel lit up: The enemy was coming. Blood still dripping from her lip, Rusalka tilted the control stick and tore through the skies.

In the blink of an eye, a bullet of light shot straight at her, just grazing her plane's frame. The shock of its passing caused the wings to groan. Following quickly after, an alien silhouette cut across her field of view.

"______"

——That *thing* flying through the sky could only be called an anomaly. At a glance, its star-shaped body almost seemed to belong in the sky, but that was just a trick of the light. And just like the creature it resembled, the enemy's true nature was that of a cold-blooded killer.

The countless tubular limbs sprouting all over its body would never let go once it latched on to its prey. But if its quarry kept its distance, the flying oddity would spray its target with an unending stream of those inexplicable bullets of light. There was simply no way to escape being knocked out of the air.

Frankly speaking, the creature's mysterious defenses utterly nullified humanity's conventional weapons—that was the implacable phenomenon that transformed a seemingly unwinnable situation into one that was truly hopeless.

——That was the essence of the unknown hostile entity known as a pillar.

This implacable enemy currently had free rein in the air. The ones she had seen almost looked like flying starfish. They were about as large as a single fighter jet, and the gray sky was filled with dozens of them challenging the pilots who had taken flight in defense of their homes and loved ones. The starfish were cutting through the air and effortlessly downing planes one after another.

It was practically death on an industrial scale—truly a nightmare come to life.

"What is sea life doing this high up...?!"

Her voice rang out, cursing the outrageousness of it all as she spun into a barrel roll, pushing her fighter to the limits to weave past the enemy, narrowly escaping certain death.

But that would not be enough to guarantee she stayed alive. Her deft maneuver had merely been a short deferral—nothing more. She would be forced to keep going all in with her life on the line again and again to have any hope of surviving.

"———"

Looking around as the combat area devolved further into chaos, Rusalka suddenly realized she could not see any more fighters in the sky. The scattered flashes of resistance that had been visible just seconds ago were all gone, and now Rusalka was truly alone.

The world fell silent, and the color seemed to drain from her vision. It almost felt like she was collapsing in on herself, until all that remained was her heart and the turmoil that lay within.

The things she saw and heard seemed meaningless, but she could still hear her heart beating.

"———"

In that moment, Rusalka was little more than an organ dutifully pumping blood.

She could not hear her instrumentation's emotionless alerts, nor could she see the storm of light projectiles zipping all around her. Even if she had heard the warnings or seen the attacks, she had no way to control her plane, since she had no arms or legs. There was nothing more she could do.

All that was left was to wait for the fatal blow to land, and then her pulse would finally sto—

"—?"

Just as she had accepted her impending doom, something clawed at the edges of her consciousness.

A faint, tickling sensation pulled Rusalka back to reality. After staring death in the face and accepting it, only to be pulled back to a merciless reality, Rusalka struggled to breathe, barely able to keep her head above an unbearable deluge of emotions.

But while enduring that hell, Rusalka realized something.

She could hear a broken transmission crackling through the useless static coming from her radio. It was a voice, repeating the same word over and over.

Before she even registered what the word meant, she unconsciously repeated it to herself.

"—Valkyrie."

——Immediately after that, light swept over the battlefield, bringing devastation in its wake.

"______"

No natural phenomenon could have caused that.

Light did not have mass. Without some very particular conditions, it could not destroy physical objects, either. And yet, that light had shattered everything in its path and punched right through those starfish that acted like they owned the skies.

Reeling from the unbelievable sight, Rusalka could only moan weakly.

Slicing through the storm of incoming rounds, that light broke through the implacable enemy head-on. Its machine gun roared as it passed the starfish, shooting bullets clad in shining light directly at the starfish's body. An instant later, the bullets struck home, and the pillar exploded in a burst of light.

The pillar's shields, which nullified all conventional rounds, had been shattered, and the resulting devastation sent its body flying backward.

A split second after that, another odd scene occurred: Something sprouted explosively from inside the pillar, revealing vibrant green leaves as a tree pushed out of it. The starfish lost its form, as if being devoured by a tree that had grown inside its body, quickly disappearing as the light faded.

It was the annihilation effect that was rumored to happen when a pillar disappeared. That had been a rumor, though, barely on the level of an urban myth, since there was no official record of it ever happening before.

Taking down a pillar was simply that miraculous a feat. Rusalka had never seen it before herself, but there was no mistaking it.

After all, she wasn't seeing it just once or twice. After watching it unfold dozens, maybe a hundred times, even the most hardheaded would understand.

Both the truth of the annihilation effect rumor and just how singularly powerful that light's power must be.

"______"

Gulping as she became little more than a bystander, Rusalka realized another thing.

That shining streak was not just light. It looked like a ball of light, but it actually had the shape of a plane. And when she recognized the shape of that plane, she was dumbfounded.

Flying around in cutting-edge fighters, Rusalka and the others had never managed to achieve anything. If the plane that so badly outshone all their efforts had been the crystallization of humanity's greatest minds working together on some brand-new machine, then that would have been easier to swallow.

——Instead, the light's true form was an ancient propeller-driven fighter.

"______"

Feeling like she was still in a nightmare, Rusalka was little more than a scarecrow gliding through the sky. A pebble resting impassively on the field of battle, staring out at the fighting going on around it.

The streak of light charged through the sky, turning pillar after pillar into trees. She could see the trees plummeting to earth and taking root in the lands ravaged by the draining effect.

It was as if life was returning to the withered landscape, like dry, cracked ground thirstily drinking drops of water.

"*—Valkyrie.*"

She heard someone's voice through the radio.

It was not just one person's voice breaking through the static, either.

"—Valkyrie. Valkyrie."

"Valkyrie. Valkyrie! Valkyrie…!"

She could hear more and more from all around her. It sounded like it was coming from far off in the distance, as if it were not just one person or a group of people but the rumbling voice of all humanity.

"—Valkyrie! Valkyrie! Valkyrie!"

"______"

Her eyes grew damp as the voices pummeled her ears, and her heart stirred.

The light arced across the sky, creating trees as it obliterated the hated pillars.

Far and wide, a burning hope spread, bringing a brilliant light to the overcast battlefield. Seeing that, Rusalka's sky-blue eyes were wide open.

It was something the army had kept hidden—

It was something capable of penetrating the loathsome pillars' defenses—

It was a display of tremendous combat prowess capable of turning the tide—

It was an ace pilot capable of shattering the pillars one after the other—

"______"

It was the dream her comrades had longed for, the wish of all the command officers peering up at the skies from the ground.

That dream, and with it humanity's hope of crushing the pillars and stealing back the skies, had come true.

And the name of that hope was—

"—Valkyrie."

In her role as observer, Rusalka murmured the word to herself just once.

3

On that day, humanity recorded what could be called their first victory against the pillars.

It was a battle where many soldiers and officers had fallen, but their first hard-fought victory gave hope to a humanity that had been cowering in fear of the pillars' menace and was an achievement to be commemorated as the opening shots of their counterattack.

—Valkyrie, maid of the heavens, who would save humanity.

That battle was the Valkyrie's trial by fire.

It was the first of what would become a glorious string of victories, a fresh page engraved in history and people's memories.

And it came to be memorialized and celebrated as the Ride of the Valkyrie, while the lives lost that day were ignored—

And the name Rusalka Evereska was merely listed as one of the pilots who happened to make it back alive that day.

Chapter 1
Second Valkyrie

1

Her memory of that moment was still shrouded and distant.

"I see, so you're the one who ■■■■■ ■■■ ■■■■."

The fragmented words seemed almost unbalanced. The reason for that was probably the calm tone of the voice that carried the weight of many years even though the speaker gave off the opposite impression.

The owner of this striking voice looked young, childish even, but his gaze was like that of a parent inspecting his child.

The dissonance of it all shook the emerging Valkyrie out of her reverie. Her thoughts dulled, almost like she had a fever, even as her eyes welled in exultation.

This was truly a mysterious place.

It was not particularly hard to see, and yet, there was an unmistakable darkness all around them. It was unclear what she was standing on, but she instinctually knew there was solid footing under her.

She was kneeling in front of a spring—Mímisbrunnr.

It was a well that possessed a divine power and could grant special blessings. Just moments ago, she had gathered some of the cool, clear water in her hands and paused briefly before raising it to her lips.

She could feel herself being released from human limits as each trickle of water passed her throat.

People metaphorically described the process of becoming a Valkyrie as rebirth, but in truth, it may have been literal as well. Or perhaps it would be more accurate to say it felt like being granted a new set of wings, something that simply could not be perceived with a human body.

She wouldn't go so far as to claim that she had transcended humanity, but she could confidently say she had crossed onto a different path from the rest of mankind.

"The path you will walk from here on will assuredly be a difficult and noble one."

A youthful, austere voice addressed her as she knelt and endured the aftershocks of her rebirth.

"You will likely be forced to see and experience a great many terrible things and more than your share of wretched nights."

"——"

"There shall come a time when you will even hear the sound of your own heart shattering as the unbearable losses continue to pile up."

"——"

"I will not tell you not to grieve. Nor will I tell you not to give in. That is a right afforded to every one of you."

No one would condemn her for open tears or faltering legs.

The young, steady voice gradually seeped into her body, circulating inside her like lifeblood, spreading through her arms and legs before returning to her heart.

Even after countless nights of loss and heartbreak, even if her will failed her and she fell to her knees, she was not alone.

She would never be alone again.

That truth and reassurance gave her strength, helping quell the trembling in her arms and legs.

"——"

"Can you stand, my child? You imbibed the well's water even knowing what an arduous and painful path awaited you. I shall grant you new wings, my beloved daughter."

As soon as she heard that solemn declaration, a large presence appeared directly behind her. Turning to see what it was, she opened her eyes wide in shock.

——Behind her was a crimson machine, a fighter plane wreathed in heavenly light.

Her breath caught at the sight of it as the voice spoke again.

"Deus ex Machinas. A Valkyrie's wings and the only means for humanity to resist the pillars."

The voice—the voice of God—proclaimed it so.

"Spread thine wings and take to the sky, Valkyrie—I, Odin, grant thee my divine blessing."

2

"—Are you Rusalka Evereska?"

"______"

When she heard her name being called, she turned around to look back down the hallway.

She sported long silver hair reminiscent of a snowy field under the full moon and sharp sky-blue eyes. Her tall and slim figure made her look like a model, but her chest was a bit on the large side. The neatly starched and pleated uniform she had on accentuated her bust, and the black stockings covering her long legs all the way up to the tight skirt of the uniform were a reflection of her meticulous nature.

She was a beautiful soldier—that was the impression most people had of Rusalka Evereska, and it was the most superficial appraisal possible. Her clear sky-blue eyes and icy beauty made an impact on anyone who saw her.

"Yes, I am Rusalka Evereska. And you are?"

"I knew it! Yeah, you look exactly the way they described you."

"You've heard of me before?"

"You betcha!"

This girl, who seemed like the exact opposite of Rusalka, nodded cheerfully.

Her golden-blond hair flowed over her shoulder down to her waist, glimmering like she was the embodiment of sunny cheer. She was shorter than Rusalka, and her figure was thinner and less curvy. At the same time, her face was sweet and charming, and more than anything, her crimson, ruby-like eyes were mesmerizing.

Her outfit was both gorgeous and seemingly easy to move in, which suited her bubbly personality. But for better or worse, they were on an army base, so it looked incredibly strange.

A girl who was the embodiment of peacetime and an unrefined, utilitarian army building. Everything about it was mismatched, and the resulting dissonance was so intense it was hard to put into words.

Of course, in recent times, extenuating circumstances were all too common, given the state of the world. Even so, there was still a responsibility to maintain a proper uniform on base whatever the situation, and Rusalka always heeded regulation dress codes.

Because of that, seeing this girl, who looked so out of place, made Rusalka deeply uncomfortable. While she wrestled with that internal turmoil, she mulled over what the girl had said before posing her own question.

"May I ask who gave you my description?"

"The bigwigs here. I've wanted to meet you for a while now, and I finally got my chance. Turns out, you really do look a little bit naughty in uniform, just like I heard!"

"N-naughty?"

"Mm-hmm!"

Rusalka had tried to deal with the girl in good faith, but her expression unconsciously darkened after hearing that upsetting impression.

No matter how you looked at it, being called "naughty" couldn't really be taken as a compliment. At the same time, she couldn't detect any hint of malice in the girl's cheerful expression.

There was a chance she had misspoken. If so, then it was just a simple mistake.

"Ummm, what do you mean by 'naughty'?"

"Huh? Isn't it obvious? The way your uniform around your breasts is practically bursting at the seams, plus that black stockings and tight skirt combo—it's almost lewd."

"______"

Apparently, it had not been a misunderstanding. She had meant every single word.

Rusalka closed her mouth at that. All of a sudden, the girl gasped, and her eyes went wide.

"Ah! I didn't mean it in a bad way! You thought I was bad-mouthing you, right? That's not what I wanted to say! If anything, I'm honestly a little bit jealous!"

"And what do you mean by 'jealous'…?"

"As in, like, envy or admiration, a sort of 'I wish I could be like that, too' feeling! Please believe me!"

The girl's expression changed in the blink of an eye as she stepped closer to Rusalka and desperately pleaded her case. Overwhelmed by the intensity of it, Rusalka simply nodded.

"Oh, thank goodness. There are just so many beautiful people who don't have any self-confidence. Or maybe they just like it that way… Well, I like that, too, I guess."

The girl folded her arms and started murmuring to herself. Rusalka didn't really understand, but she instinctively straightened her back and held her head high.

"Apologies for getting flustered. So then, what business did you have with me?" asked Rusalka.

"Eh?"

"You said you asked about me around the base. And you mentioned you've wanted to meet me for some time. However, I'm afraid I still don't really know why."

"Ah, right. That makes sense. After all, I'm the one who wanted to see you."

Saying that, the girl laughed at herself a little and then rapped herself on the top of her head. Her expression softened as she peered up at Rusalka with her red eyes.

"Rusalka Evereska—you're the top of the list when it comes to Second Valkyries at this base, right?"

"………And who are—?"

"My name is Amy."

The girl interrupted the question, pointing to herself as she said her name.

Rusalka considered the name for a moment, but it didn't ring any bells. Sensing her confusion, Amy broke into a smile before continuing.

"Even if you don't know the name, you should recognize me by another title, right? I'm the First."

"—!"

Hearing that word whispered playfully, Rusalka dramatically shot her eyes open. She could see her shocked expression reflected in Amy's crimson eyes. Amy stuck out her tongue mischievously.

"I'm the First Valkyrie, Amy. I've been wanting to meet you for a long time now."

3

"Since I'm always moving from front to front, I never get a chance to make any friends. I'm zooming to all these different places, but I never get time to sightsee, either."

"Oh, I see."

"So I'd at least like to be able to get along with the other Valkyries on the base."

"Oh, I see."

Rusalka continued replying with vague interjections as Amy beamed beside her.

Her first impression of Amy was that she was a cheerful girl. And she talked quite a lot.

Lively and talkative, a face that comes alive with emotion: She's like the exact opposite of me.

"Ah, am I talking too much about myself? You can tell me if it's getting annoying."

"No, you're still in a tolerable range."

"That's a little too honest!"

"Just kidding."

"Huh? Oh, you were kidding! …Wait, which part?"

Amy looked uneasy as Rusalka remained silent.

Just a little payback for that upsetting remark earlier. It isn't just a reaction to finding out she's the First Valkyrie. I think.

Naturally, she didn't suspect Amy was making it up. Not out of any faith in her character, of course. The reality was much simpler than that. To pretend to be the First Valkyrie would be the same as betraying all humanity.

"—It's not really that big of a deal, honestly."

"Huh?" Rusalka was taken by surprise.

"Sorry, sorry. Don't worry—you didn't say anything out loud. It's just… Well, I thought I could tell what you were thinking by the look on your face. It was just a hunch."

"…A hunch? I have a bit of a reputation for keeping a straight face."

Rusalka's neutral, impassive expression was an unchanging constant. Even her family had commented on it with some regularity since her childhood.

She was aware of the issue and was always trying to make a change, but it was rather difficult for her to achieve much progress on that front. The other Valkyries in her flight had all panned her efforts, too, with reviews like "Your face is scary" and "You're so stiff" and "Your jokes are really bad."

"What does that last one have to do with anything?"

"You can tell that much just by looking at my face? …Does that mean my efforts are starting to bear fruit?"

"Uhhh, sorry for getting your hopes up, but it's probably just that my intuition is really good. I wouldn't get too confident in yourself there."

"What a magnificent opportunity I've been afforded. It is not every day someone comes along and tells people *not* to have confidence in themselves…"

Despite her best efforts, Amy's careful response left Rusalka crestfallen.

Amy just kept smiling as she amusedly watched Rusalka touch her cheeks, trying to physically soften her expression by massaging the muscles in her face.

——Currently, Rusalka was showing Amy around the base. Right after their initial meeting, Amy had asked for a tour, saying she wanted some help, since she'd just arrived and didn't have a guide. After quickly confirming with the base commander, Rusalka had agreed to take her.

"Asking command was one thing, but I sure didn't expect you to give me the full-body pat-down." Amy seemed bemused.

"It's a necessary formality. No one gets special treatment."

"Mm-hmm. That was definitely a new experience. And I might even have enjoyed it a little bit. But…" Amy paused, giving Rusalka a bit of side-eye. "You could have just said you'd be my guide on the spot. You sure like keeping people in suspense."

"That doesn't sound like a very flattering evaluation… But as I said before, it's required, even as a formality. That said, I do agree it is a rather unproductive precaution..."

"No, not that—you should have recognized me on sight, right?"

She waved her hand, her eyes still challenging Rusalka's innocent response. But Rusalka did not understand what she was implying at all.

Seeing Rusalka's furrowed brow, Amy cocked her head in confusion.

"Wait, did you really not realize?"

"Unfortunately, I still don't. What are you talking about?" Having said that, though, a thought crossed Rusalka's mind. There were certain rumors circulating in the army's ranks. "Are you perhaps referring to the *Monthly Einherjar*, which is supposed to start publishing soon?"

"Ugh... So you know about that, too..."

"It has become a subject of gossip here on the base. From what I've heard, it's supposed to have reports on the conditions of various fronts as well as the attributes and special traits of pillars that can be found in those areas, so that information can be shared more freely within the armed forces."

"Y-yeah, that's right. That's right, but there's also this other thing..."

Amy poked her fingers together and blushed as she turned away from Rusalka. That gesture was overflowing with cuteness, but she could guess why Amy was so embarrassed.

"...I must admit I still don't understand. On an unrelated note, wasn't there also something about there being a gravure shot of a Valkyrie on the front cover?"

"It's not unrelated at all! You're doing this on purpose, right?!"

"—? No, I have no idea what you mean. By any chance, are you the one on the cover?"

"You betcha! I mean, I *am* the First, right?! Doesn't it make perfect sense that I'd be the first one featured for something like that? I'm not gonna lie, though. I definitely got a little too into it, and now that I think about it, this is actually super embarrassing!"

Amy stomped her foot as she turned red. Then she crouched down and cradled her head. Everything about her was constantly in motion, not just her expressions.

There was something about it that Rusalka found charming, like she was an adorable little animal. She held out a hand to Amy, who was a bit preoccupied at the moment.

"Ahhhhh, why did I take a job like that…?"

"Everyone has experienced a youthful indiscretion or two. I think it is entirely acceptable to set aside the moment's embarrassment and forget about it."

"Even if I wanted to forget about it, the photos are still going to stick around forever, right…?"

Taking Rusalka's hand, Amy stood up, staring at her with wide, puppy-dog eyes. Seeing her imploring gaze, Rusalka thought about how to respond.

"That's right. It's amazing what technology can do these days."

"How is that supposed to make me feel better?! …You'd understand if you had to do a photo shoot, too."

"—? If it was a request from military affairs, then I would comply."

"You say that now… Wait, your eyes are dead serious! You really are a soldier to the core!"

"Please don't compliment me too much. It will all go to my head."

"I wasn't complimenting you… I really wasn't, but… I mean…"

Rusalka cocked her head, not quite certain why Amy seemed so frustrated.

Seeing that, Amy sighed, sensing this line of conversation wouldn't get her anywhere.

"Still, judging by that response, I guess you really can't tell just by looking… We're both Valkyries, so I thought it was something you'd be able to tell at a glance. I mean, I can."

"That's…"

"Hmm, that might explain a bunch of the weird reactions I've been getting. That would be a good reason why everyone was like, *What is this girl going on about?* Guess that was my bad."

Amy nodded to herself, looking very convinced, but this was all news to Rusalka.

"You can tell if someone is a Valkyrie or not just by looking at them? How?"

"There's just a sort of feeling, ya know? If you look at me, can you sort of make out a bit of faint light? Do you feel it?"

"...No..."

It was a supremely vague explanation, but after studying Amy closely, Rusalka shook her head.

Amy's smile was dazzling, but that was something lots of people had, and that didn't seem to be what she had been talking about, either. For whatever reason, the feeling Amy had described was not something Rusalka could perceive—and she found that perfectly normal.

She didn't try to push herself. She simply accepted it as is.

That's just the difference between the First and us second generation—

"Well, it's not that impressive to begin with. I guess we can chalk it up as a special privilege for the eldest sister."

"...You have siblings?"

"Yes, quite a lot of them—including you."

"———"

"I mean, I'm the First, and you're a Second, right?" Amy flashed a big smile. "That makes us sisters."

Rusalka was at a loss. She had never thought of it that way before. Her fellow Valkyries were certainly comrades who shared the same fate, but the idea of calling them sisters was something beyond her imagination.

Amy peered into Rusalka's eyes as she reeled from the shock of that unexpected line of thought.

"Feeling embarrassed?"

"I'm astonished...or rather, perplexed? I'm sorry; I can't find the appropriate words. But if I was forced to describe it..."

"Go on..."

"I'm almost certainly older than you, so you can't be my older sister."

"Oh, come on! How unfeeling can you be?" Amy puffed out her cheeks, unhappy with Rusalka's answer. "Think about it. Theoretically, it would be totally possible for you to have a stepmother who's younger than you, right? If we're not talking about blood relations, then you can absolutely have an older sister who just happens to be younger than you. Am I wrong?"

"I don't exactly want to imagine a stepmother younger than me, either."

"I get where you're coming from, but *come on*. Throw me a bone here."

For whatever reason, Rusalka's response was not enough to make Amy stop pouting. But she also wasn't the sort of person to stay like that for long.

"Still, I was expecting that to be a rock-solid finisher. If you're still not convinced, I'll have to think about it some more for later. My family always said I get too caught up in the heat of the moment and get ahead of myself."

"I see."

"I'm not sure how to feel about you accepting that explanation so easily..."

Her expression, which had just returned to normal, suddenly wilted again. She really did wear her heart on her sleeve. Setting aside the matter of whether she got too far ahead of herself, Rusalka would certainly agree that, if nothing else, Amy was a bundle of energy.

Amy's ability to pull other people into her pace was surely a natural quality. But that wasn't why Rusalka had trouble dealing with her.

"Oh yeah, can you show me the hangar, too?" Amy's expression changed as her attention shifted to the next thing that caught her interest.

She was looking out a window in the hallway to where the base's hangar was visible outside. Inside, there were fighters being carefully prepared to take off at a moment's notice as well as—

"—Deus ex Machinas."

Rusalka still felt a sense of trepidation when she uttered that name. This time was no exception.

Lined up next to the fighters loaded with cutting-edge equipment, which would majestically dance through the sky at the hands of highly trained pilots, were ancient propeller planes. They were the only craft actually capable of fighting against the invaders that controlled the skies.

The products of the furious arms race surrounding the two World Wars were practically antiques now. Relics that once ruled the skies in a bygone era. These were Deus ex Machinas, the planes that made a Valkyrie a Valkyrie.

——The same wings of battle clad in heavenly light Rusalka had seen on that hopeless day.

"Right, right. My wings should be getting here soon. And I never really get a chance to take a close look at the other girls' wings, either."

Not noticing Rusalka's shudder, Amy squinted as she looked out at the hangar in the distance. Seeing the excitement swell in Amy's heart as she smiled made Rusalka's chest ache.

But she quickly ignored the pain and nodded.

"...Then I'll show you around the hangar. The rest of the flight should be gathering before long."

"Right, that! I was looking forward to that, too! When it comes to Second Valkyries, your flight has a really good reputation! I can't wait to hear what sort of things you all talk about!"

Amy's red eyes glimmered with open curiosity as she held her hands together in front of her chest.

"This way," Rusalka said before heading out toward the hangar.

She took long, unhurried steps, walking slightly in front of Amy.

——That way, she could hide the expression on her face as her lips moved silently.

"—First."

The whispered word faded in her mouth before it had a chance to slip out.

4

——Valkyries were the flare that God granted humanity to signal the start of their counterattack.

When written out plainly like that, it was hard to ignore the dubiousness of it all. That being said, it was undeniably true that Valkyries were a beacon of hope delivered by God.

Unable to so much as resist the pillars that had suddenly appeared, humanity was forced into a one-sided retreat. Region after region was robbed by the unprecedented draining effect, and humanity had cowered in fear of their impending destruction.

Then, without warning, a being calling itself a god made contact with humanity in their darkest hour.

* * *

"Who am I? Is this really the time for a debate? Who would you have us claim to be? The Count of St. Germain? Grigori Rasputin? Nostradamus? Aleister Crowley? Unfortunately, we are none of them. They were all human, but I, we, are not. We are a god.

"I am the great god Odin. At least one among you has surely prayed to God for help in this, thy moment of need. In response, I shall save the human race. Or more precisely, I shall grant you the means to fight."

The heads of state from around the world were gathered at an international conference to discuss how humanity would deal with the menace they faced when a figure somehow slipped through all the strictest layers of security and addressed them in a solemn, arrogant tone.

It was a wild statement that should have been laughed off, but as the self-proclaimed god said, this was no time for drawn-out deliberations, never mind jokes, and so the gathered heads of state made a shameless but resolute decision—to hear the god out.

And that choice was, without doubt, a heroic decision. Because it was the choice that secured a chance for survival.

The self-proclaimed god, Odin, had granted them the means to challenge the menacing pillars of light: Valkyries bearing the wings of war.

The one thing in the world that could stand against the pillars, and humanity's greatest weapon.

"—The First has gotten pretty attached to you, Rusalka."

Rusalka furrowed her brow as she and her comrade changed in the locker room.

This wasn't a particularly praiseworthy reaction, but she couldn't help it. Lately, this look of disapproval had been appearing on her face with increasing frequency, to the point that even she was getting tired of it.

"There's that crease in your forehead again. I'm sure you have a lot to worry about, but at this rate..."

"I'll become a wrinkly, scowling old lady, I think you said. And also how the face is a window into your personality. I remember."

"Just remembering isn't enough. You have to actually do something about it, too. Sheesh."

The second-in-command of her flight, Xenia sighed as she rested her hands on her slender waist. Her wavy brown hair had the same energy as her strong-willed blue eyes.

Her amazing figure was normally hidden under her uniform, but when she was in just her underwear, it was impossible to ignore, and Rusalka wasn't sure where she should look.

"Are you listening to me, Rusalka?"

"Yes. I really am listening, but can we finish this once we're done changing? Even if we are both women, you shouldn't just stand around exposed like that."

"What do you mean? We already shower together in the same room."

"That is nothing more than us following army regulations."

"Fine, fine."

Faced with Rusalka's entirely earnest plea, Xenia responded perfunctorily, leaning back against a locker without bothering to continue getting dressed.

"Anyway, about the First, it seems like she's going to be staying on the base for a while. Apparently, the plan is to have her work with our flight and see how much it expands our tool kit."

"—. I see. How are the others taking it?"

"Canan and Vicky are all for it. Those two tend to get worked up over whatever the latest thing is, and they're excited to meet the original Valkyrie herself. It's kind of cute."

"Then we should be careful to watch out that the First is not a bad influence on them. Thank you for the warning."

"Don't even sweat it. I am second-in-command, after all."

Xenia's round eyes drooped slightly, making her look almost a little bit lonely. But even so, Rusalka could not respond with anything other than a second "thank you."

With that, Rusalka finished changing and started to leave—

"Hey, Rusalka… Are you okay?"

Xenia called out just as Rusalka was about to leave. For a moment,

Rusalka was stopped in her tracks by the vague question, but she composed herself with a steely resolve.

"You should hurry and get changed. You won't have time to finish your meal."

"I only eat once a day. If I ate more, it'd be impossible to maintain my figure."

"I recommend you eat while you are able. A soldier needs energy to fight."

"Sure, that works fine for you, since it all goes straight to your breasts..."

This time Rusalka left to spare herself Xenia's grumbling. She could hear the sound of her second-in-command slamming a locker in annoyance from the other side of the door.

"Honestly..."

But even so, there was still a cloud lurking in Rusalka's heart. She was mad at herself for being unable to meet Xenia's eyes. It felt like her heart had been slammed instead of the locker.

They had been together for a long time, and Xenia could read Rusalka like an open book.

So much for being expressionless and no one being able to tell what I'm thinking.

The collapse of her poker face was undoubtedly related to a certain recent encounter.

"Ah, finally! Over here, Rusalka!"

A cheerful voice called out the moment she entered the mess hall.

Looking over, she saw someone waving their hand in the corner that was specially set aside—the so-called Valkyrie zone.

The eager voice and sunflower-like smile unmistakably belonged to Amy. She was patting the empty seat next to her, waving Rusalka over. Seeing that, Rusalka sighed ever so slightly and then proceeded to walk right past her.

"Wait, what? Where are you going? Could you not hear me? Heeey!"

"No, I can hear you fine. This is just me pretending to not hear you."

"Huh? Oh, it was just pretending... Wait, why?!"

"Just kidding."

Once Amy was well and truly baffled, Rusalka sat down next to her, as requested. Amy beamed, seemingly satisfied.

"You're late. I was getting tired of waiting."

"Sorry, I didn't realize you were waiting for me… I thought Canan and Victorica were keeping you company."

"I was actually chatting with the two of them until just a little while ago. But then they got a call from someone, so I ended up waiting here all by my lonesome."

Amy broke into a renewed smile as she took a sip of coffee. Rusalka scanned the room and came to a sudden realization.

It wasn't as if the mess hall was devoid of people. They were all simply keeping their distance from Amy. This wasn't because they wanted to ostracize her. It was the opposite. Amy was the most special member of an already special group.

"Times like this are when I feel the loneliest, always flying solo and moving around from base to base instead of being part of a squadron."

"…The way the military uses us Seconds is different from how they utilize the First."

"Meanie," Amy responded crossly before chuckling to herself. "Joking, joking. I know, I know. Solo operations and group operations have entirely different goals, so it makes sense. Though calling it a solo operation makes it sound more important than it really is. I mean…" She paused and gathered her breath before saying, "…I'm the only first-generation Valkyrie in the world, after all."

Rusalka was awestruck when she saw that Amy's smile did not waver in the slightest. She could not begin to imagine the weight behind that declaration.

——Valkyries were the flare that God granted humanity to signal the start of their counterattack.

And the very first one, the only first-generation Valkyrie, was—

"Amy."

She was the only one in the entire world who held that title.

From the first time she met Rusalka to when she greeted the rest of the flight in the hangar and even to when she greeted everyone after formally reporting for duty at the base—she always introduced herself that way.

"I'm the First Valkyrie, Amy."

"You don't ever say your family name, do you?"

That thought slipped out unbidden. Rusalka immediately regretted touching on a potentially sensitive topic.

There was a reason for all things. Rusalka had her reasons for being a soldier, and Amy surely had a reason for not using her family name. But Amy only shook her head.

It almost felt like she was telling Rusalka that she didn't mind. And as if to confirm that, she playfully stuck out her tongue before assuring her, "No need to worry. It's not like I have family issues…or had, I guess I should say."

"Past tense? That means…"

"Ah, my bad, my bad. That was confusing. I don't mean that. My family's doing fine. It's just that it's gotten difficult to see them."

"——"

Amy's long eyelashes obscured her eyes as she looked down, her voice trailing off by the end of her sentence.

It was easy enough to guess what she meant. It all went back to what she mentioned at the start of the conversation: She was the First Valkyrie.

Even in a crisis where all humanity needed to unite, there were still a few instances of people who acted irrationally. To avoid potential incidents and prevent anything from happening to her, the military surrounded Amy with the strictest security possible.

"And the publication of *Monthly Einherjar* would surely cause some controversy," Rusalka concluded.

"I'm not too thrilled to have that being brought back up now…" Amy flashed a wry smile as she scratched her cheek. "It looks like there's still a bit of confusion, though. It wasn't the army that separated me from my family, so I hope you aren't getting the wrong idea."

"Really? Then who…?"

"God."

Rusalka was at a loss for words. That single word cut off all conversation.

Seeing that reaction, Amy lowered her eyes slightly, wearing an expression that was a jumble of mournful loneliness, understanding, and incomprehension.

"The reason I don't use my family name is simple: I offered it up to God."

"To…Lord Odin?"

"Yeah, that's right. The All-father Odin. He said, '*Starting today, you are my child.*' I had to wonder what he was talking about when he came looking the way he did, though."

Amy covered her mouth as she giggled.

Some would have interpreted her remark as disrespectful. Odin had given humanity the strength to fight the pillars, thereby proving the existence of the uncertain and questionable concept of gods.

In other words, Amy had literally laughed at God, which under certain situations could be cause for a court-martial. But there was no way Rusalka could admonish her for it. Having seen how conflicted Amy looked just moments earlier, only an utterly heartless person could say such a thing.

Rusalka let it slide—but that wasn't why. She had a different reason for not mentioning anything—

"…How were you…chosen by God?"

"Oh? Finally showing a little interest in me? Heh-heh, that makes me happy."

"If you would rather not discuss it…"

"Ah, no, no, I'm not trying to avoid talking about it. Don't get me wrong now."

Amy shook her head as Rusalka started to sigh. She set her coffee cup on the table, a pensive look coming over her face.

Rusalka recognized that a complex swirl of emotions dwelled in her crimson eyes. Amy fell silent, seemingly choosing her words with care. Rusalka waited quietly for her to continue.

"………"

"………"

"………"

"Ummm."

The silence continued longer than she had expected, and finally Rusalka could not bear it any longer.

"If it's really that hard to talk about, then…"

"No! It's not that. I just don't know where to start… Uhhh, I mean, it's not like there's that much stuff to cover, but the beginning is complicated; that's all."

"Complicated?"

"Wellll, you know how the first time Odin showed up was at the world conference, right?"

Rusalka nodded.

Odin's first appearance before humanity was at the conference attended by world leaders one year after the war against the pillars had begun.

It went without saying, but humanity had been searching for any means to fight back with their own strength, and prayers to a deity were considered nothing more than delusional and desperate. However...

"When Odin came, he demonstrated his power by producing a Deus ex Machina capable of fighting the pillars and a Valkyrie to fly it. In other words..."

"Me."

"Everyone in the army talks about it like something out of legend."

A god bestowing humanity with a holy lance did indeed sound like it had come straight from a myth. Rusalka couldn't begin to imagine the shock of the world leaders who had experienced it in the flesh. But Amy, who had actually been there herself, simply blushed bright red.

"C-calling it something out of legend is a bit much, don't you think...?"

"Finding out God is real, and then the lance that he presents humanity turns out to be you. What else would you call that?"

"I'm begging you, please stop. I'm dying here."

The embarrassment was evidently overwhelming, because Amy's face was the deepest crimson as she desperately pleaded with Rusalka.

Still, though, with that prelude out of the way, she nudged Amy along.

"So what of it?"

"Um, in other words, it's not like I didn't already know about Odin by that point in time. Of course, I had never met an honest-to-goodness god before..."

"So...?"

"Honestly, I one hundred percent didn't believe him at first."

Amy simmered in shame as she recalled her past mistakes. Rusalka's eyes widened a bit at that, but it wasn't because she criticized her.

It was only natural to be suspicious of someone who appeared out of nowhere and started calling themselves a god.

In the end, Amy had believed Odin and become a Valkyrie, and she was still fighting on the front lines for all of humanity to this day—that was why she wasn't ■■■■■■.

"—. At first, I heard a voice in my dreams. It gradually got closer and closer, and at some point, I started hearing it even when I was awake. And then..." Amy trailed off.

"And then...?"

And then what? She met Odin and somehow ended up reenacting a scene from an ancient legend?

Ultimately, she would not get to continue her story that day.

"———"

Sirens started blaring all over the base, interrupting their conversation.

It was an alarm indicating the pillars of light, which defied the natural law of this world, had appeared inside the base's area of responsibility. The army—or rather, the Valkyries—would immediately sortie.

"That's the scramble order," Rusalka quickly explained.

"Guess we'll have to continue this another time."

Rusalka and Amy bolted straight up and briefly exchanged glances before taking off at a run. They needed to immediately change into their flight suits and get to the hangar so they could sortie. They had to fulfill their duty as Valkyries as soon as possible, to save as many as they could.

So that a Valkyrie would never be ■■■■■■ again.

——The two Valkyries, Rusalka and Amy, ran beneath the wings.

5

Amy was like a different person when she flew during combat.

"———"

Her golden wings tore through the clouds, intercepting the pillars that crossed her path, annihilating them and turning them into plants.

One of the First Valkyrie's specialties was slicing the enemy in two with just her wings, not using her guns at all. An approving whistle came over the radio from someone seeing her pull it off in person.

Common sense would dictate that slamming your plane's main wings into something while in midair was a barbaric act that would just end with your plane going down. But Deus ex Machinas made it a viable option in battle. Due to a divine blessing beyond human ken, the Deus ex Machinas far surpassed the original specs of the planes they were modeled on in every way.

All Deus ex Machinas were based on aircraft dating back to the two World Wars.

Rusalka had heard it had something to do with the weight of history and general recognition by the masses that those old planes embodied the very idea of war machines. It was in essence an article of faith, and trying to assign it some kind of logical value was pointless and impossible.

"Put bluntly, it's love."

That was the explanation she had been given when she received her Deus ex Machina.

There was no telling whether that was the truth or not, but she believed it was likely the former, as the Deus ex Machinas carried their Valkyries through the skies.

They needed to be maintained and supplied just like the planes they were based on, and they guzzled a massive amount of inefficient fuel every time they valiantly soared through the air. But they also boasted unrivaled speed, durability, and offensive power compared to their predecessors—meaning they wielded enough power to combat the pillars of light.

——Amy's Deus ex Machina, a Hawker Fury, danced through the sky as if she owned the vast blue expanse.

Normally, her plane was a silver color, but in battle, it emitted a golden gleam. It was the pride of the girl who ruled the skies, and she flew it nimbly through the swarm of pillars that looked like sea slugs, avoiding their whiplike tentacles trying to drag her down and snap her golden wings.

In the blink of an eye, she wove a spiraling path through the swarm, shooting them down all at once.

"—Splash nine tertiary pillars."

Hearing the report over the radio, Rusalka put some strength into her arm as she pulled on the control stick.

She could hear a voice howling that they couldn't fall behind, followed quickly by another voice saying to be careful and not disrupt the formation. Then there was a third voice, more distant, chiding the first two to calm down.

"_____"

But none of those had come from Rusalka.

The morale-boosting shout, the warning not to get cocky, and the calm comment reining in the others—they all belonged to other members of her flight.

It was a situation where any of those reactions was completely natural, but for some reason, nothing fell from her lips.

"—Ngh."

Gritting her teeth, Rusalka leaned into the turn as her plane banked. A single pillar that was slow to notice their approach came into view. It retracted the tentacles that were facing the other direction to bat her plane down.

"Too slow."

That was her reaction to the tentacles shooting straight at her with the speed of a flying bullet.

Once she climbed into her Deus ex Machina and put on her goggles, her field of view became wide and clear. She even had time to wonder whether she should dodge left or right before the enemy's attacks reached her.

Using that extreme focus, she slipped through the swarm of tentacles bearing down on her, aimed for center mass, then pulled the trigger. Fire erupted from her machine guns with a low, growling rumble.

A faintly glowing geometric pattern hovered around the barrels of her machine gun. The bullets passed through this field and slammed into the pillar one after the other, causing its grotesque form to shudder.

Conventional rounds would have simply been nullified by the pillar's defenses, but it was plain to see her shots were effective.

"—aaaaAAAAAH!"

At some point she had started roaring.

An unfamiliar level of emotion came rushing to the surface as she carved away at the pillar until her guns ran dry.

Her target resembled a living creature, but it was not alive, nor did it bleed. But strangely, it almost seemed to be silently begging for mercy, as if it could feel pain.

Of course, there was no way she would give these invaders any quarter.

"______"

She evaded a collision at the last moment, guiding the nose of her plane to slip past it. The pillar was covered in wounds, but it wouldn't stop moving until it was totally defeated. An unfair ability that ignored the inconveniences of living creatures.

The slug nimbly swung around, flailing its appendages like whips.

"______"

But the three craft following behind her in formation didn't give it a chance to finish its counterattack. The three of them accelerated just like she had, guns roaring as they tore into the pillar from different directions. Its tentacles were sheared from its body, and the holes in its torso became yawning gouges big enough to see through.

"______"

Broken beyond its limit, the pillar's movements suddenly stopped. For a split second, it gave off a faint light, and then greenery started swelling from inside it, forcibly pushing outward until the pillar lost shape completely.

"Annihilation confirmed."

Her lips moved as she watched it fall to earth.

When the plants hit the ground, instead of shattering on impact, they set down roots. Green buds were already starting to sprout around it. A heat welled in Rusalka's eyes.

It was only natural for that which had been stolen from the earth to be returned to the earth.

They could reach now. With the power God had granted them, humanity could finally tear open the necks of their enemies.

So—

"Evereska flight splashed one tertiary pillar."

"______"

She could hear the cool voice of the operator over the radio. The operator did her best to keep any emotion out of her voice as she reported the results of Rusalka's flight to the rest of the forces.

It was hope. She was spreading the hope that humanity's attacks could touch the hated pillars of light.

Even if…

"In addition..."

"______"

"...the First, fifty-three tertiary pillars downed."

...Even if it paled in comparison to the true hope, it was still hope.

6

"You really are amazing, Amy. Even though you're so much younger than me."

"With that big a gap, we can't just write it off as a difference in experience. That was inspiring."

"Wait, wait! Don't rub my head so hard! Argh!"

When Rusalka returned to the hangar after handing in the after-action report, she was greeted by boisterous voices.

Looking up, she saw Amy running around with a red face as two women in flight suits chased her. The tall Victorica, with light-brown hair done up in two buns, and Canan, the cool beauty with a distinctive beauty mark near her mouth.

They were Valkyries in Rusalka's flight, and at the moment, they were engrossed in pursuing the young ace pilot. When they finally caught Amy, they wrapped her in a big hug, patting her head and rubbing their cheeks against hers.

Rusalka was both exasperated and a little bit impressed at how much energy they still seemed to have. It went without saying that the two had also taken part in combat and had only just gotten back from a life-and-death battlefield. Despite that, they seemed to be having the time of their lives.

"Lots of energy to spare, I see..."

"Mrgh! If you're here, then say so, Rusalka! Hurry up and save me!"

Seeing Rusalka, Amy's face suddenly brightened, and she rushed over, breaking free from reaching arms.

"Awww, running away to the captain isn't very nice."

Victorica looked disappointed, but Rusalka wasn't very pleased, either. "I'm not sure how I should react to that..."

"Ahhh, this feeling. It's like coming home..." Amy snuggled closer.

"And you're being excessive..."

Rusalka frowned at both Victorica's complaints and the way Amy clung to her arm. Xenia just laughed as she watched from a short distance away. Rusalka glared at her second-in-command playing the innocent bystander.

"Please don't just stand there laughing. Say something, Xenia."

"What do you want me to say? The only thing that comes to mind is *Our girls sure are cute*. Was that what you wanted to hear?"

"...No..."

Rusalka felt a little uneasy about how well she and her second-in-command understood each other. Still, there was a mischievous glint in Xenia's eyes, so she gathered it was probably a joke.

Right as she reached that conclusion, she suddenly felt a weight on her other arm.

"What are you doing, Canan?"

"Just copying Amy. Is that a problem?"

"Please behave your age."

Rusalka heaved a sigh. Beautiful girls were hanging off both her arms, a situation that would have surely sparked envy in most of the soldiers on the base if they were here to see it. To Rusalka, it was nothing but a burden and uncomfortably stuffy.

"Please don't start clinging to me, too, Victorica."

"Gah! Y-you want me to be the only one left out...?"

"If by that you mean whether I'm rejecting meaningless physical contact such as this, then yes. I am leaving you out, Victorica."

"You didn't have to put it so bluntly!"

Victorica grabbed on to her anyway, pretending to collapse into tears. Ignoring the dramatics, Rusalka dexterously slipped her arms away from the other two and took a step back.

Then she looked at the four Valkyries still in the hangar questioningly.

"Why haven't you left yet?"

Amy was the one who spoke for the group. "Don't scrunch up your face so much. We were just waiting for you to come back."

"For me?"

"Yeah! It was a big win, so we wanted to celebrate together." Amy clenched her fist and held it up as Rusalka cocked her head. For a moment, she was bewildered, but after a brief pause, she brought her fist up to meet Amy's.

Amy's eyes widened a little.

"Oooooh. I'm surprised. I didn't think you'd play along."

"All I did was match you. Is that really so surprising?"

"Sorry, sorry. I just didn't expect you to be so willing. It's kind of the opposite of how you usually seem."

Rusalka eyed Amy dubiously as the girl waved her hands and smiled innocently.

From their first meeting and the confusion where Amy seemed to think that *naughty* was somehow a compliment, she had said quite a few things that made Rusalka want to register a complaint somewhere. Xenia and the others glanced at one another with wry smiles.

"Huh? Did I say something weird again?" Amy was a bit worried by their reactions.

Rusalka spoke up to assure her. "It's a rather common occurrence, so I don't mind."

"Eh? Really? So you get that a lot from other people, too?"

"To be clear, I was talking about you."

"Wait, what?"

Amy cocked her head even farther as Rusalka relaxed her shoulders and then looked down at her hand.

"I am a soldier. By necessity, I have expended a significant amount of effort to fit in while navigating a male-dominated culture."

"Navigating a male-dominated culture… Ummm."

"Not in a naughty sense."

"I—I wasn't thinking that at all! R-r-really! Not even a little!"

The way she was waving both hands so excessively warranted plenty of suspicion, but Rusalka chose not to probe further.

Noticing that, Amy asked, "Does that mean you were ordered to become a Valkyrie?"

"…Yes, that's right. That goes for most of our generation."

Xenia, Victorica, and Canan all nodded.

It was sometimes hard to tell, but they were also career soldiers. All three had been in the military before becoming Valkyries, just like Rusalka.

They had been in very different branches back then. Victorica and Rusalka were the only ones who had already been pilots. Xenia and Canan only started flying once their aptitude had been confirmed and they became Valkyries.

"Xenia was a medic, and Canan worked with comms," Rusalka explained.

"That's right. I was a top-notch operator."

Having nothing to do with herself after Rusalka had slipped away, Canan had locked arms with Victorica. With their height difference, it almost looked like she was fawning over her older sister.

"——"

"Amy? What's the matter?" Rusalka noticed her strange reaction.

"Ah! Uh, nothing! Hearing that Xenia was a medic makes a lot of sense. A medic is basically like a doctor, right? She seems like she'd be good at giving shots or something..."

"Heh-heh, for the record, I actually was pretty good. If the opportunity ever comes up, I'd be happy to give you a personal demonstration."

Xenia flashed a dangerous smile as she pretended to hold a needle. Amy shuddered and hid behind Rusalka.

"Oh-ho, do you not like me anymore?"

"N-no, it's just..."

"If that's not it...then is it maybe because you're scared of getting a jab?"

"Grgh!"

Xenia broke into a grin at discovering a new target worth teasing.

Normally, she was an upstanding person and a reliable second-in-command. Her only flaw was that every once in a while, this terrible habit of hers would rear its head. Rusalka sighed.

"Can we leave it at that, Xenia? Besides, there's no reason for Amy to be scared of needles. She is still quite immature, but to make light of her because of that would be insulting."

"Yeah, that's right! Or at least that's what I'd like to say, but could you explain what you mean by 'immature' first? How old do I look to you...?"

"Around thirteen years old."

"Wait, what?! I'm fifteen! Fifteen, I'll have you know! I'm a perfectly grown-up lady!"

Amy hopped around with her hands in the air, demanding to be treated like an adult. She was hard at work disproving her own claim to maturity, but in all honestly, whether she was thirteen or fifteen hardly changed much in the grand scheme of things for Rusalka—or the others.

Amy did not like the description, but *immature* did genuinely seem to be the best way to describe her.

"Fine. If you four are gonna act like you're all mature adults, then tell me how old you all are," Amy demanded.

"I'm nineteen years old. Just barely an adult."

"You're nineteen, Rusalka?!"

Rusalka furrowed her brow, not taking kindly to such an over-the-top reaction. If Amy was that surprised, it begged the question of just how old did she think Rusalka was before?

"Actually, I'm scared to ask, so you don't have to say anything else."

"Hey, Amy, how old does Rusalka look to you? I wanna know."

"Victorica..."

"Incidentally, I'm twenty-two. A proper lady."

Her older subordinate casually broached the exact topic that she had wanted to avoid. Rusalka glowered at her in obvious displeasure, but Victorica didn't seem to mind. Amy thought for a moment about the question and then glanced at Rusalka with wide eyes.

"...You won't get mad at me, right?"

"It would be entirely unreasonable for me to get mad at you for simply answering a question...but judging from the fact that you thought it necessary to give a disclaimer, I suppose I should assume whatever you're about to say will likely upset me."

Put that way, Rusalka decided she had no interest in ever hearing the answer.

"Fine then, just whisper it in my ear."

"That's no fair. I want to know, too." Canan joined Victorica's quest for knowledge.

Xenia wasn't far behind. "In that case, tell me, too, for future reference."

And so the three curious women all gathered around Amy. Putting aside Victorica and Canan, who tended to get carried away, what use could Xenia possibly have for knowing something like this?

Rusalka guessed it would just be inspiration for some new way to tease her.

Frowning as their whispered conversation grew suspiciously animated, Rusalka's mood only turned darker.

"Ahhh, that was a good laugh. You don't have to worry about anything, Rusalka."

"I'm sure you'll enjoy your next assessment, Victorica."

"Gah! So immature!"

"If you wish to be treated like an adult, you should behave like one. And you two, Xenia and Canan—you're acting like this has nothing to do with you, but you can expect the same."

They had no grounds to complain about an immature response when they were the ones who started being childish first.

Amy, who had managed to be the only one to escape punishment, breathed a sigh of relief.

"And you, Amy. Rest assured, I'll find an appropriately immature way to deal with you as well."

"Ehhh?! What do you mean? Wait, are you going to stop eating meals with me or stop showering with me or stop letting me rest my head on your lap…?"

"I can't recall having ever done two-thirds of that…"

Still, if she put down her foot there, that would be the end of those sorts of terrible things. At the very least, Amy seemed to have learned her lesson, given the way she slumped over in the blink of an eye.

"You too, Victorica. At least act like you're sorry."

"Fine, fine."

"Even I can tell you haven't reflected on what you did at all." Amy chuckled a little at Victorica's noncommittal response. But then she cocked her head with her finger on her cheek. "Wait, if Rusalka is nineteen and Vicky is twenty-two, then why is Rusalka the flight commander?"

"That's simple. I've been serving longer. Also, I had better grades."

"The lectures… The lectures were hell…"

The furrows in Victorica's brow deepened as she pressed a hand to her chest.

But hearing that, Amy's confusion just grew.

"...But you were already going to be a pilot, right, Vicky? So isn't it weird that the former medic is the second-in-command?"

"It isn't odd at all. Just thinking about having someone as scatter-brained as Victorica as second-in-command gives me chills. Look at these goose bumps."

"You're always so dedicated to playing the part, Captain. It's not like you really have... Wait, you really do have goose bumps!"

Seeing Rusalka's arm, Amy and Victorica started a whole new commotion. After that had run its course, Victorica pensively closed one eye.

"In the end, we would still just be dreaming of becoming pilots if the pillars hadn't shown up. Then again, it's not exactly a situation where I can say I'm happy just to be able to fly." Victorica shrugged.

"That was how desperately the army wanted to put bodies in cockpits." Canan was expressionless, but her tone of voice dropped.

——The reason they had become pilots was in large part due to the string of defeats and losses humanity had suffered when the pillars first appeared.

These incomprehensible beings were surely enemies, and the soldiers had a duty to defend the people. And naturally, when that happened, the first ones to set out and confront the enemy were active-duty pilots.

Most of them were forced to do battle with an unknown enemy. No matter how skilled the pilot, there was no way of winning against an enemy completely unfazed by their attacks. The result was undeniably tragic, but it secured humanity the time and information that had led to the present day.

After humanity suffered those losses, there was no choice but for the next people in line to fill the empty cockpits. And the ones who were next in line were Rusalka's generation, who at the time had just finished an accelerated training program.

Ordinarily, she would have been considered too young, but there was no one else to turn to. Because of that, the average age in the European armed forces and in armies around the world dropped dramatically.

The reason Rusalka and the rest of her class were already flying combat missions was because the times and the vagaries of war had forced command's hands.

So when they were asked why they were flying, the answer was complicated.

“It’s not like we are doing this against our will, though. We all chose this for ourselves.” Sensing how Rusalka felt, Xenia quietly chimed in to dispel any potential misunderstandings.

“…Yes, that’s right.” Rusalka nodded in agreement. Victorica and Canan did the same.

The situation had compelled them into these roles, but it wasn’t as if they had no choice in the matter. They had picked their paths from limited options and had no regrets, nor did they blame anyone for it.

“Well, that’s the gist of it, so I’d like to keep doing what I can.”

Victorica scratched her cheek as she smiled weakly, the aura of childishness from before nowhere to be found. Her eyes glanced over at the younger ace standing right beside her.

“You took out dozens more than we did on this sortie, right? Honestly, it would feel wrong if all I did after seeing that was just talk about how amazing you were.”

“Agreed.”

The others all nodded. Amy responded with a hesitant “huh?” but it was an undeniable fact.

“———”

All told, Rusalka’s flight had scored seven kills.

Frankly, that was a fantastic result that would make it into base’s record books. There were other Valkyrie flights deployed at various air bases on the European front, but Rusalka’s was the only one that could consistently take down five or more pillars in a single mission.

A typical battle with pillars was generally about Valkyries taking point and drawing the enemy’s attention so that civilian areas could be evacuated or friendly forces could withdraw.

Pillars were generally not engaged with the intention of wiping them out. Naturally, if they could be taken down, that was ideal, since it helped counteract the enemy’s draining effect. But that was easier said than done. Or at least it was for Rusalka’s generation.

In any case, her flight downing seven enemies was considered a truly remarkable feat. But that performance paled in the face of what Amy had accomplished.

“…Seventy-four kills,” Rusalka murmured.

That was the number Amy had shot down. Solo. It was a whole magnitude greater than what they had done. And looking at the numbers like that made Rusalka painfully aware of the difference between them.

The overwhelming difference between one who had been chosen by God and those who had not.

As Rusalka slipped into thought, Victorica suddenly clapped and said, "Oh yeah, there was another thing I wanted to ask you, Amy!"

Amy was puzzled.

"Me?"

"Yeah! I heard this rumor. Is it true you are visiting all the different bases because you're scouting people?"

"Scouting?" Rusalka furrowed her brow quizzically at the unexpected question.

She could feel Xenia's eyes homing in on her apparently wrinkle-inducing expression, while Amy turned her gaze to meet Rusalka's sky-blue eyes.

Amy promptly covered her face with her hands.

"Judging from that reaction, I guess the answer is yes?" Victorica didn't think there was much doubt.

"It's a little hard to say yes or no, exactly… Where did you hear that?"

"A cute and beautiful Valkyrie such as myself has her ways, kiddo." Victorica crossed her arms and smugly stroked a nonexistent beard.

Regardless of where she got her information, though, Amy's reaction was an obvious sign she had hit the bull's-eye. After essentially spilling the beans and drawing everyone's attention, Amy let out a little sigh.

"Don't get mad at me, please? It feels terrible that I'm basically judging all of you…"

"I don't think it's bad. It'd be an honor to meet the First's discerning standards."

"Then that means Vicky heard right. The higher-ups are planning to put together a squadron based around you," Xenia neatly concluded.

"Technically, it's more like looking for a squadron to fly with me, I think. They're still gonna keep me flying alone for the most part…"

"So you're looking for sisters in arms, then! You've been flying all over looking for comrades!" Amy smiled faintly as Victorica dramatically clenched her fists. She didn't explicitly confirm or deny it, but her reaction made it all but certain. "Well? Were we up to your standards, Amy?"

"Hmmmmm. Welllll, I dunno..."

"Oh, come on! Don't be a tease."

Amy bashfully avoided giving a straight answer when Victorica poked her cheek, demanding an explanation.

Canan followed suit by poking her other cheek. "It's fine. She's always clinging to Rusalka, so chances are looking good."

"True!" Victorica was fully convinced.

"Arrrgh! You guys really just say whatever comes to mind, don't you?!"

Amy puffed out her cheeks and glared at her would-be tormenters. The way she latched on to the two older women looked cute to Rusalka. Fitting for a girl her age.

She didn't seem so much like a fifteen-year-old who was carrying the hope of all humanity on her shoulders.

"——"

Suddenly, she remembered the way Amy had been all alone in the mess hall. There were not many who wanted to be alone, and yet everyone felt compelled to give her distance out of respect. The girl the sky loved most was forced to be alone even when she was on the ground.

It was only natural that she would want companions, allies she could fly alongside.

The way she is when they're all messing around must be the real her.

And so...

7

"How was it working together with the First, Captain Evereska?"

"——"

...And so when someone asked Rusalka that question, she hesitated for a second.

During that brief pause, several thoughts crossed her mind. Then she banished those distractions in the blink of an eye and snapped to attention like a soldier should.

"It was difficult to get on the same page as her, but I believe we are capable of working together for the most part."

"So there were difficulties with the First Valkyrie even for your flight," the base commander murmured, a look of concern chiseled on his deeply wrinkled face as he leaned his elbows on the ebony desk.

Guessing what the old officer was thinking, Rusalka responded with a short nod and a "sir."

The morning after the scramble order, Rusalka had been called to the base commander's office for a full debrief. But she had already reported all there was to report yesterday. It was clear the real focus of the discussion was not the mission but Amy herself.

"Is the whole European Command having difficulties dealing with the First, sir?"

"That's a pretty blunt way of putting it, Captain. But I can't really deny it."

He shook his head slowly as he stood up, seeming like he found it all bothersome. He stepped away from his desk and looked at the shelf on the wall, which was lined with countless files and a single picture.

In the picture was the base commander in his youth, standing alongside his fellow soldiers. The picture had been taken at the entrance of the base, back when it was still new.

"I'm not fool enough to say the old wars were any better. War is hell no matter the era. But at least back then we knew our enemies were putting their lives on the line, just like we were."

His eyes narrowed, and he stroked his wrinkled cheek before continuing in a husky voice.

"Calling it the European Command sounds nice, but the army is just a paper tiger wholly dependent on the Valkyries. We are forced to make you young women bear the fate of humanity all by yourselves."

"...That's not really true, sir, as I'm sure you are aware."

"Yes, I guess you're right."

He sighed. Rusalka understood that that had been his own form of consideration for her, but she didn't need or want his pity. She preferred to speak openly and honestly. It was true enough that Europe's armed forces were incredibly reliant on the Valkyries, but that was not quite the whole story.

"More precisely, it is dependent on the First Valkyrie, sir."

"...Of all the pillars shot down by flights under European command, approximately ninety percent are attributed to the First. She is really coming through for us, visiting every front, drumming up morale among the troops."

"______"

"Because of that, we absolutely cannot afford to lose her. That would surely lead to humanity's defeat."

"That's..." Rusalka's eyes widened at his forceful tone. "Is there some reason to believe that might be a pressing concern? Some change in Amy...in the First?"

"No, at present there is no indication of that. But there is no guarantee that will be the case forever."

The commander's ashen gaze met Rusalka's. The air in the room grew tense, and she reflexively snapped to full attention. The base commander broke the silence and said, "You may have already heard, but the brass intends to attach a squadron to the First. A unit that would accompany her as she moves between fronts and that would fly in the same battles she does."

"I had heard rumors..."

It was something that had come up just yesterday, after the sortie.

Putting that conversation together with what the commander was saying made it clear this was a measure to let the army continue its reliance on Amy. An act of desperation to prolong Amy's ability to keep flying even a little bit longer.

"If your reaction was the same as mine, then I'm sure that plan must sound shameless and craven."

"No, sir..."

His tone had dropped, losing strength, as if he could tell what Rusalka was thinking. His voice had dripped with despair and disappointment, all of it directed at himself.

And there was also a sorrow that every soldier felt to some extent. Other than Amy, who was not really a soldier, it was something that every person fighting felt.

"______"

Rusalka lowered her eyes as an awkward silence developed.

Considering the flow of the conversation, she could guess what he was about to say. And sure enough, it was exactly what she suspected.

"Captain Evereska, I intend to recommend your flight for the role."

"———"

"I heard your relations with the First are excellent. And the most important aspect of this mission is not what happens in the air…"

"It's what happens on the ground. And our relationship with her, right, sir?"

"…I have no intention of minimizing your flight's capabilities and accomplishments."

There was an earnestness in the way he chose his words. It certainly wasn't his fault that she could suddenly feel the inescapable reality swirling around her head.

"The second generation can hardly be called fortunate or blessed, given their position, but even so, your flight was quick to adapt and react flexibly to the developing war situation. I am sounding you out about this out of respect for what you have managed to accomplish."

"Sounding me out, sir? Not an order?"

"A formal reassignment would take place after I've made my recommendation to the command staff. But I wanted to speak with you personally first."

He placed his hand on the table as he peered into Rusalka's eyes. It felt like he was genuinely considering Rusalka's feelings on the matter and not just probing her. In her experience, most soldiers were earnest, but even so, humanity was in a situation where they all had to work together regardless of any reservations they might have.

"Thank you very much for discussing it with me first, sir. However, I am a soldier. I will humbly accept my orders, whatever they might be."

Rusalka stood at sharp attention, puffing out her chest.

She was proud to act as a soldier should. At the same time, it served as a statement of where she stood on the matter.

But the commander shook his head.

"While it is true that you are a member of the army, you are a Valkyrie… Your freedom and status are guaranteed under Odin's authority."

"That's…"

Rusalka's face tensed, and she was at a loss for words as the old officer continued.

"So this is nothing more than a discussion. With that in mind, allow me to reiterate."

The wrinkles on his forehead deepened as the old officer's voice took on the certain gravitas that came with age.

"Captain Evereska, I intend to recommend you as the squadron leader of the First's attached unit. Do you have any objections?"

"______"

——She should have immediately responded, *No, sir.*

His restated declaration had been lip service meant to trigger her sense of duty and eliminate the weakness that had taken root in her heart.

It was human nature to crave that sort of dramatic back-and-forth. Humans could not willingly go to their deaths without a reason. And along those same lines, they needed a reason to willingly risk their lives.

Rusalka knew she should respond forcefully, straightforwardly, and immediately.

And yet—

"—Ngh."

She could not bring herself to say that she did not have any objections.

In the moment that response was required of her to fulfill her role, she couldn't say it.

"I see, so you're the one who ■■■■■ ■■■ ■■■■."

For some reason, the words God had said when she first received her wings wouldn't stop echoing in her ears.

8

"Is it true you said you didn't want to fly with me?"

When Amy came to Rusalka's room that night, that was the first thing she said as she looked Rusalka in the eyes.

When she was hit with that question, Rusalka was shocked by the realization that it was already nighttime. She had spoken with the base commander first thing in the morning, but she couldn't remember anything else happening. It felt like she had just been lying on her bed until the buzzer for her room rang.

"Can I come in?"

"...It's a bit of a mess."

"Oooh, I've never seen you be messy before. I wanna see, I wanna see."

Sighing as Amy showed no hesitation, Rusalka welcomed her in.

Her room was located in a women-only barracks on the base. As a Valkyrie and a flight leader, Rusalka was near the top in terms of pay and status, so she had a room to herself that was impressively large by military standards, and maybe even a bit larger than she knew what to do with. There were only a few personal effects and a neatly kept bed.

Glancing around the room, Amy cocked her head.

"Ummm...where exactly is the mess?"

"Everywhere."

"What, like all of creation?"

"I wasn't speaking on such a large scale. But the desk and bed are terribly cluttered."

The sheets were slightly rumpled, and the cover was technically not properly tucked in. There were also a few unfinished documents on the table as well as a pen kept out, missing its case.

It was all left lying about, which was rather upsetting for Rusalka.

"Actually, would you mind if I cleaned up a little first? Just one hour would..."

"This would take you an hour?! What?! Are you gonna scrub everything down with a toothbrush?!"

"No, of course not. That would be unhygienic. Anyway, do you mind waiting?"

"I know that was a silly question, but is your heart really still set on cleaning?!"

Amy gave a loud "upsy-daisy!" before hopping onto the bed. She disturbed the sheets even further, the bedsprings creaking beneath her. It was practically a plea for Rusalka to simply accept the clutter for now.

"Is it that fun to torture me?"

"Does this actually bother you that much? Did these sheets save your life at some point...? On second thought, let's stop while we're ahead."

"Well, the sheets did once..."

"I said let's stop! We're leaving it there! This conversation is done!"

Her face turning red, Amy clapped her hands loudly, forcibly ending the conversation. That was when Rusalka realized she had not even turned on the light yet, so she hit the nearest switch.

Amy's golden hair seemed to shimmer in the suddenly bright room. Having trouble settling down, Rusalka moved a chair in front of the bed before finally taking a seat facing her.

"Your hair is so pretty, like the light of the moon."

Rusalka caught her breath at Amy's sudden compliment, which had come just as she was admiring the young girl's hair. It almost felt like Amy had read her mind. Feeling compelled to say something—anything—Rusalka managed to reply, "Your hair is very beautiful, too, like gleaming sunlight."

"Ah, really? Heh-heh, I'm so happy. You like my hair?"

"No, I don't really base my preferences on hair alone. From my limited knowledge, that would be akin to admitting I have a rather specific fetish."

"If you're gonna compliment someone, do it right!"

"Sorry, it was just embarrassing, so I..."

"That hit way too hard if you were just trying to cover up being embarrassed!"

Rusalka cringed. Reflexively, she touched her silver hair. It wasn't as if she had never been complimented on her hair before, but this was the first time she had been praised so poetically.

She didn't hate the moon. There was something about it being the crowning jewel of the night sky that made her heart ache.

"Still, though, I'm glad."

"You are?"

Amy broke into a smile as she stopped pouting and let her expression relax. Rusalka found it hard to keep up with her changes in mood. But her unease didn't show much on her face as Amy continued.

"I mean, you didn't turn me away at the door, and you even complimented my hair... It seems like you didn't turn down the position because you hate me."

"...It's not like I refused."

"But you didn't immediately agree, either... I'm not mad about it or anything. You get that much, right?"

Rusalka felt like she was being cornered for some reason by Amy's line of thought.

What is this vague sense of guilt?

Rusalka kept questioning herself as she stared into those ruby-red eyes. Or perhaps it was the same question she had asked herself dozens—no, hundreds of times during the half day that she could barely remember.

Why hadn't she been able to immediately answer the commander's question?

—No, it would have been far better if it was simply a matter of speaking up sooner or later. She hadn't been able to give an answer at all.

When the base commander had offered to give her some time and wait for her response, she had taken him up on his kindness. That was when she had truly lost track of time, questioning herself until Amy had come to see her.

And if someone asked what she had gained from that pointless exercise, the answer was...absolutely nothing. She still didn't know what to do. Now, face-to-face with Amy, she just felt even more lost. As her worries grew deeper and heavier, she suddenly had a new thought.

"May I ask you something?"

"Hmm? Sure, ask whatever you want. We know each other well enough for that."

Thinking back to their initial encounter more than ten days ago, Rusalka dredged up an old question. "When we first met, why were you looking for me?"

She had run into Amy, who had been all alone in an unfamiliar place. But when they first spoke, Amy had definitely said she was looking for Rusalka.

"I had thought at first it was because I'd been chosen to show you around the base, but..."

"———"

"You said your desire to meet me was related to you, so it was only natural that I wouldn't understand. Meaning your goal from the very start was to meet me."

"...Wow, I'm surprised you remember something like that so well."

Amy smiled. And the lack of denial more or less confirmed Rusalka's memory was correct. In other words, she had come to meet Rusalka with a goal in mind.

"I've thought it was odd several times. I'm not particularly skilled at getting along with people, and I lack both humor and common sense.

I certainly would like to improve in those areas, but I haven't been making much progress…"

And because of that, Amy going out of her way to talk with Rusalka was hard for her to wrap her head around. Still, she had avoided probing too deeply into the young girl's motives. Because the more she probed, the more she would be forced to actually face Amy head-on—which meant facing her own feelings head-on as well.

"Please tell me, Amy. Why—?"

"Because you made it back alive that day."

Rusalka's desperate question was met by a soft voice. She fell silent. Tension seemed to drain from the corners of Amy's mouth as a tranquil feeling suffused her being, almost like a calm sea breeze had begun blowing.

The way her expressions changed so freely, from smiles to anger and everything in between…it was everything Rusalka couldn't do. That had been her impression of Amy, but this moment changed that.

She had thought Amy's expressions freely shifted from smiles to anger and whatever else bubbled to the surface, but Rusalka could not recall her ever looking sad.

——There was even a time when I thought she had probably never cried before.

The First Valkyrie. The chosen of God who offered up her family name and received an unparalleled blessing in return,

——I genuinely believed there was no way she had ever wept.

And that was true. If *crying* was defined as "tears falling from her eyes," then she had not cried. There was probably no one who had ever seen her weeping.

"—You were the only survivor from that day who became a Valkyrie."

"——"

"That's why I wanted to meet you."

"What would you…?"

"What would I do once I did? I don't really know myself."

Amy shook her head as she smiled ever so slightly.

The tranquil aura around her faded somewhat, and Rusalka could tell she had put on her mask again—or more accurately, it was not really a mask. Amy was not smothering her emotions. If anything, the one who kept forcing her emotions down was—

"Why did you become a Valkyrie, Rusalka?"

Amy asked the same question that had been answered just last night. She had already explained it in front of Xenia and Victorica and Canan. What Amy was really asking was…

"Why did you become a Valkyrie?"

"I—I am a soldier. I have a responsibility to obey orders that come down the chain of command…"

"But you're trying to avoid flying with me."

"That's… I—!"

Rusalka reflexively stood up as Amy mercilessly pressed her, cutting off all escape routes. There was a sound as her chair fell over, but Rusalka and Amy never broke eye contact.

Even as Rusalka looked down at her from standing height, Amy didn't waver in the slightest.

The force of Rusalka's gaze was little more than a cool breeze to her. If anything, that would have been an improvement. It was entirely possible it didn't register at all.

It's—

"—It's not that at all."

Amy shook her head slowly, the corners of her eyes dropping slightly.

"———"

Rusalka thought she was already an open book. From time to time, she felt like Amy's crimson eyes could see right through her. She felt it again as she gritted her teeth.

"You've always…from the very first time I saw you…"

Rusalka didn't mean the time they met at the base.

To her, the first time she had encountered Amy—the First—had been long before that. Their first contact had been on the battlefield on the day that was now known as the Ride of the Valkyrie.

The day she had spread her golden wings in a sky filled with despair and rewrote history, a day to be memorialized—

"—Ngh."

Rusalka clenched her jaw, desperately trying to control the impulse that kept threatening to burst through her chest. To kill that shameful side of herself and return to the usual Rusalka Evereska—

"—Rusalka."

"———"

Amy called her name at just the right moment, as if she had timed it perfectly to draw her in.

She reflexively looked at Amy, her sky-blue eyes meeting the younger girl's crimson gaze.

And then—

"—Please tell me? I want to know everything about you."

9

"Rusalka! What the hell did you do?!"

"———"

Rusalka looked up sluggishly as the door to her room flew open. She was greeted by a panting Xenia, a rare sight indeed. Her usual beautifully done hair was a mess. Rusalka could see herself in the blacks of her eyes, sitting weakly on the edge of the bed.

"What is it all of a sudden, Xenia?"

"'What is it?' That's my line. What did you do, Rusalka?"

Xenia walked forward briskly until she stood right in front of Rusalka. Even then, Rusalka didn't look up, her eyes still trained on Xenia's knees.

Xenia heaved a sigh at her spineless response.

"I heard from the base commander. About us being recommended for the squadron attached to the First…to Amy."

"———"

"He also said you would be removed from our flight. And that Amy asked for it."

"———"

"I'm asking you again: What the hell did you do, Rusalka?"

Rusalka closed her eyes as Xenia pressed her. And after a bout of silence, she responded, her eyes still closed.

"—Nothing."

"There's no way that's true!"

Xenia grabbed Rusalka's shoulders and stared straight into her eyes. Rusalka felt an oddly strong emotion as she looked at her black eyes from so close.

It was the first time she had ever seen Xenia so visibly upset and yelling.

She had only met Xenia after they had become Valkyries, so it was not that long ago in the grand scheme of things, but they were comrades who had flown together with their lives on the line countless times. In terms of how close she felt to her, Rusalka would have counted her second-in-command on the same level as family. She had never seen Xenia angry like this before, and it was all because of a terrible misunderstanding.

"What did you do, Rusalka? This isn't like you at all. If something happened between you and Amy, you should have come to me..."

"Nothing happened. Really. Nothing happened between us. I'm not lying."

"——"

"Were you the only one recommended?"

Rusalka was amazed at how calmly she managed to ask that. Xenia caught her breath at the emotionless tone of that question before shaking her head.

"No, Victorica and Canan were there, too. The only requirement was for you to not be part of the flight."

"I see. I'm sure they'll be happy."

Rusalka wasn't referring to how well the two of them got along with Amy. She knew they both had their own reasons for wanting to fight the pillars.

"Though the opportunity only came because of orders..."

The answer they had given Amy the other day was not a lie. But it wasn't the whole truth, either.

——Even with Odin's power, not everyone could become a Valkyrie.

Only a select few were capable, and finding special people like Amy was like finding a single particular grain of sand in the desert. The first Valkyries of the second generation were pulled from among pilots and then from the other women in the military. Those recruits were the Valkyries who made up Rusalka's generation. They could hardly be called powerful, but they were the generation that followed directly in the First's footsteps. They were the Valkyries whose job was to hold the line until they could pass the baton to the third generation, who were chosen for having much greater latent abilities.

"Even so, Seconds have high morale. Because..." Rusalka ended up trailing off again, but Xenia continued her thought.

"Because we all joined the army before Valkyries existed. We had our own reasons to fight from the start, even if we didn't have a reason to fly at first."

"Victorica had her lover, Canan her siblings..."

"I have the homeland I lost. And you, Rusalka..."

"——"

"You joined the army to fill some hole in your heart, didn't you?"

She pressed Rusalka for her real motives in a soft, fragile tone.

The people in her flight—everyone in the army—all had their own causes. Families, loved ones, maybe even patriotism. Whatever it was, they all had a reason to fight. And they all dreamed of being able to fight together with Amy. If they could fly with the First Valkyrie, they would brave any battlefield.

That was why—

"We should go talk with the base commander directly. Or Amy. Talk things through until everyone is satisfied, and Amy takes it back. If you do that..."

"Are you really that attached to me?"

"—Gh."

A moment later, a sharp crack rang out in the dark room.

"...Just kidding."

"It's not funny... This isn't funny at all, Rusalka."

Her cheek was still hot from the slap. But Rusalka didn't touch it. There had been a brief flash of pain, but she didn't think it really hurt. If anything, she thought it had hurt Xenia's hand more.

That didn't make much sense, but it almost felt right.

"I won't go to the base commander, and there's no point in talking with Amy. I'm a soldier, and I follow my orders. You should do the same, Xenia."

"Is that really your answer?"

Xenia always seemed so composed and mature, but over the course of their conversation, she had shown Rusalka several sides of herself that she had never revealed before. Those expressions of anger, desperation, and sadness were all things Rusalka had never even imagined.

Xenia had revealed so much of herself, and yet, Rusalka refused to open up at all. And Rusalka chose to continue holding up that facade, not letting the walls come down for even a second.

"______"

Her silence was her answer. She rejected Xenia's outstretched hand. Xenia's voice trembled, unable to contain all the emotions swirling inside her, but even so, she recognized at last that Rusalka had made up her mind.

"Even though I was your wingmate."

"...I don't know how many times I've been saved by your advice."

"Liar."

That one harsh word made the sharpest cut of all, leaving a painful wound on Rusalka's heart.

Turning her back, Xenia moved away from Rusalka and put her hand on the door. She was leaving. This was a complete and total separation.

When that door closed, it would be the end of everything between the two of them.

"Xenia."

At the last second, as Xenia walked through the door, Rusalka called out. Xenia stopped but didn't turn around.

"Do you think I'm wrong?"

She didn't understand why she asked that. She had already refused to talk things through and had firmly rejected her friend's outstretched hand. And yet, something inside her found it impossible to stay quiet as Xenia walked away.

The ever-reliable second-in-command turned at her flight leader's selfish question to respond.

"Why only ask me at the very end? You already decided everything on your own."

10

That was the last time she ever interacted with Amy or Xenia.

She never saw Amy again, and she didn't speak with Xenia. But she did have some parting words with Victorica and Canan.

"I don't really get what you're thinking, but I'm not going to blame you for your decision. It must have been a hard one, right?"

Victorica had smiled and talked with her like she always did. Her manner of speech was noticeably unsoldierly, but when they parted ways, Rusalka finally realized she had been saved countless times by that gentle demeanor.

"...Traitor."

Canan, however, refused to forgive Rusalka for not joining them. There were times when she seemed to think things through logically and calmly, but at her core, she didn't hesitate to follow what her gut told her. That was exactly why she was a Valkyrie.

After bidding the two polar opposites a farewell, Rusalka was alone.

——On the day they left, she watched three planes take off down the runway.

The silhouettes she knew so well, the sisters in arms whom she had flown with so many times, were leaving her behind.

It was an odd scene that made her heart ache.

"——"

She was struck by a flash of doubt. If she had given in to it, she could have gotten into her Deus ex Machina and chased after them. But even in her moment of uncertainty, she didn't do that.

The squadron of Valkyries was headed toward the sector of the European front where the fighting was thickest to link up with Amy, and Rusalka had not been added to that force.

——Four days later, a never-before-seen type of pillar would appear on the Greek front.

It was, in effect, the first deployment of the experimental squadron based around the First Valkyrie. That battle that would come to be called Pandora's Calamity would be the European theater's greatest defeat.

Not a single Valkyrie who participated would survive the battle, first and second generation alike. Every Valkyrie who flew those skies would lose their wings—

——And once again, Rusalka was truly alone.

Chapter 2
A Wounded Crimson

1

——The first time she sat in an operator's seat, she felt nervous, despite herself.

Unlike the flight seat she was so used to, there was no belt to cinch tight over her body. There was just a heavy responsibility that weighed her down and a chair that was perfectly fine but felt oddly unbalanced to her.

Quite a few bad jokes were often repeated in the army, and one of them was that radio operators always got the best chairs in the base.

The reason for that was because a pissed-off operator made everything run just a little bit less smoothly. It was common to compare military operations to human biology. If command was the brain, and field officers and troops were the arms and legs, then operators were like the nervous system, sending signals all throughout the body. So if the operator didn't function properly, the whole body would start to fall apart.

"—Ten new pillars confirmed in the northeast sector!"

A sharp voice reported the new development as a tremor of unease ran through the command post.

They were watching the battle play out on the monitors at the front of the room, where several new red markers had appeared, immediately hammering home the severity of the situation.

The blue markers on the monitor were friendlies, and the red were enemies, but—

"What about the Rostock-Laage Valkyrie flight?!"

"They're busy supporting another unit's withdrawal! They can't come to support!"

"Incoming from 212th Panzergrenadier Battalion! It's 2nd Company! They say they'll take the new enemies in the north…"

"Absolutely not! Infantry can't do anything against pillars! They'd just be throwing their lives away…"

"They say they'll buy some time and that they're counting on us to get revenge for them!"

"—Gh! Connect them."

As reports continued pouring in from all across the battlefield, the general bitterly nodded at the operator.

The battalion was immediately connected, and a voice cut through the storm of static.

"This is 2nd Company of the 212th! Can you hear us, command? Like I said, we'll buy you some time, sir."

"This is command. We hear you—can you do it?"

"We'd just be dying pointlessly otherwise. If that's all we can manage, we could hardly call ourselves panzergrenadiers, sir."

It was a rather disrespectful tone to take with a commanding officer, but the general didn't take him to task for it. Everyone in the command post was of a similar mind, paying respects to their comrades who were prepared to face death.

In a battle where the situation could change dramatically from moment to moment, the most critical thing to have was decisiveness. The general simply did not have many cards left to play against the new enemies that had just appeared, and choosing where and where *not* to deploy the Valkyries could mean the difference between victory and defeat. And in the sectors that got the short end of the stick, he would have to fill the gap with whatever was available.

"It's already been thirty minutes since the battle commenced… The enemy will no doubt hit its limit soon. There is no way they have even ten minutes left."

"But a lot of people are going to die during those ten minutes. We can't let that happen, sir."

"…Sorry."

"Save me the apologies. We're goin' 'cause we want to. And who wants

to hear some old man's husky voice when he goes? Switch off with one of the operators, sir."

"______"

Rusalka caught her breath as the soldier on the other end called for an operator. But she swallowed her trepidation in the blink of an eye, taking over the line when the general nodded.

"—Understood. I will guide you to the location."

"Oooh, nice. I can tell you're a cutie from your voice! There's no foolin' my ears!"

"How can you be so sure? You should confirm it for yourself with your own eyes."

"Ha-ha-ha, good one! All right, we're countin' on you for directions!"

The infantry company's position was displayed on the monitor in front of Rusalka as she guided them to their target. She was leading them to a position meant to draw the pillars' attention and divert some of the enemy's forces.

But that was the same as sending them to their deaths.

"—I can hear the hesitation in your voice, pretty lady."

"______"

"I get it. Anyone would feel shaken. And I'll bet you haven't been sitting in that seat for very long—am I right?"

She was shocked at how perceptive he was to glean so much from just the way she was breathing. And as if he had picked up even that slight expression of surprise, the man laughed despite the situation he was in.

The unreserved mirth of a man willingly marching off to his death filled the line.

"Let me give you a little piece of advice. An operator naturally has to have amazing situational awareness and constantly make precise, unfaltering reports. But the most important thing is your voice."

"My voice..."

"It's hard to exaggerate how much the voice of a beauty boosts morale in the field. Plus, if an operator sounds pessimistic, then it makes sense that can spread to everyone listening, right?"

"______"

"No matter what anyone else does, we're going to be the ones dying here. So at least whisper in our ears like our lovers until the very end. We'll die for you, so let us dream of coming back alive."

The company approached their red target while he was chatting away. In less than thirty seconds, they would engage the enemy. But the tension and optimism in his voice still did not fade.

——*No, that's not true. His voice is shaking. He's actually terrified. What I should say now is—*

"So let's hear it. Any kind words for us boys about to leap into battle?"

"—I love you."

"———"

There was a moment of silence.

"Gah-ha-ha-ha-ha-ha-ha!"

A boisterous guffaw came from the other end just as Rusalka started to worry she had said the wrong thing. But the person on the other end gradually clamped down on the urge to keep laughing and regained that earlier calm.

"—I love you, too, Miss Operator."

And with that, a thunderous boom drowned out the voices on the line.

"Contact!"

The infantry and pillars clashed on the monitor as battle was joined.

Peppered by fire from the infantry on the ground, the pillars swerved from their original path, which had threatened to break through the center. The pillars' bodies glowed as they chased the infantry harassing them.

An instant later, a hail of devastating strobes of light rained down.

"—Gh."

The glowing projectiles shredded buildings and shattered roads. Her heart shuddered as she heard the echoing roar.

The battalion's plan had worked, but that meant they were in for a hideously cruel battle.

——On the battlefield, pillars used a threat level when deciding their targets. Valkyries were the top priority, followed by air units and then ground units, making for a list that seemed to prioritize whatever humanity would miss most dearly.

Because of that, whenever Valkyries or air assets got into a dangerous position, the standard strategy was to use ground units to divide the enemy's focus. This was done with the full knowledge that it was far more dangerous for the ground forces.

But if humanity didn't pick their battles like that, they would assuredly have already been ground down by the enemy.

They were forced to pick and choose people based purely on numbers and abilities, without any consideration for anything else. War was a factory that mass-produced inhumanity.

But then why? Were the people like the infantry company facing the pillars just helpless? They were able to fight on because they had their thoughts, their duty, and their dreams. And yet, she couldn't even hide a small quiver in her voice for their sakes.

"—The pillars have ceased activity! They have exceeded their limit and are undergoing annihilation!"

"Finally…!" The commander had been waiting for this moment.

The shout came from an operator observing a different monitor. It was a report that the pillars had reached their limits and the battle was over.

There was a limited amount of time that pillars could remain active. It was not fully understood, but all the energy they relied on to stay active was shared by a single swarm, and once it ran out, all the pillars on the battlefield would undergo annihilation simultaneously.

Because of that, though, combat with the pillars was extraordinarily intense. It also meant that battles tended to be decided in a relatively short amount of time. However, this generally resulted in much more widespread damage, so it was not always true that the shorter the battle the better.

The current battle had lasted thirty-seven minutes, and it had been an extremely large-scale engagement.

But either way—

"The fighting is over…"

Word was quickly relayed to the troops in the field. Naturally, even if combat operations had been concluded, they still had to conduct cleanup. Once the shooting stopped, it was time to deal with the fallout.

There were many things to do after the battle, from rebuilding to caring for casualties.

And more importantly—

"The battle is over. Thank you for your valiant efforts."

"______"

"…Thank you all…"

No response came from the gallant commander of the infantry company.

There were no blue markers left on the monitor in the vicinity.

2

——At present, the European front was where the most intense fighting was occurring. The pillars had first appeared in northern Europe and were steadily continuing their advance, driving humanity out from most of the countries in northern Europe, pushing the front line to the Rostock-Laage region.

The pillars had not only appeared in Europe, though. They had manifested in the Americas, central Asia, and Africa as well.

The fighting near the Baltic Sea that night was just one more battle in a global war.

"—That concludes the damage assessment for tonight's battle."

A cool, unflappable report echoed as the images on the monitor ran through a presentation.

Two hours after the fighting was over, casualty and damage reports had trickled into command from all divisions, and an after-action report was being conducted.

——The Hamburg base was located right in the middle of the long European front, serving a crucial role in supplying all the other bases in its area of operations.

The base was located next to a vast tract of farmland and shared grounds with the city of Hamburg. The battle that night had taken place just a few kilometers outside the city limits, and the aftermath affected the city and base alike.

"Impact on the city?" the commander asked.

"Fortunately, there was no major damage to the city itself. However, the wall shielding the city was badly damaged and has entirely collapsed in one location. It will likely take several weeks to repair it all, sir."

"It was built to protect the city, so if it did its job, then that's good enough… Make sure the repairs are carried out ASAP. We can't allow the draining effect to reach here."

The old base commander's deep, stern voice rang out as he closed his eyes. There was no response, but it was clear from everyone's faces that they all agreed.

The pillars' absorption, which stripped the earth of its vitality, was a particularly grave threat for a region that produced so much food.

There was a saying that an army marched on its stomach, and it was hardly an exaggeration. An army without supplies would have no morale.

That was what made the base in Hamburg irreplaceable.

"Any panic in the city?" the commander asked.

"The damage was limited to the greatest extent possible, so there is minimal panic among the civilian population. The removal of rubble is continuing apace, but business should resume soon, sir."

"I see… Are there any other urgent reports?"

Putting his hand to his forehead, the general looked around the room after his subordinate's report was finished. No one raised their hand. After pausing a moment, the general exhaled.

"Well done, everyone. Brief the next shift and then get some rest. You did well tonight."

And with that, the briefing was completed. As everyone briskly left the room, Rusalka's shoulders were still stiff when she also gradually made her way to the exit—

"—A word, Captain Evereska?"

"______"

The silver-haired woman—Rusalka—halted as a cool voice called out from behind her.

The one who had stopped her was a woman who had a sharp, incisive air about her. She was the one who had read out the damage reports from each sector as well as the after-action report during the briefing.

She had black hair down to her shoulders and a small beauty mark like a tear at her left eye, and she was in charge of managing the operators during combat. However, her decidedly prickly attitude toward Rusalka left a far deeper impression.

Rusalka turned and stood at attention without commenting on her attitude.

"What is it, Major Heyman?"

"Right before the end of the battle, you were charged with 212th Battalion 2nd Company, were you not?"

"______"

Straightforward and to the point—that was Major Michelle Heyman in a nutshell. Rusalka knew that about her before sitting beside her at the desks in Hamburg. But her voice held a sharper edge than usual.

Even though she tried to hold it in, Rusalka's expression tensed slightly.

She was feeling ashamed of herself and sorrowful for the infantry company that had given their lives to hold the enemy back in the last moments, questioning whether there was more she could have done.

"They..."

"Every operator has their regrets. However, we must not voice them. I'm sure you don't need me to tell you why."

Michelle's words were merciless, and there was an almost refreshing harshness to them. If an operator allowed overtly negative feelings to seep into their voice, it would hurt the morale of the troops fighting on the other end. It was just like the valiant panzergrenadier had said when he gave her courage in those precious few moments before he engaged the enemy.

Right as Rusalka was about to thank Michelle for her concern—

"—However, you do not have any right to feel those regrets."

True to form, she hammered Rusalka with a vicious rebuke. They both had the same role as operators, but Michelle's eyes conveyed her utter disdain for Rusalka, and she made no effort to hide it—it was a scorn that would not go away.

"Captain Evereska, you..."

Rusalka made no effort to defend herself as Michelle started to continue. For a moment, there was a flare of emotion in her eyes, almost like the frustration she—

"—That's enough, Major Heyman."

But a stern voice interrupted Michelle.

It was the general, who was sitting in his chair, monitoring the screens in front of him. He didn't look at the two of them as he leaned back in his seat.

"There were no issues with Captain Evereska's performance, were there?"

"...No, sir."

"Then she should receive the same appreciation for her efforts as everyone else. In addition, let's see..."

Leaving aside Michelle, whose momentum had been stifled, the base commander pondered something for a moment. But his pause was a short one.

"What do you say to taking a look around the city for a little bit, Captain?"

"Around the city, sir? But with the aftermath of the battle, is this really the...?"

"You heard the reports. The city is already starting to come back to life. The residents of the city are far more resilient than you give them credit for, Captain. So how about it?"

"...Is that an order, sir?"

Rusalka faltered, and even though she knew it was inappropriate, she questioned the general. She couldn't tell what his thoughts on the matter were, though, because he never turned to look at her. He just heaved a well-worn sigh.

"As a matter of fact, it is. Consider it an order, Captain Evereska. Go into the city, confirm the safety of the residents, and prepare a report on the progress of repairs and restoration."

"Yes, sir."

She was reluctant to go but didn't let it show. For better or worse, the base commander had given her an order. Following a commanding officer's orders was the most fundamental requirement of a soldier, and Rusalka was a career soldier. She did not want to betray that ideal.

"In that case, I will change and be on my way, sir. Pardon me."

Rusalka saluted and then glanced at Michelle. She had been silent since the general's chiding, but she closed her eyes and saluted Rusalka. Rusalka returned the salute before leaving the room.

She encountered the next shift of operators in the hallway. They passed her on either side, and just behind them was a window that looked out at the city. She could see lights here and there around the city. The reports indicated that the city had sustained only limited damage, but she couldn't tell much from just staring at the distant lights.

"Is that why he told me to check it out for myself...?"

Naturally, the general's goal had little to do with the order itself. His true motive was finding out what seeing the aftermath of the battle might inspire in Rusalka, or really just to confirm if she would experience any change at all.

"———"

And Rusalka herself was a ball of fear, too scared to check anything for herself without an order.

3

Rusalka went out into the city after steeling her resolve, only to be surprised by what she found.

After clearing the rubble from the roads and confirming the water mains, gas lines, electricity, and all the other infrastructures were in working order, the inhabitants were getting back to their everyday lives, almost as if they were competing with their neighbors.

Most of the city was already back to business as usual, and people almost seemed to be in a rush to exalt in the momentary respite of normalcy.

Honestly, Rusalka almost felt let down. Of course damage and casualties being minimal was the best outcome, but the city seemed to be doing far better than the minor disaster she had envisioned from the report. Even if it was just them putting on brave faces.

Times like this reminded Rusalka of just how resilient humans could really be. Or perhaps it was a testament to how powerful the concept of normal daily life could be.

"———"

She was wearing a coat with the collar turned up. A cold wind blew, causing white fog to form in front of her lips with each exhale. The chill breeze in the late-November air fluttered her silver hair, which glimmered like a full moon. When several people turned to look at her, she averted her eyes, wondering if her hair stood out too much.

Following the general's orders, she had changed her clothes and was now surveying the city by herself. There was still rubble-clearing work being done in various places around town. The repairs to the defensive wall were surely already in progress, and that work was also being overseen by the military, so it felt wrong for her to just be idly wandering the streets.

Of course, none of those jobs were her specialty, so the guilt was just her own creation. An effective division of responsibilities was as important at the battalion level as it was at the flight level. Those who fought had a responsibility to fight, and those who could not had their own responsibilities to look after. Rusalka had fulfilled her duty and received a new order, which was why she was currently walking around the city.

"I fulfilled my duty, huh."

She could not help scoffing at the thought that crossed her mind.

What even was her duty? Officially, she was a tactical adviser, and she served as an operator during battle. In other words, her role was to advise her commanding officer and share information as quickly as possible during battle.

Or…

"…As a Valkyrie…"

…was her true calling to fly in her Deus ex Machina and exchange fire with the pillars of light as a dauntless warrior?

"——"

Closing her eyes, she smothered that last thought.

If she could do that, then she wouldn't be walking around the city alone like she was. She would have died a noble and valiant death in battle long before that. Like six months ago, with the others—

"—Rgh."

Her eyes were downcast as she walked until one conspicuous group caught her attention.

Beautiful young women strolled side by side down the sidewalk. Other than the fact that they were all extremely beautiful, there was nothing particularly strange about them. But they were all in uniform, and they had white wing patches on their shoulders.

"——"

They were wearing the official uniform for women in the European Army, but unlike Rusalka's uniform, there was a distinct playfulness in the design. It was at odds with the strict standards and discipline the army ordinarily demanded.

But that deviation could be considered a form of consideration for the position the wearers were in, since they were not career soldiers. They had not gone through basic training, and in fact, they were like baby chicks still learning the most fundamental of things.

They were third-generation Valkyries.

The newest Valkyries to fly on the front lines while carrying the hopes and dreams of humanity. Unlike Rusalka's second generation, they had been chosen with a strict emphasis on ability. They were humanity's best and brightest hopes.

During the battle hours ago, these women had fought bravely to protect the city. They were lacking in experience and still had quite a bit to learn, but even just managing to make it back with every Valkyrie still alive was praiseworthy. They had truly done well.

After all, they had been thrown into the fray much earlier than originally intended. There were some who criticized European Command for rashly sending them in too soon, but their results and reports from the troops who fought alongside them had validated that difficult decision.

Without the efforts of the third generation, humanity's defenses would have quickly crumbled, and the world would have collapsed in the face of the pillar menace. No one could deny that.

"_____"

After spotting the figures of the people responsible for the world's continued existence, Rusalka stopped and looked around. Finding a shop at the corner of the street, she quickly slipped inside.

They had likely not had time to notice her due to her quick and decisive action.

"How pathetic..."

She couldn't help feeling disappointed in herself for skulking around in the shadows like that. She couldn't even say whether she had done it to protect herself or simply to avoid bothering them.

"Help yourself to a seat at the bar."

"Ah, thank you."

The shopkeeper had not failed to notice her when she entered. She had ducked in only to avoid the women's gazes, but it would be poor manners to leave immediately.

Besides, she had been ordered to confirm the state of the city, and this shop was decidedly a part of that same city. Not wanting to go against her mission, Rusalka sat down at the counter.

"Ummm..."

Taking off her coat and folding it on her lap, she scanned the bar from the vantage of her seat. The drunk patrons of the pub turned heated gazes on Rusalka as they got a good look at her figure. She didn't overly mind the gazes themselves, but she was at a loss for what she was supposed to do.

It was a large local pub. Nothing too fancy, just the sort of place where a construction worker or some other blue-collar regular might stop for a pint to round out the night. It was naturally the sort of place Rusalka had no experience with. The drinking age in the UK was eighteen, but despite being nineteen, Rusalka had never had any interest in alcohol. Her view was the straightforward and simple stance that alcohol merely inhibited sound judgment.

Because of that, she knew little about pubs or pub etiquette.

"Do you not know how to drink?"

"...Yes, I haven't really spent much time drinking."

"I can teach you if you'd like? The proper etiquette for a pub and all that."

A large man with a reddened nose turned toward her. His breath stank of alcohol, and his eyes were unfocused. He was unmistakably drunk.

Normally, Rusalka would have politely declined, but she had an order to follow tonight. After thinking about it for a second, she nodded.

"Then please teach me."

"Oooh, here's a cutie who gets it. Now that's something you don't see every day!"

The red-faced man raised a cheer as jeers and banter rained down from the other guests, and the pub grew lively.

"Hey, boss, an ale for my friend here. And another for me, too."

Taking the order, the bartender placed two large pint glasses filled with an amber ale on the counter. Rusalka narrowed her eyes when she got a whiff of the alcohol. At that range, she could practically feel the alcohol emanating from the bubbles in the glass.

She was about to drink for the first time, and she could feel her pulse growing oddly fast.

"Ummm, what should I do?"

"The booze is here, and you're in good company. All that's left is to just tip back and have at it."

"Sorry, an intuitive explanation like that doesn't really..."

"Huh? No, see, you can't hesitate when the booze's right in front of you. Hrm, in that case, let me think."

He pulled his glass close and pondered for a second before coming to a snap answer. He held his glass up and waited for Rusalka to do the same. And then, in a voice that everyone in the room could hear—

"—To the dead."

"______"

That was reason enough to get Rusalka to knock her glass against his before bringing it to her lips.

4

"———"

There was a stinging pain as the sunlight hit her eyelids, and she slowly woke up.

Breathing in, she felt the cool, clear morning air fill her lungs. Waking to the rising sun, she thought she was getting up surprisingly early.

What time did I go to bed last night?

"—?"

As she tried to remember back to last night, she felt something on her cheek. Touching it, she realized it was the traces of tears. She rubbed her cheek. Apparently, she'd been crying in her sleep, presumably because of a dream she'd had. She could think of two possibilities for what kind of dream it may have been, but that question soon faded…

"…Where am I?"

…only to be replaced by a new one.

She was in an unfamiliar place—a cramped, barren, concrete room. Just cold gray walls and a simple pipe-frame bed. There were bars in the small window that let in the sunlight that had woken her up. It was a place intentionally devoid of any warmth. And as if to leave no doubt about that fact, the door had iron bars, too.

It was almost like a prison, but an even more appropriate word came to Rusalka's mind.

"—The stockade?"

But that realization wasn't enough to clear her confusion.

The stockade was a disciplinary holding area, a place in army camps and bases where soldiers who had broken regulations or violated military law were held. In most cases, detainees were kept there for several days as punishment.

Naturally, depending on the severity of the offense, a court-martial might be called as well, so it was no laughing matter by any means. But even so, however she looked at it, she could not make sense of her predicament.

"Why am I in the stockade…?"

Assuming for the moment it was indeed the base's stockade, she still could not think of a reason for why she would be held there.

She was the type of soldier least likely to have anything to do with the stockade. She considered it natural to uphold the army's rules and regulations, and she didn't have any reluctance to following orders.

Given that, she would have liked to plead that something must have gone terribly wrong for her to be in there, but—

"I can't remember what happened last night..."

Putting her hand to her temple, Rusalka struggled to piece together exactly what had transpired.

She tried to work backward, but the sequence of events that would be required for her to be thrown in the stockade was too hard to surmise through guesswork, so she had to scrap that approach. Instead, she started from what she could remember.

"After the operation, I went out into the city on the general's orders. That was when I saw Natalie and the others in the street, so I ducked into a nearby shop. And then...and then?"

And then something had happened.

If that was where the missing piece was, her memories were unfortunately still dim. As she tried to grasp the thread of her faded memories—

"—You don't remember? You had a big old brawl with about twenty different drunk civilians in the pub."

As she struggled with her memories, another voice chimed in unexpectedly.

"—Gh. Who are you?"

Rusalka spun around, but there was no one there. Apparently, the voice was coming from the other side of the wall. Walking to the bars and looking out, she could not tell clearly, but she thought she could make out another set of bars next to hers. The room beside hers was surely another cell.

"In a word, we're neighbors. Hope we can get along."

"Apologies, but I struggle to see myself fraternizing with someone who would be thrown into the stockade..."

"Big talk from someone who also got thrown into the stockade."

Even though she rejected his outstretched hand, the man still belted out a hearty laugh.

His personality was more overly familiar than friendly. Rusalka preferred to maintain a measured distance with new acquaintances, so this first contact didn't leave a particularly good taste in her mouth. And on top of that, this stranger had been thrown into the stockade for some reason. That was more than enough for her to be on her guard.

"The mood got a little tense there. Don't tell me you're feeling nervous."

"No. More importantly, who are you? What did you do to deserve the stockade? Fraud?"

"You mind if I ask why you suspected fraud first of all things?"

"Because you said something earlier that I cannot let pass without comment."

It had been passed over in her initial shock, but the first thing he had said was not something she could just ignore.

"From what you said before, it sounded like you believe you know why I am here," Rusalka began.

"I just said it, didn't I? You beat the crap out of around twenty drunk civilians all at once in town last night."

"There is a flaw in your statement."

"What?"

Rusalka calmly boxed the man in, prepared to checkmate him.

"I would never start a fight with drunk civilians. And I do not partake in alcohol because it impairs one's judgment. That is simply the kind of discretion expected from an officer. So your statement must be false."

"No, no, no, no. You definitely did. You were one hundred percent drinking, and you absolutely did start a fight. That's why you're here."

"You have already been proven wrong. Checkmate."

"Just listen, will ya?"

She had destroyed his argument with irrefutable logic, but he refused to give up.

"Are you still clinging to such a preposterous claim that I would actually get into a drunken brawl?"

"C'mon now, don't give me the whole 'last thing I remember is literally anything but going into a pub' spiel. I can personally confirm the exact moment you started drinking."

"We have two differing statements, and yet there is only one truth."

"How can you be so confident if you can't even remember?!"

It sounded distinctly like the man was scratching his head in frustration. He appeared to be quite attached to his theory, but Rusalka couldn't find his claim even remotely plausible.

There was a saying that anything one man could imagine, others could make real, but there were limits. Rusalka had practiced hand-to-hand combat as part of her basic training, so it wouldn't have been impossible for her to deal with drunken amateurs. But even if it was possible, there was still a significant missing piece.

"Let us suppose that I did in fact enter a pub, and I will even allow, for the sake of argument, that I did in fact avail myself of alcohol. What then? How would that lead to a large fight? What could possibly...?"

She was about to say, *What could possibly make me do something so stupid?* when—

"Valkyries."

—a single word made her stop.

"_____"

"The reason you got into a fight was because of an issue involving Valkyries, Captain Evereska."

The man on the other side of the wall used her name. And as she fell silent, he continued:

"Or perhaps I should call you the Broken Valkyrie."

He tore into Rusalka's old scar—though no matter how much time passed, it never fully closed. A searing pain shot through her.

"I suppose this is where I say checkmate?"

"...That's rather heartless of you..."

"What's good for the goose is good for the gander."

There was a wry laugh from the other cell as the mood in the air lightened slightly. That change was what made her realize how much tension had been permeating the air. And also that despite what he said, it had been his consideration for her that had introduced a modicum of calm.

Indulging in his thoughtfulness a little, Rusalka sighed heavily and closed her eyes.

"You...can call me whatever you like. Whatever it is, I can take it."

"Is that so? Don't mind if I do then, love."

"I would prefer not to be defamed."

"You mean you consider that defamation? Learn to take a joke..."

She did not particularly feel like listening to a lecture on humor from someone who would interrupt a serious conversation to derail it like that. But regardless of how she felt, the man continued:

"Anyway, you have a lot of different titles, Rusalka Evereska. The hope of the second generation. The mother of Valkyrie flight-based tactics. And on and on…"

"You seem quite knowledgeable about me."

"Anyone who's been in the army for a few years knows at least that much. You're pretty famous, as I'm sure you're aware."

For better or worse, and whether it was fame or infamy, she was very conscious of that fact.

——Rusalka was well known in the European Army. She had been an ace pilot in her own right, and her Valkyrie flight had achieved prodigious results in battle as well. She had also been instrumental in developing the tactics regularly used on the European front ever since their inception. And she was the Broken Valkyrie, who had abandoned her flight that had mastered her tactics, only to fold up her wings—

"And to top it off, I got into a brawl with a bunch of civilians in a pub? I'm sure that will earn me a shameful new title as well."

"Oh, so you're willing to believe my story now?"

"…It's become more plausible…"

She had denied it before, but now she lowered her eyes, accepting that it was likely true. She still couldn't remember what had happened, but it was entirely believable that she might have gone off in a fit of rage when she heard that word, if her judgment had been impaired by alcohol. And if anything, she had gotten off easy if the stockade was all the punishment she had to look forward to. A fight like that would be an unprecedented scandal for the military.

"It would appear I've made a fool of myself."

"It was really something, all right. Even if the booze made you fuzzy in the head, your body didn't miss a single beat. But…"

"But?"

"If you think it's embarrassing to vent everything on whoever happens to be around, then I guess that part would be pretty embarrassing."

When he put it that way, there was nothing she could say. And there really wasn't any other way to put it. She had vented her bitterness at her own lack of virtue on whoever happened to be around her in a drunken fit. She could not imagine a worse thing for her to do.

"It looked pretty rough, but if something happened, you could always try talking about it? We're both locked up here, and I can keep a secret. I can listen awhile if you want?" he offered.

"Talk…? With you…?"

"Where'd that tone come from? Why so suspicious?"

She had not intended on being so obvious about it, but that had been her plain and frank reaction.

Either way, they were hardly even acquaintances. In fact, since she still couldn't remember last night clearly, she had effectively only just met him that morning. He was hardly the sort of person she felt comfortable having a heartfelt conversation with. Something like that was the equivalent of baring her soul. And she had no intention of being so lax as to expose herself like that to someone she barely knew.

"Sometimes there are things you can only talk about with people you don't know that well," mused Alejandro.

"Really?"

"How should I know? I just said it. I think there's probably something to it if you want an outsider's perspective on something, though."

It was hard to tell whether he really wanted to persuade her. But surprisingly, that vagueness helped ease her wariness.

Rusalka furrowed her brow, telling herself not to get caught up in his pace.

"If you still can't accept it, then just pretend I'm a wall that can nod along while you talk to yourself," was Alejandro's suggestion.

"I don't believe walls can nod along to anything."

"Use your imagination a little, will ya? Anything one man can imagine, others can make real. That means it could be a thing, right?"

"——"

"Hmm? What is it?"

"Nothing…"

She was surprised to hear him bring up the same saying she had thought to herself. And at the same time, she could feel the tension in her shoulders fading a tiny bit. She almost felt foolish for being so obstinate.

"Anyway, just give it a shot. And if you still aren't convinced when it's done, you can wring my neck for revenge."

"Very well."

"That was a little too quick for comfort."

His response felt rather cowardly.

It wasn't as if she had conceded there was a logic to what he said.

She most certainly had not. But she did sort of feel like running her mouth a little bit.

Perhaps it was even a bit of an extension of her desperation from the night before—

"But now that I'm trying to talk, I don't really know where to begin..."

"As long as it's about you, say whatever you want... Also, sorry if it sounds like I'm coming on to you."

"Can the wall stop talking, please?"

"To be clear, walls don't have necks to wring!" The man sounded a little sullen as the springs on his bed creaked. "If I can make a request, then... Why did you become a pilot?"

"———"

Rusalka paused for a moment at the surprising question. She had been asked why she joined the army and why she had become a Valkyrie countless times. But it was her first time being asked why she had chosen to fly. Because it was so strange and so unexpected, her lips started to move on their own.

"—The first time I saw a plane was when I was still a young girl."

5

Rusalka had joined the army before the pillars first appeared.

Born in a rural village in the north of Europe, she had been raised in the warmth of a loving family with her parents and two older brothers. She was aware she had been blessed with a happy upbringing.

She had been allowed to do what she wanted and was a little bit spoiled, since she was the youngest child. It wasn't in her nature to indulge in the privilege of being the youngest, however. Even back then, she had been just as inflexible and serious, just as humorless and unexpressive. Her family never hesitated to tell her as much, but it didn't change no matter how much time passed.

They had lived in a rural-enough setting that the local school had been several hours' walk each way, and hardly any other children her age had attended. She had abstractly known that cities existed, but the thought of actually seeing one had been like a dream. It had almost felt like cities were some imaginary place the adults whispered about in stories and rumors.

——Her world changed when she was eleven.

On that day, a propeller plane flying in the vast sky up above was forced to make an emergency landing in the wide-open field outside her school. Despite experiencing some kind of mechanical trouble, the pilot managed a splendid landing, and Rusalka's eyes were stolen away by that bright-red plane.

The fuselage was such a vivid red that it almost looked like a blazing fire. It was love at first sight.

Almost everyone who lived anywhere remotely close gathered to see if the plane could somehow be repaired. Rusalka watched the pilot working on the plane for days on end.

One day, after having seen Rusalka come by so many days in a row, the pilot finally asked her a pointed question:

"Do you like planes?"

She reflexively nodded, but she immediately regretted it. The subject of the red propeller plane was starting to become taboo in her home. Lately, that had been all she could talk about, and her parents were naturally not thrilled to see their young daughter so excited over a big hunk of metal.

She was the youngest child, but on that point, they refused to look the other way. Her brothers were on her side, but they were just children, too, and there was not much they could do for her. In the end, she was forced to bottle up her dream as an aimless impulse ate away at her from the inside.

That was why she regretted reflexively nodding. If it had been a leading question, and he was working together with her parents, then that would be the end for her.

But while she shivered at the possibility of such an outrageous imaginary conspiracy, the pilot broke into a grin and looked genuinely happy.

"—You don't say! That's great. I love planes, too."

——After that, she would visit the pilot often and listen to his stories. The middle-aged pilot was happy to tell her all sorts of stories. Because of that, she eventually told him she wanted to fly in a plane someday, too.

"Ahhh, that's a great dream."

And he didn't laugh at her dream. He listened while a little girl living in the middle of nowhere feverishly talked about her dream of flying, and he didn't laugh at her.

——On the day he finished his repairs and flew away, the pilot gave

Rusalka a gift. It was an old, faded set of dog tags. Thinking back on it, it was hardly the sort of thing anyone should be giving a young girl. But she would never forget how she felt in that moment. She swore to that pilot that someday she would soar through the sky, too.

The pilot didn't say he would be waiting. He didn't promise to meet her again someday, either. And thinking back on it, he had never even said his name.

But she didn't need any of that.

"The sky's the meeting place, and there's no such thing as too late or too early—that's enough for any pilot."

And with that, he grinned and took off.

Rusalka watched him go until his plane disappeared way off in the distance. And time passed as she continued to believe that someday, somehow her chance would come—

"And now I can't even fly in that sky anymore."

Rusalka's breathing was ragged as she muttered weakly.

The rash and ignorant girl who had been driven by dreams alone was gone. In her place was Rusalka, who had put untold hours of work into making that dream a reality.

She had weathered her family's objections, left her hometown, and joined the army even though she was a woman. She had been forced to thread a needle to become a pilot despite the odds stacked against her for being a woman, but she devoted herself to her studies and training to earn that right for herself.

And she had believed that sometime in the future, she would get her chance to fly through that same sky as the pilot from her youth.

But then the pillars of light had appeared, and she had gotten her chance to fly far earlier than expected in a way that she never wished for.

"I didn't get to fly because I was chosen but because there was no one left to fly."

Her promotion to being an active pilot had simply been the consequence of a sudden change in circumstances. Countless valuable pilots had been lost fighting the pillars, making it expedient to rush Rusalka and her class into cockpits after a crash course.

And while she was flying like that, Odin appeared, and the First

Valkyrie was born. That was around the time Rusalka became a second-generation Valkyrie.

"I didn't have any special talent. I had just been thinking about it longer than everyone else, because I've always been thinking about flying, even when I wasn't allowed to fly. That was why I figured things out a little bit before the others."

She had even been proud of it. She was glad to be recognized. Anyone who had their efforts acknowledged would feel a desire to improve themselves even further. And Rusalka was no exception. She had been proud of what her team had accomplished, of what Xenia, Victorica, and Canan had achieved.

——And as those days went by, everything changed when she met Amy.

"The First Valkyrie, huh."

For the first time, the man said something as Rusalka's back straightened.

He could not see it, of course, but it was something she needed for herself, to give herself a moment of pause.

Amy's smile flashed through her mind, the girl who seemed to always have such a bright golden aura to her.

Flying together with her was an important mission any pilot in the world would have considered an honor. And yet, Rusalka hadn't been able to bring herself to do it. In fact, of all things, she had—

"The great Valkyrie who even offered up her family name to God… no, to all of humanity."

"Don't talk about her like that, please. That wasn't her at all. Amy was just…"

She would smile when she was happy, get upset when people teased her. But she would never let anyone see her sad—outside that one moment.

"——"

Rusalka stopped there, unable to say anything more.

Amy had come to her room that day, and they had spoken. But she would never tell anyone else what had been said.

"You'll talk about everything in the first half of your life and then just give me total silence? I guess the rest is only for paying subscribers?"

"Paying…? No, I have no intention of seeking profit…"

"You wouldn't know a joke if it walked up and kicked you right in the ass. Not that it matters, I guess." There was a bitter laugh as the man changed tacks. "It looks like we'll have to continue this story some other time."

Just then, there was a loud screech as the iron door opened. There was a sharp, clicking bootstep as a young man in uniform appeared in front of Rusalka's door. Judging from the insignia on his arm, he was one of the military police charged with watching the stockade. He stood at attention and addressed her through the bars.

"Captain Rusalka Evereska, you are to be released in accordance with regulations. Please step outside, ma'am."

She reflexively stood at attention and saluted. Seeing that, the soldier unlocked the door, granting her freedom. Feeling almost let down, Rusalka stepped out and headed toward the exit.

"Cooling your head for the night… No, I guess it's just sleeping off the booze? It must be nice being a Valkyrie, getting off with only that much."

Annoyance crossed her face as the man's sharp tongue hit her back on the way out, so she decided to get a look at his face for herself.

But—

"Would you mind looking this way?"

"Unfortunately, I got caught up in a certain someone's rampage yesterday and am not looking too great. I'd rather not have anyone remembering how I look right now."

"Mrgh…"

The man was lying facedown on the hard bed. All she could tell from that angle was that he was tall and that he had dirty-blond hair. Held hostage by guilt over something she still couldn't remember, she found it impossible to insist he turn around.

"So you would have me leave without knowing the face of the person who I told so much about myself?"

"I remember your face perfectly. If the chance arises, I'll be sure to give you a call."

"So you don't plan on telling me your name, either."

"Isn't it more romantic this way?"

Rusalka sighed.

Face aside, it had been a long time since she had exchanged promises to meet again with someone whose name she did not know. And she had never actually managed to meet that pilot again. What was going to come of this promise?

"You can trust me to follow through. I'm a guy who keeps his word."

"...I'm not sure that line has the effect you want when you're refusing to even turn around..."

But even so, he insisted on remaining hidden. He simply waved his hand at her as she headed outside.

"I'm sorry, but may I ask you something?"

After she stepped outside and basked in the cool morning air for a moment, Rusalka turned to the young MP watching over the stockade. He snapped to attention. She was sure he was having a bit of trouble with how exactly he should address her.

"What is it, Captain?"

"Where should I go now that I've been released?"

"No orders were passed along to me, ma'am. You may do as you please."

"As I please..."

Rusalka couldn't believe this would all end with just that based on what she knew of what she had presumably done. She had gone into the city on the general's orders, and in the process of carrying out those orders, she had consumed alcohol while on duty and even started a bar fight. It was honestly bad enough that she was mentally prepared to receive a dishonorable discharge.

If nothing else, she had to go apologize in person for her transgressions.

"Though going to do that while I still don't even really remember what I did would probably just make things worse..."

At the very least, she could not imagine a proper justification for what she had done the other night. But even if it would be the last thing she did before her discharge, she felt she should properly take responsibility.

"Apologies for bothering you. Also, about the man in the cell beside me..."

Her tongue froze as she started to ask who he was. The guard looked puzzled as she paused for a moment.

"...No, never mind. If you'll excuse me."

Rusalka shook her head, deciding it would be poor taste to ask. He looked a mess, but he had declared that he would keep his word. She decided that robbing him of the opportunity to follow through wouldn't be very fair.

Besides…

"…It's just a little bit, but…"

…she really did feel a tiny bit lighter after talking some.

Grateful for that, her feet felt a little bit lighter, too.

6

Rusalka had secured a seat in the corner of the mess hall for lunch.

"Is it true you got drunk and started a fight, Rusalka?"

"———"

And the girl sitting next to her did not mince words at all.

Glancing over, she saw a refined but unexpressive face. The short girl had olive skin, light-purple eyes, and long black hair. She had on a uniform, but it was hard to shake the feeling that the uniform was wearing her more so than the other way around. She looked like a student trying hard to appear older than she was, and in truth, she was still school-age. If Rusalka recalled correctly, she was just sixteen. But she looked even younger than that, which made it feel even less like she had any business wearing a soldier's uniform.

"Did you hear me?"

"…Yes, I heard you, Alma Conturo."

"Just Alma is fine."

The young girl looked up at Rusalka. There was no trace of emotion on her face, which was something they had in common. Another similarity was the way they both were eating lunch in a corner of the mess hall away from anyone else.

"Of course, I'm alone due to a breakdown in relations. Surely you don't have a need to do the same?" Rusalka openly asked.

"Did you want to eat dolo?"

"I'm not sure what that means. I can't help but feel it an extraordinarily painful description of my situation."

Rusalka wondered whether it was just her interpretation as she started to eat. Following her lead, Alma started to nibble away at her food as well.

The people nearby made no effort to interact with them. It wasn't as if the mess hall was deserted. The other soldiers were simply avoiding them. Or more specifically, avoiding Rusalka.

She had thought she was used to people tiptoeing around her, but the feeling had escalated in an unexpected way after last night, making her belatedly realize she still had some sense of herself as a normal person. Though even that seemed almost like an observation from afar.

——Her status at Hamburg base had always been complicated.

She was a Valkyrie unable to fly, not because of any physical issue but because of an emotional problem. That was the reason why she was called the Broken Valkyrie and why most people had such a low opinion of her.

For better or worse, she was difficult for the people on the base to deal with. And on top of all that, she had gotten into a drunk bar fight with civilians. Not only was it a bizarre action, given her usual behavior, but it was also unprecedented for a Valkyrie to be thrown into the stockade for something like that. It was only natural for the people around her to distance themselves even more.

"I understand it is completely my own fault, but..."

Rusalka thought back on her actions as she took stock of the discomfort and agitation pointed toward her from all directions.

She had thought it a lonely scene when she had seen Amy by herself in the mess hall in the past, but experiencing it for herself, the emptiness eating away at her heart was far worse than she had imagined.

Which only made her regret how she had treated Amy at the time even more—

"So what was it?"

All of a sudden, Alma's voice interrupted her moment of reflection and her meal. Rusalka finished swallowing a bite of cheese and penne as she cocked her head.

"What was what?"

"Dementia?"

"You don't have a filter, do you...?"

She furrowed her brow at Alma's innocent question before massaging her forehead.

She was struck by the thought that it had been a while since she had worried about wrinkles on her forehead. She was sure her current sentimentality had something to do with all the talking she had done in the stockade that morning.

"By all accounts, I did indeed get myself in a pub brawl with civilians. I don't recall it happening, though."

"Because you took concentrated damage to the head?"

"Or due to the effects of alcohol. Unfortunately, either might very well explain the symptoms."

"...That's surprising."

Alma touched her napkin to her lips while Rusalka was forced to agree with her frank assessment.

Both the fact that she had consumed alcohol and that she had become drunk were things she would never have imagined. And then to get into a fight in the pub to top it off... She could only imagine she had been bewitched somehow.

Still, the evidence all pointed to the truth of the situation.

"So it would be better for you not to be seen with me. Not unless you want others to start spreading wild rumors regarding your association with me."

"What, like the two of us going out to play around with men every night or something?"

"In a word, yes."

Alma snorted. It was a weak, disinterested response, but that was just how Alma was sometimes. She often held to positions that got her labeled a maverick or eccentric.

Victorica and Canan both had tended to flout regulations a little bit, but they'd still been career soldiers, and that core identity had never wavered. But Alma was different in that regard because she was a third-generation Valkyrie.

Unlike the second generation, who were chosen from among the ranks for having even the minimal level of compatibility, the third generation were elites handpicked from all around the world for their potential. They were different from Rusalka's generation, who had been soldiers before becoming Valkyries. This generation had been made Valkyries first and foremost.

It could be considered one aspect of a Valkyrie's divine blessing that from the moment they awakened as a Valkyrie, they were capable of naturally operating the Deus ex Machina they were granted by Odin. Just as there was no bird born without knowing how to use its own wings, the Valkyries instinctively knew how to control their own wings as well. That was also why Xenia and Canan had been able to fly so comfortably with Rusalka and Victorica despite coming from different branches of the army.

Of course, there was variation in skill, born of each individual's unique experiences and senses, but even that was made up for to some extent by the Valkyrie's natural compatibility with her machine.

Because of that, the third generation's military experience was extraordinarily limited. They had undergone the most basic of crash courses and been told to learn the rest in the field. That was proof of just how bad the war was going and could even be considered a truly foolhardy decision by military leaders. That being said, just like the shameful but resolute decision the world leaders had made to believe the self-proclaimed god who had suddenly appeared, that reckless choice had led to a miraculous result, allowing the army to hold the line.

The main force currently holding the European front together was the third generation of Valkyries. Because of that, the third generation tended to have a strong sense of pride and strongly identified as Valkyries.

Consequently, they generally took a poor view of Rusalka, who was infamous for abandoning her role as a Valkyrie, which meant the way Alma interacted with her normally could almost be called heretical.

"———"

Alma apparently didn't concern herself overly much with all that, though, as she sat beside Rusalka, her cheeks near bursting with food as she focused on her lunch. Her stance toward Rusalka had been the same ever since she was deployed to Hamburg base. She did not always spend time with Rusalka, but if their schedules happened to overlap, she would sit with her during meals.

And Rusalka understood that even that tiny connection had been an enormous help to her. That was probably why she had not insisted on trying to distance herself from Alma.

But that mutual understanding was only shared by Alma and Rusalka—

"—You seem quite at ease given what happened last night."

Naturally, not everyone was so understanding.

"———"

A sharp, clear voice thundered out. It was a fierce tone that drowned out the noise of the mess hall and forced those who heard it to listen.

The owner of that voice was brimming with drive, to the point she almost seemed the embodiment of a bolt of lightning.

Her bright-red hair was neatly tied back, and her prim expression conveyed a natural-born refinement. Her eyes flared angrily as she put her hand on the table and glared at Rusalka.

Looking back into her amber eyes, Rusalka set down her fork.

"Were you having lunch as well, Natalie Chase?"

"Why, yes, I was. However, having seen you, I couldn't simply sit still. Just what were you thinking last night?"

Her sharp gaze shot straight through Rusalka, trying to probe the depths of her heart. She was another of the third-generation Valkyries at the base. In addition to being the flight leader of the base's Valkyries, she boasted overwhelming talent for being a Valkyrie and demonstrated an excellence as a pilot that marked her as a promising prospect in the future once she had time to grow into her role some more.

She was the model third-generation Valkyrie. She had chosen to become a Valkyrie for the sake of humanity and had a powerful sense of pride and duty. And also—

"For a proud and noble Valkyrie to be thrown into the stockade of all things… It's inexcusable."

—she was one of the people who made no effort to hide the animosity she felt toward Rusalka.

"———"

The way she made no effort to hide how she felt about Rusalka was refreshing. Not because open animosity was easier to endure than just having everyone avoid her, nor was it a masochistic desire to have someone blame her for what she did.

If she had to describe it, it was because she felt that the way Natalie behaved was more agreeable than her own demeanor. The way Natalie was so comfortable loudly declaring something was wrong if she thought it was wrong. Rusalka sensed she was probably jealous of that confidence.

"Are you listening to me?"

Natalie's eyes narrowed in annoyance as Rusalka remained silent. Snapping back to reality at that verbal prodding, Rusalka shook her head.

"Pardon me. You came over so suddenly that I was surprised."

"...Still acting like this is someone else's problem, I see. Do you have any idea just how grave your actions last night were?"

"Grave?"

"Quite. Surely even you must have realized how unprecedented it was."

Having it pointed out so plainly, Rusalka didn't have an answer for her.

In truth, she had reported to the general immediately after she had been released, fully expecting a dishonorable discharge. She had apologized for what had happened last night and waited for his verdict.

But to her surprise, her sentence had only been to provide a written explanation and a formal apology. Put bluntly, it was a punishment so lenient it might as well have been an acquittal, and it would almost certainly earn cynical comments about how Valkyries were afforded special treatment. Even Rusalka herself felt she was receiving special treatment.

As Rusalka fell silent, Natalie crossed her arms and sighed.

"You are in a complicated position to begin with. But even so, the problems you cause do not merely affect you. Even if you cannot fly anymore, you are still..."

"...I'm not a Valkyrie any—"

"I'm well aware of that!"

Before she could finish, another thunderous shout suddenly split the air of the mess hall. Half a second later, Natalie covered her mouth with her hand, as if she had not intended to shout. There was an awkward tension as—

"...You're too loud, Natalie."

Alma glared at Natalie in annoyance as she covered her ears. Natalie lowered her hand.

"...Please do not make me repeat myself anymore, Alma. You shouldn't fraternize with her so much. It sets a bad example."

"Example? You want me to go along with everyone else? Why?"

"Why must you be so unreasonable...?"

Natalie's lips sank into a frown as Alma cocked her head in confusion. It looked like things might explode between them at that rate, but having flightmates wear at each other's nerves like that served no one.

"Natalie is correct, Alma. She is just being a good friend." Cleaning up the remnants of her lunch, Rusalka picked up her plate and stood to leave.

Alma seemed displeased as she looked at Rusalka.

"You're my friend, too."

"______"

Rusalka couldn't say anything in response. Her expression remained unchanged as well. She just silently nodded and turned to Natalie.

"Natalie, I truly regret what happened and am seriously reflecting on how it happened. I will not let something like it happen again."

"Of course. It should never have happened in the first place even. However..."

"However?"

"You still refuse to say anything in your own defense."

Rusalka's eyes widened as Natalie crossed her arms and glared, seemingly annoyed at Rusalka's response.

She was a proud girl. Even when dealing with someone who was entirely in the wrong, she would grant the accused an opportunity to explain themselves. But Rusalka merely shook her head.

"This is just the natural conclusion."

"—Argh. That's not what I meant at all..."

Natalie's voice grew slightly ragged as Rusalka responded while averting her sky-blue eyes. But after the angry outburst just moments earlier, she soon closed her mouth.

Rusalka quickly took her leave and went to return her plate and silverware.

"______"

Looking around, it was plain to see that the three of them had made a scene. Rusalka had become even more infamous since the morning, and she was determined not to get the two of them caught up in any nasty rumors.

"It would be nice if I could just blame it on the alcohol, but..."

Even if she couldn't remember what had happened because of the alcohol, her trip to the stockade could hardly be chalked up to the same weak excuse. The main issue was probably her inability to find anyone else to blame for her guilt.

And with that thought, she walked out of the mess hall by herself.

——There was one person who watched her leave before heaving a long, heavy sigh.

"...Why must you always look like you've given up on everything...?"

After making that wistful observation, Natalie sat down where

Rusalka had just been moments ago. Her hand touched the seat, feeling the warmth Rusalka had left.

"Pervert..."

Natalie glared at Alma's blunt comment. It turned out she had more to say.

"You know... You should stop furrowing your brow like that. Your personality shows on your face."

"Where did you hear that?"

"It's just a saying you can hear anywhere."

"Hmph... Whatever..."

Natalie avoided Alma's gaze, looking down through the long eyelashes that rimmed her eyes. Her intense lightning-bolt-like aura slowly faded. And without that dazzling thunder, all that remained was a young woman.

"...Why does she insist on never saying anything...?"

"You're annoying, Natalie, so can you go somewhere else?"

"How rude."

Natalie's expression softened as she propped her head up at Alma's blunt appraisal. Meanwhile, Alma quietly went about eating the remainder of her lunch, which was starting to get cold.

7

After leaving Alma and Natalie, Rusalka wandered aimlessly around the base.

She couldn't find any place where she could calm down. Her always overly serious demeanor had long troubled her, and it meant that in a situation like her current one, she did not know how best to make use of her time.

"I was already a burden, but..."

She was fed up with the awkwardness of so many gazes she could feel in the distance. Word of her scandal last night had spread all through the base. She had no way to know how exaggerated the rumors had become, but if she had to hazard a guess, she was probably becoming known as the former Valkyrie who picked a fight with civilians and didn't get any kind of punishment for it.

"The worst possible rumor I can imagine..."

There had surely never been a Valkyrie with such a notorious reputation. At the very least, Rusalka could not remember anyone who came even remotely close, and she was the second-generation Valkyrie who had served the longest in the army.

It was possible the army was in the process of covering up her scandal. Not that that would make her feel any better, though. Being thrown in the stockade for a night, a written apology, and two days of discipline. That was the extent of her punishment, but it was probably just a measure to avoid letting this develop into a major disturbance.

Ultimately, she wouldn't be welcome at her post, but she couldn't bring herself to stay hidden away in her room, either, so she was wandering around the base—

"———"

She caught her breath when she realized where she had walked without thinking.

"The hangar..."

The maintenance crews in jumpsuits were rushing all around, getting things in order. The pilots had gotten a brief respite after the fighting ended, but it was clear from the maintenance crews' ghastly looks that they had been working through the night to make sure the main force the army could wield against the pillars—the Valkyries' Deus ex Machinas—would be ready to be on station again as soon as possible.

The Deus ex Machinas were essentially sacred relics granted by God. But they required the same maintenance as the models of plane they were based off, which meant they needed a lot of work hours in order to continue operating at peak performance.

And battles in the sky were not fought by Valkyries alone. For them to fully realize their potential, they needed support from other units as well. Having to keep the modern airframes maintained and ready to go as well was why the maintenance crews were constantly laboring around the clock.

These technicians were working themselves to the bone to keep things going just so that the wings needed to fly across the battlefield were ready to sortie at a moment's notice. And it went without saying that Rusalka had no business getting involved here. Even if she was just sitting out of the way, it would only make her and the work crews uncomfortable. She turned to leave—

"—Oh, if it isn't the Broken Valk. Been a while since you showed your face here."

"______"

—but she was stopped in her tracks by an unexpected, husky voice. Bitterly, Rusalka realized she had tripped up. If she had kept moving, she could have just pretended she hadn't heard the voice and been on her way. But she had stopped. And the person calling out to her had noticed that moment of indecision.

"Hey! Wait, wait, wait! Don't ignore me! C'mon, get over here."

"Chief Technician Reever..."

Brisk, determined footsteps approached Rusalka. Resigned to her fate, she turned and was greeted by a tall, smiling man standing right in front of her. His eyes were brimming with curiosity and anticipation.

"I heard! You got into a royal mess down at a pub in the city, right? Ha-ha-ha, not too shabby."

"Yes, I well and truly botched things."

"Oh? It looks like you're taking it harder than I would've thought."

The man who put his hands to his cheeks and wriggled his hips as Rusalka's shoulders slumped was Chief Technician Roger Reever—the head of Hamburg base's maintenance crews and a grizzled veteran.

At almost 190 centimeters tall, he had a slender, well-toned body; bright-brown hair that had been permed; and a pink headband. He had an unusual appearance but was incomparably skilled when it came to maintenance. Rumor had it that if not for him, the base would be able to keep only half as many planes operational as it did, and he was widely considered to be one of the main figures holding things together from the shadows.

Rusalka glared at him. "Watch out. If you get too close to me, you might end up getting thrown around, too."

"Ha-ha-ha, looks like you're really smarting. What's the big idea, showing me such a cute side of yourself?"

Sighing, Roger put a finger to Rusalka's chin, nudging her face up. And when she did, his long eyelashes fluttered.

"Having a bad night with liquor is something that happens to just about everyone as they grow up. What's it matter if you make a mistake every once in a while? That just means you're human. Your reactions are usually so alien it can be hard to tell if you're really human in there."

"I certainly never intended to be so removed from normal behavior that my humanity would be brought into question."

"Ah-ha-ha-ha, good one."

She hadn't meant it to be a joke, but for some reason that was how it had been received. For the first time, Rusalka realized just how annoying that could be.

Noticing Rusalka's mild irritation building, Roger raised his eyebrows. "Hmm? You seem like you've changed a bit."

"Huh?"

"It's not connected at all to what we've been talking about, but you're actually showing a bit of emotion today. That liquor may have been just what the doctor ordered."

"———"

Rusalka touched her cheek. It didn't feel like her expression was any softer than usual. And if anything, she felt more depressed than normal.

"Or if it wasn't the liquor, then…maybe it was a guy?"

"It was not."

"Oooooh? Shooting the theory down straightaway? Usually, you get up on your high horse before denying it."

Roger's unseemly smile widened when she reflexively dismissed the possibility.

But it was a boorish suspicion. She did not feel aggrieved at his probing. It was such a spectacularly misplaced guess that the events that morning in the stockade did not even cross her mind.

"Well, if you're that insistent, then I suppose I'll believe you. Aaanyway, the reason I came over here…"

"Wh-why did…?"

"—Your Spitfire."

The air around Roger changed the instant those words were spoken. Rusalka froze, as if a spell had been cast on her. She gulped.

"I've kept your Deus ex Machina properly maintained. It's ready to fly whenever you might need it."

Roger crossed his arms, almost like he was hugging his elbows, as he glanced toward a certain corner of the hangar. She saw a Deus ex Machina waiting quietly there beneath a gray sheet.

"———"

An enormous, conflicted mass of emotion welled inside her. Joy and anger, sadness and guilt. It felt like she had experienced the entire gamut of emotions all at once.

At the very least, there was no mistaking that even as emotionless as she was, her feelings were all being called into action. That was just how much that plane meant to her.

——That Deus ex Machina contained all the feelings and thoughts she had for the sky.

"A Deus ex Machina can only show its true potential under the guiding hands of the Valkyrie to whom it was given," Roger began.

"———"

"Only women can become Valkyries...and only young girls at that. They receive their Deus ex Machina from God, and they just rely on their innate proficiency to figure out the controls. It's only natural."

Roger was talking about the initial scheme that had been introduced when Valkyries were first born. It had been tested countless times, and there had even been experiments where air force pilots had flown in the Deus ex Machinas Odin had granted the Valkyries.

But—

"Divine power, huh? Wonder of wonders, only the plane's chosen Valkyrie can properly wield it," Roger mused.

If a Deus ex Machina was flown by any pilot besides its designated Valkyrie, it would be nothing more than an ancient propeller-driven plane. It was a steadfast rule that applied even when Valkyries exchanged Deus ex Machinas.

In other words, there was a single Valkyrie meant for each machine. That was the unwritten rule.

"As is, she's just wasting space in the hanger sitting over there," Roger said, bringing up Rusalka's machine again.

"...Why are you maintaining her?"

"What's this? Are you perhaps interested in little old me? Sorry, sorry. Just kidding."

Waving off Rusalka stilted question, Roger shifted gears and thought about it for a moment.

"I suppose it would sound cooler if I said it was because I believed you would fly again someday, but I can't say I'm overly confident in seeing that happen."

It was lighthearted, but Roger made it clear that he didn't have a lot of faith in Rusalka's return to the skies. She couldn't help flashing a wry smile at his straightforward response. In his own way, he was being considerate of her.

And seeing her smile like that, Roger's expression softened.

"So I suppose the most honest answer is that it's just habit. There's a plane there, so I'll make sure it is maintained. And I'll make sure it gets repairs. And I'll make sure it's ready to fly."

"———"

"And that's because I know how to fix planes. But fixing people's outside my area of expertise."

In one sense, it was a cold response. Rusalka lowered her eyes and bit her lip.

I really don't have any right to be here—

"—That was why I was so surprised when I heard about yesterday. Have you maybe managed to recover some?"

"Huh…?"

Rusalka looked in wonder as the topic somehow managed to make its way back to that. For a second, it felt like static interrupted her thoughts, but she quickly adjusted, which left her wondering if she was being teased again as she met Roger's smiling eyes.

But she couldn't sense any ill intentions as he stood there calmly. If she just assumed he was good at hiding what he was thinking, there would be no end to her doubts, but…

"Why would my scandal last night have any connection with me recovering? If you believe alcohol has that much power, then perhaps you are suffering under the delusions of an alcoholic?"

"It's not very nice to say something so twisted—and after you looked so cute when you were crying."

"Wha—?!"

Roger winked as he held a finger to his lips. Before she realized it, Rusalka's cheeks were burning.

What did he mean by that?

"…When you say 'crying,' are you by any chance using the word the same way I do?"

"I'd like to say that's a pretty awful attempt to dodge the issue, but I guess it was also some really terrible liquor. Anyway, yeah, I mean exactly what you think I mean when I say 'crying.' You understand, right?"

Roger traced a finger from his eyelid down his cheek as Rusalka froze. He had no reason to lie about something like that out of nowhere. At least, she was mostly sure of that. And Rusalka had noticed the dried tears on her face that morning in the stockade.

She had assumed it had been a dream, but—

"What did you see last night…?!"

She had been forced to conclude that she had gotten into a fight with civilians in a drunk fit based on circumstantial evidence and other people's testimonies, but that was apparently not all that had happened.

Just how much had word of her disgraceful behavior spread around the base?

Rusalka stared at her hands as Roger shrugged.

"I couldn't say. I was busy last night, so all I saw was when you were being thrown into the stockade. I didn't get to see the decisive moment…but I did see you crying."

"W-was I shamefully crying out of fear of the crime I had committed…?"

"Well now, what do you think?"

Rather than malice, this was his idea of an earnest response. He seemed to be testing her, but really, he didn't know the answer to her question. In which case, there was only one person she knew who could answer her question.

"Pardon me, Chief Reever, but I'll be going now. I've decided where I should visit next."

"Oh yeah? I have more work still, so I won't stop you…but are you okay?"

Rusalka looked up, finally deciding where she should head after wandering aimlessly most of the day. When she heard Roger's question, she glanced back for just a second.

——Her eyes darted to her beloved plane, sitting in the corner of the hangar beneath a sheet.

"Yes, for the moment at least."

She hesitated for only a split second before she nodded. And then she stood at attention, facing the maintenance chief's all-knowing gaze, which seemed to see right through her.

"For now, I am going to go settle up with my tears from last night."

8

"—I'm pretty sure the promise was that I would find you. Sheesh, you just don't understand proper romance."

The door burst open, and Rusalka came to a stop in front of the iron bars as the man grimaced.

He was tall, with dirty-blond hair. She hadn't been able to get a proper look at him that morning, but now she could see that he had deep-blue, almost sapphire-like eyes and a scraggly, unshaved mustache that suited the hint of wildness that touched his smirk.

When she finally got a good look at him, it almost felt like she was standing in front of a caged lion. Not because he looked particularly savage, but there was something about his presence that evoked the creature. For some reason, he had that sort of imposing aura about him.

"______"

——Rusalka had returned to the stockade in search of answers about last night.

And he had apparently not expected her sudden visit, either, because he didn't have a chance to turn around. Thanks to that, she could finally stand face-to-face with the man who had acted so haughty that morning. And yet…

"What is it? You must have wanted something if you bothered coming all the way over here, right? Why not try saying something?"

"Is it because you are inside a cage that you look like a lion?"

"Wha—? Wait, wait. I told you to say something, but I meant let's have a conversation. How do you expect me to play catch with you when you come lobbing a bomb like that? Besides, I'm more of a football guy."

The man responded without getting up from his seat on the bed, just looking out at her from behind the bars. He was being held for a full day, unlike Rusalka, who had been released after a few hours. That just drove home again how differently Valkyries were treated compared to regular soldiers, but she put a lid on that thought for the moment. She had something she wanted to ask the man in the cell.

"You said you were with me at the pub where I started a fight last night, right?"

"Huh? Ah, yeah, that's right. But is that really what you came here to ask? After all this, you still don't believe me?"

"I believe you regarding that part. The military police confirmed as much."

"That isn't believing me, then. It just means you went and got evidence."

He ruffled his hair with his hand in exasperation.

Unfortunately, that was the sort of thing Rusalka preferred to be absolutely sure about, so she would rather he just let that part go. Either way, she had gotten confirmation that he had been there that night. All that remained was—

"Could you please tell me about last night in a little bit more detail? According to your story, I started to go wild when the topic of Valkyries came up..."

"Whoa, there. You should be precise when it comes to reports. Let's review, Captain Evereska."

"——"

"I can't hear you. Or is it just that your memory is lacking when it comes to topics you would prefer to avoid?"

He dramatically raised his long legs high up before bringing them down to rise to his feet in a single, smooth motion. He slowly approached the door and looked Rusalka in the eye through the bars.

Rusalka was taller than average, but this man was even taller. There was such a large difference in their heights that she was forced to look up slightly when standing right in front of him. But mysteriously, she didn't feel intimidated. She simply stood tall and continued to listen.

"If it's about this morning, I'm quite confident that the exact statement I made was '*The reason you got into a fight was because of an issue involving Valkyries.*'"

The quiet, careful correction he spoon-fed Rusalka triggered her memory. Remembering their exchange that morning, she was forced to acknowledge that he was correct.

It had only a slightly different nuance, but it was not uncommon for imprecise language to have a significant impact on meaning. And in the army, it was absolutely necessary to accurately repeat an order to avoid errors in transmission.

"The reason I went wild was an issue involving Valkyries."

"But why are you so interested in what happened last night? You got out after half a day. The brass decided to let this go without it turning into a big scandal, so why are you here digging it up again?"

"...The dried-up tears..."

Rusalka touched her cheeks. The man furrowed his brow at that, while Rusalka glared straight at the wrinkles on his forehead.

"I—I heard that I was sobbing."

"...What, that? You were still plenty pretty even if you were crying."

"But I'm nineteen...almost twenty at this point. And a career soldier to boot. For me to do that in front of other people..."

And to sob in terror of the consequences of a crime I committed of all things.

Hearing that self-admonition, the man nodded and closed one eye as he said, "I see..." For a moment, Rusalka tensed, on edge about what he might say. But what followed was not a taunt at all.

"You think it's normal for a soldier to not feel free to cry? It's a bit frustrating, but there's a kernel of truth to that, I suppose. But what about a Valkyrie?"

"Huh?"

She had come to find out why she had cried. She had been prepared for him to make fun of her for it even. But he didn't comment on her motive at all.

It had only been for a short moment, but he had seriously thought about what she said before responding.

So she decided to do the same as the man behind bars continued his line of thought.

"The current Valkyries are mostly third-generation Valkyries chosen for their potential. They're not soldiers at heart; they're Valkyries first and foremost...so they should be free to cry, shouldn't they?"

"Even if that were true, I'm different. I'm a second-generation—"

"—Valkyrie."

Rusalka froze at his decisive conclusion. And she also realized that even if he had not said it, she would have. Even though she denied it time and time again to everyone who tried to say otherwise. Even though she had decided she didn't have the right to call herself a Valkyrie anymore.

She gritted her teeth as a swell of powerful emotions surged inside her.

"—'I am a Valkyrie.'"

His words caught her off guard. Her mind ground to a halt as unease cast a shadow over her thoughts. She stopped breathing, looking straight ahead. The man's gaze remained unchanged as he looked down at Rusalka and spoke.

He repeated it again:

"'I am a Valkyrie.'"

She furrowed her brow in confusion, unable to grasp what he was getting at. It was an unpleasant feeling. She couldn't explain why, but it was uncomfortable on a deep level because she could not understand what he was doing.

"...What is your point?"

So she finally decided to ask him directly. And faced with her desperately searching question, his response was incredibly simple.

"That was what you said while you were crying and rampaging around the pub."

"—!"

She wanted to say that was impossible, but she couldn't. She couldn't remember. She had no evidence to disprove his claim.

——*No, there is proof. The proof is how much my heart aches.*

The pain in her chest. As long as that shame remained, she would never be able to say something like that, no matter how broken her spirit. She shouldn't have been able to utter those words.

"You..."

Her voice was trembling in pain, but what was she even trying to ask? She didn't understand it herself. And no one else could possibly know, either. Before her question could take form, something happened—

"______"

——All of a sudden, alarms started blaring across the entire base.

"That's... It can't be...?!" Rusalka could hardly believe it.

These were emergency sirens she had heard so often she had lost count long ago. Sirens that triggered an instinctive unease, forcing everyone listening into a tense state of alertness. There was no mistaking what they meant.

——A pillar must have been detected by the base.

"But we just pushed them back last night!"

She paid no heed to the weak, almost pleading voice that escaped her lips. That was just how devastating it was to have to face pillars two days in a row. They had driven the pillars back the other day because they had kept their enemy occupied until their time limit was up. A second attack coming so soon would mean they wouldn't be able to depend on that rule anymore, which was gravely concerning.

And more importantly—

"The only people on base capable of enduring another battle so soon are..."

"Evereska!"

"Gh!"

As Rusalka thought back to the attrition and exhaustion of last night, despair started to well in her heart, but a sharp voice called her back to her senses. Spinning around, she realized the blond man had called her name.

As he looked at her through the bars, there was a seriousness to his gaze that he had not shown before.

"Quit grumbling and get to your post!"

"...Who are you?"

"Those are orders from a superior officer. There are things that only you can do right now."

The man's voice pulled her back to reality, but she was immediately unsure how to deal with him. But he was already looking far beyond the moment. He had decided to worry about his own situation later and focus on pummeling Rusalka with a powerful sense of responsibility.

"Do your duty, Rusalka Evereska!"

"Yes, sir."

He seemed an expert at issuing orders, and Rusalka quickly accepted his latest one, dashing out of the stockade. She left the military police behind as they started shouting while the sirens blared.

"I'm going to my post! Take care of him!"

She didn't explicitly tell them to release him. But it was an unspoken agreement that people in the stockade would be let out in the event of an emergency. There was no sense in letting them die because a stray round from an air raid hit the stockade, and more importantly, the base would be shorthanded no matter how many people they scrambled to find.

"I should also..."

Rusalka trailed off as she rushed away, not waiting to see the young military police officer nod. But for a moment, her feet were unsure where exactly that was.

She was currently a tactical adviser attached to the command staff as well as a radio operator, so her natural place would be in the command post. But when the image of her crimson Spitfire flashed through her head, she hesitated.

"—No."

But that indecision lasted for only a moment. After a split second, it was clear what she had chosen. She didn't run to the hangar; her destination was the command post. This was the natural conclusion.

The army had to operate as a single organism. The head had its role, as did the arms and legs and organs. If one part decided to act independently on a whim, the entire organism would cease to function properly.

She was just one of the cogs in the army's machine. And a cog's role was to rack its brain and figure out how best to work in sync with the rest of the machine's moving parts.

In order to do that—

"Alma…Natalie…"

She prayed the two girls she had left in the mess hall would fight hard.

They were still inexperienced Valkyries, but they were Hamburg base's strongest assets in combat.

Fortunately, none of the Valkyries' Deus ex Machinas had been damaged in the fighting yesterday. The base's overall readiness had been badly degraded, but the key Valkyrie flight had been unscathed and should be able to fight in almost-peak condition.

"If it's them, I'm sure…"

Unlike Rusalka, they could make the correct choice.

Even as she clung to thoughts like that, she ran through the base as the sirens continued to blare. She was greeted by the grand scene of the entire base scrambling to get to their positions and do their jobs, everyone's hearts racing from the sudden alert.

She was filled with awe at the way humans could act when they knew exactly what their duty was and set out to do it. The way they ran in hopes of making their dreams come true. To Rusalka, the army was a gathering of people like that—people truly worthy of respect.

Even as she acknowledged that at some point, she had slipped off those same rails.

"—?"

Moreover, when soldiers who had such a powerful drive hammered into them stopped moving to look up at the sky in shock, they always stood out like sore thumbs.

"——"

Looking over to see what had caught their attention, Rusalka inhaled sharply. Subconsciously, she slowed and then stopped, too.

She couldn't peel her eyes away from it. There was a pillar of light to the east of the base, just kilometers away from the city proper. It was natural. Whenever pillars appeared, that pillar of light was always there, too.

But the towering, colossal figure slowly appearing from inside the pillar of light was different. It was obvious for all to see that it defied common sense. And Rusalka knew exactly what it was.

"A secondary pillar..."

Chapter 3
Because the Sky Is There

1

——Natalie had the utmost confidence that she was one of the chosen.

"______"

Changing into her flight suit in the locker room, she quickly pulled back her red curls. The sirens were still wailing all through the base, and she could hear the frantic rush going on around her.

She took a deep breath while touching her hair to clear her mind. It was a routine she had developed for herself to maintain her mental balance. If she couldn't think clearly at critical moments, then she had no hope of reaching her full potential.

The person she modeled herself after was someone known for always having calm and collected tactical judgment, and Natalie did her best to live up to that ideal. Her routine was just one of the tools she had personally developed as part of that effort.

"Get my Deus ex Machina!"

Running into the hangar, she leaped into her plane, which the maintenance crew had already readied.

Her beloved machine, which had seen her through dangerous skies just last night. Its beautiful silver fuselage evoked the image of a shooting star. She had been completely enraptured by its beauty when she first received it from Odin. Fortunately, it was in peak condition. The chief technician had personally finished tightening the last bolt as the engine roared in exultation, as if it were raring to fly and do battle again.

"If so, I'm certainly of the same opinion."

It was a joy to be able to fight for her homeland. She had been born and raised there, and she fully intended to grow old there, too. She would fulfill the duty that came with being chosen by God and grasp that future with her own two hands.

"Valkyrie Natalie Chase, taking off."

Natalie's Deus ex Machina raced down the runway and leaped into the air. The planes of her flight followed her into the sky one after the other.

Other pilots were already in the sky, exchanging fire with the pillars—fighter jets flown by regular human pilots instead of Valkyries. Their goal was not to shoot down pillars so much as disrupt and delay their advance. In other words, they were running interference for the Valkyries. And thanks to their hard fighting, the initial attack of Natalie's flight made it in time.

"———"

From her cockpit, she could see a swarm of pillars spreading out into formation as the sun set in the distance. The enemy was the same type as they had fought the day before, called fireflies for their similarity in appearance to the small insects.

The pillars took many different forms, but all the ones that resembled insects shared a similar sturdy exoskeleton. That carapace could even withstand the attacks of Valkyries, so taking them down required careful aim at joints and gaps, which made them particularly dangerous enemies.

"But there is no need to fear as long as we know the type we are dealing with."

The most dangerous thing about fighting pillars was how they could change their form and fighting style from battle to battle. Consecutive days of action put a massive amount of strain on the European front, but if the enemy didn't have enough time to tweak their designs, then that meant both sides were operating without as much preparation as they would have liked.

There were a lot of enemies in the air, but that was all.

"This is Waltz 1. Waltz 2 and 3, take the right. Waltz 4, with me on the left. Scatter the enemy."

"*—Roger!*"

"...Do you copy, Waltz 4? Waltz 4...Alma!"

"I heard you."

As she pressed her one unresponsive flightmate, the familiar unconcerned response finally came back over the line.

You could at least respond when I'm talking to you!

Irritation swelled in Natalie's chest. Orders and rank were absolute in the army. At the same time, it was still necessary to take ability into account. Natalie calmed herself, reminding herself not to get too high-handed just because of her formal rank.

"Even if you hate me, I am the flight leader, Alma. Please follow orders. Actions that disrupt the flight's ability to coordinate are unacceptable."

"Who said I hate you?" That response was unexpected, and for a second, Natalie was at a loss for what she should say. Taking advantage of that opening, Alma continued. *"Also, there's something inside the pillar—inside that light."*

"Huh?"

Eyes widening, Natalie looked to the edge of the battlefield—to the pillar of light visible a few kilometers away to the east of the city.

——As the name indicated, the unknown enemies appeared whenever a pillar of light manifested.

In most cases, the pillar of light would suddenly erupt from the ground, and countless pillars would swarm out from inside it as it remained inactive throughout the course of the battle.

The pillar of light itself wasn't affected by physical attacks. It couldn't be blown away even by the most powerful explosives the army could bring to bear. The pillar of light would stand inviolable for the duration of the battle, and after a set amount of time passed and the pillars had undergone annihilation from lack of energy, the tower would disappear as well.

Because of that, in most cases, soldiers tended to not pay any attention at all to the pillar of light once a battle started, since the structure itself didn't attack. And Natalie had been no exception.

And so—

"—Ah."

—when she looked closely to check what Alma had pointed out, she gasped hoarsely. Surely countless other troops on the front were staring wide-eyed at the same scene. The sight burned itself into the consciousness of everyone there.

"_____"

A giant shadow gradually appeared from the sinister pillar of light towering over the surrounding area. It was a creature with a green shell that had an almost metallic luster. Its arms had multiple joints and ended in sharp scythes—five of them on either side of its body. It had red compound eyes and emotionless features.

Natalie shuddered in dread, not because she had lost heart but because of how impossibly large and overwhelming the creature's presence was.

"That's..."

Hearing the quiver in her voice, she inhaled as she took in the enemy's full appearance. It resembled a praying mantis. Of course, that was only true on a superficial level. No praying mantis had ten arms, and the enemy's size was incomparable to any insect.

It was gargantuan. Far too massive. It was easily fifty meters tall and could stroll past the wall built to protect the city without any difficulty at all. And that enormous enemy's presence meant something terrifying.

"—A secondary pillar."

Desperation crept into her voice. The pillars that Natalie and the other Valkyries usually fought were small entities called tertiary pillars. Their sizes varied somewhat, but by and large, they were around the size of an aircraft, and while conventional weaponry didn't work on them, they couldn't even begin to compete with a modern jet in maneuverability.

What made tertiary pillars a threat was their numbers and the fact that most of humanity's arsenal had no effect on them. But with the rise of third-generation Valkyries, they had become an enemy that could be fought and beaten.

The course of the war had begun to turn, and humanity had finally won itself a small bit of hard-fought hope.

But that hope and humanity's greatest wings had been crushed by a secondary pillar.

It was the loathsome enemy that had sheared humanity's wings. Boasting an offensive and defensive capability a whole order of magnitude greater than a tertiary pillar, it was an overwhelming menace that left utter destruction in its wake.

There was only a single record of a secondary pillar ever being defeated—when the First Valkyrie had fought like she was possessed and managed to take one down at the cost of her own life.

It was the foe of all Valkyries, an incomparably powerful enemy that had been beaten only once before.

——This was how the battle that would go down in history as the Defense of Hamburg began.

2

Everyone in the command post was at a loss for words as they registered the overwhelming presence appearing on their monitors.

"——"

The big main monitor at the center of the room displayed the field to the east of the city, where the pillar of light had appeared, as well as the enormous monster that was slowly emerging from it—the secondary pillar.

Instinctive survival alarms rang in the back of their heads as the sinister and imposing mantis-like design and ominous compound eyes glared down at humanity's domain.

Pillars came in a multitude of forms, but every one of them mimicked a life-form on earth. It almost seemed like a sick joke. Or perhaps the invaders were boasting that all life on earth belonged to them.

"The enemy is deploying tertiary pillars! This is..."

One of the signal officers gulped as he saw the points of light scattering across the screen. Those pinpricks spread until the whole display was a solid red. The swarm of tertiary pillars that was deploying around the secondary pillar was more than double the throng they had seen last night, and they were surrounding the city in a show of force.

The enemy was sending in a secondary pillar right where the effects of consecutive battles would be most felt. It was an all-out offensive to cut off any hope of retreat. It was a simple but effective brute-force push.

——*Wait, is this really just brute force? Is this actually a strategic deployment?*

"_____"

If the thought that crossed the minds of the officers in the command post was true, then that would be horrific.

Until that point, the enemy had shown no indication of any kind of rationality or strategic consideration in its actions. That was the only reason humanity had managed to barely hold on despite their weak position and fight back using tactics and strategy.

But if that stopped being the case, if the pillars began to manage even a clumsy form of strategic coordination, how would humanity be able to respond?

Even at the best of times, a secondary pillar's appearance was enough to rock the entire army. If the enemy also started maneuvering on an operational level…

Hamburg base was the lifeline of the European front and a position humanity had to hold no matter what—

"—Keep your heads about you!"

Just then, a stern shout rang out, shattering the panic that was filling the air. It was the base commander, standing in the center of the command post.

He had probably come running at full speed when he heard the alarm. But there was no unease detectable in his voice or expression as he looked around the room at all the faces of the command staff.

"Do not falter. If we waver here, the whole army will follow."

"_____"

That alone was enough to change the mood. No matter how hopeless the situation might seem, a commanding officer always needed to remain calm. And that applied to the radio operators, who would have to convey the general's orders to the rest of the fighting troops.

"It's hard to exaggerate how much the voice of a beauty boosts morale in the field. Plus, if an operator sounds pessimistic, then it makes sense that can spread to everyone listening, right?"

The words of the commander of the infantry company who had plugged the gap during last night's battle with his and his men's lives crossed her mind.

Michelle had not been their operator, but she had heard the exchange while listening as backup for a new operator.

She had found it a horrifically cruel and deeply moving confession. And when she thought about how that new operator must have felt when she heard it, how much it must have hurt…

For a second, she glanced at the empty seat, but she quickly abandoned all unnecessary thoughts. If the general was going to set aside his feelings to perform his duty, then there was no excuse for her to do differently. Michelle snuffed out her emotions and resolved to fulfill her role with an icy calm in order to make sure that the confusion and unease in the command post didn't worm its way to the brave soldiers on the front lines. So that it would not reach the Valkyries flying through such harrowing skies.

"—2nd Squadron, 71st Squadron, Valkyrie flight—you are cleared weapons hot!"

There was no trace of fear or panic in Michelle's voice as she announced the opening of the battle.

3

The bullets of light grazed her wings as she executed a sharp barrel roll to evade.

She was engaged in a close-range dogfight, just barely dodging the enemy's attacks. Natalie would be lying if she said she didn't prefer that sort of combat, but it wasn't because she got any particular thrill out of it. It was because the more attention she drew to herself, the less danger her comrades would have to face.

"And at such short range, stray rounds aren't quite as concerning."

By drawing the enemies toward her, she could guide their attacks upward into the sky above. As the shots missed her Deus ex Machina, they disappeared off into the distance, swallowed by the setting sun. Then she repeated the same maneuver on a dozen or so pillars, weaving through the gaps in their formation.

Her guns growled as shock waves rippled through the air, and three tertiaries dissolved into light particles and disappeared. Catching that out of the corner of her eye, Natalie continued without letting up, charging into the salvo of light rounds fired at her and acting as a decoy by flying straight through the enemy's formation.

The pillars' mysterious glowing projectiles were still not fully understood, but it was at least known that they were high-density masses of energy. If one hit, it would wreak havoc just like any shell or bullet.

Because of that, stray rounds naturally became a concern. Even if Natalie dodged a spray of fire, it would still do real damage if the shots hit the ground.

As a Valkyrie, she carried the hopes of all humanity on her shoulders. What was demanded of her was to perfectly carry out her role. In other words, she had to pitch a perfect game.

And to that end—

"—That's it! Nice and bunched, just like that!"

After she executed a sharp 180-degree turn and threaded the needle, the enemies turned their focus to her. Following her through her quick turn, the cluster of tertiaries all accelerated.

It was like a scene from a nightmare as their eerie, emotionless compound eyes all focused on Natalie, and they gave chase with a speed matching a fighter plane.

But if that was a nightmare, then humanity had been experiencing that nightmare for a long time already. And the reason Natalie and the other Valkyries were fighting was so they could put an end to that nightmare.

"—Gh."

She clenched her jaw so tightly a little trickle of blood ran down the corner of her mouth. It wasn't very elegant. She clutched at the control stick of her plane as she ascended in a spiral at blistering speed.

The fuselage creaked under the strain, and she could feel herself being crushed against the seat she was strapped into. Gritting her teeth through the pain, Natalie's amber eyes glimpsed the moon.

And then—

"Alma!"

"You don't have to shout."

A black point appeared in the middle of the full moon. In the blink of an eye, Natalie swerved away and rapidly decelerated, snapping to the side. And the tertiaries that had been chasing her couldn't match the extreme maneuver.

Even if they were unnatural creatures, they weren't capable of breaking the laws of physics.

——Then a black death came swooping down on those dozen pillars.

What did they think of the steadily approaching darkness? It was a question that could never be answered, since it was not even clear that pillars were conscious in the first place.

But either way, the result was simple.

——There was an enormous explosion, almost like the sun had somehow risen again, followed by the expansion of a big black cloud.

The explosion thundered in the air, sounding almost like the end of the world had come as the fireball kept expanding and consumed the formation of pillars, catching a couple more on the edges of the blast, annihilating all of them.

"Every time I see it, it's still such an absurd amount of firepower…"

Natalie's lips twisted in a mixture of awe and exasperation.

——All Deus ex Machinas were based off propeller planes from the two World Wars.

The peculiar choice was supposedly connected to the weight of history and humanity's faith in these machines, but the details had never really been made clear. Either way, each Valkyrie was given a different set of wings based on those relics of another age.

For example, Natalie's took the form of a Spitfire. In terms of actual combat performance, it was incomparable, but it was an exact copy in every other respect.

If nothing else, old propeller planes were certainly better than some unknown technology that no one knew how to repair or maintain. Because of that, the European Army and all of humanity had simply accepted it at face value.

According to Odin, each Deus ex Machina reflected the abilities and skills of the chosen Valkyrie. Even though Valkyries usually flew in flights of four, their planes were often all different makes and models. But because of that, they were able to pull off unusual tactics, like what Natalie and Alma had done.

Natalie's Spitfire flew at high speeds, disrupting the enemy formation and nimbly shooting down her targets while dancing through the air. Meanwhile, Alma's Lancaster, a sluggish, heavy bomber, wielded the sort of overwhelming firepower capable of utterly annihilating the enemy.

These two planes were the core of the flight that Natalie commanded.

Naturally, they were not the only Valkyries in the flight. To make full use of their capabilities, they needed help from their wingmates to manage the battlefield.

They also needed to work together with the non-Valkyrie air units, which fought desperately to buy them time and to make sure that the pillars' attacks did not reach any innocent civilians or their homes.

The Valkyries would use that precious time to exterminate the enemy.

"Well done. Let's prepare for the next group."

"Don't get cocky. Also..."

"What?"

"I don't like that it's not moving."

Even with her vague comment, there was no mistaking what Alma meant. Far in the distance, the secondary pillar was simply standing there next to the ominous pillar of light. It wasn't just lethargic; it hadn't moved at all since it first appeared.

"—What is it thinking?"

It was a question Natalie had thought dozens of times before when dealing with pillars.

Just what were the pillars thinking?

But while that question had a broad range of philosophical interpretations, she meant it in a much narrower sense this time. She was wondering why the secondary pillar was just standing by and watching ominously.

"———"

Looking at the battlefield, the European Army currently held the upper hand.

Naturally, Natalie's flight was putting up a good fight, but even the regular pilots, which had no means of dealing damage to the enemy, were managing to hold the line well. She was starting to think that maybe they had gotten more skilled after persevering through the battle last night, but she quickly realized that was far too arrogant and presumptuous of her.

The ground forces were performing well, and from the reports, it sounded like the evacuation was proceeding apace.

Everything was going smoothly, and the surprise battle was going in their favor. But all of that was overshadowed by the uncanny presence of that secondary pillar. It almost felt like it was depriving them of all good fortune with its mere presence.

That was a testament to just how menacing it was.

"If we could at least get permission to engage it..."

Natalie could feel a dryness in her mouth as she murmured this.

At present, the general's orders regarding the secondary pillar were to wait and see.

It wasn't moving or making any attempt to attack. And since conventional weapons didn't work on it, the only ones who could engage it were Natalie's Valkyries. But put another way, that also meant no one other than her flight could provoke it.

Because of that, they had been forbidden from making any attack runs on the secondary and were supposed to prioritize eliminating the tertiaries instead to whittle down the enemy's fighting power.

And that was the correct decision. The tertiaries actively engaged in combat were clearly causing more casualties and more damage to civilian areas than the unmoving secondary.

Natalie didn't hesitate to follow those orders and focus on eliminating the tertiaries because she understood the sound reasoning behind them. But—

"—I have a bad feeling about this."

"Agreed."

For once, Alma agreed with her.

She could hear the uneasy voices of the other two members of her flight through the radio as well. This wasn't the sound of the side currently winning the battle.

Maybe it was just an unease that only Valkyries could pick up on. If so, then did that mean they were the only ones who could feel this sense of impending doom?

"But—"

She rushed another group of enemies, machine guns roaring as she gracefully wove through a gap in the cloud cover. As she did so, she turned her thoughts to the command post in the rear for a moment, almost as if praying.

——If only Valkyries can sense it, then I'm sure...

4

The secondary pillar that had appeared immediately after they engaged the enemy had still not moved.

"______"

Ever since blowing their minds with its sudden, dramatic appearance on the battlefield, it had not made any notable movements.

The tertiary pillars had of course been active like normal, and the Valkyrie flight had performed splendidly in driving them back. But the secondary's eerie silence presented a major threat for the course of the battle.

"What is it thinking...?"

The general held his hand to his mouth, murmuring so that no one could hear him as he pondered the situation.

The Valkyries and the rest of the ground and air assets were doing outstanding work, and the European forces had an overwhelming advantage at the moment. But no one out there fighting believed it would end so simply, and the general felt those same doubts more strongly than anyone else.

"Gh."

Gritting his teeth, he struggled between two choices.

Judging from the current situation, it had been correct to forbid attacking the secondary. Because it had remained inactive, they had been able to deal with the tertiaries and limit casualties to the greatest extent possible. But it was also true that they couldn't afford to leave the secondary there indefinitely.

——Defeating the secondary was not the goal of their current operation.

From that perspective, it would be logical to just focus on defense and wait until the enemy's time ran out. While the path of least resistance was not the same as prudence, mistaking reckless valor for bravery would also needlessly invite misfortune.

But even so—

"Commence attack on the secondary pillar."

"______"

A silent tremor ran through the command post as the general made his decision.

Everyone paused their work for a moment, and a silence that was unimaginable in the middle of a frantic battle filled the room. As his subordinates turned their gazes to him, the general nodded gravely.

"You heard me. Direct all forces to begin attacking the secondary pillar."

Several people gulped as he handed down his order.

Naturally, they understood that continuing to buy time and wait for the enemy to reach their activity limit was the path of least resistance. And they understood that the general had surely considered every aspect of that safe choice for several minutes.

Because of that, there were no objections. And after an incredibly brief delay, they immediately prepared to give the attack order.

"______"

Having made such a crucial decision, the general massaged his forehead and exhaled.

Hamburg base was a crucial cornerstone for the European front, a foundational part of humanity's resistance. As a man who had been entrusted with the management of such a crucial base, he was often tormented by the question of whether he had made the correct decision.

But the die was cast. All that remained was to push onward and find out if the right number came up.

"Valkyrie flight, your priority target is now the secondary pillar." An operator contacted the Valkyries, passing along the new order to make a run at the secondary.

They were likely the ones most put off by the creature on this battlefield. The general couldn't say whether they would be glad or object to the new order.

Soldiers wouldn't disobey orders, but they were different. And he had no choice but to rely on those girls, who did not even know why he had given the order he did—

"—Ah."

Suddenly, the general noticed someone gasping.

He glanced in the direction of the sound, his eyes narrowing. It had come from the analyst tasked with tracking the secondary pillar. The analyst was watching the monitor as his eyes widened.

"General, movement from the..."

He had surely been about to say *secondary pillar*, but he never got to finish his report.

——The next instant, a massive impact rocked the command post, ripping the heart out of the army.

5

"Wha…? Gh!"

A plume of black smoke rose from Hamburg base in the rear as Natalie's throat clenched.

Her first thought was to wonder what had happened, but she immediately realized it was actually exceedingly simple.

The command post had been struck by the enemy. The one place that must never be allowed to come under attack had suffered a grievous blow. But the way it had happened made no sense.

The tertiaries were being pushed back by Natalie and her flight. There was no way even a stray round could have reached the command post, never mind an intentional attack. What had hit the command post was one of the secondary pillars' giant scythes.

"———"

Natalie's thoughts froze as she considered the incomprehensible.

Ever since it had appeared, the towering giant had done nothing but stand next to the pillar of light. But it had taken decisive action the instant she received an order to attack it.

It still hadn't left its starting position. It had merely raised one of its arms and swung. Nothing more. And yet somehow, the scythe had crossed an impossible distance and connected with the command post.

It was too absurd to even imagine.

"Natalie."

Alma's voice pulled her back to reality. Even in their current situation, her voice was as neutral as ever, which helped Natalie remember to breathe again.

"Panic is spreading, and command got hit. What should we do?"

"What…?"

"You're the flight leader, Natalie."

Natalie caught her breath, the true weight of that position finally crashing down on her.

They couldn't get in contact with command, and there was little hope of getting new orders for the foreseeable future. For a moment, she worried about the safety of the people in the command post, but she quickly shook her head.

She couldn't afford to worry about anything else in her current situation. In the absence of standing orders, officers in the field were supposed to assume command. In other words, Natalie's judgment took precedence.

"—Commence the assault on the secondary pillar. We cannot allow it to circumvent us and cause any further damage."

"Roger."

Alma immediately acknowledged Natalie's directions, even though she usually never seemed to be listening. It was almost annoying how receptive she could be in a situation like this.

And yet, it's reassuring to hear her response.

Natalie turned toward the secondary as she received acknowledgments from the rest of her flight, aiming her guns right at the mantis's compound eyes.

Perhaps sensing the sudden hostility directed toward it, the secondary turned its head toward Natalie. A red glint flashed in its compound eyes as it tracked the Valkyrie, and five of its arms creaked.

The fifty-meter-tall pillar swung its scythes wildly across the space in front of it like so many wrecking balls. The tiniest amount of contact would cause massive destruction. Goose bumps formed all over Natalie's body as she raced into that unprecedented storm.

Natalie sharpened her senses, welcoming the close-range fight. It felt like the Deus ex Machina was an extension of her body. And relying on that intimate connection, she dodged one swipe after the other, finally breaking through.

"Guns, guns, guns!"

Her weapons roared to life, spitting fire right into the pillar's face. She emptied everything she had in her attack run, but Natalie's Deus ex Machina didn't boast high firepower. That one barrage had little hope of toppling the enormous secondary.

But the smallest of leaks could sink the greatest of ships. Damage slowly but surely added up.

And Natalie's aim was—

"Huh?"

The bullets that should have shattered the pillar's shiny green shell had disappeared. Not because they had been deflected or blocked. They had quite literally disappeared. And as her eyes widened in shock at what had happened—

"—*Aaah!*"

"Shannon?!"

She heard her comrade's scream over the radio.

The scream had come from a Valkyrie in Natalie's flight who was flying behind her. Her Deus ex Machina had caught fire, and her wings wobbled badly.

Natalie's first thought was that she had been hit by enemy fire or grazed by one of the secondary's scythes, but that was not it. Because the damage to her Deus ex Machina was unmistakably damage caused by a machine gun.

"It can't be..."

Seeing the telltale bullet holes, she felt a chill run down her spine.

The attack on the command post and what had just happened. It had been Natalie's attack that had damaged her comrade's Deus ex Machina. The bullets she had fired at the secondary had somehow vanished and plunged into her flightmate's craft.

In other words—

"It can change the vector of incoming attacks?!"

Natalie's voice cracked as she deduced what was happening. Then, as if wanting to reinforce the shock and terror she felt, the secondary swung one of its scythes high. Natalie steadied herself in the cockpit, but it was meaningless. The scythe's aim was the base several kilometers away. As it lowered its arm, another plume of black smoke rose from the base.

"______"

There was no mistaking it.

Their enemy had some ability to bend space.

Secondary pillars had been observed only a handful of times, but in every instance, they not only sported a size several hundred times that of a tertiary, but they also wielded some sort of special ability as well.

It varied from secondary to secondary, and apparently this pillar's unique ability was warping space. Taking full advantage of that, it had reached out several kilometers away to hit the command post as well as redirect Natalie's attack to one of her comrades.

In other words—

"Our attacks can't touch it, but its attacks can pass through any defenses...?"

If that was allowed to stand, it would turn the battle into a one-sided massacre. The situation was already going pear-shaped. And more importantly, Natalie realized the biggest potential problem.

"Alma! Don't attack it!"

"———"

"The enemy is warping the space around it. If your Grand Slam redirected toward the city..."

Alma's bomb could do more damage to the base or the city than even the secondary's scythes.

Though it was hard to control, Alma boasted the strongest firepower of their forces. Her Lancaster had the greatest ability to inflict wide-scale destruction out of all the Valkyrie aircraft.

With their trump card sealed, they would struggle to overcome the secondary pillar.

"What do we do, Natalie?"

This time Natalie didn't have a response for Alma's question.

"———"

If their attacks wouldn't work, they should consider withdrawing and immediately start making the necessary preparations. But should they return to the base, which had just come under direct attack? How extensive was the damage? She had no information to rely on. And if their forces pulled back, the pillars would surely continue attacking. Either way, they would end up getting run down.

In which case, even if they couldn't defeat the secondary—

"There is no one else who can take it on. So..."

"Buy time until a retreat?" Alma asked.

"—Yes."

Though it was hard to say whether their haphazard plan would even get that far.

She could feel her heart aching at the decision. It was a heavy responsibility for the one who had to make the final call. Natalie bit her lips as she endured the pain, and she glared at the secondary.

Its compound eyes looked emotionless, but she focused as much as she could to glean something, anything about the enemy's intentions.

"*—lie Chase.*"

"—! A transmission?! Are the comms fixed?!"

Just as she had been about to launch herself into the fray again, she heard a voice through the static, and she leaped at it, desperately clinging to hope.

"This is Valkyrie flight Waltz 1! Requesting response! Command?!" Natalie called out, imagining the reliable base commander on the other end. There was a moment of silence on the line.

"*No, the command post has been destroyed. General Barkley has been killed in action.*"

"——"

Natalie forgot to breathe as the cold report came in. The general was dead, and the tension in Natalie was on the verge of snapping. At this rate, her iron heart would collapse and her will to continue fighting might shatter—

"*—Consequently, I am assuming command. Follow my orders, Waltz 1.*"

—but the next message kept her from tumbling into despair.

"Wh-who are you…?"

"*Me? I'm Alejandro. Alejandro Ostley.*"

"——"

The man's voice was deep and brimming with confidence.

The reason Natalie caught her breath at his announcement was not just because she was overwhelmed by his drive, though. It was because she recognized that name.

Alejandro Ostley. It was—

"The mastermind of the Miracle at Lamia!"

"*I'm honestly not a big fan of that title…*"

Natalie's voice unconsciously went up a pitch as Alejandro barked a bitter laugh on the other end. But he quickly pushed past it.

"*Still, if it'll help here, then I guess I should just accept it. Now then, it's time to start our counterattack.*"

The static cleared as he said that.

Alejandro's voice reached every unit on the battlefield. All communications had been thrown into chaos from the attack on the command post, and the chain of command had been on the brink of total collapse before he began addressing the entire area of operations.

"All forces, can you hear my voice? I am Alejandro Ostley, and I am assuming command. General Barkley has been killed in action. I repeat, General Barkley has been killed in action!"

Alejandro said his name while reporting the general's passing. There was no avoiding a drop in morale when everyone learned that the base's commanding officer was dead. In some situations, the loss of a leader could make it difficult to reestablish an organized battle line and could even lead to the full collapse of the front. But Alejandro prioritized sharing the truth to avoid further muddling the chain of command. He continued speaking, reassuring the troops who were growing restless and worried.

"The situation right now is bad. The enemy is strong, and we're getting ground down one-sidedly. But miracles can happen."

"...Miracles."

A commanding officer had no business talking about needing a miracle to win, but for better or worse, the soldiers believed in gods and miracles. Not so much out of a particular religious faith or awe toward the divine. It was more like a lucky charm or a ward against jinxes.

And Alejandro had told them they needed a miracle to win. None other than the peerless hero who had been the mastermind behind the Miracle at Lamia, the officer synonymous with miracles in the army—that very same Alejandro Ostley had just said miracles could happen.

That was—

"—And if it's a miracle we need, then I'll make one happen."

How would one even begin to describe such a spurious statement made with such utter confidence?

Unlike the special abilities of the secondary pillars or the powers that Odin had imbued the Valkyries with, Alejandro's power was unique to humans.

His words gave the army, which had been on the verge of breaking, the strength to keep fighting. And Natalie and the other Valkyries were no different.

"Sir! We are..."

"I understand the situation. We have to figure out the enemy's trick. Until then, you need to keep its attention. You can do it, right?"

"——"

It was barely a question.

The confidence and expectation in the way he asked that lit a fire inside Natalie. Pushing all extraneous thoughts in her head to the side, she focused everything she had on a singular goal.

"Yes, sir. Leave it to us. Valkyries, let's do this!"

Her voice excitedly rose as she led her flight back into the secondary pillar's range.

——And so Hamburg base's counterattack began.

6

"——"

The blond playboy standing in the middle of the rubble-filled command post—Alejandro Ostley—crossed his arms.

He had assumed command out of necessity, but his makeshift headquarters was just a mound of debris and corpses, and the enemy was an unparalleled menace: a secondary pillar.

Things were bad no matter how he looked at it. Particularly the last bit about the secondary. Alejandro had been through a bad experience with a secondary before. The idea of having to clash with one again made him wonder if the nightmares would ever end.

It was enough that he wanted to curse his fate and question whether there really were any gods, but—

"At least the food in the stockade was really good. I guess we can call it even."

That idle musing drew a laugh from his subordinates, who were frantically rushing all around him.

The one silver lining was that Alejandro's direct reports had not suffered any casualties in the base attack. They had been standing by in the rear, since their commanding officer had been thrown in the stockade, and that had turned out to be a stroke of good luck.

When the alarms started blaring, Alejandro had been released, and the junior officers who had served with him for a long time followed his orders without delay. Their quick reaction speed had prevented the complete cratering of morale. The Valkyries were reacting well, too. There were plenty of reasons left to be able to keep their heads up.

"Th-the secondary pillar..."

"Oh, you're up and moving about? You were lucky."

Alejandro pulled his focus from the monitor displaying the current state of the battle when he heard a familiar voice. He watched an operator with black hair shake her head as she stood up.

She was one of the survivors who had been buried in the rubble. Her expression warped in pain as she scanned the battered command post.

"Right after the general gave the order to engage the secondary pillar, it started moving, and then..."

"Oh, you remember that, too. Good. Saves me time not having to explain things. The fighting is still ongoing. Normally, I would want to get all the casualties out of here, but..."

Alejandro glanced bitterly at the entrance to the command post. Following his gaze, the operator turned to look as well. And there she saw the completely ordinary steel door at the room's exit.

"Huh?"

However, what should have been behind it was completely missing. Past the doorway was something that should have been impossible—lush green plants and a thick canopied forest.

Of course, there was no way the command post was normally connected to a forest.

"Seems like it's connected to that secondary's bizarre ability. Space around here has gotten warped. Right now, there's no telling what parts of the base connect to where anymore."

"——"

Alejandro nodded in affirmation of her entirely understandable shock. The fact that he and his subordinates had managed to reach this place had been largely luck. The warping on the base had occurred right after he reunited with his subordinates at the stockade, and they had miraculously managed to arrive at the command post after passing through several different bends in space.

And thanks to that, he had gotten there right before General Barkley died.

"______"

Alejandro glanced over at the row of dead bodies lining one of the command post's walls. Less than 20 percent of the command staff had survived the attack. And because they couldn't do anything else for them yet, the deceased had been lined up and covered with coats. Among their number was the base's commanding officer, Major General Logrev Barkley.

He had been on death's door by the time Alejandro reached the command post. Gasping for air, he had entrusted command to Alejandro before breathing his last. It was almost a miracle that he had held on that long, refusing to die until he could entrust his duty to someone else.

"No, that wasn't a miracle."

Alejandro didn't believe that everything came down to fate or chance. He wouldn't deny that the whims of fate and the luck involved in being at the right place at the right time could be deciding factors, but everything began when someone had the determination to take the first step.

That was exactly why…

"All the repositioning is going to badly disrupt the chain of command. I need someone familiar with the base. I understand you've been injured, but I need your help."

His request was directed at the woman whose face had gone stiff from everything that had happened. Slowly, she shifted her focus to Alejandro.

"You're conscious, obviously. Is your head clear? What's your name?" Alejandro asked.

"—Michelle. Michelle Heyman."

Alejandro nodded at the clear response, which was far better than he could have hoped for.

"All right, then, Michelle. Let's get to it. My crew are a rough lot unfortunately, and I need someone who can take care of more delicate tasks."

"Yes, sir. Understood."

Ignoring the pain racking her body, she stood up and returned to her post. Alejandro watched her courageous figure before returning his attention to the monitor.

On the screen, it was clear that all the troops, and the Valkyries in particular, were putting up a valiant fight, desperately trying to turn their disastrous position around.

But the situation was still undeniably awful. And the biggest reason for that was—

"The terrain's become a jigsaw puzzle. That secondary really pulled a fast one on us," Alejandro complained.

Doors, hallways, and stairways no longer connected to the locations they were supposed to. In a situation where it was impossible to move freely, the army wouldn't be able to coordinate the way it desperately needed.

If communications had been severed as well, the European Army would have completely melted away without even putting up a proper fight. But even with their resistance so far, that fate was drawing ever closer.

We need to do something to normalize communications and movement, but—

"—Colonel! There's a call from outside the base!"

"Now? Who the hell could that be? Put them through!"

It was an unnatural occurrence right when they were tackling a crisis. Normally, that would cause a moment of pause, but Alejandro did not hesitate at all to take the call.

"This is Alejandro. I've assumed command of the base. Who is this?"

"——"

"—? We're a bit busy here. If you don't need something, I'll deal with you later."

There was a brief silence on the other end as Alejandro furrowed his brow. But he sensed a breath, as the other end did not want to lose contact after finally getting through.

"Apologies, I was a little taken aback after hearing a voice I didn't expect."

"—That voice…"

"This is Captain Rusalka Evereska. I have a report for the operation's command staff."

Alejandro raised an eyebrow as the name and voice on the other end clicked together. And then he fell silent, waiting for her to continue. Taking the hint, Rusalka continued.

"I have figured out the secondary pillar's trick. Unfortunately, it requires an analog solution, so you should get a map."

7

——Earlier, when Rusalka first spotted the secondary pillar…

"—A secondary pillar."

The shock of what she was seeing pierced her whole body. She completely stopped moving, almost like she was in a trance. Soldiers all around her froze as well, all other thoughts falling away after catching a glimpse of the imposing specter visible in the distance.

The secondary pillar was covered in a green carapace and had five pairs of long arms tipped in scythes. It was an imposing figure that exerted a menacing pressure powerful enough to crush a human's spirit.

Rusalka was no exception. If anything, it was even worse for her because of how massive the secondary pillar loomed in her past. Because humanity's greatest enemy, a secondary pillar, had…

"Amy…"

The name of the girl who was a crystallization of her regrets slipped weakly from her lips.

The First Valkyrie, humanity's greatest hope, her savior from the Ride of the Valkyrie, and the hero who had taken down the only secondary pillar ever defeated in human history at the cost of her own life.

It had been a secondary pillar that had killed Amy, Xenia, Victorica, and Canan.

"——"

Why had a secondary pillar appeared here all of a sudden?

A fierce revulsion filled her head as she cursed the irrationality and outrageousness of it all. But however much she wanted to beg and plead, the reality of what she saw didn't change.

Deep down, she knew it had been bound to happen sooner or later. With the emergence of the third generation of Valkyries, humanity had stopped faltering in battles with just tertiaries. Because of that, more secondaries had started to appear. It was only a matter of time before they would appear again on the European front—the site of the harshest fighting in humanity's great struggle.

Because of that, it was practically a given that she would encounter one at some point. Once it did happen, all that remained was to summon the will to fight back.

"I..."

She clawed at her chest and gritted her teeth, gathering the courage to fight against that grotesque monster—

"Do your duty, Rusalka Evereska!"

"Ngh."

The reprimand that had gotten her moving just minutes ago flashed through her head as she remembered to breathe again.

Breathe in. Breathe out. She repeated the action, taking one deep breath after another until the tension slowly melted away. And then she finally started to move again.

Committing herself to that momentum, she started running for the command post before her legs could stop again.

She chose not to consider whether it had been the man's voice or the order that had compelled her to act.

"They're already engaging the enemy...!"

High in the sky above, she saw jets circling, pulling the enemy's focus away from the city and the base. Their job was to draw the tertiaries' fire and limit the amount of danger the Valkyries and anyone on the ground would be exposed to.

Since conventional weaponry didn't work on pillars, they were little more than decoys. The pilots were risking their lives to lure the enemy in and make them give chase. Their battlefield was in some ways even more difficult than the one Valkyries endured. But it was thanks to their efforts that Valkyries could fight to their full potential.

"———"

Above the clouds, the pillars chasing the fighter jets were shot from behind and enveloped in flames. The trees bursting out from inside the shattered pillars consumed the remnants before plummeting to earth.

It had been a Deus ex Machina with a gray fuselage that lit them up. One of the Valkyries in Natalie's flight had perfectly timed her shots.

Rusalka was the one who had suggested trying that technique when the young Valkyrie had been struggling to improve. The girl had an incredible amount of potential that shined brightest when she could operate with the support of allies.

Fortunately, she had been open to hearing Rusalka's advice and clearly taken it to heart. Even though it must have been mortifying to take advice from a Valkyrie who had folded up her wings.

But even as Rusalka became enthralled by the emotions she was feeling, the Valkyries continued to score victories.

Natalie made tactical breakthroughs, always heading wherever enemy forces were thickest. The direr the situation, the better she performed.

Alma's bombardment attack had a large area of effect that took full advantage of all the enemies her flightmates concentrated, utterly wiping out anything that came within range.

And the other Valkyries were impressive as well. Their flying wasn't flashy, but they steadily and reliably whittled down the enemy's numbers with their teamwork.

The battle was steadily turning in the European Army's favor.

But that was all overshadowed by the eerily patient secondary pillar standing still in the distance.

"It's not making any effort to act. What is it after…?"

The secondary cast a shadow over the whole battle, even though it hadn't made a single move since it first appeared. From what she could see, the Valkyries hadn't attacked it, most likely on orders from command. That could certainly be considered the right choice.

The secondary hadn't done anything overtly threatening yet, and it wasn't participating in the general attack. Because of that, the defenders had been able to focus on clearing out the tertiaries, which dramatically limited the amount of damage that could have occurred. So in a sense, they should be grateful the secondary wasn't moving, but…

"I have a bad feeling…"

A vague apprehension was growing in Rusalka's heart. She couldn't put it into words, but she thought it was the wrong choice to let things proceed this way.

——Was there some reason the secondary was simply watching and waiting?

"_____"

Certain insects were known to lie in wait for hours or even whole days to catch their prey.

The pillar was only mimicking an insect's appearance, of course. There was no guarantee it was copying its predatory instincts as well. But even so, perhaps its actions had something in common with its form's inspiration. If so, then it wasn't just on standby—

"It's gauging its prey…?"

But the Valkyries it should have considered the greatest threats were already in the sky. So what was it after if it was ignoring them?

There was no way there was anything more important than the Valkyries on the battlefield, unless—

"It can't be."

Rusalka suddenly took off as she felt a dangerous premonition.

——The pillars' current assault was already far removed from the standard playbook.

So how could she be sure the enemy wouldn't make the optimal choice? If it understood humanity, had formulated a strategy, and was waiting for an opportunity to strike, then the best move it could make right now was…

"We have to abandon the command post right away—"

Running down the hallway, she burst through the steel doors to warn the core of Hamburg base about the terrible possibility she had realized.

But what greeted her was not the general's stern figure.

"Huh…?"

A green conifer forest filled her field of view. The gears in her head ground to a halt at the completely unexpected scene. And without any concern for her shock, the situation suddenly changed, taking a dramatic turn for the worse.

"—Wah?!"

A thunderous explosion rang out behind her. She immediately turned around, just in time to see black smoke rising into the air. It had come from the center of the base—from the building that housed the command post. The very same place she had been on the verge of entering.

The upper half of the base's headquarters was blown away, and the building itself had sustained tremendous damage. It was clear at a glance that the command post itself had been hit. But Rusalka's eyes widened as she struggled to figure out how it had happened.

What had hit it? And why was she standing in a forest so far away from the base? How in the world had this happened?

"I can't just stay here..."

It was an inexplicable situation, but Rusalka immediately started running to get back. The command post would need help after that attack. She needed to help the survivors and make sure the chain of command did not collapse—

"—Agh?!"

As she left the forest and raced down the slope, there was another sudden shift in her field of view. She frantically put her hands against the gray wall that had appeared in front of her without warning. She gritted her teeth at the shock that went through her arms before immediately looking around.

She quickly realized she was now standing in the middle of a road in Hamburg proper.

"First the forest and now the city..."

She had been in the forest just ten seconds earlier, only to now end up kilometers away in the center of the city. The massive distance had been crossed in the blink of an eye.

It was clear something unnatural was taking place. She had moved from the base to the forest to the town in a matter of seconds.

——*No, it's not just affecting me, either.*

"Wh-what the—?! Why am I in the city?!"

"Aaah! What happened...? I was just going into my room!"

"Waaaaaaaah! Papa! Mamaaaaa!"

Panicked screams, shouts, and wails filled the air. The cause of this pandemonium was the same teleportation Rusalka had just experienced.

At a glance, there was no defining characteristic to the people who had been affected. There were soldiers and civilians, men and women, young and old. It was not a large-enough sample size for her to make a confident assertion, but it didn't seem to be affecting only certain people.

In other words—

"It isn't triggered by movement. Certain areas are being linked somehow."

Just like the command post's entrance had led to the forest, the edge of the forest had connected to this street. Space was being warped, changing the very lay of the land. That would also explain the trick behind how the base had been attacked even though that seemed impossible.

"The secondary pillar's ability…!"

The secondary was still glaring down at the European Army from its position next to the pillar of light. Its emotionless red compound eyes were like a hunter tracking its prey—it was then that Rusalka became sure her instinct had been right.

If she had only reached the command post a little bit faster…

"Now isn't the time for regrets…"

Shaking her head, she roused her flagging spirit. The world would not stop and give her time to wallow in self-pity. People would keep dying every moment she stood still. There was no time to get drunk on despair during a battle.

"—Time to go."

Even though she still didn't know what she should be doing, she hurled herself forward, running with all her might, not allowing herself to stop for even a second.

8

"—Not this one."

Though she had set aside her regrets for the moment and was in motion once again, Rusalka kept running into more strange twists in space. It felt like the secondary was laughing at her.

Trying to get back to base from the center of town, she passed through a civilian's house, a graveyard, and even wound up back in the forest.

"—Not here, either."

It almost seemed like she was watching a bad movie as disconnected scenes flashed by in quick succession. These passages were caused by unnatural rifts in space, so even when she crossed massive distances, it happened in the blink of an eye and didn't tire her at all. But the mounting impatience and unease she was feeling robbed her of composure and ate away at her nerves.

"—What do I do?"

She could see Natalie and the other Valkyries struggling against the secondary overhead. But on closer examination, Rusalka could tell their movements were not as sharp as they should be. There was a hesitation in their attacks and evasive maneuvers. They were fighting without any guidance due to the destruction of the command post. All the decision-making responsibility had fallen on the flight's commanding officer, Natalie.

She had a strong sense of duty and an impressive amount of self-awareness, but she was still just sixteen. She was too inexperienced to be comfortable shouldering the lives of everyone on the battlefield all of a sudden.

"—Wagh."

Rusalka had focused too much on the sky above and lost track of the ground below.

Opening a door in front of her and stepping through without paying attention, she lost her footing and fell straight into water with a splash. After a moment of panic, she realized she must have been transported to a lake near the base.

"———"

Using the light from the surface to determine up and down in the shadowy depths, she launched herself off the bottom of the lake.

She was skilled at swimming, but that had been the most dangerous warp yet. It would have been fatal for anyone who couldn't swim. As soon as her head broke the surface, she started treading water and looking for the shore—

"—? Is that a voice?"

She swung around, searching for the source of the sound she was hearing. It seemed like a child screaming. Her heart began to race as she kicked the water and hurried over toward the voice—

"—Gh!"

Right as she was swimming, another warp occurred. She reached out to keep from falling over.

"This is..."

The floor she had landed on was flooding. The water reached just below her knees. It was apparently connected directly to the lake, which explained where all the water was coming from. It looked like a civilian house somewhere in town, but it would only be a matter of time before it was flooded.

"H-hello?"

As Rusalka confirmed the situation, she heard a child's trembling voice in her ear. Turning, she saw a little boy around ten years old holding his knees as he sat on top of an off-kilter bookshelf. He had probably climbed up in fear of drowning when the house started rapidly filling with water.

It was clear the scream she had heard in the lake had been his.

"Hey! You, the lady who's drenched! You okay in there?!"

And right as she noticed the boy, Rusalka heard someone through the wall. It was a man's gravelly voice calling from outside the flooding building. Looking over, she saw part of the house had collapsed, and the voice was coming from the other side of the rubble.

"I'm safe! The boy inside is, too!"

"Really? That's a relief. After that first impact rocked the base, a huge piece of shrapnel came flying this way and crashed into the door. I'm tryin' to move the debris, but…"

"Yes, that isn't really a realistic option."

Judging from the poor condition of the house, they would need heavy machinery to clear a path, but there was no hope of that, given the current situation. That meant she couldn't count on help from the outside.

"Looking at the force of the current, it would be difficult to go against the flow…," gauged Rusalka.

The warp Rusalka had passed through connected to the lake, but she couldn't see herself being able to swim back that way while carrying the boy. Going with the current and finding a gap in the rubble would be the simplest solution.

"——"

Taking a deep breath, Rusalka stuck her head beneath the surface of the water, following the current in search of some exit. Finally—

"There is a gap the two of us should be able to clear, if just barely. Do you think you can hold your breath and hold on to me for a little while?"

"Waghhh…"

Rusalka approached the boy on the shelf and explained that she had found a way out, but he was struggling to make a leap of faith. Meanwhile, the water continued pouring in. It was almost at her waist now. Sooner or later, they wouldn't be able to breathe anymore. Or the building's structure would give out and collapse completely, unable to endure the force of the rushing water.

"——"

She could hear the man from before and several other voices outside desperately trying to clear the rubble. It was obvious they wouldn't make it in time.

"I understand it's scary. But if all you do is wait for others to save you, nothing will change. If you want to be saved, you have to reach out your hand, too."

"I—I do...?"

"Yes, that's right..."

She paused for a moment, seeing herself in the terrified boy. The Rusalka who had rejected Amy's outstretched hand. Who had rejected Xenia's outstretched hand.

"—You have to reach out and grab on to whoever's trying to help you."

But she swallowed her momentary hesitation and continued talking to the boy, trying to reassure him. Hearing that, he gulped and then slowly held out his hand to Rusalka.

"May the wings bless you for your bravery," she recited.

"Wings?"

"The great wings that protect the sky for you and your family and your friends and all the good people of the world."

Even though she knew it must look awkward and clumsy, she forced herself to smile for the boy as she took his hand. And then, holding him close, she turned to the escape route. The water was up to her chest. There was no more time, but she didn't feel worried.

She was surprised at how calming the thought of that blessing was—

"—Bwah!"

"Oooh! They made it out!"

Popping her head out of the water, she and the boy emerged from the cellar at last. A pair of burly arms grabbed the boy and pulled him up.

"Thank you for that," Rusalka said gratefully.

"Don't be ridiculous. If anything, we should be thanking you. Are you hurt anywhere?"

"You needn't worry. I'm not injured... Though we did run into a little trouble on our way out."

When she had been following the current, Rusalka had just barely managed to slip through the gap in the rubble while holding the boy and had been in real danger of getting stuck. If it had been any tighter, big breasts would have been the death of her.

"C'mon, gimme your hand."

Accepting his help, Rusalka was pulled out of the water, too. Totally soaked, Rusalka shook her annoyingly clingy hair and stood. Finally getting a good look at her, the man furrowed his brow.

"I thought I recognized your voice. You're the one from last night…!"

"—? Have we met before?"

"Yeah, at the pub. Guess the drinks weren't too good, since you don't seem to remember a thing."

The big man scratched his head bashfully as he mentioned meeting her the other night. She inhaled slightly at that, struggling to respond:

"Is that so? Either way, it's good that you seem safe and sound. Have you all been rescuing others?"

"We ain't doing anything special. I just rounded up a couple of muscle heads, and we've been trying to pull people out of collapsed buildings… Besides, it ain't like we can run away right now."

The man glared at the pillar visible in the distance.

It seemed they were generally aware about the warped space and were trying to deal with the fallout somehow. And the fact that they had chosen to save people in this situation rather than run away in a panic was worthy of praise. But—

"We're just doing this because there's nothing else we *can* do. It's pathetic," bemoaned the large man.

"…Is that really true?"

"What?"

The man cocked an eyebrow at that. Noticing his reaction in her peripheral vision, Rusalka narrowed her eyes as she wrung her jacket dry.

After having warped several different times, there was something about the movement from the lake to the house—or more specifically how she had ended up there—that was bothering her.

It was—

"Miss…"

As she was thinking about that, the young boy came over. He looked a little bit tired, but he walked right up to her and lowered his head.

"Thank you for saving me."

"That's my job. I'm a soldier. Any soldier would have done the same."

"But you were the one who came to save me. So..." The boy raised his soaked head and looked directly at Rusalka. "Thank you for finding me, Miss."

Rusalka's eyes widened. His plain and simple gratitude hit her right in the heart. Catching her breath, she averted her sky-blue eyes.

"...You said before that there was nothing else you could do, right?" Rusalka asked the big man.

"Huh? Yeah. You can call it rescuing people, but it ain't gonna solve any real problems."

The man looked uneasy as the topic of conversation turned back to him.

And there was a certain truth to what he was saying. No matter how many times they pulled people out of the rubble, there would be no end to it until the battle was over.

But—

"In that case, would you be willing to cooperate with me? We might be able to change this situation."

"——"

"I understand it's difficult to blindly take me at my word. And I'm not completely sure of myself, either. But I believe there is at least a chance of victory..."

Rusalka was trying to say that she wanted to get them all out of this disastrous situation. She had come up with a plan, but she couldn't execute it by herself. She needed more people. And that meant she needed their help.

"Damn, you really are one unpredictable babe. Just full of surprises."

"...Eh?"

"You don't have to look so desperate. We'll lend you a hand if that's what you want. I said it before, right? We're only doing this because there's nothing else we can do. If you're saying there's another way, then we're all ears."

The gruff-looking man broke into a smile and looked around. The other civilians who had all gathered to help the child nodded when they met his gaze.

"——"

Rusalka was taken aback as the man turned toward her again.

"Let's do this, Valkyrie. After all that talk last night at the pub, it's time to see what you're made of."

"...What was I crying about at the pub?"

"Huh? You don't even remember that?"

The man scratched his cheek as his determination fizzled and transformed into awkwardness. But sensing the earnestness in her gaze, he heaved a sigh.

"Honestly, that was our bad. We had a few too many and let things get outta hand. It wasn't right sayin' those things to someone like you, who's fighting for us... Like telling ya to get your shit together and all that."

"———"

"That's when you sent my ass flying. Sayin' '*Valkyries are heroes.*'"

I really said something that embarrassing with a straight face?

Rusalka could feel shame well inside her, but the people around her were reacting differently from how she expected. The man's face drooped, like he was embarrassed at what he had done, and the other men all looked the same. She was only just realizing how many of them had actually been at the pub.

"And you were right. Of course you were. So let us help you. If we can do that much, then maybe we can make up for last night and that cheap booze."

The man extended a hand. While she was still trying to decide how to react, she felt something grab her sleeve. She looked to see what it was, only to find the boy also holding out his hand for Rusalka.

"Take the hand reaching out for you, just like you said, right?"

"—Yes, that's right."

Urged on by the very same words she had told the boy, Rusalka quietly turned and accepted the man's handshake.

"Thank you for your help. I will make sure you don't regret it."

"Yeah, I'm countin' on ya, hero. Or should I say, Valkyrie."

Rusalka struggled to respond as the man shook her hand, a look of anticipation on his face. But she felt something unmistakable.

She turned to the boy.

"It is dangerous to stay here. You should go with one of the adults. I have to do my duty."

"Okay! May the wings bless you!"

"—Yes, and you too."

She nodded at his little prayer and then peered up to the sky.

The Valkyries were still fighting the invaders without any reinforcements. In order to break the impasse and change the flow of battle.

"We'll do whatever it takes, so tell us: What do you want us to do?" The big man was ready.

To protect the city, to stand a fighting chance, Rusalka turned to the men, and—

9

"—With the help of volunteers, I have created a map detailing both the positions of the spatial distortions and the locations they currently connect. An analog analysis of the results is ongoing as we speak."

Rusalka was scrawling notes across a map of the city. It was a massive sheet of paper that had been hanging in a factory she had arrived at after crossing through several different warps. The map had details of the forest and lake and other areas in the vicinity in addition to the city itself. All that was missing was a map of the base. Without that, she couldn't finish her analysis, but—

"Fortunately, I serve directly under the command staff."

"Wait, the base map's definitely confidential. Are you saying you revealed that to civilians?"

"Yes. The pressing nature of the situation necessitated desperate measures. Is that a problem?"

Rusalka's defiant response was met with a laugh from the command post.

"No, if you judged it necessary, then it must have been warranted."

It had been less than twenty minutes since she had requested help from the civilians. In that time, a new officer had assumed command of the base and reestablished the command center after the attack, and he was now praising her actions.

She had been surprised when she recognized him as the man from the stockade, but when she heard his name, it all made sense.

"You're a nasty man, Lieutenant Colonel Ostley."

"You weren't the only famous person around here is all. Don't go getting testy on me now, Captain Evereska."

They both made their positions clear by addressing each other by formal rank.

The soldiers manning the command post filled out their map, following Rusalka's directions. And there were astonished gasps as they confirmed all the notations.

——Rusalka's plan was to use incredibly straightforward human-wave tactics to deal with the warps in space.

The warps randomly connected different places over an area spanning several kilometers all around the city, but the physically disconnected areas were still connected somehow. The lake water flowing into the house and the child's screams reaching her in the lake proved as much.

In other words, the wiring was messed up, but it was still possible to walk straight through from one side to the other. Given that, it seemed obvious that what they really needed to know was which areas connected where. A guide to find the path.

"So you used people as pathfinders. Standing people at the edges of the warps to serve as signposts. And with guides, you can minimize confusion and panic."

"Like a guide for someone arriving at the base for the first time. It's still not so simple that I would claim we can move freely now, but simple navigation shouldn't pose such a problem anymore."

"But still, even if you figured that much out, it can't have been easy to pull off. And there's a battle still raging. You did well to convince the civilians to help you."

There was a tone of admiration in Alejandro's voice as Rusalka closed her eyes for a moment.

It went without saying, but the battle going on overhead was not just some unrelated concern for the people on the ground. If the Valkyries or fighter jets, or even the tertiaries, took a hit, they might well crash into the city. It was a situation where civilians should have moved to shelters. But the first man Rusalka had asked as well as several other civilians had all chosen to help her instead. Without them, she would never have been able to complete such a detailed map.

Alejandro's surprise was fully warranted. And if she had to explain it, she had only one answer.

"Everyone has the right to fight for the things they want to protect."

"...Either way, I'll send the updated map data to all units. We should be able to get things moving again with this. All that's left is..."

"Yes..."

Rusalka and Alejandro were surely both looking up at the secondary towering in the sky.

They were making good progress on curbing panic and confusion on the ground. The next task was figuring out how to deal with the giant secondary.

Overhead, the Valkyries and the regular fighter pilots were all actively engaging the secondary and tertiaries still in the sky. But as long as they didn't have a way to deliver a decisive strike, the situation would continue to gradually turn against them. And the source of that problem was also the source of the strange bends in space, which had not only disrupted the base's functionality but had also caused a tremendous disturbance for the people on the ground—

"According to reports, space is being warped in the air as well. An attack by the Valkyrie flight got caught in one and somehow hit an ally. They're currently engaging in a delaying action, but..."

The unspoken implication was that they would reach their limit soon. Either they would get shot down when their focus lapsed or be forced out of the action when they had no more fuel left. But there was no guarantee they wouldn't bump into some lethal bend in space when they tried to touch down for refuel and resupply.

They needed to solve the disconnects in the air, too—

"What on earth are you hesitating over, Captain Evereska?"

"Michelle?"

A woman's voice suddenly cut in. It was a familiar voice that she immediately recognized. In fact, it was one she was used to hearing through a radio. Michelle had been the operator for Rusalka's flight back when she was still flying.

And just when Rusalka had stopped moving in order to think, Michelle pleaded with her.

"You aren't thinking about this like it's someone else's problem, are you? As if the sky wasn't your battlefield...?"

"Michelle? Your voice is... Are you wounded?"

Detecting a note of anguish in her quivering voice, Rusalka quickly realized the cause. Considering where her post was, Michelle must have been in the command post when the secondary's attack hit. With that much force, there was no way she would have escaped unscathed.

Ordinarily, she should have been recovering in a bed at the very least.

"I'm not what you should be concerned about right now!"

"——"

But she had no patience for Rusalka's interest in her condition. She had always been so cool and collected, regardless of how dire the situation, so Rusalka was speechless at hearing her flare up. However, Michelle didn't stop there.

"My injuries are irrelevant... Even if I wasn't injured, I still wouldn't be able to fly. I still wouldn't be able to fight."

The pain in Michelle's voice took a sharper edge, but she endured, putting even more force into her words.

"But that's not true for you!"

"I..."

"We would fight if we could... I know I would... But I can't! You're the only one who can! You're the only one who has wings, Rusalka!"

"Ngh."

Michelle's words pierced her heart.

A loud, hacking cough followed the desperate plea. Rusalka shuddered at the sound of the bloody wheezing, but Alejandro chimed in, reassuring her.

"She's okay. Just got a little too worked up. But she meant what she said."

"I...I know that..."

Rusalka didn't want to be so thickheaded that she failed to understand Michelle's heartfelt plea. And it also explained the confusion she had felt about Michelle's actions up to that point.

She had probably wanted to share those thoughts with Rusalka any number of times from the moment they had first met again at Hamburg. She had said it countless times already even.

"*——Unlike me, you can fly, can't you?*"

It would not have resounded so strongly if it had been said out of anger or hatred or offhand annoyance. It would have just been fuel for the fire of self-hatred that already tormented Rusalka. But the emotion in Michelle's words was completely different. Her voice was filled with sadness and aspiration.

——From the bottom of her heart, Michelle was genuinely remorseful that Rusalka Evereska could not fly.

"What was it you said? Everyone wants to be able to fight for the things they care about?" Alejandro tried to recall.

"——"

That wasn't exactly what she had said earlier, but he had gotten the gist of it. Rusalka didn't want to argue over semantics and waited in silence to let him finish his thought as he continued in his usual self-confident tone:

"I'm the same. We all are. That goes for everyone at the base. And I'm sure it's the same for the civilians who helped you, too. Everyone wishes they were in your shoes."

"In my shoes… You mean as a Valkyrie?"

"Yeah, that's right. But that's just us burdening you with our own selfish expectations."

"Eh?"

Rusalka's eyes widened, and she put her hand to her chest. There was no way Alejandro could see her, and yet—

"Bet you've got a pretty shocked look on your face right now. But the weight of everyone's hopes and dreams is too heavy. You can't get off the ground carrying that much baggage around. Why do you think birds are so lean? It's so they can fly, right?"

"——"

"Whether you fly or don't, and what burdens you carry or don't, that's for you to decide, Evereska. Whatever you choose, humanity can take responsibility for it."

She was taken aback by how he so easily brought all of humanity to the table. Her lips cracked, and a little laugh escaped.

"Aren't you supposed to tell me to take responsibility for my own actions there?"

"If it was something you could be expected to carry, then I would have. So if everyone wants to fight to protect the things they care about, then…" Alejandro paused for a moment before he asked, *"…What is it that you love?"*

"——"

It almost felt like she could see him staring straight at her through the radio. She looked up at the sky. The air units were engaging tertiaries as the fighting continued. But in that moment, her eyes were trained far beyond that as she took in the wide-open skies above.

The setting sun was starting to fade, and a few stars were barely visible in the distance.

She looked up at the sky she had once yearned for. The sky she had given up on somewhere along the line.

The endless blue skies she had yearned to melt away into—

"What's precious to you, Rusalka?" Alejandro asked again.

And this time, Rusalka did not hesitate to respond.

"It's—"

10

—Run.

"Over here! It's forest past here! Watch your step!"

—Run. Run. Run.

"This way leads right into a wall! Don't crash into it!"

—Run. Run. Run. Run. Run.

"Straight ahead! Straight ahead! If you go straight—"

—Run.
—Run. Run. Run.
—Run. Run. Run. Run. Run.

—Run!

"Chief Technician Reever!"

"Rusalka?!"

Seeing Rusalka dash into the hangar, Roger's eyes widened in surprise.

Not unreasonably, either, since she had not appeared from the entrance to the hangar. She had slipped in through a window and rolled across the floor.

Shaking her head to get the leaves out of her hair, she ran over to Roger.

"Is my Spitfire ready?!"

"—Gah. Of course! It's always ready to fly!"

He had a moment of shock at Rusalka's intensity, but it faded as soon as it appeared, and he flashed her a thumbs-up, pointing to a corner of the hangar in the same motion.

Rusalka's beloved crimson Deus ex Machina was sitting there, waiting.

"I got word from the command post. It's ready to go whenever you are."

"Johnny on the spot, like always."

With Roger's seal of approval, Rusalka sprinted to her Spitfire. She caught the pair of goggles one of the men in the hangar threw to her and quickly put them on. She hadn't made any preparations to fly. Even a novice would know it was suicidal to go up into the air like that. But she didn't have time to change into a flight suit, and the path to the changing room hadn't been mapped out, either. She had not even changed out of her soaked uniform yet, so it was just all around too late to be worrying about something like a flight suit.

"Rusalka! I'm worried about how much ammo the others have left! If possible, get them to touch down for a resupply!" Chief Reever called out.

"I'll let them know. Please stay clear."

Fuel concerns aside, the fact that no one had touched back down for a resupply yet was worrying. Concerns about spatial distortions were preventing safe landing, but it was dangerous to keep flying without any means to fight back, too.

She needed to determine a safe way to land for the people who had been in the air since the start of the battle and share it with the others. All the more reason she needed to get into the air as soon as possible—

"——"

She slipped herself into the cockpit with practiced ease, fastening the harness and putting on her flying cap and goggles. She reached out to check the gauges, and that was when she noticed it. Her fingers were trembling. She couldn't move.

"Gh..."

She had gotten that far by buckling down and forcing her weakness aside. She had gotten there without losing her nerve.

And yet, this now that I'm sitting in the cockpit?

"——"

Roger and the maintenance crews who were watching her leave started to look perplexed, sensing something was off when her engine hadn't turned on yet.

Rusalka scolded herself, telling herself to not worry them like that. But even so, her arm refused to move—

"You are a Valkyrie, Rusalka."

"—Ah."

That was when an encouraging voice spoke to her through the hangar speaker.

Even though there was no way the command post could possibly see what was happening, he still knew somehow.

The mastermind of miracles, Alejandro Ostley, continued:

"The sky is the place you dreamed of. So fly, Rusalka! You're going to be like Amy, right?!"

"—Argh. You promised not to tell anyone that!"

Gritting her teeth, Rusalka finally started moving again as he revealed what she had talked about that morning in the stockade. The hand that had frozen stiff, refusing to listen to her at all, finally started working the controls in the cockpit.

The engine turned, and her machine roared in joy.

"...Sorry for keeping you waiting."

She apologized to her beloved plane for making it spend so long gathering dust on the ground. Naturally, Roger and the mechanics had kept it in perfect condition, so the dust was just metaphorical.

"You weren't the only one wasting away, gathering dust, though. I was, too."

Closing her eyes, Rusalka exhaled.

The entrance to the hangar opened in front of her, and the Deus ex Machina's wheels started rolling. She steadily picked up speed—

"Give 'em hell, Rusalka!"

Roger's deep voice boomed out, followed by shouts from the rest of the maintenance crew.

It was too heavy to fly carrying the weight of everyone's expectations and hopes. Alejandro had been right.

But even so, that was exactly what she'd decided to do.

* * *

"Rusalka Evereska, taking off."

Her crimson plane spread its wings, dancing through the sky once again.

11

"Gh…! Shannon's frame can't take much more! Alma, support her!"

"You'll be defenseless if I do."

"Just do it!"

Natalie was desperately looking all around her, giving orders even in the midst of a dogfight with bullets of light closing in on her from all sides, doing everything she could to support the rest of the Valkyries in her flight.

Alma hesitated for a second when Natalie gave that order, but she obeyed and went to support Shannon. Natalie desperately wove and evaded as the enemies intensified their attacks on her instead.

With Alejandro's encouragement, morale had risen for a while. Natalie and the other Valkyries were fighting the good fight, of course, but the pilots in the fighter jets were valiantly drawing the attention of the enemy, too. The outlook was grim, though.

"The distortions…"

From the bits and pieces she had heard over the radio, she could tell it was affecting the ground as well. There was mass confusion in the air and on the ground as the secondary lured various groups into friendly fire.

Because of that, every unit was struggling to support one another, and the civilians were having trouble reaching the shelters.

Natalie gritted her teeth at the dire state of affairs.

"How much longer do we have to wait? We could really use a miracle here."

Natalie hated herself for so desperately clinging to that hope. She hated the laziness of leaving it to someone else to figure out how to solve the problem and not thinking for herself.

Just then—

"Natalie—"

Natalie exhaled at Alma's vague message. Was it someone in a pinch? Or the secondary doing something new? Either would mean another blow to their position in the battle. She would have to limit the damage as best as she could.

"—Ngh."

Perhaps that timidity and inattention had affected her wings, because there was a slight disturbance in her plane's evasive maneuver. A split second later, a light round grazed one of her wings, and her plane cried out, hampering her ability to move freely.

She didn't even have time to say anything.

The tertiaries right in front of the restlessly evasive Natalie had been waiting for that moment, and they sprang into action, ready to pounce on an opportunity to take down a Valkyrie.

There was no way out. Natalie could tell immediately with her peerless spatial awareness. And she also realized that meant this would be the end of her short life.

"———"

As doom drew near, Natalie reflexively closed her eyes. Even though she knew that was equivalent to giving up, to cutting off any possibility that might still be available to her.

And because of that—

"Only a fool averts their eyes in the face of the enemy."

Natalie was the only one who didn't see the crimson Spitfire flying straight up from below.

"Eh…?"

The red line swerved through the air, machine guns roaring as lines of fire erupted from its wings.

The next instant, a hole opened in the swarm of tertiaries closing in from the front. It was a small opening, but that was more than enough for her to slip through.

Natalie dove into the gap, desperate to escape her impending death sentence. The firefly-like tertiaries batted their wings, accelerating in an attempt to keep Natalie from escaping their encirclement, but they were uncoordinated, and several ran into one another, causing cracks to form in their shells.

Natalie gasped as she saw fragments of light scattering from those collisions. And then that voice slipped into her ears again.

"You would do well to remember that pillars can be damaged when colliding with one another or when hit by another pillar's attacks."

A stream of bullets mercilessly poured into the fractures that had formed in one tertiary's shell. The shots were weak enough that they would have been deflected by the shell, but they slipped through the breaks and slammed home, striking the tertiary's core.

The next instant, the tertiary disappeared in a flash of light that lit up the whole sky.

"You can make them crash into each other in midair? That's..."

"It was common practice among Seconds. Our planes don't have the firepower to crack the enemy's defenses head-on. A bit of wisdom gleaned by the weak through trial and error."

The voice responded again to Natalie's stunned murmur.

A sudden intruder—no, she knew who it really was who had stormed onto the battlefield. The crimson Spitfire tearing through the night sky was the same Deus ex Machina that had been biding its time in a corner of the hangar, waiting for its master to finally return.

"—You've woken up again at last."

"—? I don't recall being asleep."

"I didn't mean it like that!"

"Just kidding."

For a second, Natalie was dumbfounded. She wanted to berate Rusalka for not taking this seriously enough, to ask how she could be so at ease in a battle where a moment of carelessness would get someone killed. But she hesitated, given what had just happened moments ago.

"Do you mean to say you're able to remain composed even in a battle as intense as this?"

"It has nothing to do with that at all. It's just something an old friend taught me."

"Is that what it is?"

"Yes. The worse the odds get, the more important it is to crack wise."

Natalie was half amazed and half dumbfounded by that tall order. She looked over to her side again, seeing both the crimson Deus ex Machina and the unmistakable silver hair in its cockpit.

"I'll be counting on you, Captain Evereska!"

"You're the flight leader, so do as you wish."

Natalie's heart was dancing on edge at Rusalka's polite response.

It was probably because she was lined up, wing to wing, with Rusalka's Spitfire. With the plane she had chased after and dreamed of flying with ever since she had been chosen as a Valkyrie.

"How did you manage that attack just now, Captain?"

Natalie shook off those jitters of excitement as she followed up with a question.

She and the others had been holding back in order to avoid friendly fire, due to the high amount of spatial distortions. But it looked like Rusalka had attacked with confidence that hers wouldn't be redirected.

"It's simply psychological warfare. The enemy can't freely warp space however they like. That much is clear from the fact that everything on the ground is still technically connected."

"But my shots hit Shannon's plane..."

"It must have positioned the tertiaries in locations it had prepared beforehand with spatial distortions. That's what caused your shots to hit Shannon."

"———"

"From the enemy's perspective, that only needed to work once. After that, we would be forced to stay on guard against it, unable to attack freely. This secondary is a crafty one."

If that was true, it would be unthinkable. What she said pointed to a dire possibility. A possibility that the pillars might be able to think, make plans, and execute those plans.

"No, there's no point in trying to deny it anymore."

The enemy had challenged them to a fight the very next day after the last battle. It had even sent in a secondary, an enormous commitment of fighting power. And it had even dealt a massive blow to the command post in its very first attack. To continue in the assumption that pillars were mindless and couldn't act strategically would be starry-eyed optimism.

"You're quite adaptable."

"...Don't treat me like a child. There is no time for complaints in the air. Do you have any ideas for how to defeat the enemy, Captain?"

"Naturally. I have a few, but..."

Considering the situation, it went without saying that continuing to fight a delaying action in hopes of the enemy reaching the limits of its energy would be extraordinarily difficult. She wanted to believe Rusalka had some kind of plan if she had returned to the sky, but—

"It's Alma Conturo."

All of a sudden, a man's voice broke into their line. Alejandro. His forceful voice caught her attention, and it took a split second before she realized what he meant. But just as she realized the answer he was getting at, Rusalka also spoke.

"I was also thinking that was the only choice."

"We don't have time to waste getting things set up. She's the only one here with the firepower to actually damage that secondary. What do you say, Conturo?"

"———"

Alma had been silently listening to their back-and-forth.

With the Grand Slam munition she had loaded on board, it might actually be possible to break through the secondary in one shot.

"But if we fail, her bomb might go off inside the city."

"If it comes to that, then we've already lost this battle, and that was just all the fates had in store for us," Alejandro stated simply.

"Gh! Are you really just going to give up like that?!"

"Of course not. And I don't think it will come to that, either. I just trust in our fate."

Alejandro laughed at Natalie's fiery response, but there was no laughter in his voice when he continued in a quiet, confident tone:

"I believe that if we exhaust every last bit of our wisdom, every last ounce of our strength, and don't give up even at the bitter end, that fickle goddess of fate will come through for us—miracles are just the last bit of spice at the end."

Such was the resolve of the man who had shouldered the responsibility of command at the drop of a hat. The man synonymous with miracles was explaining what it took to draw fate to their side.

There were a few seconds of silence.

"—Got it. I'll do it."

"Alma..."

"I'll do it because my friends are asking me to—get me to the enemy."

Her request was sent out to the whole army, but to Natalie's ears, it sounded like a personal request of her. She had assumed Alma hated her, but during the battle, Alma had told her she was wrong, and now she was asking her for help.

Natalie caught her breath.

"—Of course I will! Who do you think I am?!"

"You're too loud, Natalie."

"How rude!"

Alma slowly started to climb as she responded bluntly to Natalie's enthusiasm.

She had already dropped one Grand Slam. She had only one more left. She would have to hit the secondary with that one shot and put an end to the battle. They would need to do whatever it took in order to deliver her into position and draw the secondary into her sights. Reaching that conclusion, Natalie glanced to Rusalka, who was flying beside her.

"I'm transferring command to Captain Evereska."

"Natalie, that's..."

"You aren't a waste of space anymore. The colonel is correct. This is not the time to be obsessing over positions when we have to give our all. Please take command."

Rusalka had a far superior track record in the use of flight-level tactics and was better suited to take command because of her experience. But Natalie wouldn't have yielded command merely because of such a surface-level conclusion.

"—I've waited a long time to be able to fight under your command."

Now that they had finally managed to fly together, she could finally convey how she really felt.

12

——I'm focused.

"———"

The air was clear, and it almost felt like she could see beyond the night and into the next day. The wind sounded distant and calm, soothing her heart as she flew through such a furiously deadly battlefield.

"It's odd."

She had flown so many times before. Fought the same incomprehensible enemy more times than she could count. She couldn't remember them all anymore. And every battle had been desperate. She had always maintained a calm facade, but on the inside, she had very little composure to speak of. That was just Rusalka's limit, and the simple truth of the matter for second-generation Valkyries.

So how could she be so calm as she rode out to fight again?

"—Ah, that's why."

Something about it felt familiar, and she suddenly realized why.

It was similar to how she had felt the very first time she had taken to the skies for battle. Though she never would have wished for it to happen that way, her heart had soared when she had been made a pilot and ascended into the sky like she had always dreamed. When she had felt that exaltation, she had prayed she would get to fly again in that same sky.

She had finally remembered that feeling, and having regained it—

"—May the wings bless and protect you."

She offered up a prayer for the others as she nudged the nose of her Deus ex Machina down and accelerated. The flight followed her as one, diving into the enemy's ranks.

The swarm of hovering tertiaries' lights danced wildly, swaying to the left and right. She wove among the incoming fire, twisting her plane to evade, treading a fine line between life and death.

There was no distortion in space in the areas where the tertiaries were active to prevent friendly fire on the pillars' side. Rusalka's analysis had been correct, and the flight shot down one enemy after the other, turning them into bursts of light and plant life.

"______"

Clutching the control stick, Rusalka focused entirely on evading enemy fire.

Unfortunately, there was a fundamentally insurmountable wall between the capabilities of second- and third-generation Valkyries. But that was only limited to their Deus ex Machinas' offensive and defensive abilities. Skill and craft were another story.

While Rusalka did not have enough firepower to finish off a tertiary on her own, she had survived in these skies, stalked by such powerful enemies, longer than anyone else in the world.

It had been like that in her old flight, too.

"I'll take the lead and draw the enemy's fire. Use that opening to take them down."

It was a particularly dangerous role in a Valkyrie flight, resolutely leading the enemy around by the nose. Natalie had been the one shouldering that role, but her experience could not begin to compare to Rusalka's.

More importantly, Rusalka had no choice but to rely on her comrades, since she didn't have the strength to shoot down the enemy by herself.

"Now!"

At Rusalka's sharp order, a hail of bullets rained down from the sides, pelting the defenseless tertiaries strung out in a column behind her. They had focused too much on her and lost track of their surroundings.

The cost of inattention was a heavy one, and the tertiaries would not get a second chance. Shattering into bursts of light and greenery, they fell to the earth, returning the life that had been stripped away. The absorption's effects were grave, so every little bit that could be returned mattered.

And it was also payback for the atrocities the pillars had perpetrated.

"That was too easy..."

One of the Valkyries murmured in awe as she followed Rusalka's orders.

Obviously, she was a member of the third generation, so she had several times the firepower that Rusalka did. There was no way that was her first time shooting down a tertiary, either. She had almost surely already shot down more in her short career than Rusalka ever had.

The reason she was so shocked at fighting with Rusalka was because of how effortless it felt.

"Natalie studied the tactics well, but..."

In Natalie's case, her superb spatial awareness had gotten in the way of her playing the role of the decoy. Her vision ended up nagging at her like someone who could hear a gnat buzzing right next to their ear. In addition, it was hard to leave an enemy to others when she was capable of shooting it down herself. Because of that, her movements were always a little bit flat when playing the decoy.

But Rusalka didn't have that vision, nor did she have that attack power. And the decoy tactics had originally been designed for second-generation Valkyries. There was no way Rusalka, the pioneer of those tactics, wouldn't be able to execute them perfectly.

"———"

And Rusalka was performing her old role with a much greater precision than she had in the past. There wasn't any sign that she had grown rusty despite how long it had been since she had last flown. Her comrades—no, her younger sisters—gasped at the skill with which she soared through the skies.

It was only natural, though. Even when she hadn't been flying, there was not a day that had gone by without her thinking about the sky. Even when she tried to put it out of her mind, she couldn't help herself. Ultimately, not a single day had gone by where she had not thought about flying and how to fight.

"All that time I thought I wasted is just another weapon."

She just barely dodged the incoming tertiary fire by nudging slightly left or right. Her bright-red fuselage flew freely all around the sky, and the more it annoyed the enemy, the better.

Natalie and the others shot down the enemies clinging to her tail, turning them into bursts of light and then green. And as Rusalka led the tertiaries around by the nose, her Deus ex Machina closed in on the secondary.

"———"

Instead of swinging at Rusalka to specifically swat her down, it unleashed a single horizontal slash.

The scythe split the wind, tearing through the sky without concern that some tertiaries in the way were caught up in the attack.

Faced with that line of death, Rusalka had two choices—up or down.

Her decision was immediate and her movement near instantaneous.

Up or down seemed like the only way to go at first, but both were wrong. The correct choice was to keep going straight forward.

"You like forcing people into 'heads, I win; tails, you lose' choices, don't you?"

Most likely, she would have crossed a distortion and ended up in a deadly position whether she dodged above or below. Or maybe she would have even been transported right in front of a wall and died immediately in the unavoidable crash.

Either way, she won her bet. The scythe barely brushed the top of her cockpit, tearing off the canopy as it passed, leaving Rusalka's silver hair fluttering in the wind. Blood ran down her temple where a fragment had struck her.

It didn't matter, though. There was no pain. Her heart felt like it was about to explode, but for some reason, her lips curled into a smile.

"Ha-ha."

A laugh slipped past as her sky-blue eyes stared straight into the secondary's red compound eyes.

Right up against the enemy's body, she suddenly shot upward. It looked like she was flying straight up the secondary's torso, but the enemy would not attack at that range.

Or rather, the secondary could not attack at that range.

"—Gh!"

A fusillade of light rounds flew at Rusalka as she climbed the secondary's torso. But they were all slow, slow, slow. Far too slow. There was no way they would be able to hit her.

It hadn't practiced enough, hadn't studied enough, wasn't self-aware enough. It didn't love the sky enough.

"You think you can hit me with a joke like that?!"

Rusalka howled as she clenched the control stick. The Gs were adding up as she accelerated, but she didn't care at all. She just glared into the secondary's compound eyes as she ascended.

The light rounds could not keep up with her, just like she had planned. And having missed her, they crashed straight into the secondary's torso one after the other.

"—Ghhhhh."

Did it hurt? Was it mad? There was a strange sound from the secondary.

The praying mantis it was based on didn't normally chirp in the wild. That was another mark that it was an unnatural simulacrum—and either way, its punishment had only just begun.

"Second wave! Now!"

"Aaaaaaaaah!"

Again, the Valkyrie flight fired as one on Rusalka's order.

About ten seconds earlier, they had detached from Rusalka and spread through the sky, and now they were aiming their fire on the compound eyes that had been focused on the crimson Deus ex Machina, letting loose with all they had.

Friendly fire from the tertiaries was striking its torso, while the full force of the Valkyries' guns was spraying into its eyes. During that onslaught, the secondary completely lost sight of Rusalka.

—That was when she zipped right by its face, intentionally flying a provocative route across its field of view.

Seeing that, the secondary raised a scythe into the air, desperately trying to catch her. If it swung, it would hit Rusalka and all the tertiaries around her—

"Alma Conturo!"

Just then, Alejandro's voice rang out, calling for the girl who had been circling in wait above the desperate battle. Her Lancaster dove down—and she unleashed her last Grand Slam.

"——"

The seismic bomb fell in slow motion, blocking out the moon. And finally, the bomb that boasted the greatest destructive power of conventional weapons, second only to nuclear warheads, approached the secondary before it disappeared.

Just before the secondary was caught in the expected blast radius of the Grand Slam, the bomb was swallowed up by a distortion.

If it fell into an area around the city or the base, that would be the end of everything, but—

"Checkmate."

"Checkmate."

Coincidentally, Rusalka and Alejandro had the same reaction.

The very next moment, the Grand Slam reappeared…right next to the secondary's waist.

Ironically, it was the very same distortion that had led Natalie's shots to hit Shannon. Because of that friendly fire incident, they had been able to determine the exact location of the distortion.

In other words—

"You lost because you showed too much of your hand," Rusalka declared.

She escaped the secondary's zone of control just as a fireball engulfed the air behind her.

—An enormous explosion shattered the night sky, swallowing the secondary in a swirl of flames.

"——"

A hellish inferno sprang up, consuming the secondary and all the tertiaries in the vicinity. The destructive shock wave flattened everything around it as Hamburg was treated to the world's most intense fireworks display.

As the flames and black smoke cleared—

"That can't be..."

—Natalie saw a silhouette still standing, shrouded in black smoke. There was shock and despair in her voice, but she could hardly be blamed.

For it to still be standing, even after all that—

"No, this is—"

"Finish it, Rusalka!"

Just as Rusalka shook her head, the radio crackled with Alejandro's agitated voice. Hearing that, Rusalka exhaled.

"Roger!"

Swinging around, she dove straight into the smoke, charging right at the silhouette. As she approached the smoke, the secondary's figure gradually came into view. She could not see all of it, but miraculously, she managed to keep track of its movements.

A scythe aimed right at Rusalka swung upward, slicing through the billows of smoke. It was an attack the secondary had not shown before. It had been consistent up to that point in only swinging its scythes downward or in horizontal slashes. But it was not an intentional change in attack pattern so much as a last resort forced upon it by the situation.

"—I can see it."

She could see the secondary through the tear in the wall of smoke. Its green shell was lined with fractures from withstanding the full force of the Grand Slam, and all the tertiaries that had been caught up in the explosion had already undergone annihilation. The enemy was battered, bruised, and barely standing.

It had lost six of its scythes, and it was using two of the remaining ones to hold itself up to avoid falling completely. It was leaning unsteadily, which was why it had been forced to rely on a rising attack from below. And that swing missed.

Shrouded in wind, Rusalka closed the distance in the blink of an eye. There was no space between her and the giant figure.

"AAAAAAAAAAAAAAAAAAAH!!!"

Rusalka started shouting as she charged the enemy.

Was it to spur herself on? —No, it wasn't that. Her soul was telling her to roar.

Her soul, her resolve, the very core of her being, and her wings were all screaming for her to sink humanity's fangs into the incomprehensible invaders that dared trespass on their skies.

Her Valkyrie instinct was screaming. Howling. Roaring madly.

And seeing the secondary's emotionless compound eyes right in front of her—

"—Heh."

—she tilted the nose of her Spitfire up into a sudden ascent. The tertiaries following her could not keep up with her sudden turn, and they crashed head-on into the fractured shell of the secondary.

It was like a pileup on a highway as they slammed into the secondary one after the other. And finally, finally its shell cracked wide open.

—That was when humanity saw it.

"There's a globe of light inside the secondary…?"

Looking down from on high, she saw a shimmering ball of light floating inside the secondary's torso. It looked like there was some kind of coin floating in the middle of the orb.

Rusalka—and all the Valkyries there—instinctively understood just what that was: the pillar's weak point. If they could shatter that, it would mean their victory.

And as if sneering at their brief moment of hope, the orb of light faded, gradually disappearing inside a distortion in space, threatening to turn their battle into a farce—

"—I won't allow it!"

But Natalie Chase wouldn't let the secondary escape so easily.

Late off the blocks when Rusalka rushed the secondary, she still managed to follow the trail Rusalka had blazed. Natalie was the only one in position to threaten the weak point that had been revealed.

The machine guns on her gray Spitfire erupted. An instant later, the bullets slammed into the glimmering orb, mercilessly shredding it.

"———"

The light swelled as the orb cracked and then finally shattered. The secondary raised what sounded like a pained scream. And as that echoed over the battlefield, something amazing happened.

"The pillar—"

There was a dumbfounded voice on the radio, but there was no need to figure out whose voice it was. No one had the presence of mind to bother. They all turned their eyes to the pillar of light in the distance.

As the secondary's scream hung in the air, the pillar of light lost its shape, fraying at the edges. The light fractured and then broke into countless pieces before finally disappearing.

In other words, it was the pillar's complete defeat and—

"Rejoice..."

—the secondary's final death throes, the tertiaries' silent annihilation, the pillar of light's brittle, fragile end. As everyone watched that, an intense, powerful voice called out to all the troops through their radios.

"*—This is victory! For us and for all of humanity!*"

"—!"

Hearing that, Rusalka's eyes widened and her hand clenched. She shouted for joy as a swell of emotion rose in her breast.

"———"

The spreading cheers all drowned her individual cry, swelling up all across the land below her—no, it was not just from down below; they were coming from the sky as well.

The pilots, the Valkyries—everyone in the air was cheering, too.

The cheers from the ground and the sky merged, becoming a song of victory. And as they spread, the secondary's screech finally ended, and it lost its form completely. A tree consumed the remnants of light coming from the crumbling orb and began to sprout, but it was nothing like when a tertiary was downed. A gargantuan tree hit the ground, and a rampant growth spread out all around it, breathing life back into the barren earth with a wave of vibrant foliage and flowers.

It was the first time humanity had ever seen anything like it.

"Amy..."

With the emergence of the third generation of Valkyries, there had been minor victories. But this was the first time a pillar of light had been toppled with the total defeat of the pillars that it had spawned.

At the very least, it was a feat that had never been managed by a Valkyrie other than Amy.

"Valkyrie."

She heard someone's feverish voice.

Not from the radio but from the ground below. A massive crowd of voices had become one and somehow reached her ears. The people on the ground below were shouting up at the Valkyries in the night sky above.

"Valkyrie. Valkyrie."

And now, through the radio, the voices from the command post reached Rusalka's ears.

"Valkyrie. Valkyrie."

"Valkyrie! Valkyrie! Valkyrie!"

The chants that Rusalka had heard once before, back before she had been a Valkyrie herself. When she had felt empty as she watched Amy, who was so different from her, flying calmly through the skies.

How did it feel now?

"Valkyrie! Valkyrie! Valkyrie!"

"——"

She quietly took a breath. The battle was over.

Humanity had been pushed to the brink. They had just endured a massive, unprecedented assault by the pillars. But they had repelled the attack and defeated a secondary pillar for the second time in human history. It was a day to be celebrated.

—And so the curtain fell on the battle that would later come to be called the Return of the Valkyries.

Chapter 4
Sigrdrifa

1

"You're the one who contributed the most, Natalie. You finished it off."

"No, you deserve the most credit, Alma. Without your Grand Slam, we never would have revealed the secondary's weak point."

"It's you."

"It has to be you!"

Sparks flew as Alma and Natalie glared at each other.

They were in the command post of Hamburg base. The base was still showing much of the damage it had sustained during battle from the day before.

Having survived the fierce fighting, the Valkyries had been ordered to get some rest, and they had slept like logs. They were called to the office of the base's commanding officer the next morning, and they had just gathered when Natalie and Alma started getting into it.

Their argument was heated, but it was a strange one. They were both trying to argue the other was more deserving of the highest recognition for their feats in battle.

"It's funny. Normally, people would be fighting to claim the honors for themselves," Alejandro mused, propping his head up and enjoying their argument.

"That seems wrong in its own right..." Rusalka sighed and turned to the two girls. Her sky-blue eyes glinted. "Behave yourselves. Where do you think you are?"

"——"

Her strict rebuke was enough to get Alma and Natalie to stop at once. She nodded at the two of them when they turned to face her before continuing:

"You are third-generation Valkyries… I'm aware you were sent out into battle with less-than-minimal training that could hardly be called a crash course, but even so, this is inexcusable."

"Ack…"

"So harsh…" Alma groaned.

The two of them froze at Rusalka's genuine reprimand.

Rusalka seemed satisfied that they had finally realized how unacceptable their argument was, given where they were standing, but Alejandro's smile only deepened as he added his thoughts to the mix.

"I wonder who's really failing to be considerate here? Well, it's nothing new that all the Valkyries are problem kids. Not much point worrying about it now."

"—? That is a rather unsatisfactory evaluation," Rusalka protested.

"Just let it go. It'd be a pain in the ass if we got stuck here all day. I'll entertain your grievances later."

She did not really appreciate how he said that, either, but it was technically an order from a superior officer, so Rusalka reluctantly acquiesced.

Alejandro grimaced, not failing to notice Rusalka's grudging acceptance.

"Ummm, so then why did you call us here, sir?"

In Rusalka's stead, a small girl with her hair split into two braids raised her hand. She did not look quite as young as Alma, but there was still some immaturity to her face. She was one of the Valkyries in the flight who also fought hard during the battle.

Rusalka had the same question. The only people in the room were the Valkyries who had flown yesterday and Alejandro, who had assumed command of the base during the battle.

"I'm still pretty tired and sleepy honestly, so I'd like to have a chance to recover, ya know…?" the small girl griped.

"Well, I'll be damned. We've got us a live one here. I know it's just temporary, but I am technically your commanding officer," Alejandro said in exasperation.

"Maybe I'd be more awestruck if you were some superhuman being."

The young Valkyrie dodged his complaint with a calm attitude, like she was the real big shot. Seemingly taking a liking to her, Alejandro let out something between a stifled chuckle and a sigh.

"So you know what you think and you aren't afraid to say it, huh. I like it."

"My plane's all beat up, too. It'd be pretty rough if the enemies came a third day in a row."

"Whoa, there. I've got enough nightmare fuel as it is." Alejandro shrugged. And then he winked as he turned to Rusalka. "Well, even if that did happen, I'm sure Rusalka can manage something with all her wisdom and bravery, right?"

"There are limits to how much you can squeeze from wisdom and bravery. I can take twenty men in a bar brawl, but I can't fight a war without my plane."

"——"

The eyes of everyone in the room widened. Looking from face to face at their reactions, Rusalka pointed to her lips.

"I was joking just now. Was it hard to tell?"

"If you've gotten over it enough to be able to joke about it, then that's what's important. Getting back to the topic at hand, though… Honestly, the idea of another assault by the pillars is not a laughing matter."

On that note, Alejandro stood and looked at the lined-up Valkyries. He leaned over the ebony desk and punched his palm to his chest with a smack.

"If they came at us two days in a row, there's no guarantee a third attack isn't coming. But fortunately, this time they didn't simply retreat—they were entirely annihilated. So there's good reason to believe there won't be another fight so soon."

"But even that isn't certain," Rusalka noted, following his line of thought.

"That's right. So we need to figure out how to get back on our feet ASAP. Regarding your Deus ex Machinas, the maintenance crews are hard at work on them right now. But they've been working around the clock for two days now, so efficiency has dropped like a rock."

"Then what are your intentions, sir?" Natalie's shapely eyebrows furrowed as she struggled to see how the situation could be improved.

Alejandro clapped his hands, as if he had been waiting for that question. "This is the crux of the problem. Honestly, it is going to be difficult to get Hamburg back to full operations in the near future. The command staff has been decimated, and it will take time to rebuild the wall around the city, too."

"So then what can we do…?" Natalie wondered aloud.

"—Push the front lines forward?"

"Exactly."

Alejandro snapped his fingers and winked at Alma for guessing correctly. Alma didn't respond, and Rusalka's reaction was chilly as well, but Natalie was different. Her lips quivered with excitement.

"So that's how it is. It'll take time to restore the base, but we can't just abandon the ground we fought so hard to hold. With retreat out of the question, the only path is forward," Natalie concluded after some further thought.

"Ooooh. How'd you figure that out, Alma?" asked the other young Valkyrie.

"I thought the idea of pulling back because we can't fix the base was meh, so why not go forward instead?"

"T-trying to figure everything out with that brute animal instinct of yours again…"

Natalie, who always tried to approach things logically, simply could not wrap her head around Alma's instinctual reactions. If anything, Rusalka was more on Natalie's end of the spectrum, so she understood. But rather than sympathizing with Natalie, she focused on the subject at hand.

"Pushing the front lines forward? …Is that really possible?" Rusalka openly questioned.

"It certainly won't be easy. And I'm sure some will laugh it off as idle fantasy. But you all took down a secondary pillar. There's no arguing with that fact," Alejandro assured them.

"———"

"You managed to do something that no one other than the First has done before. You've pulled off something amazing enough to go above and beyond the expectations of the brass…and the entire world."

Alejandro looked at them as he crossed his arms resolutely. Natalie and the others gaped at the scale of what he was saying.

"The expectations of the world…," Natalie murmured.

"You have carried the hopes of the world as Valkyries before now. But this is something far weightier than that. It's a special class, even among Valkyries."

It was an idea that was too great for simple words to convey. And the Valkyries other than Rusalka stiffened at that. Even Alma furrowed her brow, as if dwelling on some thought. And Natalie, who always had a powerful sense of duty, had surely been hit with a heavy shock.

"Humanity's hopes…on our shoulders." Natalie quietly tested the words.

"Yep. How's it feel? Heavy?"

"…I wouldn't have it any other way."

There was a moment of hesitation, but Natalie still managed to respond confidently. Her strength of will was dazzling to Rusalka. Her electrifying way of life was truly fitting one who would fly while bearing the hopes of humanity.

"Sigrdrifa."

Suddenly, Alejandro screwed up his face and said something that Rusalka didn't understand.

It was a word she didn't recognize, and she furrowed her brow when she couldn't parse it. Seeing that, Alejandro continued:

"Sorry. It's only natural you wouldn't know. It's the name of an operation that had been developed in the upper levels of the army."

"An operation?"

"Yes. The brass had developed a plan for a potential counterattack to reclaim areas controlled by the pillars, and the name for the squadron that would serve as the core of that counterattack is Sigrdrifa."

"——"

Hearing that, astonishment and understanding colored Natalie's and the others' faces.

But it meant something more to Rusalka. She understood it immediately. That plan had been originally designed for Amy and her squadron.

A squadron centered around the First Valkyrie that would reclaim the lands seized by the pillars, with the ultimate goal of defeating the primary pillars.

——That was the true form of Sigrdrifa.

"I was personally tasked with forming this new squadron. The brass is looking for a miracle, and by chance and with a lot of help from all of you, I managed to make that happen for them. So now I've gotta pull another rabbit out of my hat."

"—I would like to join Sigrdrifa, sir!"

As Alejandro scratched his head, Natalie's hand immediately shot up. He was taken aback when she suddenly stepped forward and volunteered, her cheeks red with excitement. Natalie was breathing heavily through her nose as she leaned forward even more.

"Alma contributed the most in this battle, but I did land the last blow on the secondary pillar. I am sure I will be of service, sir."

Natalie's sense of duty was on fire as she made an appeal for her usefulness. Her upright personality was on full display as she still refused to yield in her belief that Alma deserved the most credit for defeating the secondary.

Natalie turned to look at Alma.

"Alma! You made the most distinguished contribution, so you should be putting yourself forward as well! We have a duty to take responsibility for our actions."

"Natalie is the one who did the most..." Alma grimaced in seeming annoyance at Natalie's meddling. But the bitterness soon faded. "But if I can go to the front lines, then that's what I want."

"I'd have it no other way!"

Natalie broke into a happy smile as Alma indicated her willingness to join.

Surprisingly, the two of them seemed almost like friends. And latent abilities aside, their current fighting capabilities were well aligned as well.

"Just hold your horses. Your desire to volunteer is commendable, and I acknowledge your enthusiasm. But I said it before, didn't I? I was personally tasked with forming the new squadron. Your enthusiasm has nothing to do with it."

"...Do you mean...?"

"Do you mean to say we're not qualified...?"

Alma and Natalie paled in disbelief. There was a mysterious gleam in Alejandro's eyes as he watched them.

But Rusalka just heaved an ostentatious sigh. "It is poor taste to play tricks like that, sir. Please don't tease these young pilots."

"Rusalka...?"

"Neither of you needs to worry. The command staff will be the judge of which of you contributed most to this victory, but regardless of who receives that commendation, there is no way either of you would not be chosen. You both contributed greatly to the defeat of a secondary pillar, and Sigrdrifa will need members with those sorts of achievements to have any credibility."

The Sigrdrifa plan required Valkyries with precisely that sort of world-class track record in order to get off the ground. It had originally been drawn up with Amy's name to lend it weight, and now it would finally get a chance to see the light of day.

"Sheesh, it's no fun when you can see through everything. I can't hide anything at all, can I?"

And Alejandro broke into a smile, all but confirming her deduction. His attitude was like a playful lion, but Natalie and Alma were not amused.

Laughing at their reactions, Alejandro glanced over to Rusalka.

"Incidentally, it sounds like you're of the same opinion. That Sigrdrifa should be made up of the people who contributed most to the last battle."

"Is that not just fundamentally obvious? If anything, it would be illogical to try to keep them out. If I were the commanding officer, I would make the same decision."

"Right? Well, it's a relief to have your seal of approval, too. If that's how the person of interest feels, then it makes things easier on me as the one giving orders."

Something about the way he said that caught Rusalka's attention. And she quickly realized why when she met Alejandro's eyes.

"You can't be serious..."

"It was your swift discovery that helped reveal the true nature of the secondary pillar's ability, and it was thanks to your efforts that went above and beyond the call of duty that we were able to restore the base's ability to function so quickly. Furthermore, your contributions in leading the Valkyrie flight and assisting in the defeat of the same pillar are undeniable. And while you yielded the final blow, your final push was what ultimately revealed the enemy's weak point."

"———"

"I've already talked with the brass—the one who contributed most in this battle was none other than you, *Major* Evereska."

Alejandro looked Rusalka in the eyes as he announced her new rank.

Unable to face her reflection in his clear-blue eyes, Rusalka looked away. But even though she looked away, there was no escaping what he was asking of her.

She had said it herself—that it was only logical that whoever had been judged to have contributed most would be chosen for Sigrdrifa.

But—

"I folded up my wings once before already. Who could—?"

"—I can accept that decision."

As Rusalka tried to find an excuse, Natalie immediately cut in. She was holding her arms and looking away from Rusalka.

"If you hadn't gotten the army back on its feet, the damage we suffered would surely have been much greater. There would have been little hope of restoring the city and the base…and in the worst case, we might have been completely defeated."

"———"

"Hypothetically at least. Even without your guidance, we would surely have claimed a narrow victory."

Natalie's face turned red as she refuted herself as an afterthought. There was a trace of her pride in the fact that she limited it to only a narrow victory, refusing to acknowledge any possible result other than victory.

"I agree. Rusalka deserves it."

"Ah, then me too."

With Natalie's assertion over, Alma tacked on her approval, as did the third Valkyrie who spoke with a decidedly relaxed tone of voice. The two of them waved their hands as they acknowledged Rusalka's meritorious actions.

Honestly, it was a mysterious feeling.

"You always shunned me, though…," Rusalka protested.

"…You were irritating, yes. But when the time came, you stood and contributed to our victory in your Deus ex Machina. What could there be to hate about you?" Natalie held firm.

"But I'm just a Second. My abilities are lacking in every area compared to you..."

"Are you mocking me?! After you flew that elegantly— Argh! Why do I have to try so hard to compliment you?! Unbelievable!"

Natalie stamped her foot, at wit's end dealing with Rusalka's stubbornness. Seeing the swelling indignation that would have had Natalie biting her handkerchief if she had one, Rusalka was finally cornered.

——*No, it isn't quite that.*

"Is it heavy? Carrying all humanity's hopes? Or..." As Rusalka questioned herself, Alejandro had a question of his own. He paused for a moment before continuing. Rusalka eagerly awaited his next words.

"Or is it because of the name Sigrdrifa?"

Rusalka inhaled sharply at his soft question.

Just how good could one man be at jabbing right into the depths of people's hearts?

That pointless thought let her forget how dry her lips were for a moment.

"What is there to hesitate about, Major Evereska? You are..."

"Natalie."

When Rusalka did not immediately respond, Natalie looked irritated and started to question her, but Alma grabbed her sleeve and shook her head, stopping Natalie.

"This is for Rusalka to decide."

"—Gh. I just can't understand it."

With her strong sense of duty, Natalie could not comprehend why Rusalka was hesitating. But the fact that she at least tried to understand was a demonstration of her virtue.

"Could I ask you to give just a little bit of time before I respond?" In the end, Rusalka wanted a chance to think on it.

"Yeah, I'll wait. But I'm not gonna wait till I'm old and wrinkled."

"It won't take that long—not this time."

She ignored his joke as she looked down at her hand.

"Well then, looks like things are allll nice and settled now. You guys do your best." The laid-back Valkyrie was ready to excuse herself, but Alejandro wasn't letting her go that easily.

"You're acting like it's someone else's business, but you're joining the squadron, too."

"Huh?" Shannon Stewart, the girl who had tried to wrap things up neatly with a clap of her hands, tilted her head.

She would also be a member of the newly formed Sigrdrifa.

2

—Unsurprisingly, the restoration of the city was not proceeding nearly as smoothly as it had two days earlier.

"That's to be expected, I guess."

She could still feel the damp ground and puddles beneath her feet as she absentmindedly looked around the city.

The general had ordered her to observe the city two days ago, but this time she had gone on her own initiative. The man who had given her that order, Major General Logrev Barkley, had died honorably in service during the battle.

At the time, she had not really understood why he had given her that order, but—

"He was probably trying to get me to realize exactly what was resting on my shoulders."

Like many others, General Barkley had lamented the fact that Rusalka had folded up her wings and been dwelling on her pain. That was why he had done so much, for better or worse, to get Rusalka moving again.

"Even though I was such a difficult subordinate to deal with… I can only hope I will be able to live up to his expectations."

It must have been a challenge for him to take care of a Valkyrie who had been an ace, only to fold up her wings. But he never once treated her badly. It made her realize again just how great the general was, and she resolved herself to keep her head high going forward.

"Ah! Miss!"

As she adjusted her posture, a high, loud shout rang out.

The boy Rusalka had saved the day before was waving his hand as he ran over, kicking up slashes of water as he crossed the puddles. They had parted ways almost immediately after meeting last time, back when they were both still drenched from head to toe.

"Hello. You look like you are doing well," Rusalka said in greeting.

"Mm-hmm. I didn't get hurt at all thanks to you. You got the bad guys, right?"

"Yes, I did. Apparently, I even earned a commendation for contributing the most to victory."

"Wow! I don't know what *commendation* means, but that sounds amazing!"

The child clapped his hands in innocent excitement, and amusement lit Rusalka's eyes. She had meant it as a joke, but when she actually found herself saying it, something about it struck her far harder than she had expected. Before he could ask her any more questions, she glanced around.

"Are you by yourself? Are your parents...?"

Just then, she caught herself, realizing she had potentially asked a very inconsiderate question. But the boy didn't notice her concern as he scratched his head.

"I'm alone right now, but it's fine. Mom and Dad both came back. Our house fell down, though."

"O-oh. That's a shame."

"It was because of all the water."

The boy seemed half sad and half defiant at that fact.

Rusalka closed her eyes. It was a relief that his family was safe, but her choice of topic had been careless to say the least. It was not at all uncommon to suddenly and violently lose family members in this day and age. The fact that the two back-to-back battles had turned out to be a massive victory for the European Army did not change that fact of life.

"Even when we win, it always takes a toll..."

The higher-ups in the army and the people in the city were all excited by yesterday's triumph, but there had been losses, too, even if those losses were not publicly acknowledged.

"———"

Rusalka felt a sort of emptiness from that realization. And that she felt that way struck her as almost arrogant. But she also suspected it was just a taste of the loneliness Amy had felt.

Amy had guided the forces of humanity to victory on countless battlefields, but she'd never been able to save everyone. Rusalka wondered if it had hurt her every time she'd seen the shattered towns and all the people busily trying to get back to normal, or if her spirit had been so strong and noble that she'd never experienced that heartbreak.

——Even as she thought that, she knew all too well that it wasn't true.

"Miss? Are you hurt?"

A child's intuition was a powerful thing. That innocent gaze seemed like it could see right through an adult's clumsy deceptions.

The boy had easily recognized the anguish she had been trying to keep hidden and was sincerely worried about her. Rusalka shook her head and relaxed her lips.

"No, you needn't worry about me. This is just a pain I will have to grow used to."

"...That's so sad. It hurts, right?" The boy was teary-eyed as he looked up at Rusalka's smiling face, looking her straight in the eyes. "If it hurts, then I can pat it for you."

"——"

"Wah!"

The boy was surprised when he was suddenly enveloped by a comforting warmth. Struck by his kindness, Rusalka had unconsciously given him a hug.

Pathetic as it was, she had been taught something important by this boy for the second time in as many days. She was filled with immense gratitude. She was thankful that she had been able to save him.

And she would have more chances to experience that same feeling in the days ahead. Even if it would just be once or twice. Even if her struggle amounted to little in the end.

This is why I am fighting.

"—Be good to your family. I'm glad you made it through safely."

3

Leaving the boy, she walked the streets for a little while before steeling herself to enter the pub.

When she pushed open the swinging door, a bell rang. Looking around the gloomy room, she saw the owner standing behind the counter. His eyes widened slightly when he saw her. Rusalka stepped inside with a nod.

"You are open quite early."

"...It's getting to be evening. About time the folks running around outside'll start feeling like a pint. Best time to earn some money."

"So it would appear. I'm glad your shop is still standing."

"I got lucky. It's in better shape now than how you left it after that brawl."

"I'm sorry; I still can't remember it."

The owner offered a shrug and a "that's impressive" to her confessed memory loss. Turning, he poured a glass and set it gently on the counter.

"This...really looks like milk," Rusalka observed with apparent confusion.

"That's 'cause it is. I'm not pouring a regular drink for someone who doesn't know how to hold their liquor."

"I know how to drink it. You just lift it to your mouth, pour some in, and then it passes through your throat."

"That's downing it. That's not what drinking is. Besides, if you fly off the handle again, there's no way I can stop you by myself... Was your boss okay after that?"

"Boss..."

Staring at the glass of milk, Rusalka looked to her unreliable memories to try to figure out what he meant. But her memories of that night were still lost to the ether and entirely unsalvageable. But from what she knew of what happened afterward, there was a natural explanation.

"Do you mean the person with me who was also taken away?" Rusalka asked.

"Hmm? Yeah, I think I heard he got thrown in the stockade."

"...Yes, he's fine. He's currently sitting in the best seat in the base, even."

"Is that so..." The barkeep nodded slightly in acknowledgment.

Taking him up on his hospitality, Rusalka lifted the glass of milk to her lips. As she did, the general gist of what must have happened that night finally clicked in the back of her mind. Which would also be why she and Alejandro had both been thrown into the stockade.

"Evenin'." The barkeep greeted the new guest as the bell at the door rang. And then his eyebrows arched. "Oh? Speak of the devil. Were you waiting for him?"

"—?"

Rusalka arched her eyebrows in confusion. Turning, she saw a tall, blond man stepping through the door of the pub and immediately spoke up.

"That's a hideous misunderstanding, and I feel obligated to correct it for the sake of my honor."

"Hey! I don't know what you're talking about, but I can tell you're already bad-mouthing me. Also, you shouldn't be bothering civilians. Don't go causing him any more problems."

Rusalka heaved an ostentatious sigh as he sat on the stool next to her like it was the obvious thing to do. "Colonel Ostley..."

"What do you have to sigh about? Right when I was thinking to myself that I haven't seen you around the base, here you are, slinking away to a pub. Looks like you've got a promising future in the army after all," Alejandro said as he flashed a carefree smile.

"To be honest, I'm not particularly enthused with that appraisal. And this is not alcohol. I'm quite capable of learning from my mistakes."

"Really? Or did the owner just give you milk because he was worried about what you'd do?"

"...I won't deny that..."

Even if the barkeep had not given her milk, she had had no intention of ordering anything alcoholic. But she was sure Alejandro wouldn't buy that excuse, so she gave up trying to explain herself as her gaze sharpened.

"And what brings you here, Colonel Ostley? Shouldn't you be quite busy handling everything back at base?"

"Isn't it a pain to keep saying 'Colonel Ostley'? You can just call me Alejandro."

"Why are you here, Colonel Ostley?"

"Ha-ha-ha." Something about her stubborn response triggered a cascade of amused laughter. "My subordinates are all supremely competent, so I was told to leave to get out of their hair. Given that, I had little choice but to take a look around town."

"It is hard to reconcile that first part with you popping into a pub in such high spirits."

"Really? You mean this isn't exactly what the soldiers you knew were like?"

"That's..."

Rusalka did not have a reply to his counter. Taking her brief silence for an answer, Alejandro grinned like he had just pulled off a great prank. He held up a finger to the barkeep.

"A pint of ale for me, boss."

"You're quite comfortable in this setting, aren't you?"

"I can tell you're desperately trying to make me out to be some bad soldier, but we both know you hesitated just then. So no, I'm not going to quit drinking—check and mate."

"——"

Rusalka could only meet his banter with indignant silence.

The lack of conversation carried on for a while, with only the sound of the bartender pouring Alejandro's drink punctuating the silence. Finally, the bartender placed the pint on the counter.

"—To comrades."

"—To comrades."

Rusalka reluctantly joined Alejandro's toast. If it was to comrades, to the dead, then she had no reason to turn it down.

Rusalka sipped her milk, feeling bitter that everything seemed to be playing right into Alejandro's hand. After a short while of drinking in silence, he spoke up again.

"So how about it? Going to be able to make a decision?"

Half a day had passed since the conversation that morning. On the one hand, he hadn't given her much time at all, but on the other hand, it also wasn't particularly rushed.

"Wouldn't it be more normal to give me a bit more time?"

"I like to think I'm on the more patient end of the spectrum, but unfortunately, when it comes to this, I can't really afford to wait much. I have to keep scrambling, looking for new potential."

"New potential..."

"Finding Valkyries worthy of carrying the hopes of the world and tapping them to become members of Sigrdrifa."

"——"

Alejandro downed half his ale in one gulp before setting the glass on the counter. Rusalka hesitated for a moment as she watched a drop of condensation trickle down the outside of the glass.

"Am I really one of those?"

"Do you even have to ask? With all the titles you've earned and everything you've done, you think that's still not enough?"

"My self-confidence is…"

"You still can't believe in yourself, huh? Yeah, that's definitely a personality thing. Honestly, I can't understand it at all. I've been like this since I was born. Never not been sure of myself."

"That's hard to comprehend. Have you really never doubted yourself?"

"Nope."

Rusalka couldn't help chuckling at how easily he answered that.

Alejandro was always looking straight ahead at what he needed to do, his eyes never clouded by doubt. Not even when burdened with such a sudden, heavy load as taking over as the interim base commander in the middle of battle.

Not only that, he was leading Sigrdrifa and standing on the front lines of humanity's war for survival.

"…I doubt I could ever stand in that position."

"If you need to hear it from someone else, I can say it, too. If you hadn't noticed what was going on, none of our forces would have been able to maintain even basic unit cohesion. If you hadn't flown, there is no way all the Valkyries would have made it back alive. And if you hadn't been there fighting, there's no way we would have taken down the secondary. The reason it was decided that you were the one who contributed the most to that battle is because of all the things you did. You have every right to be proud of what you've accomplished."

Alejandro rattled off a glowing list of her achievements as he held his glass. Praising her distinguished service during the battle and how she had filled a crucial role, he gave her a push by saying how she had indisputably saved the day.

It was all—

"That's a rather scathing way to put it."

It was all a painful bed of thorns for Rusalka, and he surely knew that. After that one comment, she fell silent.

"———"

"At the end of the day, the things people say are still just words. You're the one who has to make this decision for yourself. If you were the kind of woman who couldn't do that, then maybe someone else could decide it for you. But that's not you. When it comes down to it in the end, you decide things for yourself—just like she did."

"She…?"

Alejandro seemed to be looking off in the distance. Rusalka furrowed her brow as he seemed to be thinking of someone far away. But he didn't respond. Instead, he finished his drink in a single gulp. Setting the glass on the counter with a heavy thud, he said, "Boss, another pint for me. And one for her, too."

"Is that ale…? W-wait, I'm not drinking…"

"Quit whining. This is an order from a superior officer. I'll have you thrown in the stockade for insubordination if you don't obey."

"You— That's an abuse of power…!"

Rusalka's voice quivered, but Alejandro snorted shamelessly.

The barkeep looked disapproving, probably out of concern for what Rusalka might do after having a drink again. But Alejandro just flashed him a lighthearted grin.

"Don't worry. I'm not gonna make her drink enough to go wild. And it's up to her to decide whether she actually drinks or not anyway."

The barkeep sighed before preparing his order. Finally, he placed two pints of ale on the counter. Seeing the glasses filled to the brim with alcohol, Rusalka gulped.

"What do you mean, it's up to me to decide?"

"Exactly what it sounds like. I said it was an order, but you're the one who chooses to obey or not. Just like how you're the one who chooses to drink or not. Life is a series of choices, Rusalka."

"______"

"You have to make a choice in order to do anything. Sometimes people try to talk their way around this by saying they choose not to make a choice, but in the end, that's just another choice. And if you ask me, making a choice means reaching out to grab something of your own volition. A choice doesn't mean much if you're just losing things left and right."

Rusalka froze when faced with the pint glass while Alejandro reasoned with her. He made no move to take his own glass, waiting for her to make her decision.

Time passed slowly, and condensation formed on the side of the glass before leisurely trickling down. The silence that filled the room was interrupted only by their breathing. Then Rusalka suddenly realized something.

"…Is this a continuation from the stockade?"

"Yeah, a bit of advice and talking things through. Unfortunately, we know each other a bit more intimately now, though..."

"That isn't quite right. You already knew me quite well yesterday, Colonel. And I'm not fond of how you phrased that, either."

"Don't go getting mad about every little clause tacked on to the end of a thought." Alejandro smiled wryly before tapping his finger on the counter. It was in time with her heartbeat, and something about it felt awfully nice. "What did you think after looking around the city?"

"What did I...? ...I thought the scars from the pillars run deep."

"That's true, but people are strong. Did that thought not occur to you, too?"

It was true she had been struck by the resilience and resolution on display as she watched the people working to get back on their feet and restore the city.

Rusalka fell silent, and Alejandro's eyes narrowed.

"With Sigrdrifa moving from place to place where they're needed, you'll see this same scene time and time again. And you'll also taste that same sense of accomplishment as well as that same powerlessness."

He laid out the conflicted emotions she was feeling.

——No, he was not just reading her thoughts. He probably felt the same thing himself.

He felt the same accomplishment from protecting the people and the city and the same powerlessness at not being able to protect them all. Just like she felt.

——For a moment, she saw Amy's face in his.

"Grrr."

She clenched her jaw. And when she opened her eyes, she grabbed the glass in front of her and raised it to her lips in one quick motion. The ale had a numbing effect as it passed her throat and spread through her body. It almost felt oppressive as she gulped it down. And finally, Rusalka slammed the empty glass on the counter.

And then—

"—I said something I never should've said."

—she finally put the source of her regrets, which she had bottled up inside, into words.

4

"—Please tell me? I want to know everything about you."

She could still remember the moment Amy had asked her that like it was just yesterday. As if time had stopped and she were living that moment over and over again.

She saw it in her dreams every night. She saw Amy whenever she closed her eyes. The night Amy came to her room, the way she had sat on her bed, smiling up at her.

The night her commanding officer had asked her if she would fly together with Amy. Rusalka had refused, only to stand face-to-face with Amy looking like she understood everything.

——Even in that final moment, she had never stopped smiling.

"She said she came to our base because she wanted to meet me. Because I was the only survivor from the Ride of the Valkyrie who also became a Valkyrie."

Rusalka remembered how Amy had run over to her with that easy smile. The young girl who had pestered her to show her around the base while wanting to talk about so many things.

Amy had run circles around her so many times. She was uninhibited and free, always thinking of things Rusalka never could have even imagined. Never behaving herself, even for a moment, always causing problems for Rusalka, who she happily dragged along behind her.

It was so out of character for Rusalka that she had to go back to when she was still a child with her parents to remember the last time she had been led around like that.

"I'm sure she was genuinely trying to get closer with me. I don't think she ever once distanced herself from me. She was always sincere."

She could still remember how sharp Amy's gaze was when she sat in her cockpit. Like an arrow loosed from a bow. She was just a normal girl when she was on the ground, but in the air, she transformed into a goddess of war, mowing down the invaders who dared fly in her skies. That change in character and her overwhelming strength stunned Rusalka every time she bore witness to it.

The way she flew through the sky with more composure than anyone else… It was something every Valkyrie and everyone who ever yearned to fly dreamed of at least once.

"She was close with the rest of my squad, too, and it was charming to see how they got along. It was a complicated situation, but they could probably be called friends."

Xenia, Victorica, and Canan all interacted with Amy in their own ways.

A motherly figure, a friend, and an older sister. There wasn't anything false about their friendships.

Even though Rusalka tried to warn them to maintain an appropriate distance, the three eluded all her efforts at professionalism: Xenia looking on from a little ways away, enjoying herself while Rusalka was at a loss for words as the other two constantly conspired with Amy.

Their bonds were real, and that was why they stuck with Amy all the way to that final battle.

But Rusalka wasn't able to go with her, and she wasn't there for that fateful day—

"When my commanding officer asked me about it, I didn't have an answer. He offered to give me some time, like now, but when he said it wasn't an order, I immediately had an answer."

If it was an order, she would have obeyed because she did not have a choice. But the moment she was told it was not an order, she instantly knew what she wanted to do. It was obvious from the fact that she would have obeyed only when she didn't have a choice in the matter.

"I didn't want to go with Amy."

It was true that she liked Amy. She enjoyed talking with her, was surprised by how she viewed the world, and learned a lot by being able to observe her strength up close.

All of that was true, and yet she still couldn't go with Amy.

"…Why not?" Alejandro gently nudged her along after having listened in silence up to that point.

Rusalka licked her dry lips, looking for the words inside herself—

"Why couldn't you go with Amy…with the First?" Alejandro asked again.

"Because…"

"———"

"Because I hated the First Valkyrie."

She clearly remembered the sin she had committed that night. Remembered what she had said to Amy. The feelings she had kept bottled up, that she had decided should never see the light of day…those emotions had gradually forced their way out until they burst the dam in her heart.

She had said those same words to Amy while she sat on Rusalka's bed that night. When Amy had asked why, Rusalka had told her, *"Because I hate the First."*

"…You survived that day. That was the battle that proved the First Valkyrie's strength, that signaled the start of humanity's counterattack. You're one of the witnesses who saw what happened."

"Yes."

"Why would you hate Amy? I don't believe for a second that it was some roundabout suicidal ideation. And I can't see you hating her for not letting you die fighting there, either."

Alejandro was right. Rusalka had never once wanted to die. And she had never been plagued by the thought that she would have been better off dying on that day.

But when she had seen those golden wings dashing gallantly through that lonely sky—a sky so devoid of life she had felt like the only person left in the world—a thought had crept into her mind.

"Why didn't you come sooner? Why couldn't you have been just a little bit faster…?"

That thought had consumed her heart as she flew all alone through the dark skies. It was not something that should ever be voiced. A thought that she should never have spoken.

Why had she said such a cruel, heartless, merciless, inconsiderate thing?

How could she say something like that to Amy, who tried with all her might to save the lives scattering to the winds all around her? How could she ask why she hadn't come sooner?

Why hadn't she come before Roy, Harris, Mullane, and Ed died?

They had all been good friends and reliable comrades. They had their bad points: Roy was always chasing skirts, Harris would wear the same socks for days on end, Mullane incessantly complained about food, and Ed was meticulous and fastidious to a fault. But none of them ever looked down on Rusalka for being a woman or treated her any differently than any other guy in the squadron. They treated her like one of them and flew together with her, trusting her with their lives, just like she trusted them with hers.

When she was left all alone in that empty sky, after they were all gone, she couldn't help but think the unthinkable.

"I knew better. It's a famous story. How Amy tore herself away from the people trying to stop her from going out that day and rushed onto the battlefield."

Dozens of pillars had appeared, and the battle seemed hopeless for humanity. Amy was the cornerstone of humanity's fighting strength. Their decision to try to protect her made perfect sense. But Amy broke free anyway and raced to join the battle, saving countless lives in the process. One of whom was Rusalka.

And yet, after being saved, Rusalka's response was, *"Why didn't you come sooner?"*

"Even though she saved us."

She had erred just that one time.

With the younger girl sitting there right in front of her, asking so bluntly to hear what Rusalka really felt. In that moment, with Amy's blue eyes trained on her, as Rusalka was saying the most pathetic, most shameful thing possible, she knew she was making a mistake.

She was filled with guilt, and in any other moment, she would have surely averted her eyes. But she was looking at Amy. And she saw it.

——She saw sadness in the eyes of the girl who bore the fate of the world without ever letting the pain show on her face.

"I'm sorry."

The sadness disappeared like it had never existed after she said those words.

But she had made Amy apologize. A girl who hadn't done a single thing wrong. Who had nothing to apologize for.

Even though Rusalka was the only person who had survived that battle and was able fly in the same sky with her. Even though she should have been the last person in the world to hurt Amy like that.

* * *

"I never spoke to Amy again after that night. I don't know what she felt… I constantly thought about talking to her again someday."

But she had been robbed of that opportunity. She would never get another chance.

She should have known it already. Ever since she had lost so many friends since that first battle. There was no guarantee that the person you were talking to today would be there tomorrow.

"And now I'm supposed to stand in the same place Amy did? That's… I…"

"You can't do it?"

There was a sob in Rusalka's voice as Alejandro quietly interrupted. Rusalka sucked air several times as she nodded.

She had felt it particularly hard earlier when she had seen the shattered streets and the flurry of activity filling the city. When she saw the same scene Amy had, she was confronted once again by the enormity of the bond she had broken.

So she—

"I won't tell you to fly in order to atone for your sins. Amy wouldn't have wanted that, either."

"…Colonel…"

"Yeah?"

"Did you know Amy?"

Rusalka finally voiced the question that had been so slow in coming.

He had called her by name several times in the course of the conversation. It didn't sound like someone who only knew of her, and she couldn't let it go without asking.

"How do you think I managed to pull off something like the Miracle at Lamia?" Alejandro scratched his cheek. "It was because Amy and her squadron covered our retreat."

"———"

Rusalka looked down as Alejandro answered matter-of-factly. He was right. It was obvious.

His famous miracle had been the evacuation of a city attacked by a secondary pillar, an operation that involved safeguarding a huge number of civilians. And that was the battle where Amy, Xenia,

Victorica, and Canan had fallen. His miracle was something the army had concocted to balance that tragic news with a man-made triumph. Alejandro Ostley was nothing but an artificial hero.

"But I don't care whether it's all an illusion or not. Either way, I gained the power to fight back. I got Sigrdrifa."

"——"

"Honestly, I had intended to come see you sooner. But it's hard to get around without causing waves when you're treated like a hero. I only managed to make it out here when General Barkley called me in."

"The general...? No, you said you had intended to come see me?"

It reminded her of the time when Amy had first spoken to her. Alejandro nodded.

"Yeah, Amy left me a message for you. Though it's not really as special as that makes it sound, I guess. I had an opportunity to talk to her, and she was worried about you."

"Amy was... About me?"

"You weren't the only one who wanted to talk face-to-face again."

Rusalka froze when she discovered a messenger she never even dreamed of.

She was scared to ask what Amy had said, what she had left behind. But—

"You can always choose not to ask," Alejandro suggested.

"...But you would still just choose to tell me. Right?"

"Damn straight. You really do see right through me."

Alejandro declared without hesitation that he was going to be touching her heart whether she liked it or not.

It was a little late, but she realized her first impression of him as a lion in a cage had been right on the money. He acted friendly and personable, but his true nature was undoubtedly that of a lion. He didn't show any leniency and had a majestic bearing that inspired those around him to be more like him.

And on top of that, he didn't hesitate to extend a helping hand to pull up others. He was proudly aloof and kept himself apart, but when it came to his determination, he resembled Amy.

That was probably why he had gotten close enough to Amy that she would discuss Rusalka with him.

"She talked about you. This girl named Rusalka, who she had left behind. How you were moody, not honest about your feelings, despite being so straightforward and frank when it came to everything else. About how your personality was totally contradictory."

"______"

"About how you told her the things that she needed to hear that no one else would ever say. And about how you were her best friend."

"—Ah."

Rusalka had been determined to take the message head-on, no matter how harsh it had been. To at least atone what little she could by facing up to it honestly.

"—Aghhh."

To resolutely accept whatever came.

But that resolve didn't last for a second.

Hot tears poured from Rusalka's wide-open eyes. No matter how much she wiped them away, there was no end to the tears.

"She wasn't mad at you. And while she was sad, she didn't wallow in it, either."

"Ugh, ahhh…"

"So you don't have to feel tied down by it. I guarantee it."

"Wh-what good is…y-your guarantee…?"

"Always ready with a comeback, even when you're bawling your eyes out."

Alejandra smiled as Rusalka made the expected quip, even as she sobbed uncontrollably. He made no effort to comfort her.

"______"

If the point of comforting her was to make her stop crying, then he knew he had made the right choice. Sometimes the tears just needed to flow.

"Boss, can I get another pint?"

"______"

"And another one for her, too."

He ordered another round for them both as Rusalka kept crying.

And the bartender, who had been watching in silence, the only observer to their conversation, heaved a little sigh and then started pouring two more pints.

5

"Oh."

When she saw how Rusalka looked, the black-haired woman stopped in her tracks.

They were inside the base's barracks, and Rusalka was on her way to her room. Naturally, she recognized the woman who stopped to look at her—it was Michelle.

Rusalka inhaled slowly when she saw the bandage around Michelle's head and her arm in a sling.

"How are your injuries, Michelle?"

"I was lucky to escape with just this much. My console's position in the room is what saved me." Michelle's expression was stiff as she responded.

It was miraculous that she had managed to survive when so much of the command post had been devastated by the secondary's attack. More than half the command staff, including General Barkley, had been lost in the strike.

She was surely being tormented by the memories of all the people around her who died. If Rusalka had been in the command post at the time, there was no telling if she would have survived.

Spelling out her thoughts, Rusalka said, "But I'm not the kind of person to think I was lucky not to be there."

"Of course not. You're..." Having gotten that far, Michelle's eyes narrowed. Her expression tensed slightly as she focused on Rusalka's face. "...Your eyes are red. Have you been crying?"

"Uh, no, this is..."

"You seem to have just come back from outside. Were you checking the city? Did someone yell at you out there or...?"

"...It would be far more bearable if that were all it was."

Michelle averted her eyes, understanding what Rusalka meant.

If the civilians whose homes and lives had been destroyed vented their anger and frustration at Rusalka or the other soldiers, then they could accept it and regret the fact that they had not been able to do better.

But the boy who had lost his home and the bartender at the pub had not blamed her at all. And neither had the other people in the city or Alejandro. All she had gotten was praise and gratitude. And Rusalka couldn't handle that. Particularly not from people who were still looking to the future with hope, despite the terrible losses of lives and livelihoods.

"This has nothing to do with any civilians," Rusalka clarified.

"But to the best of my knowledge, you crying like that has..."

"It's all Colonel Ostley's fault," Rusalka reported concisely, putting a finger to her eye, still feeling the traces of shed tears there.

She had no intention of telling anyone else about what he had shared with her or the regrets she had revealed to him while crying her eyes out. It was too embarrassing and pathetic. The only people in the world who knew those things were Alejandro and the man behind the bar.

"So you don't need to worry about... Michelle?"

Just as she was about to finish her explanation, she felt something was off about Michelle's silence. Michelle's expression stiffened, and she touched the mole at the corner of her eye as she ruminated on what Rusalka had said.

"Colonel Ostley made you cry?"

"—? Yes. What of it?"

"There are several points I would like to ask more about in detail, but I suppose the takeaway is that the mastermind behind the Miracle at Lamia is not the man of character he is reputed to be?"

"I'm not sure what impression you got from what I just said, but I don't think there's much room for argument that he is an unconventional officer and lacking in common sense."

"...That is true..."

Michelle nodded, as if convinced by that explanation.

Judging from her reaction, it seemed like Alejandro took the same attitude with everyone, and that conclusion made Rusalka all the more exasperated with how troublesome their commanding officer was.

But—

"I cried and cried, and now I feel relieved... I haven't been able to cry for a long time."

"...Does that...?"

"Yes."

Rusalka nodded at the barely formed question. And just that was enough for the woman who had known her since the days she had been leading her own flight.

She knew whom Rusalka had cried over and to whom she had raised a glass.

"And I can confidently say that it was only thanks to his encouragement that I was able to cry, and that I was able to fight."

"...Then what will you do now that you've flown again?"

"———"

Still badly wounded and fighting through her own pain, Michelle pressed Rusalka on what she would do going forward.

Rusalka thought for a moment. If she had not spoken with Alejandro that night, she probably would not have been able to answer. But—

"Will you join the colonel's Sigrdrifa plan...?"

"—I'm going to keep flying."

"Ah..."

Rusalka answered confidently, putting her hands on Michelle's shoulders as she started to lean forward. Their faces were close enough to feel each other breathing. Rusalka looked Michelle straight in the eyes. And as Michelle breathed in, Rusalka continued:

"I will be one of the members of Sigrdrifa."

"———"

She spurred her resolve by saying it explicitly and without hesitation.

She had said something terrible, regretted it deeply, and then folded up her wings in shame and guilt. But the sky had been there the whole time, waiting for the moment she would spread her wings once again.

"...Finally..."

Rusalka was shocked by Michelle's weak response.

It was a hoarse sigh of relief. And it had come from Michelle of all people. Her frozen expression finally melted, softening as she averted her eyes.

"You've finally returned, Rusalka."

"I guess I really kept you waiting."

"Yes, you did."

Michelle's lips slipped briefly into a barely visible smile. But it was gone as soon as it came, and she stepped back, putting some distance between her and Rusalka. She turned to walk past and continue down the hallway. As if declaring that they had said enough.

"Michelle, just one thing."

"What is it?"

Michelle did not turn around.

"Could you be my operator again, like before? The situation is different now, and it will no doubt be difficult."

Michelle almost stopped but kept on walking in the end.

"That's quite the shameless request."

"Yes, it is. I've decided to try being just a little bolder from now on."

"—I'll take it under consideration."

With that curt response, Michelle turned the corner and disappeared down the hall. Rusalka watched her go and then breathed a sigh of relief.

And—

6

"I see, so you're the one who ▪▪▪▪▪ ▪▪▪ ▪▪▪▪."

It was something that had tormented Rusalka over and over and over again. Hiding in the mists of her memory, something that she wanted to avert her eyes from, to wish away.

But it resounded in her dreams every night, never letting her forget the sin she had committed.

"I see, so you're the one who ▪▪▪▪▪ ▪▪▪ ▪▪▪▪."

That solemn voice. That haughty voice. That voice filled with mercy. It repeated those words over and over. And finally, Rusalka remembered what she had felt when she had been told that.

That moment was when she stopped averting her eyes. It was when she acknowledged the mistake she had made.

——And it was because her sin had been forgiven by none other than the girl she had hurt most.

"—I see, so you're the one who hates the hero."

* * *

The fog cleared on the words that had tormented Rusalka so many times.

Yes, Rusalka had hated the hero.

She was surely the only person in the world who had hated that noble and earnest young girl.

Even after becoming a Valkyrie herself and flying with the same noble mission that Amy had, that hatred had always dwelled deep in her heart.

She had believed that she had done something unforgivable. That there was no pardon possible.

But Amy had forgiven her and accepted her.

And she had surely had that same carefree smile, that same mischievous glint in her eyes, and that same voice that always ravaged her heart.

Because she had so much love hidden away in that small little body.

Because she was Rusalka's best friend.

"—I see, so you're the one who hates the hero."

But still, calling Amy a hero was almost laughable. She had always hated being given such grand titles.

There was supposed to be a promotional pamphlet made with her on the cover, in order to spread the word about the things she had done and extol her beauty. But that project was put on ice when she died.

Afterward, the person in charge of making it had visited Rusalka. He had come to give her a picture. The picture that was going to be the cover of that illusory magazine.

It was a picture of Amy blushing, looking terribly embarrassed.

The girl who seemed so special both on the ground and in the air looked like any other girl her age inside the confines of that photograph.

The morning after the fog of memory cleared in her dream, Rusalka pulled out the photograph that she had always kept tucked hidden away in her desk.

She pinned it on the corkboard hanging on her wall—next to all the reports on the fighting around Europe.

——She could hear Amy's miffed voice, saying, *At least put me in a nicer place than this!*

7

——The sun streamed through the window that morning, too.

The early broadcast started as the people on the base slowly woke up and greeted the new day.

Traces of the battle were still fresh and visible as everyone gathered on the parade grounds in front of the flag.

Every soldier stood at attention. And standing in front of them were the beautiful and reliable Valkyries, who bore the hopes of humanity.

Natalie Chase looked proud.

Alma Conturo seemed emotionless as always.

Shannon Stewart appeared sleepy more than anything.

The maintenance and support crews were gathered in separate lines. Among them were Chief Technician Roger Reever, the mainstay who made it possible for the base to have such an extraordinarily high operational readiness rate, and Major Michelle Heyman, her arm still in a sling as she stood with a group of operators who looked nervous.

A man walked forward, looking entirely at ease despite facing the full assembly of Hamburg base.

Blond-haired, blue-eyed, and tall, he sported a scraggly mustache, still unshaven—this was the new commanding officer of the base.

The commanding officer charged with overseeing the European army's front lines, Lieutenant Colonel Alejandro Ostley.

"Thank you all for gathering so early. The only reason we made it through the other day was thanks to all your valiant efforts. We lost many friends in that battle, Major General Logrev Barkley among them."

The troops listened as Alejandro began speaking from the platform. There was no anger or grief in their eyes, just a soldierly resolve and an intense focus.

"We do not have time to stop and look back. We have to keep moving forward while storing the gratitude we have for our lost friends in our hearts. In order to win a better future for all humanity."

A quiet heat spread through the audience. And seeing that, Alejandro cleared his throat.

"And with that, I'll spare you my bad attempts at this kind of speech. No matter how I say it, it's not going to change the promises we made our comrades or the future we are fighting for. Am I wrong?"

"______"

"The battle the other day showed us something. Starting now, we will be pushing forward. Humanity has been forced to retreat for too long. That humiliation ends now."

Alejandro really was good at capturing people's hearts.

He had an intense passion in his voice that gradually but forcefully drew in anyone listening to him, sparking a similar intensity in their hearts until they were looking ahead with him, cloaked in the same intensity of purpose before they realized it.

"Sigrdrifa."

That word filled the soldiers' ears, seeping into their heads and into their souls.

It was the name for the maidens of war who would take flight and do battle to reclaim the skies from the pillars of light. The women who would spread their wings and soar high above to carry on the wishes of their fallen comrades and fulfill the hopes of every living person. Sigrdrifa—the wings of victory.

"That is the name for the winged Valkyries who will fight for the future of humanity."

Sigrdrifa—the wings that had been broken once before would rise again for the sake of the world. Wings that would rejoin the battle, having survived the fateful Flight of the Valkyrie and the Return of the Valkyrie. And befitting that name, they would wage war to reclaim those sublime, clear-blue skies for all future generations.

"This is the commissioning ceremony of the commander who will lead that force, the commanding officer of the Valkyrie Squadron Sigrdrifa. Step forward, Major Rusalka Evereska."

"Yes, sir."

Called forward at the end of that theatrical performance, Rusalka looked straight ahead. Taking her place next to Alejandro, she stood tall as the gazes of the troops, the maintenance crews, the operators, and above all, her fellow Valkyries focused on her.

"Rusalka Evereska, reporting for duty as the commanding officer of the Valkyrie Squadron Sigrdrifa."

Beneath the wide-open skies, there wasn't a single cloud in her eyes as she accepted her commission.

8

——Somewhere, there was a dark, dark room.

It was an odd place, containing a vast space with a towering ceiling. And yet, for some reason, it felt definitively closed-off from the world.

There were several rows of seats all lined up in front of a large screen—it might take a moment, but anyone would think it a theater after examining the room. But while there were well over a hundred seats, only a single one was filled.

There was a single small figure in the center seat right up in the first row. The figure quietly ran a hand through his black hair and let out a long, tired sigh.

"—So you've finally started to move, Sigrdrifa."

It was a murmur that imparted how long it took for this moment to come. But the voice sounded young, even childlike.

The shadowy figure was small, and there was a childish charm to his face.

The black-haired boy had a handsome face, and a black eye patch covered his left eye.

His voice was tinged with joy and fear as he said one more thing:

"—Ragnarök draws near."

Afterword

Hello! Welcome to any new readers! And to those of you who have read my other work... What am I supposed to say here? Thank you for your continued patronage?

Apologies, my absentmindedness is shining through with blinding force from the very start. I'm the author, Tappei Nagatsuki.

It is an incredibly personal thing, but this is the first time I've ever introduced myself as just Tappei Nagatsuki in an afterword. The reason for that is that I originally started out writing light novels on the web before eventually being approached by a publishing company about the idea of adapting my story for an actual book.

Because of that, I would always sign with the pen name I used online in my web novel, too, and this book is the first time I've stepped away from that.

This was a moving book for me as the author, but what did you think of it? I hope you enjoyed it.

This book is a spin-off of sorts, a prelude to the main work, *Warlords of Sigrdrifa*.

You may be wondering, *Where is that main story, then?* If you are picking up this book on release day or soon after, then no one will have seen the main story yet.

The reason for that is because *Sigrdrifa* is an original anime that will be broadcast after this book is released! *Original anime* has such a nice sound to it. It just makes the heart dance in excitement. And I danced while I wrote this as well.

Just kidding.

Warlords of Sigrdrifa is an original anime that I have contributed to by writing the scripts and working on the overall structure of the series.

During the initial planning stages, it started with just three really basic foundations of manga, of "Open skies! Fighting girls! Something dramatic!" and things just took off—pun fully intended—from there. And now it has finally reached the light of day.

The first piece of all that is this book. That's a lot of pressure.

Writing a spin-off prelude before the main series even releases is certainly an aggressive approach, but I personally love exploring the past arcs of stories, so I'm all for it. Please have fun looking forward to seeing just how the characters here will make their appearances in the anime!

And just as you would think from this being part one of two, these characters and their stories will show up in the next volume as well. What battles, struggles, and sorrowful good-byes wait in store?! I hope you'll enjoy the struggles that lie in wait for Rusalka and the others… Hold on. Isn't that just a lot of bad stuff? I suppose that's what a story is.

It's always darkest before the dawn. I'm sure you all enjoy dramas. I do, too. We have that in common. That's why I'm sure you'll love the next part, too, friend!

I won't keep you waiting too long on the next part! Depending on when you pick this up, it might even be out already, and I can meet you again in the afterword of that volume!

So having made that energetic announcement, I'd like to take a little bit of space to thank all the people who have helped place this book in your hands.

To my editor Ono, thank you very much for waiting for me to finish the manuscript with an archaic smile even while everyone was worried about such a tight schedule! You were a lifesaver during the proofreading and corrections phase. I hope you'll continue granting me your wonderful help as this new series continues! But seriously, please and thank you.

To the illustrator, Takuya Fujima, thank you for such a lovely illustration of Rusalka and Amy! And thank you as well for contributing character designs for the anime! As a fellow lover of less intensely colored characters, we were like two horses in harness, pulling together!

Thank you to Takaaki Suzuki for your help with the military setting and research. I've been in your debt from the very start of this project. We worked through the night together just three days after meeting. Thank you for all your help supervising the general setting of this book!

Fujima and Suzuki are also working hard with me on the anime, and it would not be an exaggeration to call *Sigrdrifa* our baby!

And also to all the people in the editorial offices of Sneaker Bunko and to the proofreaders and the people at various bookstores, without whom this book would not have been published. It is truly thanks to you that this book made it to publication.

And to all the people involved with the creation and production of the anime, thank you all. All of you working day in and day out to create something special has been the greatest motivation to me as an author. I can't wait to continue our work and make *Sigrdrifa* a hit!

And finally, my greatest thanks to you readers who have picked up this book. This story continues in the next book and creates a foundation for the contents of the anime! I will be doing my best in hopes that you will enjoy the future developments of this series!

Let's meet again in the next book! Thank you so much!

April 2020 (while at work furiously writing the next book)

Rusalka (pt. 2)

Prologue
An Ancient Lullaby

1

——It had always felt strange to me, even from a young age.

Why did my sister and I have such different personalities? We were identical twins and raised in the same environment together, so why?

"That's because there's more than one way to look at things."

That was Father's response to my childish confusion.

I could feel his warmth against my shoulder as he sat next to me. His answer made sense to me, but my spirited younger sister, sitting on the other side of him, was not satisfied with that.

"Ehhh? If we see things differently, won't that mean arguments? We'll end up fighting with each other."

"Well, that might happen from time to time. Do you not like the idea of fighting with your sister?"

"Of course not. I don't like starting fights I know I'm going to win."

Father chuckled a little at her unshakable confidence.

"That's a wonderful principle to live by. Listen here, both of you. You mustn't hate anyone indiscriminately. From time to time, people might do something you don't like, but that's—"

"That's not all there is to that person, right? I know, I know. You've told us that a million times already."

"Ha-ha, sorry about that."

It was something we had been told many times before. My sister puckered her lips in annoyance from hearing it so often, but even though I had heard it just as often, I didn't feel any of her irritation. That was yet another way the two of us were different.

"You and your sister are both a little different from most people, but as long as the two of you stick together, you'll be fine. You can make up for each other's shortcomings and support each other."

Father patted both of us on the head with his reassuring, strong hands. I liked when he did that. And I liked my sister's sullen face as he did it, too. I liked the fact that she couldn't argue with that final conclusion Father always finished with.

"Understand, you two?"

Both of us nodded like always.

Seeing that, Father's expression softened, and he broke into a gentle smile.

"There's my beautiful girls."

And I liked when he said that, too.

2

"———"

Sensing that something was a little bit off, she slowly opened her eyes.

Wispy clouds laced the clear sky. A soothing breeze blew as the early-summer sun shone down just after noon. She had apparently dozed off, lulled to sleep by the tranquil ambiance.

It felt like she had dreamed of a memory from long ago during her brief nap. Putting her hand to her eyes, she felt a small tear fall on her finger. It was an almost nostalgic feeling.

"—Sister."

As she dwelled for a moment in her emotions, someone called out to her from behind, addressing her with a dignified tone of voice that spoke of an iron will. It was undeniable that the speaker possessed an unflappable mental fortitude that didn't waver at much of anything. In fact, she couldn't recall ever having seen her younger sister shaken or unsteady.

"Are you listening to me?"

"I'm listening. Sorry, I just had a dream from long ago."

"You don't have to apologize. If anything, I'm the one who's usually dreaming."

"Hmm? I didn't mean to be accu—"

"I know! I know! Argh!"

When she tried to apologize for being inconsiderate, her sister's hands literally covered her mouth to stop her from interrupting. The tussle caused a bit of a stir, as the younger sister leaned over the seat from behind, drawing the attention of the other passengers.

They were making a scene in a bus currently on the road. It was only natural that people would stare.

The bus's destination was a large nearby town, and there were around twenty people on board. There were no stops along the way. Everyone had their own reasons, but they were all headed for the same location.

"It's obvious this is pretty much the only place around here that even resembles a town," her younger sister muttered, as if perfectly guessing what she had been thinking.

For a second, she wondered if she actually had read her mind, but when glancing over, her sister just responded with an exasperated, "You're just an open book—that's all."

She was the only one who ever said that, though—

"What good sisters you are."

As she pondered that, the polite older woman sitting beside her spoke up. She had a tranquil expression on her face that was filled with well-worn smile lines as she glanced at the two of them.

"You have quite the strong resemblance. Are you by any chance twins?"

"We are. I mean, yes, ma'am, we are. I'm the younger one, and the unreliable-looking one here is my older sister. Though most people guess the opposite."

There was something funny about watching her switch to a politer tone that she was clearly not comfortable with at all. But when she noticed her older sister's expression softening, she issued an annoyed "what?"

The older woman cut in and said, "Now, now, don't fight. Where are you coming from?"

"We've been moving from place to place from up north. But that's how it is for everyone, right? I'm sure you…"

"Yes, from farther north, and east as well. It's just not livable out there anymore…"

The older woman turned her lonely gaze down as the younger sister quietly averted her gaze out the window.

The sky was still clear and bright, but there were not many people left who could call those blue skies beautiful and majestic. Not in Europe at least.

—The open skies had become a symbol of terror.

"——"

It had been more than a year since northern Europe had fallen under enemy control. Humanity's habitable lands were gradually being stolen away. To survive, people departed their homelands, enduring with the help of others in the same position as they fled to other countries. But no matter how far they ran, the enemy's advance seemed unstoppable.

Everyone realized it, even though they pretended not to.

—Extinction was slowly but surely closing in on humanity.

Just like with the older woman, nearly everyone on the bus was a refugee from one land or another. And she and her strong and reliable younger sister were in a similar position, too.

However, in their case, they never stayed in any one town. Theirs was a never-ending life on the run.

"I see, I see. Sisters always stick together, eh?"

"Heh-heh. That's right. My older sister might look like she has her act together, but she's utterly hopeless without me."

Her younger sister and the older woman had continued chatting comfortably while unease filled the older sister's heart. Her sibling was a force to behold, hitting it off with the older woman in less than a minute.

She had a talent for getting other people to smile. It was a natural gift. But not every innate gift was a blessing.

"—Dear?"

Suddenly, the older woman's voice rose in surprise. Looking back, the girl saw her younger sister had suddenly leaned all her weight against the back of her seat. She caught her sister's body and cradled her just before she collapsed entirely.

Their neighbor looked shocked at the practiced ease of her movements. She lowered her head slightly.

"My apologies for giving you a scare."

"N-not at all. It's not a problem. But is she well?"

"Yes. It is almost like a chronic disease of sorts…a sort of spasm where my sister suddenly falls asleep. There is nothing actually wrong with her body, though, so please do not worry. But more importantly…"

"More importantly?"

"—Please tell the driver to accelerate."

Struggling to keep up with the unexpected developments, the older woman let a bewildered "what?" slip out.

It was only natural, but she didn't have time to explain everything carefully—

"Leave the two of us behind and take shelter. Just go straight into town."

Saying that, the older sister slung her bag over her shoulder, lifted her unconscious sister in her arms, opened the window of the bus—and leaped out.

Because of the rules of inertia, leaping out of a car driving at speed was practically suicidal. But the older sister's long, slender legs touched the ground as she spun her body in a big circle, dispersing the shock and softening the impact as she landed safely on the road. She took a short breath.

Her long blond hair swayed in the wind, and the water bottle in her bag sloshed loudly, but she was uninjured. And her sister was also safe and sound in her arms. But she was quivering.

——Having a nightmare.

"—Don't stop!"

After checking on her sister, she shouted to the bus up ahead. The driver had started to brake to check on the seemingly suicidal sisters, but he could not afford to do that. And the people on the bus soon realized why.

A dazzling white light suddenly appeared from inside the large forest off to the east. It took on a cylindrical shape that shot up into the heavens. A pure tower of light.

Despite its beauty, it was a loathsome symbol of disaster to all humanity.

"—A pillar."

Murmuring softly, the older sister adjusted her grip on her younger sister. The bus started accelerating, gunning it to escape the pillar that had suddenly appeared. The elder sister saw the older woman at the back window of the bus, looking apologetic and worried about the two of them. She was grateful for that kindness.

Both of her hands were full carrying her sister, so she couldn't wave. Instead, she lowered her head deeply, and while it was by no means her specialty, she kept a smile on her face to reassure the kind stranger. The only thing they could do was pray for each other's safety.

"I suppose I should pray that any good fortune we might have should be given to you all."

With that, she started running, cutting a gallant figure with her sister still cradled in her arms. She headed away from the road and in the opposite direction from the pillar in the east, into the forest stretching west from the road, in order to throw off the enemy's search as much as possible.

Even though the younger sister was slender, the older sister was running faster than should have been possible for someone carrying another person. In fact, she was sprinting at a speed even a well-conditioned soldier would have trouble matching.

"———"

Her sister's sleeping face was all twisted up. She was clearly suffering in the confines of a nightmare. And as if laughing at the younger girl's distress, the tower of light behind them began to spawn enemies.

She was not fool enough to look back and let her speed drop. Either way, they would end up coming into view before long anyway. Because they were the ones the enemy was after.

"—Hljóðs bið ek allar helgar kindir."

She picked up speed as she crossed into the woods, and what crossed her lips was not a cry, nor a condemnation cursing the world for its unfairness, but a song.

Singing in a whisper, she wove ancient lyrics passed down through the ages from long, long ago. It was a song of prayer. Their mother had sung it for them as a lullaby, and her mother had sung it for her.

"—Meiri ok minni, mögu Heimdallar. Vildu at ek, Valföðr."

Her sister stirred in her arms, her pained expression easing slightly.

The little sister had always liked that song. Not to sing it herself, though. She liked to have their parents, or sometimes her older sister, sing it for her. And that had never changed.

Just as the fact that they both cherished and cared for each other had never changed.

And so—

"—Vel framtelja forn spjöll fira, þau er fremst um man."

She kept singing as their flight continued—across the green earth, through a world being drained of life, beneath a sky dominated by light.

Running on and on and on until the end of the world arrived.

—Never knowing whether their flight or the world would end first.

Chapter 1
Sigrdrifa Reborn

1

——Cutting through the white clouds, the crimson Deus ex Machina stuck close to the enemy's back.

"——"

Before her instruments could even alert her that the target was in her sights, her instincts told her to fire, and so she pulled the trigger. The machine guns on her wings emitted a roar as a stream of lead careened into the enemy. It had hardened defenses that wouldn't be dented by conventional weapons of any kind, but thanks to the Deus ex Machina, the divine blessing bestowed upon the Valkyrie piloting the plane was extended to the ammunition as well, and they pierced right through the enemy's shell like it was glass.

There was a high-pitched shattering sound, too, followed by an explosion of light, proof of the enemy's destruction.

"*—Splash one tertiary pillar.*"

The remnants of the enemy transformed into particles of light, a visual confirmation of its defeat, just as the report came over the radio.

The sharp, cool voice announcing the result over the radio was calm. There was no excitement or emotion at shooting down an enemy. To some, her voice might have been disappointing, but to the pilot of the Deus ex Machina, it was just right.

She preferred to save all unnecessary excitement and high spirits for after combat was concluded. More importantly, getting excited about shooting down a single enemy would be a terrible misunderstanding of the current state of the battle.

"Remaining enemies?"

"One hundred forty-one hostile contacts."

An emotionless count was the response, but she didn't loosen her grip on the control stick. In the past, she had felt her spirit break at the sheer number of enemies and cursed her fate. But now she didn't have to confront her own weakness like that anymore.

"—Alma! Now!"

"...You're too loud, Natalie."

Over the radio, an excited voice and a calmer one shared a quick exchange. The next moment, a massive explosion bloomed in the skies.

"_____"

The clear-blue expanse was swallowed up by a tremendous flame and a wave of destruction, and for just a second, it felt like the world might be ending.

Just as she registered that surreal scene, her eardrums were pummeled by the delayed sound of the explosion. It was a tremendous blast that seemed to shake everything, including the sky outside her cockpit, as dozens of enemies were enveloped by the blast and consumed.

It was a Grand Slam dropped by Alma Conturo's Deus ex Machina, a Lancaster bomber. The most powerful single attack humanity could bring to bear against the pillars. It scorched the enemies mercilessly through their protective shells, completely annihilating them.

It was powerful enough that it could even take down a larger secondary with a single strike in the right circumstances, but it was not a weapon of finesse, and positioning was crucial to avoid causing friendly fire with its blast radius. Because it was so difficult to be sure of that, for a time Alma had been left behind by other Valkyries.

But now—

"What do you mean?! I'm merely providing adequate support!"

"I can see that. Your voice is still too loud, though."

Despite those great results, an argument quickly filled the communication channel, pushing satisfaction at the result of the strike to the background for later.

Natalie Chase, a Valkyrie in Alma's squadron, was getting into it

with her after that powerful attack so dramatically changed the tide of the battle.

They were the same age and had become Valkyries around the same time, and since joining the same squadron, they had developed an excellent rapport in combat. Alma was heavily specialized in inflicting damage, while Natalie aided her by providing skillful situational analysis and high maneuverability.

Natalie could draw the enemy's focus with her Spitfire, setting up a sector on the battlefield where they could be sure that allies would not get caught up in Alma's massive attack, allowing Alma to focus wholly on delivering her battle-ending bombs.

Ever since they started refining that tactic, their results had been off the charts.

However—

"Could you not just communicate more clearly that you're properly keeping track of my movements! Without that—"

Alma cut Natalie off and simply said, *"You're annoying. Is that clear enough?"*

"You are so—!"

Despite their compatibility in the air, there was no end to their arguments.

But even as they went at it, Natalie was still skillfully covering Alma's retreat to the rear now that Alma had unleashed her trump card and run out of munitions. They were certainly a strange pair.

"I'll still have to give them a talking-to when we get back down, though."

While giving their teamwork a bit of side-eye, the pilot of the crimson Deus ex Machina turned her attention to the enemy again.

Sadly perhaps, her plane was significantly less powerful when compared to Alma's and Natalie's, particularly in terms of offensive potential. It was almost fatally insufficient, but she had given up on lamenting that difference or feeling bad for herself long ago.

"—Ngh."

Leaping sharply into hostile airspace, she slipped through a narrow gap, cutting a path that brought her close to another enemy. As its focus shifted to her when she passed, it almost felt like their eyes met.

"——"

It was a being with a pitch-black shell covering its whole body, and short feelers and horns protruded from what would have been its head. It flapped the wings growing from its back. It looked similar to a flying ant drone, but its body was more than three meters long, and its jaw was fully capable of tearing apart a fighter jet.

—The unknown enemy beings commonly called pillars.

That was the name of the opponents they were facing off against in the air, and the enemy of all humanity currently menacing the world. The only means available to challenge the pillars were the Valkyries. They were the wings Odin had granted humanity, giving them a chance to fight and save themselves in the face of total extermination.

"Hah."

She exhaled, making a point to keep breathing as she caught the pillar's focus. All of a sudden, the sound of the wind, the rumbling of her engine, the pounding of her heart, and the constant noise of her rushing blood returned at once.

Turning her plane, she caught the enemy's attention as she wove through the miniscule gaps between enemies trying to block her way. The moment she slipped between enemies and got a 360-degree view of the sky around her, it felt like she had threaded the needle.

Her plane was far weaker in both offense and defense compared to her peers. That was her limitation. So all she could do was trust in her senses and the instinct for fighting that she had cultivated with all her experience—

"—Gh!"

Behind her, one of the pillars that accelerated to stay on her tail suddenly slammed into another pillar, badly cracking both of their thick shells with a pained howl. The pillars' outer shells were stout, impenetrable for even the most powerful conventional weapons. The only things capable of piercing them were attacks that came from Deus ex Machinas piloted by Valkyries—and friendly fire from other pillars.

Unable to fully utilize the former, her only reliable means of attack was the latter. Because of that, she would dive into the enemy ranks, disrupt their focus, egg them on until they followed her, and cause as much collateral damage as possible.

And once the enemy had been thrown off-balance—

"Falling in behind Major Evereska."

"Get wrecked, you damn bugs!!!"

A refined, graceful voice and a spirited roar rang out at the same time as two more planes slipped into position behind the pillars still chasing her. By the time the pillars noticed the looming threat, it was far too late. She pulled up into a steep climb so that only the distracted ants were in the line of fire—

"———"

A merciless stream of rounds easily shattered the pillars' shells and slammed into their bodies.

Torn apart by a storm of lead, the pillars' wings, legs, and torsos were shattered. Without so much as a groan, they transformed into particles of light, scattering as they fell to earth.

"The pillars have reached their activity limit. They are withdrawing."

Just as ten more pillars had been added to the mission score, the coolheaded operator's voice chimed in with the report that the battle was over—their enemies were pulling back, proof that the Valkyries had won.

"—Checkmate."

A single word crossed her lips as she looked out at the scene before her.

She had let that out subconsciously, and she scolded herself for such an exuberant reaction. The enemy had merely withdrawn for the moment. It was not as if any definitive conclusion had been—

"—Yeaaaah! We did it! All that's left is mopping up the stragglers!"

"Lisbeth, don't get ahead of yourself. You could learn a thing or two from Major Evereska."

"Ha! Spare me the lecture, Leili!"

"———"

Hearing such a youthful exchange after catching herself, she felt a little guilty. It was nice to be held up as a model pilot, but less so when she had just messed up herself.

Either way, she couldn't really ignore it once she heard them.

"Don't let your guard down until all the pillars have disappeared. Remain on standby at the rally point until further orders. Return to base in formation once we get the all clear."

"—Roger."

That drew a response from the entire squadron. They stayed on station, waiting for permission to withdraw from the mission area. During that period, the remaining pillars turned into light one by one before being absorbed back into the tower looming over the forest in the distance to the east.

The tower of light standing in the distance was essentially a frontline base that spawned pillars of all shapes and sizes. There was no indication where one would appear next, and since they cropped up without warning, there was no way to stay ahead of them. However, there did appear to be a rule the pillars followed when they advanced: They never appeared in the middle of large cities or suddenly pop up behind the front lines of humanity's armies.

But even so, they were an enemy that could not be communicated with that advanced without warning, regardless of time of day. That alone was menacing enough to slowly wear away at the nerves of humanity's fighting forces.

"——"

The tower of light gradually faded from the top down, disappearing.

With the frontline base disappearing, the grunts had no choice but to follow suit, and countless winged ants dissolved, taking the distracting buzz of their wings and their twisted black silhouettes with them, concluding the battle.

"—No more hostile contacts on radar. Please return to base."

The same cool voice that had been in contact throughout the battle reported the end of combat operations over the radio, and the pilot nodded, even though the operator could not see her. She nudged the control stick and turned her plane toward the base—

"Well done, Major Evereska."

Her lips broke into a smile at the curt acknowledgment.

2

Returning her Deus ex Machina to the hangar, she leaped from the cockpit with a light step. She removed her aviator hat and shook her head, her streaming silver hair shimmering in the sunlight.

Undoing the top button of her flight suit, she felt an immediate release, followed by relief. She took a long, deep breath as her well-endowed bosom was finally freed from its tight confines.

"Hey, good-looking. Catch."

All of a sudden, a voice called out from the side of the hangar, and the silver-haired beauty—Rusalka—caught an object that had been tossed her way. Looking down, she saw a cute pink water bottle with a flowery pattern on it, a bold statement of its owner's tastes.

"Thank you, Chief Reever."

"Don't be like that. We're friends, aren't we?"

The tall, well-toned man smiled as he put his hand to his cheek. His light-brown hair was held back by a pink hair band. Rusalka was on the tall side for a woman, but he was still much taller than her. He was Roger Reever, the chief technician who headed up the maintenance crews at the base. He was a maintenance fanatic, running a hangar with incomparably exacting precision.

Charged with overseeing all maintenance at humanity's forward-most outpost, Holm base, he was almost single-handedly keeping the Valkyries' Deus ex Machinas running, making sure the only effective weapon humanity had against the pillars could take to the skies at any time. And on top of the natural relationship between a Valkyrie and the maintenance crews, he was also a close friend of Rusalka's.

Indulging in his kindness, she brought the bottle to her mouth. She was greeted by a warm, sweet flavor that seemed to make her exhaustion melt away.

"That's quite delicious. Your tea has reached a new level."

"Humans are constantly improving, after all. That goes for more than just serving tea. I'm getting better and better at repairs and maintenance, too. It won't be long before I break free from all human limits."

"That's amazing. I can't wait to see how far you'll go."

"Thank you, sweetie. On an unrelated note, is it okay if I get my hopes up, too?"

"—? I don't really mind, but are you asking me for something?"

Rusalka cocked her head at Roger's roundabout question. Before Roger could answer her, though, the situation cleared itself up.

"Again with that?! Gimme a break already!"

A shout split the air inside the hangar, pausing the general hustle and bustle for a moment. The outcry had come from a pair of girls facing each other in a corner of the building.

One was a lively-looking girl with short black hair, while the other had long, almost translucent blond hair—they were both young, still in their mid-teens.

"...Those two again?"

"Those two again."

Roger nodded as Rusalka's shapely eyebrows furrowed deeply.

There was more than a little exasperation and resignation in her voice, proof that this wasn't the first time she had dealt with this exact problem. The two of them arguing in the hangar was not a new development. In fact, they got along about as well as water and oil. Their arguments could be heard in the hangar, in the barracks, in the mess hall—pretty much anytime and anyplace they happened to be.

"Is this really the state of Sigrdrifa, fighting on humanity's front lines...?" Rusalka lamented.

"It would be a disaster if any outsiders happened to hear them. But getting them to work together is your job, so do your best, Squadron Leader."

"Executive officer of the base and squadron leader besides...I really should have turned those positions down when I had the chance."

"What? Nooo, what are you even saying?"

Rusalka sighed as she put her hand to her forehead. Roger fired back immediately before waving his hand lightly as he headed for his post to examine Rusalka's Spitfire.

In other words, he was telling her to do her job like a professional. As chief technician, he would maintain their planes, so as squadron leader, she should...

"...I suppose I should discipline my ill-mannered pilots."

Rusalka rolled her shoulders, sighed to herself once more, and then started walking over to where her pilots persisted with their unsightly bickering.

"Just accept it already! I got more kills than you! That's proof I'm better. Grades from back during training don't mean a damn thing anymore!"

"I didn't say anything about old results, Lisbeth. I merely said there would have been fewer dangerous situations if you would just put more effort into working together with the people around you."

"That's their fault for not matching my pace! Why do I have to slow myself down for people weaker than me?! If we lose because of that, whose fault—?"

"—That's enough."

The two of them were in a heated argument over what had happened in the battle they had returned from. In and of itself, their observations contained some valuable analysis, but the location, optics, and several other aspects of how they were going about it were problematic to say the least.

In order to explain that to them, Rusalka cut into their conversation, starting by silencing the loud dark-haired girl—Lisbeth Crown. Grabbing the back of her head in a vise grip, she lifted the small girl into the air.

"Ghgyaaaaa!"

"Aren't you the very model of a proper soldier, holding a debriefing right after the battle. However, our speech and conduct, and even our presence, are deeply tied to strictly classified military secrets. Please learn to consider the appropriate time, place, and occasion for your conversations."

Lisbeth's feet fluttered as she writhed under the powerful grip threatening to crush her skull. As Rusalka continued chastising her, she smiled kindly at the other girl—Leili Haltija—who watched in mute shock at the terrifying feat of strength.

Seeing Rusalka's smile, Leili turned pale and snapped to attention.

"Y-yes, ma'am. Ummm...Major Evereska...I'm sure Lisbeth is reflecting on her outburst, too..."

"Th-that's right! Lemme go! Lemme go already, Major Kong... Ghgyaaaa!"

"Really? You call this reflecting?"

"I'll—! I'll make sure she understands, ma'am! Please have mercy!"

Leili pled for clemency, finding it unbearable to watch as Rusalka gave the unrepentant Lisbeth more encouragement to reconsider her actions. It was clear Leili was far more mature than Lisbeth.

"Very well. I'll leave it to you. But if you are going to take responsibility, you need to follow through."

"Y-yes, ma'am! I swear it."

Trusting Leili's spirited acknowledgment, Rusalka released Lisbeth's

head at last. The younger girl collapsed to her knees as Leili caught her, bringing a definitive end to their argument.

But Rusalka couldn't help feeling terribly empty at resorting to force to end their quarrel.

"Is this all just a result of my inability to communicate properly…?"

"I suspect there is probably a more relevant point for you to improve on than that, Major…"

As Rusalka closed and opened the hand that had been tormenting Lisbeth, she heard a familiar voice address her from behind. Turning, she posed a question. "What exactly is my shortcoming, then, Natalie?"

"About that. If I might make a suggestion from an ordinary point of view…I suppose I would call it a lack of confidence and a difficulty with interpersonal relationships."

"…So then it is because I'm inarticulate…"

"I don't believe that's necessarily connected to your alarming reliance on physical force."

The girl with bright-red hair tied back—Natalie Chase—crossed her arms as she made that comment. She was a member of Sigrdrifa and another of Rusalka's subordinates.

Rusalka raised her eyebrows at Natalie's suggestion as she considered her hand.

"That's true. I've gotten in the habit of relying on strength because it is efficient, but I should be using my words, given my position. I'll reflect on that going forward."

"I understand the feeling well, though. Those two are quite the troublesome nuts to crack."

"I suppose that's to be expected of the outstanding talents the commander scouted for us."

While Natalie commiserated with her, Rusalka let an idle complaint slip out. Though in her case, her complaints tended to rest somewhere in the gray zone between irony and actual praise.

"The commander…" Natalie rolled the phrase around in her mouth a bit. "He's certainly eccentric, but he has a sixth sense when it comes to people. And when it comes to judging someone by their abilities rather than looks, he's quite reliable."

"Yes, that's true. But…"

"But there's a limit to all things, right? We're soldiers fighting on the front lines for all humanity... There must be some standards to maintain the dignity of the International Peacekeeping Organization."

"Exactly! That's exactly right."

Rusalka was in total agreement with Natalie's frank assessment.

Indeed, Alejandro Ostley, the base's commanding officer and the overall commander of the Sigrdrifa task force, was an unconventional officer who did not really fit into any preexisting molds.

A large number of the soldiers gathered at Holm base under his meritocratic system would have been drummed out of the service for various reasons in a peacetime military. Given that he had brought them all together and consistently achieved concrete results, there was no arguing that his finds were not capable.

In fact, if he had not been the commanding officer, it was doubtful Sigrdrifa would have been able to operate as smoothly as it did, and there was little chance that Rusalka would have ever become its squadron leader, either. That was just how much of an outcast she was on the European front.

But the situation had changed, and she was able to fly again. And the impetus for that had been none other than Alejandro, a fact for which she was eternally grateful. However, Rusalka was still terribly tormented by the cost of his involvement.

Since—

"Colonel Ostley's frivolousness can only be called a failure of character, especially as the commander of a base who is supposed to be a role model for all the soldiers under his command. Pushing practically all the paperwork onto his executive officer and wandering around the base at all hours. And even forcing me to drag him out of pubs in town..."

"A-ah, I see. That sounds quite troubling..."

"Yes! It really is! He's unbelievable."

"...Kicked the hornet's nest..."

Rusalka started listing all of Alejandro's sins at length, the menacing look on her face overwhelming Natalie as the olive-skinned girl next to her—Alma Conturo—murmured a languid comment. Alma looked up at Rusalka with a seemingly expressionless face and tugged her sleeve.

"Rusalka, he's calling for you. The commander."

"The commander? Then I'll go after the briefing to—"

"Don't worry! We can take care of that."

There was a disapproving look on Rusalka's face, but Natalie emphatically interrupted her. She had always had a strong desire to get ahead, so she most likely wanted to make a proper impression and demonstrate her position to the newcomers, Lisbeth and Leili.

And Rusalka could not be sure how long she would be tasked as the squadron leader for Sigrdrifa, so she decided to respect Natalie's initiative.

"Understood, then I'll leave the briefing to you, Natalie. Alma, help her out in case anything happens. And you, too, Shannon—I see you hiding back there."

"...If you insist..."

Rusalka smiled wryly at Alma's standard low-energy response before saluting the two girls. They saluted back as she quickly left the hangar for the changing room.

Changing out of her flight suit, she headed to the base commander's office. She would not have minded just going straight there, but given that she was almost certainly going to be met with a snide comment if she did, she decided to avoid that possibility altogether.

Watching her quickly leave—

"Th-thank you for that, Alma...," Natalie murmured gratefully.

"It's just a hornet's nest... Rusalka's enjoying it—her current life."

"I think that's quite problematic all on its own. After all..." Natalie turned around, stopping there. Following her gaze, Alma turned around as well. Behind them was the line of Sigrdrifa's Deus ex Machinas, fresh from the battlefield. Looking at them, Natalie clenched her hand, pressed against her chest.

"...We're on the front line for all of humanity. And the major is our Sigrdrifa, the one guiding us to victory."

3

"What, you showered first? Splendid, splendid."

"It was either that or suffer another one of your snide remarks, sir."

"Snide remark? What, me? I never said anything about you smelling bad. Just that you had the scent of a woman freshly returned from battle."

"It's not an issue you can resolve with careful phrasing, sir."

Rusalka's eyes narrowed as she took umbrage with his indelicate response. The handsome blond commander—Alejandro Ostley—grinned like a lion.

They were in the office given to the commanding officer of Holm military base. The man sitting in the chair behind the desk with an air of brazen audacity had none of the solemnity and gravity befitting his rank and position. There was no denying that the unique atmosphere he cultivated was part of why he was beloved by his subordinates, but—

"It would perhaps be better if you carried yourself with some awareness that you are standing at the front line of all humanity, Colonel. Could you please conduct yourself with a more appropriate attitude in order to provide a proper example to the troops?"

"That's a tough ask. What exactly would a more appropriate attitude be?"

"If I might be so bold… To start with, wear your uniform properly, properly shave yourself, stop leaving all your work to your subordinates, maintain an upright and dignified posture barring exigent circumstances, cultivate your subordinates' strengths while identifying their weakness—"

"Wait, wait, wait, wait, wait. If I did all that, I wouldn't be me anymore. That would just be someone else entirely."

Leaning over the desk and propping his head up on an idle hand, Alejandro looked nonplussed as Rusalka counted off the traits she wanted in an ideal commanding officer. He continued as he leaned back comfortably in his seat.

"Just learn to love the officer you've already got. I'm everyone's base commander, a father figure, a first among peers, and a big brother."

"…Be more studied than anyone else while also spurring others to constantly improve themselves. And also, drink with more moderation and eat your vegetables without complaints."

"You were still going?! You might as well just tell me to step down so someone else can take over and be done with it."

"No." Rusalka stopped her enumeration after Alejandro let loose with an exaggerated complaint. "There is no replacement for you, sir. That is our greatest problem."

After all the abuse he had just endured, Alejandro's eyes sparkled at that. But no matter how much she disliked that response, Rusalka wasn't the type to lie.

No matter how many flaws he had that she wished he would correct, Alejandro had more than enough qualities to recommend him—indeed, ignoring his flaws, he had qualities no one else could match: his innate instinct for skillfully handling his subordinates and a nigh superhuman mastery when it came to dealing with pillars. His natural ease and jovial character were good for morale as well, almost like he was a man born for leading soldiers in wartime.

That was Alejandro Ostley, the man in whom the International Peacekeeping Organization (IPO) had placed their hopes.

"Ooooh, so that's it. I'm irreplaceable, huh? Looks like you get it, too."

"Yes, sir. So, given that you cannot be replaced, there is no choice but for you to change yourself. I will summarize all my requests and provide them to you in writing."

"You know, there's always the option of just accepting me for how I am, right, warts and all?"

"I would hardly call that a feasible option when it is wholly unreasonable..."

"Don't say that with such a genuinely confused look."

Alejandro seemed to be enjoying himself as he shrugged in the face of Rusalka's dubious expression. But she refused to back down.

"I look forward to the day when you finally give in to my demands, sir. When that time comes, I will personally comb out your hair."

"You're definitely the type who remodels all your lovers to suit your preferences. It's scary to imagine what might happen, given your thoroughness."

Trembling at Rusalka's faint smile, Alejandro changed topics, putting both his elbows on the desk as the childish glint in his blue eyes disappeared. "First of all, well done out there. Let's hear your report. How is the squadron doing?"

The air around him changing in the span of a single breath, Alejandro transformed into the imposing war hero befitting his position.

Rusalka straightened, struck again by how stunning his transformation could be, even if she thought it was utterly unfair.

"We successfully pushed back the host of tertiary pillars without any losses. In the near future, we will likely encounter the secondary stationed in this region. Natalie's and Alma's coordination and proficiency continue to grow by leaps and bounds. Though as ever, their bickering is..."

"That just goes to show how well they get along. Are there any issues with coordination in the rest of the squadron? There's talk about some Valkyries from Japan coming over. Officially, they're reinforcements, but—"

"But the true purpose is to share knowledge with new Valkyries, right? From the data you gave me, several of them seem to have significant potential, but..."

Approximately twenty Japanese Valkyries would be traveling from the distant land of the rising sun to join their base's personnel. On paper, they were a crack force of highly skilled Valkyries who had achieved impressive results. They were unmistakably junior in terms of training, but their aptitude was undeniable and apparently a sight to behold.

"The state of war in the region, geopolitics, and all sorts of other things play a part. Asia has suffered relatively little impact from the pillars so far. Unlike Europe, where a crash course scramble for pilots was the only choice, they've had the leeway to choose and train only the cream of the crop."

"I hadn't expected girls even younger than Alma and Natalie, though."

"I doubt anyone feels especially good about it. But they were volunteers, and there's no arguing they have top-class aptitude. We can't afford to ignore that potential."

Rusalka was ashamed of the current state of affairs, but she buried that away in a corner of her heart. Alejandro and all the other soldiers felt the same regret.

"...Returning to the report, regarding Alma...," Rusalka said with some hesitation.

"Go ahead."

"She is still somewhat of a concern, but she has grown less distant from the rest of the squadron compared to before. She had felt depressed about lacking a role before, but she has become significantly more cooperative."

She was never much for talking, and it could be hard to tell with her usual expressionless demeanor, but Alma had a strong drive to fight for humanity. And unlike before, now that she could fully wield her abilities for the cause, she was gradually starting to rise into contention as one of the top aces among Valkyries.

"However, she still needs support from Natalie for the time being."

"Still, her, a top ace, huh? Imagine that. In that case, she's going to have to work a bit on her public speaking skills in order to be a proper role model for all the rookies looking up to her."

"She has her own positive traits. There's no need for a girl her age to force herself to change. And the next generation of Valkyries can surely learn a lot just from seeing how she flies."

"That's a pretty different response from the one I got..."

"Please don't expect to be treated the same as a teenager, sir."

Rusalka sighed as she protested his peevish protest. It wasn't the sort of attitude a grown man should have, but she also knew it was just another of his ploys to tease her, so she ignored the bait.

"Questions about Conturo aside, there's no need to worry about Chase and Stewart. Their stability is impressive. Stewart in particular. She's almost too unflappable," Alejandro concluded.

"She was always the sort of pilot who could keep her cool even after taking a hit, but since joining Sigrdrifa, she's gotten more and more reliable every day. Perhaps it's because she has grown to trust the people around her."

"Or maybe because she's taken to being a role model with rookies joining the team."

"——"

Rusalka remained silent as Alejandro had a hollow laugh at that. Gauging her reaction, he shrugged a little.

"I'll admit they're a handful."

Just that was enough to make it clear they were both thinking about the same subject: one of the biggest problems the Sigrdrifa Valkyrie squadron was dealing with.

"So? Are we going to be able to use the rookies Crown and Haltija?" Alejandro asked, finally broaching the topic.

"In the air? Or on the ground?"

"Both, obviously. Not that I'm worried about the air side of the question. I trust my eyes. I wasn't running around the continent looking for top recruits for nothing."

"Yes, that certainly isn't the most pressing problem."

Rusalka nodded as Alejandro physically pointed to his eye in a show of extreme confidence.

The latent potential of all the new Valkyries he had found was undeniable, and their future performance would far outstrip what Rusalka could offer. And among his recruits, Lisbeth and Leili were particularly ahead of the pack. They had so much potential, it was possible to dream that they might even eventually reach the level of the First, if they could fully utilize their innate power and instincts.

However, while they possessed indisputable talent, their behavior on the ground was intolerable.

Rusalka launched into her explanation, saying, "Viewed individually, Leili doesn't have any major problems. However, there is a concern that anytime she's paired with Lisbeth, her inability to cooperate might become a problem."

"Because she has such a talent for adjusting to her wingmates, even if she can work well with less skilled Valkyries, her balance gets thrown off when she's paired with someone with similar capabilities."

"As for Lisbeth, she makes absolutely no effort whatsoever to work with Leili or anyone else for that matter. From a squadron leader's perspective, her egotism is unacceptable."

"She lost her family to the pillars. There are more than a few people in the army who joined up for revenge. She was a good fit for a Valkyrie, and there aren't many people who can match her ability."

Alejandro pensively closed an eye as he raised Lisbeth's background.

It had been just under two years since the war with the mysterious invaders had begun. The havoc caused by the still entirely unknown enemies increased every day, all around the world. Ironically, the more they advanced, the more casualties there were, which led to even more people volunteering for the army. Lisbeth had been one of them.

"______"

Alejandro Ostley's force was fighting day and night to reclaim stolen land on the European front. Having been tasked with such a heavy burden, the IPO had also given him free rein to place any Valkyrie under his command.

The force he had gathered represented the greatest concentration of humanity's fighting power, Sigrdrifa. And—

"—That makes you, the squadron leader, my right hand."

"Reluctantly."

"You've gotten a lot less respectful with me lately."

"I've learned that attending to your moods is a waste of effort, so I've chosen to devote my time to more productive pursuits."

If she was being more honest, her reluctance was really just lighthearted jest.

His words and his decisiveness had guided her when she had been scared to fly and unwilling to climb into her Deus ex Machina, stuck in limbo between being a Valkyrie and not feeling worthy of the name. At the end of the day, she was quite proud to be flying under his command.

That said, she had no intention of telling him that until after the war was over—

"You're even more of a romantic than I am."

"—? What do you mean, sir?"

"Forget it. So is there anything you need me to do about Crown and Haltija?" Brushing off her question, he furrowed his brow while pondering the topic at hand.

"No, sir." Rusalka shook her head. "Their training is part of my job. I won't neglect my duty."

"…You seem awfully excited about it. Don't bully those two girls too much."

"I would never. It's just…"

"Just…what?"

"I can't deny a certain excitement at the thought of inflicting all the various hells I suffered as a rookie on them."

"Well now, aren't you just the model of a soldier!"

That probably was not intended as the literal praise it sounded like, but Rusalka didn't bother digging into that line of thought. She just saluted and then turned to leave.

"I'm looking forward to your results. I'll be counting on you, Rusalka."

Rusalka sighed slightly as Alejandro left her with his usual parting words.

"Yes, sir, I know. Since, by whatever quirk of fate, I've ended up as your right hand."

Whatever quirk of fate that had been with them ever since they shared a pint in that pub.

4

"So is it true that you and the colonel are getting it on, Major?"

"Wha—? Lisbeth?!"

And with that blunt question, Rusalka's renewed spirit was balanced on the precipice yet again.

They were in the mess hall at Borne base, in the corner reserved for Valkyries. That question came just as Rusalka had come over to eat with her subordinates.

The opening salvo was Lisbeth's, immediately followed by a chiding from Leili.

Rusalka's sky-blue eyes narrowed as she stared down Lisbeth, who was smirking at her. Feeling curious gazes from others as well, she responded flatly, "Not even remotely."

"What?! Really?!"

"Why are you so shocked, Haltija?" asked Rusalka.

"Ugh, um, apologies, ma'am…"

Leili must have been pretty badly shaken, since she totally forgot her usual decorum. Her cheeks turned red as she apologized, and Lisbeth chuckled at her.

"You're the kind of girl who's a sucker for fads, aren't you, Leili? Always tryin' to act cool, but look at you now."

"H-how rude…! Take that back. You take that back this instant, Lisbeth!"

"Ha. Screw that, little miss perfect. Not until you admit I'm better than you."

Lisbeth gestured with her fork provocatively as Leili's eyebrows arched in unbridled anger. An explosive situation had formed in the blink of an eye, and a nervous mood filled the mess hall.

"We're eating here. And there are others watching as well. Need I remind you of your manners? Again?" But while the people around them were watching nervously, Rusalka quietly interrupted their argument. Perhaps recalling what had happened in the hangar from the dangerous tone of her voice, the two of them immediately fell silent.

"And that question as well. You two are both promising prospects the task force commander scouted personally. He is responsible for you, and your actions reflect on him. Both the good and the bad. You should think carefully about what that really means."

"…Yes, ma'am. There is no excuse."

"——"

Faced with Rusalka's reprimand, Leili apologized. However, Lisbeth was sulking in the seat across from Leili, sullenly refusing to open her mouth.

"Lisbeth? I couldn't hear you."

"Fine, fine. I get it! I get it, Major! Satisfied?!"

Lisbeth slammed the table as she stood up. Glaring at Rusalka, her eyes had a decent edge to them, but for someone who had been in the armed forces as long as Rusalka, there was no way that would be enough to get her to back down.

"Just what I'd expect from a major who worked her way up from the bottom. The howls of a little girl aren't enough to get a rise out of you." Lisbeth scoffed.

"I won't deny that. It sounds like you have some thoughts you'd like to share, though."

"Damn straight, I do! Of course I do!" Thumping her chest, Lisbeth turned her fangs on Rusalka. She almost looked like a growling stray dog. "I should show respect just 'cause you've been in the army a long time and you've got a fancy rank? There's no way I can do that. 'Cause you're way weaker than I am, Major."

"Lisbeth!"

Leili sprang out of her seat, sharply scolding Lisbeth. But Lisbeth's face just curled into a sneer as she snorted.

"What? Aren't you thinking the same thing? *Major Evereska's ability as a Valkyrie is clearly lower than us newcomers*, was it?"

"That's… But that's different from showing proper respect to a superior officer. Even you…" Leili trailed off.

"I'm right! I don't have money, and I didn't go to any special schools, so why do you think I am standing here? Because I've got talent as a Valkyrie. 'Cause I've got a talent for killing the enemy!"

Leili caught her breath at Lisbeth's menacing response.

It was an incredibly narrow-minded perspective on things, but there was some truth to it as well. The reason Lisbeth was in the army despite not even completing the dramatically condensed basic training was because she had one-in-a-million potential as a Valkyrie. And in terms of sheer combat strength, she had already caught up to Rusalka, and even surpassed her in some respects.

——To the point that she viewed herself as an instrument for killing the enemy.

"I won't ever acknowledge anyone weaker than me. You can grab my head with that vise grip of yours as hard as you want, but that's nothin'. The gaping hole in my heart hurts way more, and the only thing I can do to fill it is kill every last one of those bastards…!"

"——"

"You think I can do that while taking orders from people weaker than me? Why don't you reflect on your own strength and come back after, Major."

Lisbeth's eyes were filled with derision as she glared at Rusalka, as if she was staring down an enemy. Saying her piece, she picked up her tray and made her way out of the mess hall.

"W-wait, Lisbeth! Ummm, I'll talk to her, Major, so…"

Leili frantically cleaned up her tray as well and chased after Lisbeth. The other Valkyries nearby all watched awkwardly as the unpleasant scene unfolded.

"…Haaah…"

And left alone at the table, Rusalka massaged her brow and heaved a heavy sigh. It was a pretty intense explosion. Taking the brunt of that youthful impulsiveness, she was left with a hefty sense of disappointment in herself.

"She really let you have it, didn't she?"

Natalie carried her tray of food over with a grimace on her face. She sat next to Rusalka as the two empty seats in front of them were filled by Alma and Shannon. Surrounded by her subordinates from her time back on Hamburg base, Rusalka broke into a big smile.

"You saw, huh?"

"With that big of a performance, it's only natural you'd draw attention."

"They got you, Rusalka. You let them walk all over you."

Rusalka looked a little embarrassed at Natalie's and Alma's comments. Her expression drooped a little bit as she looked at the clock.

"A bit late for your meals, no?"

"Wellll, about that—we were giving the rookies some time to themselves. Figured they were still in the phase where they would want to talk among themselves," Shannon explained.

"I see."

"If anything, I was surprised to see you trying to mingle with them. I was afraid it might spark an odd mood if we did. Actually, it sort of did end up that way from the looks of it."

That easygoing stream of consciousness was Shannon Stewart's unique way of communicating. But her thoughts and the things she focused on were always on point, and she could wield that perceptiveness in combat as well.

Which was why Rusalka winced just a little bit. Because it meant she had no excuse.

"Well, given it's you, ma'am, I'm sure you were going along with them in order to give them—or more specifically, one of them—a chance to vent."

"That's how it was with you, too, Natalie," Alma pointed out.

"I—I was not just venting! In my case, it was a reasonable protest founded on genuine chagrin and indignation!"

Natalie faced Alma head-on, strongly objecting at being grouped together with Lisbeth.

And as she watched them, Rusalka thought back to her old relationship with Natalie. Before Sigrdrifa was formed, when Rusalka had not flown in a long time, Natalie had been strict and forceful in confronting her. But now she understood the reason behind her belligerent stance at the time.

"Natalie's attitude toward me back then was..."

"Love, definitely love."

"Right, love... Wait, love?"

"No, it wasn't!!" Natalie yelled at the top of her lungs.

Tripped up by Shannon's perfectly timed interjection, Rusalka's conclusion got twisted, and Natalie went bright red. Natalie then turned to the provocateur and pointedly interrogated her, demanding, "Shannon?" But Shannon simply took a sip of water and made a point of obliquely avoiding her eyes.

"So what are you going to do?" Ignoring the exchange going on over her head, Alma continued on the previous topic. Alma pointed to herself as she asked her question in a flat voice. "Want us to talk to the rookies?"

"——"

"That reaction is upsetting..."

"Sorry, I was just surprised."

Rusalka had stared in shock at Alma's unexpected proposition.

It was a proposal for them to interject themselves into Rusalka's problem. And Alma was not much for proactively seeking out interactions with others in the first place, so for her to suggest that...

"You've changed as well, Alma."

"No. I've always been nice."

"That's true."

Natalie looked like she wanted to say something but prudently decided not to butt in.

The attitude of her reliable juniors—no, sisters—caused Rusalka's expression to relax a bit.

"I appreciate the thought, but please leave them to me. I'm the squadron leader, so I have to live up to the responsibility that position comes with."

"Okay. Good luck, then." Putting her hand to her well-endowed bosom as she said that, Alma nodded in response. The way that she accepted it without digging in was just like her. Seeing that, Natalie and Shannon glanced at each other and shrugged.

"If you are going to insist, then allow us to observe you in action."

"If it looks like it's not working, then just say so quickly. It's kind of turning into my job to be there with some follow-up lately."

Natalie's response was stiff and unsociable, while Shannon just breezily waved her hand, both imparting their own sort of encouragement as Rusalka nodded.

She had been tasked with this job by Alejandro and her younger sisters, so she wanted to properly follow through for all of them.

"And more than anything, there's the very valid question of why I'm still flying when I'm clearly lacking in firepower. I wouldn't be able to face my old comrades if I let that go unanswered."

The three of them had their own responses to that. But Rusalka knew that the reason they did not try to defend her overaggressively or fret about her was because of their faith in her.

That was why she had said that—to spur herself to not let things remain as they were.

5

"Still, though, I think the major's going to have a hard time with them."

After they watched Rusalka clean up her tray and leave, Shannon murmured the thought pensively. Despite her lackadaisical manner of speech, she was very sharp.

Natalie looked up from trying to get Alma to eat everything on her tray. "Then perhaps we should help out, too?"

"Mm, that's probably gonna be a little hard. Leili aside, Lisbeth is openly hostile with the major, and that's probably just something that'll have to be settled between the two of them."

She took her time getting to the point, but her answer was clearly sound. The reason Natalie wanted to grimace in frustration was because she knew Shannon was right.

"You're the squadron XO, Natalie. You worried? Or upset? Thinking of staging a coup to graduate from being second-in-command?"

"Please don't joke about something like that. What happened before is in the past. Right now, I hardly have any complaints about the major. Though I do have thoughts about her insisting on being so self-deprecating."

"It's love."

"Yep, definitely love."

"No, it is not!!"

Natalie indignantly grabbed Alma's and Shannon's ears for teasing her again. The two of them were still yelping in pain when Natalie sighed.

Unlike the Rusalka who had been unable to fly, Natalie thought highly of how she handled being the squadron leader for Sigrdrifa and didn't believe her management of it had any glaring oversights.

She believed that with time, Lisbeth and the other rookies would come to understand just how large Rusalka's roles really were, and she expected they would change their opinion of Rusalka eventually. But—

"I..."

"—? What is it, Natalie?"

Alma furrowed her brow when she noticed Natalie's eyes narrowing slightly.

Natalie shook her head at her friend's question. "The battlefields change and our roles change, but the worries never go away... We've cleared out quite a large number of pillars from around Holm base, but the crux of it all still hasn't shown itself."

"...Mistletoe..." Alma grimaced as Natalie nodded curtly.

Mistletoe—the code name that had been assigned to the secondary pillar that currently stalked the region around Holm base. It was the powerful enemy the Sigrdrifa task force was hunting under Alejandro's command.

In addition to small-scale tertiary pillars, large secondary pillars had also been dispatched to counter Valkyrie deployments around the world.

And among those secondary pillars, Mistletoe had a particularly powerful special ability. Sigrdrifa had already fought with it twice but hadn't managed to finish it off in either encounter.

They couldn't move on to another battlefield with such a dangerous pillar still lingering around. Because of that, they were stuck in a holding pattern, unable to advance, which was the primary cause of the impatience and unease currently plaguing the base.

"The longer we let it get away from us here, the worse off things get for all the other fronts... Mgh."

"Worrying about it and praying about it aren't going to make the enemy decide to show up. You're overthinking it."

Shannon smushed Natalie's cheeks between her hands as she started pondering the wider European front. Revealing a look that she would normally never let anyone who knew her see, Natalie shuddered.

"Wh-wh-wh—…?"

"You've aaalways been a worrywart since back in training."

"Stories about Natalie? I'm interested."

"Really? In that case, I have pleeenty to tell."

"You two…"

Alma's eyes were sparkling with excitement as Shannon broke into a grin. At a loss for how to deal with her friends, Natalie heaved a sigh.

But because of that, the darkness that had been encroaching on her heart moments earlier had already dissipated.

"Sheesh, if that was your aim from the beginning, there must be better ways to go about it," she muttered softly to herself.

After all, if she actually tried to bring it up, they would obviously deny doing anything of the sort.

With such reliable comrades, it felt silly to try to put up a facade. It was like her heart was always laid bare when dealing with them.

——Which was all the more reason she needed to be particularly careful when around them.

"Natalie? Are you mad?" Alma asked.

"…I'm not mad. I'm exasperated. You've reached a respectable position in terms of abilities, but you two still act like trainees. At this rate…"

"At this rate, what?"

Alma cocked her head, and Shannon also had a quizzical expression. Seeing that, Natalie gently put her hand to her chest.

"It will be a problem if the major has to keep worrying about you two on top of everything else. Right now in particular, when she's struggling to deal with the rookies constantly at her throat, you should avoid adding to her burden."

"Your suggestion will be taken under consideration going forward…"

"That's a rather uninspiring response—you mustn't cause more problems for the major, Alma."

Her expression softening, Natalie put her hand on Alma's cheek. Alma narrowed her eyes at the ticklish feeling, but even though she furrowed her brow, she did not reject Natalie.

"Yep, it's love."

"I told you before—that's not it!"

"Owww."

Her hand shifted from caressing to pinching. Alma's cheek stretched more than she expected, and she almost lost herself for a moment in curious testing.

"Hey, Natalie." Watching the two of them horsing around, Shannon had one eye closed, and her expression was a bit different from her usual disinterested look.

"Are you hiding something from us?"

"When put that way, I suppose I'm having trouble hiding all my general daily annoyances with you two."

"——"

Shannon fixed her with a steady gaze, and Natalie returned it with a steady gaze of her own. Finally, Shannon relented.

"Fine. In that case, I'll keep out of it and leave you to your business."

"N-no fair. Don't just leave me here."

As Shannon tried to escape, Alma, with Natalie still pinching her cheek, grabbed on to her shirttail. Shannon's expression displayed a clear and obvious disinterest in getting dragged back into it.

6

——And just as Rusalka's subordinates had feared, the situation really showed no signs of improving.

"It really just isn't going well..."

Her well-defined brow was wrinkled as Rusalka dwelled painfully on her lacking abilities.

She had put on a brave front for Alma and Natalie, but her interactions with Lisbeth really were not getting any better.

Of course, from Rusalka's perspective, she could not afford to just spend all her time training rookies. In addition to serving as the squadron leader of Sigrdrifa, she also worked as Alejandro's right hand, however unwillingly, and that meant she had to divert some of her attention to the management of various aspects of Holm base.

She got some help with all that from Alejandro's subordinates, who had been with him longest, as well as Major Michelle Heyman, the leader of the radio operators and Rusalka's exclusive operator during combat. Even so, it was still an enormous amount of work.

She made a point of making time while dealing with all that to interact with Lisbeth and Leili, who was trying to help in her own way, but they were still like oil and water.

"Ability as a Valkyrie, huh...?"

Looking down at her hand, Rusalka reflected on the, by now, very familiar insult.

It had finally reached a point where, when it came to ability as a Valkyrie, Rusalka, the last active-duty second-generation Valkyrie, could not match anyone from the third generation or the even newer cohort that Lisbeth and Leili were a part of. They were fundamentally different in terms of raw power, which opened an insurmountable gap between Rusalka and them.

In the fighting just the other day, the number of enemies Rusalka had shot down was far fewer than any other member of the squadron. Lisbeth gloating about getting three times as many kills was still fresh in her mind as well. Of course, the number of aerial victories was not really a measure of how much someone had contributed to humanity's survival, but—

"It won't be long before they pass me in total kills, too."

In terms of her entire career, she had flown more than ten times as many missions as them, but they were already closing in fast on her total number of enemies shot down.

But Rusalka was not feeling particularly vexed by that.

"———"

In the past, she had felt envious of her younger sisters, who had joined her in the sky later, a powerful jealousy of what gifts they had been granted.

She knew now that it was probably a sort of heroic ideation out of a desire to make up for the guilt of being the only survivor and a regret for the horrible thing she had said to her best friend.

But it had been Alejandro who had forced her to realize the error of her ways. It was precisely because she had been saved by him that she wanted to convey to Lisbeth somehow just how dangerous it was to fly through the skies fueled by hatred and dwelling on dark, negative emotions. But as ever, she refused to listen to Rusalka because Rusalka was weak, leaving them stuck in a peculiar impasse.

Maybe I really should just eat my words and ask Alma or Natalie for some help with this...

"I wouldn't really mind if it was only my reputation at stake here… But I don't want to betray his trust. And if something happens to Lisbeth first, it might be too late."

It was simple to declare she would handle it herself, but actually making that happen was turning out to be far more challenging than she had imagined. And so she started thinking about possibly asking for some help.

Natalie had offered to assist at any time if she wanted it, but considering all the factors at play, Rusalka was surprised to find herself thinking Shannon might be the right one for the job. Alma had her own strengths as well, so Rusalka hoped she wouldn't take it personally that she had been cut from the list of options from the outset.

"Maybe I should try talking to Shannon about it tomorrow."

Most likely Shannon would be put out a bit, since she tended to dislike getting involved in annoying jobs, but at a root level, raising the unit cohesion of the squadron was for her sake as well, in a way.

As she considered how to convince Shannon with that sort of rhetorical argument, Rusalka opened the door to her room. She thought back to what had happened that day in order to write her daily report before going to bed.

And then with gratitude for another day coming to an end—

"It's been a long time, my child. Have you been well?"

An unexpected voice greeted her as soon as she entered her room. Her breath caught in surprise.

It was not an issue of someone being there or not or the door not being locked. The reason she gasped was not because she had a surprise visitor but because of who that visitor was—and because of the awe she felt when face-to-face with that familiar figure.

"What is it, Rusalka? Do you not recognize me?"

"N-no, of course I do. I was just surprised to see you here."

Rusalka frantically shook her head as he cocked his head slightly. Then belatedly, she knelt and lowered her head in a reverent bow.

There was a clear and dramatic line between that and the standard military salute that indicated an instinctive submission to the figure before her.

MONTHLY

Naturally, since he was—

"I am grateful to be granted a visit by the great Lord Odin."

Hearing that, her visitor—Odin—flashed an almost inhuman smile as his one visible eye narrowed slightly in apparent amusement.

He was the All-father, the one who had reached out and made contact with humanity when they were on the verge of outright collapse while struggling with unknown enemies. A real live god who had made himself known.

Humanity had teetered on the brink of destruction when they discovered they had no way of dealing with enemies that were alien in every which way and totally unaffected by all the weapons they brought to bear. That was when Odin appeared before humanity and gave them the means to fight the pillars—Valkyries.

Ever since, Odin sided with humanity and cooperated with the IPO, continuing to awaken those girls with the aptitude to become Valkyries and sending them to the front lines.

Naturally, this meant every Valkyrie had received Odin's divine blessing from him personally. It was as true for Alma and Natalie as it was for Lisbeth and Leili. And Rusalka was no exception.

Rusalka had also become a Valkyrie by directly receiving his divine blessing.

"______"

If Valkyries were the irreplaceable signal flares declaring the start of humanity's counterattack, then he was the deity who gave birth to those Valkyries.

But why was he here—?

"Is it that hard to understand why I would be here?"

"—Ngh!"

"There's no need to be so shocked. It's a simple feat to read something floating on the surface of a human heart. And you're my adorable daughter. It's only natural for a parent to understand their children's inner thoughts, is it not?"

Odin shrugged, smiling. Each and every one of his friendly, endearing gestures only served to increase Rusalka's wariness, though, and she was finding it increasingly difficult to breathe.

"Hmm. I have so many daughters who feel at ease in my presence, which only makes your reactions all the more precious, Rusalka. You need not steady yourself so. Even if I am unmistakably a true deity."

"Thank you very much for your kind consideration, Lord Odin."

"So formal. You could always go for something with a bit more filial love imbued, like Father."

"That's..."

Rusalka was at a loss for how to respond to Odin's proposition.

Part of it was concern about being a bit discourteous to a self-proclaimed god so casually, but there was a more fundamental problem, and that was how he looked.

Honestly, it was just too weird to call someone who looked like that Father—

"——"

The figure sitting on Rusalka's bed, legs crossed—Odin, the deity hailed as humanity's greatest guardian—looked like a small boy who couldn't possibly be more than twelve or thirteen years old.

He had a black eye patch over his left eye, and his wide-open right eye had a striking red iris that Rusalka could see herself reflected in. He looked like a mysterious, bewitching boy with an indescribable mystical allure. His voice and gestures seemed almost childish as well. While Rusalka assuredly was struck by a sense of awe whenever she met with him, she simply couldn't bring herself to call him Father.

"Haaah, you too, huh?"

Having sensed her strong resistance, Odin shook his head.

"My daughters all have different relationships with me, but not a single one of them will call me Father. Is this appearance really so lacking in gravity? If so, I suppose I may have made a bit of a mistake."

"No, you need not feel bad, Lord Odin. I believe your appearance is very... It's very adorable. I do not dislike it."

"Oh? Is that so? I see, I see, so you have a thing for little boys, then. You seem pretty close to Alejandro, so I had assumed your interests lay somewhere along those lines—"

"Both of those theories are incorrect."

She immediately interjected as Odin hypothesized with an amused look on his face.

Her expression paled as she realized that her reflexive response had been very rude, but Odin's eyes widened just a little bit at her instinctive denial before he burst into laughter.

"Heh-heh, that was a pretty over-the-top response. As for whether it was your supposed interest in young boys, Alejandro, or both, well, perhaps I shall refrain from probing too much."

"You may probe either if you wish. Both are extraordinarily disheartening suppositions to leave unchallenged."

Again, she was struck after the fact by the thought that she might have been speaking rather impudently, but she also hesitated to correct her statement in order to maintain a firm and resolute stance against either accusation.

And with the retreat of the overwhelmingly solemn atmosphere that had filled the room when she first noticed Odin, Rusalka finally managed to find the presence of mind to look back at him.

Odin was rumored to have lived since ancient times, but his appearance was not only quite young; he also dressed in casual attire that only emphasized his childish image. He was wearing modern apparel with bright colors that made him seem like an energetic young boy and not an ancient, solemn god.

If she was forced to say whether the outfit suited him, she would have to say it did, but—

"—Oh."

"If it is difficult for you to converse, then I'll do this. It should be a little easier now."

With that remark, Odin was suddenly clad in a beige-colored robe. It looked like a mantle from olden times, and while everything else about Odin's image seemed to take a modern feel and design, it certainly helped impart the sense of an old, eternal presence.

"Your expression has changed. In a good way, my child."

"...What brings you to see me today, Lord Odin? I can't imagine you would go out of your way to visit random Valkyries. And I'm..."

"Not a special Valkyrie? Less powerful Valkyries... As I recall, you girls were called Seconds."

Odin touched a slender finger to his chin as his eye glimmered eerily. Rusalka tensed, feeling like he was peering into the depths of her heart with that red eye.

Odin wasn't wrong, of course. Unlike before, Rusalka no longer viewed her lack of power as a second-generation Valkyrie as such a terrible flaw.

But it was entirely natural to believe that Odin would direct his attentions and favor on those Valkyries who were the most skilled and performed the best. Just like with Amy, the First.

"It was unfortunate what happened to Amy. But that does not mean my love for my daughters would fade, nor would I favor any one in particular over the others. A god's love cannot be measured in human terms."

"Reading my mind again?"

"You should realize by now that you have a tendency to let your feelings show, as surprising as that might seem. Even if your expression doesn't change, it still shows in your eyes. Your eyes are blue like the skies, and they can change easily, just like the sky."

Rusalka raised her hand to one of her eyes at that. It was something she had never heard before.

As she covered an eye for a few seconds, making them both one-eyed for a brief moment in time, Odin's lips relaxed just a little bit.

"My child with hair like a moon's tear and eyes like the sky, I have come to you this evening with a request."

"—A request for me…Lord Odin?"

"Yes. None other than you."

Rusalka's eyes widened slightly in surprise as she remained kneeling, and she lowered her head again in reaffirmation of her submission to Odin.

"Whatever it is you desire, Lord Odin, if I can be of service."

"You need not worry. There is no one more appropriate than you for this. Have faith in Odin's eye, which sees through all. Though having said that, my eye is imperfect and hardly sees much of the future anymore."

Shrugging, Odin narrowed his eye, as if lamenting the limits of his power. But he quickly hid that disappointment and raised his hand, pointing to one side of the room. There was nothing but a wall there—his finger was pointing to something beyond it.

"In the forest a few dozen kilometers to the southeast is a man-made structure that was abandoned decades ago. A facility nestled deep beneath the ground."

"A facility in the forest…"

Mapping the base's surroundings in her head, she had a general idea of the location of the structure Odin was referring to. An underground facility that had been abandoned decades ago was likely some kind of air-raid shelter from the war or something along those lines.

"There are two sisters hiding there in hopes of staying away from human settlements. I want you to retrieve the two of them and protect them. Can you do that?"

"Sisters? Protecting civilians is, of course, our job. But..."

"I understand your confusion. Why would I go out of my way to ask you specifically to rescue two sisters who were left behind, right? The reason I can't move myself is simple. Were I to act, it would become far too large of an event. It would no doubt incite those tiresome pillars, and I can't allow the two of them to become caught up in the fighting that would almost certainly ensue."

"Who are these sisters that you would take such an interest in them, Lord Odin?"

His voice remained flat and steady, but it was incredibly obvious how attached he was to the pair. Just when it seemed odd how long Odin remained silent when she pointed that out, he spoke again.

"Yes, I suppose there are several ways to choose my words here, but...those sisters are both daughters of mine."

"—You can't mean...Valkyries who deserted?"

From how Odin looked, the worst possibility came to mind as she pressed him for information.

Valkyries received a divine blessing from God, were granted Deus ex Machinas, and flew through the skies to carve out a future for humanity. But not everyone who received that blessing was able to continue flying wholeheartedly forever.

There were those whose hearts had broken after numerous battles against the pillars and deserters who refused to fly as well. The IPO had a policy of tacit acknowledgment of their unique circumstances, and starting with the third generation, when a Valkyrie deserted, they were not court-martialed or brought up on any sort of charges.

But that was merely a judgment by humans made with consideration to the sheer weight of what was being demanded of Valkyries. It would not be that surprising that a god like Odin might come to a different decision regarding how to handle them.

But if Odin was planning to have her tie up some deserter Valkyries to bring back and force them to fly against their will, then however disrespectful it might be, she was going to have to voice her opinion.

However—

"Worry not, Rusalka. I have no interest in chasing down those who have fled. It is a harsh thing to say, but forcing those whose wills have broken back out onto the battlefield will only result in more wasted deaths. I don't wish for that, either."

"I…see… In that case, it seems all the more reason to ask: Who exactly are these sisters?"

"I said it, didn't I? They are, without a doubt, my daughters. However, they are not quite there yet."

"In other words, they have that much potential? That's…"

Rusalka finally understood what Odin was asking of her.

Every Valkyrie had been granted her blessing directly by Odin. However, every Valkyrie from the second generation onward had been volunteers who had passed tests gauging their aptitude.

There were none whom Odin had personally chosen from among humanity as being suitable to be a Valkyrie—none since the First. Since Amy.

"Save those sisters, Rusalka. Both of them will play critical roles in determining the outcome of Ragnarök. They are crucial and irreplaceable to humanity."

"Yes, sir!"

Tasked with a role far beyond anything she could have imagined, Rusalka felt her soul trembling as she responded.

Deep in her chest, she felt an intense sense of exaltation at being given such a task, alongside the hope of renewing humanity's counterattack against the pillars.

As that feeling filled her whole body, Odin nodded to Rusalka.

"I'll form a rescue team and go find those sisters right—"

"No, that won't do. Why do you think I came all the way here to meet with you specifically?"

Rusalka had envisioned telling Alejandro and then putting things in motion immediately, but Odin stopped her in her tracks. Unable to answer the god's question, Rusalka's eyes widened.

"Why is that? I intended to join the rescue team myself, so…"

"The existence of those two girls cannot spread beyond the absolute minimum who need to know. At this base, just you and Alejandro. And…hmm, I suppose Natalie and Lisbeth."

"Natalie and…Lisbeth, Lord Odin?"

If those were his choices, then obviously he had some reason for it, but even so, Rusalka could not help but find the choices indecipherable.

Rusalka and Natalie were the squadron leader and executive officer for Sigrdrifa. It was not generally considered a good idea for both of them to be absent from the base at the same time. And for Lisbeth to be the last one rounding out the team—

"Dissatisfied?"

"No, sir. If you believe it is necessary, then we will face this mission with just those members."

She had her questions and her doubts. But there was no hesitation in her reply.

Odin smiled deeply, satisfied by her response.

"Then I'll leave you to it. I have high hopes for your success, my child."

Chapter 2
The Brafford Sisters

1

The heavy rains had just lifted, so the ground in the woods was a muddy quagmire.

Vibrant green foliage hung heavy with droplets of rain, and even the slightest jostle would bring the water down in a little baptism. In small amounts, it could be considered cute and fun, but when the leaves moved, it was usually because of whole branches rustling. There were enough droplets falling to fill her cupped hands, enough to leave anyone passing beneath the boughs completely drenched.

"———"

It wasn't the time of year when simply getting wet would lead to chills, but there was no guarantee that the sunlight that helped to dry her would continue indefinitely. Using the hiking tricks they had picked up during the past few days, she slipped beneath the drenched leaves while watching her feet as she headed for the watering hole she had found.

Because of the rains, there was a chance it had swelled with runoff, so whenever she went to retrieve water, she was careful to pick a point upstream where the water flowed clear and clean. Her companion was also quite picky about how clear their drinking water needed to be, which was all the more reason to go upstream and avoid stagnant ponds. She touched the water bottle at her hip, checking it was still in place.

"Honestly, we should probably distill everything, even if it isn't still water."

She surprised herself to realize the pun she had happened to stumble into.

"Distill...still...water."

Rolling it around in her mouth, she thought it was pretty funny. She decided to share it when she got back to their hideout to see what her companion thought.

"I can't just stand here thinking about random stuff all day."

Tamping down her urge to get a move on, she kept her footsteps light while walking swiftly and cleanly along the muddy slope. As the scenery gradually shifted into a familiar area, she reached her goal—the watering hole.

Fresh water was running through a crevice in the rocks, trickling down the slope from there, feeding into a large river that extended into the forest. Fortunately, the long rains did not seem to have had too significant an impact, and she was able to collect water without any trouble.

"All right, that should do for now. All that's left is—"

Feeling the heft of the water bottle as it sloshed a bit, she started to turn back the way she came. Suddenly, she cocked her head. Ignoring the beautiful golden hair that fell on her slender shoulders, she narrowed her eyes as she felt a presence. Turning in its direction, she listened closely.

It was faint, but something was disturbing the calm of the forest. She straightened out and raced up the slope in the direction she had come from, forgetting all about the joke she had come up with.

2

"Wgh?!"

Rusalka stopped and turned around when she heard the yelp behind her.

She had lost count of how many times it had happened, and every time, it was exactly the same: Lisbeth making the trees rustle without paying attention to where she was going and subsequently getting drenched in a huge deluge of her own making.

"Could you please just listen to my instructions, Lisbeth? I won't claim you could have avoided all this, but it certainly would have dramatically decreased the number of times it happened."

"Grrr… Don't make me keep repeating myself, either. I have my own way of doing things. You don't have any right to complain about how I do 'em!"

"I see. Is that so?"

Lisbeth fired back with her usual spirited response, but Rusalka just slowly shook her head.

"Sadly, if we leave things up to you, we won't make it in time. We are already behind schedule as is. From now on, I have to insist you get with the program and do things my way."

"Wh-what right do you have?!"

"Squadron leader, executive officer of the base… If you're looking for titles, I've got a few, in case you've forgotten."

With Rusalka resorting to appeals to authority, Lisbeth's waterlogged jab was weak. Natalie looked exasperated as she threw a towel over Lisbeth's short black hair from behind and started drying her head with an ease that came from plenty of practice over the past few hours.

"Maybe you should have drawn the line a little bit sooner, Major? There's an eastern saying that even a Buddha loses patience by the third time."

"I don't intend to go around saying I'm more patient than a Buddha, so I suppose I'll be a bit more decisive next time around. More importantly, we can't afford to mess this up."

Currently, they were deep in the forest a few dozen kilometers away from Holm base.

Since they had been sent out to look for what was seemingly an underground air-raid shelter or something like that, they had left their car behind a while back and had been walking through the woods, following a compass, for hours.

At this point, Natalie felt compelled to say, "Still, I am beginning to question if those two girls we're looking for are out here somewhere. It just looks like animal trails out here to me…and not much of that, either, to be honest."

"If you look closely, you should be able to tell the tracks where the grass has been stepped on…but with the rain this morning, it might be difficult for untrained eyes."

"Untrained eyes… Major, are you a professional when it comes to hiking?"

"My hometown was in the forests of northern Europe. Walking through the woods is like a stroll in my backyard."

Taking advantage of that experience, Rusalka had been guiding the other two through the forest. Always check your footing; clear openings in the foliage to make a path; speak up regularly to keep track of where everyone is.

Without any one of those things, the difficulty inherent to moving around out in the wilderness went up dramatically.

"Your home was in the forest…," Natalie murmured.

"Surprised?"

"Ah yes, a little bit. You carry yourself with such refinement that I had simply assumed you had been instilled with a classical education from a young age."

"Ha, it doesn't surprise me one bit!"

While Natalie was shocked by Rusalka's background, Lisbeth, her hair still wet despite getting toweled off some, sneered with her canines showing.

"Your stupid gorilla-like grip makes a lot more sense, knowing you were raised in a forest. I'm sure you trained by climbing trees and drumming those— Ugwaaaaa!"

"Again with those insults…!"

Natalie clenched the hand that had been drying Lisbeth's head just moments ago and proactively dished out a little bit of punishment for the blatant disrespect Lisbeth leveled at their squadron leader. Lisbeth crumpled to the ground, bruised but unbowed as Natalie lowered her head slightly.

"To be clear, I do not share this child's opinion, Major."

"You don't need to worry. You and Lisbeth are different. Even if you think I'm like a gorilla, you at least have the courtesy to keep it to yourself."

"In the first place, I don't think you're like a gorilla!"

Acknowledging Natalie's frantic plea, Rusalka's lips softened slightly into a small smile.

Then she thought again about Odin's task—the sisters who would impact the fate of humanity.

"I suppose it should be called a revelation from Lord Odin himself. Since he suddenly appeared in my room last night, the surprise and awe of it won out over gratitude, though."

Lisbeth still could hardly believe it. "To enter a lady's bedroom without her permission... The thought process of mythological beings is difficult to comprehend."

"...But there's no denying his concern for how the battle between humanity and the pillars is going. Lord Odin truly wishes for victory in Ragnarök. That much was made quite clear." That night, he had disappeared after having entrusted the sisters to Rusalka, so it would not have been that strange to think it just a dream, but... "I'm still not sure whether to praise Colonel Ostley's decisiveness or be astounded by his impulsiveness..."

When Rusalka had reported the contact from Odin that same night, Alejandro had ordered the search and rescue of the sisters on the spot, then tasked Rusalka with the mission.

Thinking back on it, she remembered something about Alejandro's demeanor when he had given that order. Ordinarily, there tended to be an undertone of flippancy to most of his orders, but he had looked quite serious that time. He was an officer, so she would prefer he always act with such gravity when doing his job, and for once, her wish had been answered.

She had also conveyed Odin's inexplicable team choice—Natalie and Lisbeth—and surprisingly, he had given his seal of approval relatively easily as well. Because of that, they had been able to go out on the mission with the people Odin had chosen, but—

"Natalie aside, for Lisbeth to be the third member... I don't think this is his way of ordering me to take this opportunity to rectify my lacking guidance, but..."

She could not tell what Odin or Alejandro, who had given the team his seal of approval, were thinking.

They were regularly checking in with the base via satellite phone, but the details of the operation were strictly limited to Alejandro and her operator, Michelle, just like Odin had wanted. But because of that, she hardly felt comfortable mixing official and personal matters by pressing Alejandro on the radio for his reasoning.

Naturally, Alma and Shannon had a lot of questions about why Rusalka and Natalie were out on some secret mission, but they would be able to clear all that up once it was over.

Since—

"This is the first time Lord Odin has chosen a Valkyrie himself since the First. We must have them lend their strength," Rusalka concluded.

"...But are we really gonna be able to use them for anythin'?" Lisbeth muttered as she crouched next to Rusalka, still nursing her head after enduring Natalie's disciplinary blow. "Seriously, though. I dunno how much talent or whatever they're supposed to have. I mean, if a literal god is telling us to recruit them, then I guess it's probably a helluva lot, but still...they've been running away, right?"

"...They are living in a forest far removed from other humans, so that is highly likely."

"Then doesn't that just mean they've already given up in their heads? Tellin' someone like that to fight...that's pointless. No matter what *Father* might say."

Lisbeth's sarcastic term of address and the way she spoke were coarse, but she stood by her beliefs, and she held to a certain logic that Rusalka could understand.

Lisbeth had much greater aptitude as a Valkyrie than Rusalka. But she was not flying around fighting as a Valkyrie because of that unbridled potential. She was doing it because she had chosen to fight the pillars of her own volition.

"———"

This time, Natalie didn't have any follow-up. That alone was proof that she believed there was some logic to what Lisbeth was saying as well.

The willingness to fight that came from within. That fundamental desire was the one thing shared by all serving Valkyries regardless of where they were born or how they were raised or anything else.

Lisbeth and Natalie, and Rusalka as well—they had all chosen to fly of their own accord.

But—

"—I wonder how it was for Amy." Rusalka murmured this to herself as she remembered her friend's vibrant smile.

Amy had talked with her about a lot of things. Almost all of it was stuff Amy had one-sidedly shared with her. Rusalka had never really probed much herself. So she wondered how it had felt for the first Valkyrie, a girl who had been so considerate of others.

What had she been feeling when she accepted Odin's offer and accepted the role of signaling the start of humanity's first counterattack? Of course, Rusalka no longer had any way of finding out—

"—Gh!"

"What happened?"

Suddenly, just as she was sinking into thought, Rusalka swung around and asked what was wrong. Natalie and Lisbeth were shocked by the sudden reaction, but she did not have time to respond to them.

She could feel a tingling at the nape of her neck, an instinct cultivated from her youth in the outdoors. It had served her well in combat as well, and it was telling her something strange was approaching.

And it seemed to be coming closer at high speed as well, dashing up at them from somewhere below—

"Natalie! You and Lisbeth get behind me…!"

"Major?!"

Rusalka immediately pulled her pistol and prepared in case a wild animal was charging them.

Because of the absorption effect of the pillars, the number of animals living out in the wild had dramatically reduced, but many dogs and other creatures had gone feral with the rapid retreat of humanity emptying entire regions. Rusalka lowered her hips and steadied the handgun, prepared for the possibility of being set upon by feral dogs.

There was a sound of something breaking through the foliage—

"—Hmm? Ah, it was people."

What appeared from the greenery was not a feral animal but a beautiful girl.

Her striking blond hair was tied back, and her clear-blue eyes looked like they contained the vast skies in them. Rusalka had often been complimented on her eyes, but even so, this girl's eyes seemed enchanting.

From head to toe, she had a delicate beauty, as if a god had gone out of their way to shape such splendor. For a moment, Rusalka couldn't help wondering if they had just encountered something supernatural out deep in the forest.

"______"

However, what surprised her was not the girl's great beauty. It was because she looked impossibly familiar.

Since—

"—Amy?"

—she looked just like the friend she had hurt so badly, who she should never have been able to meet again.

3

The question Rusalka could not help asking aloud elicited four very different reactions.

The girl herself widened her eyes slightly in shock, and Lisbeth was shouting angrily as Natalie pushed her back behind cover. Natalie's face froze as she looked over at Rusalka. Rusalka's change in expression was dramatic.

"———"

It was because Rusalka was the most shaken of all by the question that had slipped out.

This was the shock of confronting someone who could not have been there, who she should have never been able to meet again.

There was a still moment of silence following their reactions. The first to return to her senses was the blond girl who had touched off the encounter in the first place.

"Apologies, but I am not Amy, whoever she might be."

"—Ngh."

Rusalka's throat clenched a little as the girl denied it.

She calmed down after hearing the apology, and as the composure she had lost gradually came back, her field of vision returned to normal, and slowly she realized the distinct differences between the girl in front of her and Amy.

Their faces were remarkably similar, but the air about her and the tone of her voice were quite different from the Amy she knew. Unlike Amy, who had been so slender and dainty, this girl was taller, with a more mature build.

But more than anything, her expression was heavy. Amy had almost always had a smile on her face.

"Major!"

As Rusalka slipped into thought, comparing the girl in front of her to Amy, Natalie's sharp voice brought her back to her senses, and she quickly confirmed the current situation.

This girl was not Amy, but she might just be one of the two sisters Odin had tasked them with finding and protecting. Thinking that, Rusalka lowered her gun—

"My companion was quite clear about not coming into contact with anyone, so apologies for this as well."

With that up-front disclaimer, the girl leaped away. Rusalka immediately reached out, but the girl slipped through her fingers and was quickly retreating deeper into the forest.

"Screw that! I've had enough of this forest shit!"

Lisbeth sensed an opening and dashed forward with a predatory agility. Using her explosive momentum, Lisbeth immediately gave chase. With her unhinged animalistic charge utterly removed from all the fundamentals of military hand-to-hand combat training, she would have gotten a zero, or maybe even a negative score, in any kind of formal evaluation. Still, she managed to get ahold of the girl's clothes.

"Gotch— Ngh?!"

Technique aside, Lisbeth's attack at least got high marks for decisiveness, but the girl evaded her grasp and gracefully swiped Lisbeth's legs out from under her, sending her flying. It was a textbook throw that was the product of disciplined training. The only reason Lisbeth groaned as she hit the grass instead of being knocked out entirely was because the girl had been kind enough to give her a chance to soften the fall.

"I have no intention of injuring you as long as you will just leave me alone."

"W-wait! Don't..."

Seeing Lisbeth go down, Natalie was shocked but immediately drew her gun and shouted a warning. She instantly took aim at the girl, whose eyes narrowed as she stared down the barrel.

"You can't shoot that."

"—Ngh!"

Natalie had been through training, but she had never shot a living creature, let alone a human.

Marking her hesitation in seconds, the girl leaped into the trees. Natalie's expression tensed for a moment, but as expected, she couldn't pull the trigger.

Lisbeth shook her head as she pulled herself up. "Argh…why didn't you shoot?!"

"It's not that simple to just shoot someone! She's a person! More importantly, what should we do now…? Major?"

Natalie put the gun back in her holster as she shouted at Lisbeth and then looked to Rusalka for instructions. But she quickly noticed something off and furrowed her brow.

Looking around, she couldn't see Rusalka anywhere.

"Major?! Where did you…?"

"—If you're looking for me, I'm over here."

The tension was plain in Natalie's voice until she got a response from the trees in the distance. Lisbeth and Natalie were shocked as they turned in that direction.

As they did, they watched as Rusalka slowly appeared from the direction where the girl had run off. She was carrying the girl who had escaped, held tight between her arms.

"I somehow managed to settle things without letting her get away. Positional advantage was the deciding factor."

Rusalka shook her head blankly as Natalie stood there, speechless. The girl Rusalka had caught was worming around, still trying to slip away, but after quickly realizing Rusalka's arms would not budge at all, she slumped, crestfallen.

Seeing that, Lisbeth shook her head as she stood up.

"I feel you," she said to the girl. "Positional advantage, my ass. Everyone knows a gorilla's the strongest animal in the forest."

That was an utterly disrespectful thing to say about her superior officer, but it also contained an awe that hadn't been present before.

4

She had grown up in the outdoors, so she was simply superior when it came to maneuvering in the woodlands, due to a wealth of experience.

Rusalka was insistent that that was the true decisive factor, but no matter what she said, Lisbeth wasn't having any of it, and it didn't seem to convince the girl she had caught, either. To top it all off, even Natalie was doubtful.

"To the best of my knowledge, your individual fighting ability is on an entirely different level, Major, but…that has nothing to do with aptitude as a Valkyrie, right?"

"I…don't think so? I don't really feel any particular difference in physical abilities now compared to before I was a Valkyrie."

"Right. Neither do I."

Natalie, who had recently gotten much closer to Rusalka, suddenly seemed a little bit more distant than before. Rusalka was feeling that acutely as she kept an eye on the two girls in front of her—Lisbeth and the girl she had caught.

The girl's arms were tied with rope that they had brought with them, and Lisbeth was not taking any chances with their impromptu prisoner.

"You keep trying to get away. You just dunno when to give up, do you?"

"It's true. The people I admired were all seemingly gallant and great, but…it is difficult to actually live up to their examples," the struggling prisoner agreed.

"Huh? Quit it with that logical sort of explanation. It makes my ears itch."

"Your ears? In the forest, there are many small insects and parasites that can burrow into your hair and ears. Perhaps that's the real cause."

"That's not what I'm talking about!"

Maybe they naturally didn't get along, but a volatile situation was developing between Lisbeth and the girl. Rusalka sighed a little as she watched it grow worse with each passing comment.

"Apologies for being a little bit violent before. However, I would ask you to please not misunderstand. We are soldiers… We have no intention of hurting a civilian," Rusalka tried to assure the girl.

"This child behind me has rather poor methods of restraint for a soldier…"

"What'd you say?!"

"That's because she is not a proven soldier yet, just a baby chick," Natalie said with a sigh.

"What'd you say?!"

Lisbeth's head whipped back and forth at their exchange. Natalie put her hand on Lisbeth's neck, telling her to stop it.

And then Natalie turned back to the girl who was watching them with a stiff expression. "Have you not heard of Valkyries? That's who we are."

"...I've heard of them. Winged maidens of battle, granted power by God to fight the pillars."

Rusalka and Natalie glanced at each other at the unexpected response. The girl then peered at Lisbeth.

"You look quite different from what I imagined... I honestly thought you might actually have wings on your backs."

"You think we fly like that? We fly in planes! What a dumb thing to say!"

"Dumb? I think wings would look quite nice on you, though..."

"Asshole..."

Lisbeth turned red as the girl teased her, but the girl also seemed genuinely confused why the Valkyrie was upset by her comment. Natalie and Rusalka glanced at each other again as it looked more and more like the two of them just didn't mesh well.

In the end, Natalie and Lisbeth changed places, and they proceeded without further incident.

"Who the hell is she...? I didn't think there could be anyone who pissed me off more than you, Major."

"I'm impressed you can say that to my face... But I think I have to agree that there is something strange about her."

Their prisoner had great physical capabilities as well as the skill to take full advantage of them. And the throw she had used on Lisbeth was a type of throw commonly taught by the military. It was also notable that for someone apparently living out in the forest, her clothes were incredibly clean, and she was maintaining her hair as well.

Rusalka would just have to set aside the fact that she seemed to resemble Amy for the time being.

"My name is Natalie Chase. May I ask your name?"

As she was thinking that, Natalie was trying to forge a more cordial relationship with the girl. Rusalka was left to reflect on having forgotten such a simple and obvious point.

"My name is Claudia. Claudia Brafford."

"Claudia Brafford...that's a lovely name."

Natalie glanced over at Rusalka as she repeated the name.

However, neither her given name nor her family name was familiar to Rusalka. In fact, other than the general location, Odin's oracle had been essentially *You'll know them when you see them.*

He had not been wrong. Rusalka certainly had recognized her the moment she saw her. From the moment she laid eyes on Claudia, she was sure that she was one of the sisters they were looking for.

Part of it was how much she resembled her unforgettable friend, but the biggest reason was her Valkyrie instinct, which had been ringing in her head the whole time.

Natalie and Lisbeth must have felt the same thing.

"We're repeating ourselves, I know, but we have no intention of causing you any harm, Claudia. However, we did come into this forest looking for you and for your sister," Rusalka explained.

"Me…and my sister…?"

"Which means you both are here. There's no mistaking it." Lisbeth snapped her fingers at that, a nasty look on her face as she approached Claudia. "There's no point trying to hide it. If you don't want to suffer, then just spit out where your sister is."

Natalie felt like she had to ask, "Why are you acting like some two-bit villain?"

"Sorry, but I have no intention of selling out my sister. I won't say a word, even if you torture me."

"And this one's just as stubborn…"

Lisbeth was a genius at making situations worse, and Claudia was quite intent on maintaining her silence. Struggling to deal with how everything seemed to be spiraling out of control, Natalie pushed Lisbeth aside.

"My humblest apologies. Please pay no heed to her thuggish outburst. Our goal is to safeguard you and your sister… We have no intention whatsoever of causing either of you harm."

"Really?"

Claudia was stunned at the difference in warmth between Natalie's earnest plea and Lisbeth's outburst.

Rusalka nodded slightly as Claudia glanced at her. "Natalie is correct. We were tasked with protecting the two of you."

"What could the army possibly want with us?"

"…No, the army didn't request your safeguarding. That was God."

"——"

"Lord Odin ordered us to protect you and your sister."

Hearing that, Claudia's eyes widened slightly. That was only natural. Just a few years earlier, even most religious groups tended not to go around proclaiming they were acting on a direct revelation from a god.

But for the first time since the dawn of history, a god had presented himself before all humanity. Even those who had not seen him personally knew his name.

"Lord Odin..."

"Yeah, you know, that guy, everyone's beloved father. From what I've heard, apparently you and your sister are supposed to have some big ol' role in determining the outcome of Ragnarök. That means we're gonna have to bring you back with us."

"The way she described our circumstances is rather lacking, but that's more or less the gist of it. Do you have any idea what it might be about?" Rusalka asked.

Claudia peered down at the ground. Rusalka and the other Valkyries exchanged glances as she seemed to ponder the complicated question. Finally—

"...I'm sorry, but I can't show you to where my sister is."

With that, Claudia stopped walking and stood there, turning around in front of them.

"The hell do you mean you can't?"

"I meant what I said. I would like my sister to be left alone. In exchange, I'll go with you."

"...You mean you'll take your sister's place?"

Claudia nodded at Natalie's question.

"Yes, that is what I am proposing. You may take me with you. Even without me, I'm sure my sister will be able to live on without much trouble."

Rusalka was unsure how to interpret that valiant declaration.

Naturally, to be in accordance with Odin's revelation, she couldn't accept Claudia's proffer. But she didn't like the idea of dismissing her determination, either.

In the end, an awkward silence prevailed between the two sides, until—

"—Ahhh, I was wondering if something had happened, since you took so long coming back, but I guess you impulsively jumped to conclusions again."

Claudia was waiting quietly for a reply when her determination was disrupted not by Rusalka, Natalie, or Lisbeth but by someone else entirely.

"———"

Her arrival was entirely outside Rusalka's expectations.

She appeared from the foliage right between the four of them and heaved a sigh as she took in the situation.

"I have a vague idea of what might have happened… I'm sorry. Sister must have said something strange and caused you all trouble, right?"

"You must be…" For Rusalka, there was no doubt.

The girl shrugged, her blond hair hanging over one shoulder in a braid, her face a mirror image of Claudia's.

From her features and the way she spoke, it was clear at once who she was. And all but confirming it, Claudia said, "Shiri."

"Yes, yes. As you can probably guess by now, I'm Shirin Brafford—the other sister you all are looking for. The one who actually has her wits about her, for the record."

She flashed a wink as she playfully responded to her sister's call.

5

"You're always so extreme, Sister. What person in their right mind would leave their one and only younger sibling all alone in the forest without a word? Considering my condition, I would have died for sure."

"No, I put some actual thought into my decision, in my own way…"

"Then your thought process was wrong, and you should reflect on your mistakes."

"…Understood."

Overwhelmed by her younger sister's baleful glare, Claudia hung her head in contemplation. As she took in their exchange, Rusalka was unsure where to go from here.

Some time had passed from their decisive exchange in the forest, and they had changed locations to facilitate a proper discussion. Because of that, Shirin had invited them to where she and her sister were currently living.

"Is this an old bunker?" asked Natalie.

"Hmm? Ah yes, probably. Now that you mention it, I used the sign out at the front as firewood. Sorry about that."

"...W-well, it is an emergency situation, so that's understandable."

Natalie's expression froze at Shirin's unabashed response. There was a cup in her hands that looked a lot like it had been fashioned by hand, and there was steam rising from the warm tea poured inside.

Considering the obvious lack of supplies, she had to work up her nerve to bring the cup to her lips.

"Hmm...? That's a rather gentle taste..."

"Did you think I would serve guests muddy water? Too bad. I'm rather particular about my tea. I insisted that we bring some proper tea leaves when we left. Thankfully."

Shirin smiled as she raised her own cup of tea to her lips. Much like Natalie's reaction and Shirin's proud declaration suggested, it was quite an excellent cup of tea with a refined taste and strong fragrance.

"What tea leaves are these? And there's something particular about how it was made as well, yes?"

"These? Ah, it's a special blend from a supplier..."

Shirin was glad to delve into the topic as Natalie expressed a keen interest in the tea.

Meanwhile, Rusalka sipped at her portion as she scanned the underground bunker that had formerly been a shelter but was currently home for the Brafford sisters. It retained only the barest minimum level of functionality as a place to live, but it had also been sparsely decorated.

It certainly matched the description Odin had given her, but the sisters had been living quite a spartan lifestyle in what she had imagined must have been a pressing and precarious situation that had been forced upon them.

Nonetheless—

"We didn't come here for pointless chatter. We already explained it to the older sister. Do we really have to go through it all over again with the younger one, too?"

Lisbeth shattered the peaceful atmosphere, almost seeming like she was looking for an argument. She was masterful at ruining the mood, but she undeniably helped get the conversation moving, since she was always trying to get on with things.

Rusalka focused her attention back on the sisters, Shirin and Claudia, turning to face them.

"My deepest apologies for my subordinate's poor manners. In addition, please allow me to explain the situation again. The reason we have come to find the two of you as well as the request behind it—"

"Ah, don't worry. You don't have to bother with that. You're messengers from God, right?"

Rusalka's eyes widened as Shirin waved her hand slightly, interrupting her.

That was certainly the crux of it, but had she heard that from Claudia in the forest at some point? That alone would have been insufficient as an explanation, though. Just how much did she know?

"It's hard to explain, but just think of it as if I heard it straight from your head. Anyway, as for that god's invitation…after careful deliberation, I don't suppose you would be willing to accept a polite rejection, would you?"

"…Could I ask you to explain your reason?"

"A father's last request. He warned us not to go along with gods who were strangers."

Shirin stuck out her tongue a little, soundly rejecting the request. And Lisbeth unsurprisingly snapped at that.

"Save the sleep talking for when you're actually sleeping, princess. I don't feel like playing along with your bad jokes."

"For various reasons, I do sleep more than the average person, true, but I don't believe I actually talk much in my sleep."

"You—!"

Shirin didn't seem at all bothered by Lisbeth's anger, and quickly hitting her breaking point, Lisbeth started reaching for her. But in a matter of seconds, Claudia was standing in front of Shirin, ready to protect her younger sister.

"Outta my way. I needa have some words with your sister over there. I'm not playin' around."

"I apologize for Shiri's rude way of putting it, but it's true that the reason is our father's last words."

"Oh, your pops must have been something! What, was he some kinda psychic?!"

The two of them were staring each other down and came incredibly close to each other, but neither was willing to yield a single step. But hearing something she couldn't let pass without comment, Rusalka broke into the conversation.

"Wait just a minute, please. Your father said something about this day coming?"

"Not specifically this day as it happens. '*The two of you are special, so a visitor might come for you some day. But I don't want the two of you to accept their invitation.*' Sort of like the *Tale of Princess Kaguya*. Are you familiar with that story? It's an old tale from Japanese folklore," Shirin explained.

"I suppose my education was a bit lacking, but unfortunately, I haven't. I'm not sure about this Princess Kaguya, but…your father said that you are special? Do you know what he meant by that?"

"Yes, it's rather obvious, since neither of us is remotely normal, after all."

Shirin pointedly touched her own arm, not hesitating at all to answer Rusalka's question. Hearing that, Lisbeth scoffed, thinking she was just jerking them around again.

She had laughed at Shirin unironically acknowledging that she was special, but Shirin didn't seem upset about that reaction. She just looked at Lisbeth—

"—Ah, your family was killed by the pillars. So you became a Valkyrie for revenge. You cared a lot about your younger brother, didn't you?"

"…What?"

"My condolences. I know the pain of losing your family. But could you please stop burning everything around you with the flames of your wrath? It's very misdirected."

"—Nrrrgh!"

Shirin's emotionless words elicited a dramatic reaction from Lisbeth.

There was a sound of flesh and bone crashing as Shirin shut her eyes. But the source of the noise—Lisbeth's fist—had not reached her. It landed square on Claudia's cheek.

"Lisbeth! Stop that at once! Are you hurt, Claudia?"

Pulling Lisbeth away, Natalie checked immediately to see if Claudia was okay. Claudia rubbed her cheek with the back of her hand and gave a small nod.

"Yes."

"I'm sure you could have evaded that or blocked it…," Natalie said quietly.

"I didn't want Shiri to be punched. But I won't deny that she hurt her. All I could think of was to offer my own cheek instead."

"Tch!"

Hearing that, Lisbeth scoffed again. She didn't apologize or say anything else before turning and leaving the room.

"Argh! Why would she…? Major, leave Lisbeth to me. Could you please take care of Claudia?"

"Yes. I'll leave her to you, Natalie."

Natalie was steaming mad as she chased after the young Valkyrie. Rusalka wet a handkerchief with her water bottle and pressed it to Claudia's red cheek.

"I'm sorry for my subordinate's actions… Even after we promised again and again that we had no intention of hurting you."

"Oh, good point! I shall demand an apology and compensation! What should we have them do?"

"Shiri."

"Fiiine. Sheesh, it was just a joke. You're so serious."

Just as she started trying to mess around, Shirin was stopped dead in her tracks by a single word from Claudia. Shirin swung her legs around as she sat on a wooden box.

"That wasn't very nice of me. I don't suppose you'd believe me if I said I didn't intend to hurt her?"

"No, I'm sure you had no malice. But how did you learn about her past? The only people who should know why she volunteered are me, my commanding officer, and Lord Odin."

"Whoa there, you're forgetting the most important person of all—Lisbeth herself."

Rusalka was struck by an odd feeling when Shirin made that obvious correction. However, she caught her breath as she quickly realized what Shirin was getting at.

That would explain Shirin's preternatural abilities of observation. Something beyond just simple eyesight or hearing.

"Mind reading? Not reading lips but actually peering into thoughts…"

"Correct. You're much more flexible than I expected, Major. My first impression of you convinced me you would have trouble with these sorts of things."

"I've had a god come directly to my room, and I fly around in the sky in a magical propeller plane. And I'm fighting monstrous, supernatural enemies to boot… I've long since grown tired of being thrown for a loop by insisting on holding on to my preconceptions."

"I see. Yeah, that makes sense. Heh-heh, you got me there."

Putting her hand to her mouth, Shirin broke into a delighted smile. After watching her innocent reaction, Rusalka turned her attention to the older sister.

"Is this what you were referring to when you mentioned your father's last words and claimed that neither of you is normal…?"

"Yes, Shiri has been able to read people's thoughts from birth. And I…"

"You?"

While acknowledging that they had abnormal abilities, Claudia hesitated to put her own ability into words. Even with Rusalka pressing her, she seemed at a loss.

Perhaps annoyed by the hesitation, Shirin just sighed.

"Sister's specialness is simple. She has far, far more endurance than the average person and impossibly fast reflexes. She can run for two days straight and still be perfectly fine."

"That's…amazing. I would love for the people I work with to be able to learn from that."

"Whoa. Hey, Sister, this major is dead serious about that."

Shirin pulled at her sister's sleeve as Claudia's eyes widened slightly.

Seeing their reactions, Rusalka furrowed her brow, wondering if she had said something strange.

If she was being frank, infinite endurance would be incredibly convenient. There were a lot of things about being a soldier that came down to tests of endurance. If that could be improved by daily training and a thoughtful diet, then their performance would only get better.

"I think it's only natural to have that sort of thought…"

"The fact that you honestly think that means you're doing a job where it's normal to think like that, right? Ugh, all the more reason to pass on it."

Shirin's face puckered in disinterest as she stuck out her tongue.

Rusalka felt that the way she put it was rude, but she could not deny the validity of the point itself. Of course, she didn't want to force them to come along if she could help it.

At least part of the reason why Odin wanted the two sisters so much was surely because of their unusual abilities. But infinite endurance and mind reading... How would that help in the fight against the pillars?

"Could the reason possibly be to try communicating with the pillars in hopes of finding a path to peaceful coexistence...?"

"Ah-ha-ha-ha. That's a conflict-resolution strategy straight out of fairy tales. But sorry, that's impossible. They don't have any hearts. And also..."

"And also...what?"

"——"

"Shirin?"

Shirin had fallen silent in the middle of her sentence. And there was no response when Rusalka called her name. There was a quizzical look on Rusalka's face as Shirin's body suddenly started trembling.

Shirin was sitting on a wooden box, but as she started to fall over, Rusalka immediately reached out her hand. But Claudia was even faster, propping up her sister's shoulder and keeping her from collapsing.

Rusalka breathed a sigh of relief, but—

"This is bad."

Claudia's soft murmur only raised more questions.

Ignoring Rusalka's reaction, Claudia quickly wrapped her arm around Shirin's body and easily lifted her up. And then she turned to Rusalka, who was still looking on in surprise.

"Pillars have appeared. You should hurry and call back the two who went outside."

6

"Goddammit!"

Lisbeth unleashed a full-strength kick on the tree right in front of her. Her leg bounced back from the force of the shock, numb, but it did not do anything to soothe the nauseous anger brewing in her stomach.

In thrall to her rage, Lisbeth clenched her fists painfully tight.

"Lisbeth."

As her fingernails bit into her palms, a voice called out to her from behind. It was an obnoxiously familiar polite voice. Natalie.

Lisbeth had trouble dealing with Natalie, who was both her senior as a Valkyrie and also much closer to their commanding officer, Rusalka. Alma was easier for her to get along with, even though she never had any idea what Alma was thinking, since at least she didn't aggressively go out of her way to get involved in Lisbeth's business, unlike Natalie.

Because of that, Lisbeth stubbornly refused to respond to Natalie. Seeing that, Natalie sighed.

"It's not just the major, either. You should respond to your seniors. Just because you're irritable is not an excuse for ignoring me."

"——"

"Did what Shirin say upset you that much?"

"—Argh! And what do you know about me?!"

Still not turning to face Natalie, she vehemently fired back at the question.

"They're both freakin' weirdos. I can't tell what the hell the older one's thinking, and the younger one is even harder to read. And to top it off..."

"...She correctly guessed your past?"

"—Gh! ...So you knew?"

Lisbeth reflexively turned around, staring unblinkingly at Natalie. Seeing that, Natalie smiled and said, "Oh dear," as if finding her reaction strange. "Judging by your reaction, it's simple enough to infer that much... And even without that, there are many victims of the pillars among those volunteering to become Valkyries."

"Gh, so it was a leading question..."

"I don't think what I said was all that devious, though."

Her smile took on a hint of wry bitterness as Natalie touched her hand to her neatly kept red hair. Even in the middle of the forest, she looked as prim and proper as ever. Even though she had the same uniform as Lisbeth and Rusalka, there was a certain quality to the way she wore it. And that was just one more thing that annoyed Lisbeth.

"Don't give me that look like you've got it all figured out. Like my wonderful senior with her stylish looks and her aristocratic family could possibly understand how I feel."

"If it were impossible to understand each other because we were born to different lives, then mutual understanding would never be possible anywhere or with anyone. And while my concern for my appearance stems in part from my personality, it's also because I believe it is part of my responsibility as a Valkyrie."

"As a Valkyrie?"

Lisbeth's eyebrows arched at the unexpected response. To her, it seemed obvious that a Valkyrie's role was to fight pillars, so what did hygiene or fashion have to do with anything?

Seeing that thought plainly in her reaction, Natalie asked, "May I?" as she put a hand to her chest. "We are humanity's hope, the one and only means to truly resist the pillars. All around the world, people are looking to us. You know that, right?"

"What, so don't let them see us being sloppy or messy? We're putting our lives on the line out here. As if we have time to worry about what people around us think—"

"—The only reason we are able to fly so freely is because of the people around us."

Lisbeth reflexively tried to fire back, but Natalie interrupted her with a quiet response. Lisbeth's next words caught in her throat as Natalie looked her straight in the eyes.

"Ordinarily, the military is a male-dominated organization. All soldiers have the resolve to fight on the front lines for the sake of others, and they take pride in that. And we are stealing that away from them when we fly."

"But...that's just how it is."

"Yes, you're right. That's simply how it is. However, they still have to fly and fight on the battlefields where there are no Valkyries, even though they have no hope of victory. In order to protect the people."

"——"

Lisbeth had no response.

The math was simple. There weren't remotely enough Valkyries to be able to respond to every single battle with the pillars. Their enemy was one that appeared seemingly at random and could show up at any point of the many fronts, and there were not enough Valkyries in the world to deal with them wherever they appeared. This meant that to hold the line and protect the people near battlefields that didn't benefit from the support of Valkyries, many soldiers made the ultimate sacrifice.

There were a great many people who bravely rose to face an enemy they had no way of defeating.

"The reason they can keep flying and fighting is because of their resolve and pride, to be sure. But people can't live on tragic heroism alone. People need hope, too—we are that hope."

"——"

"It would be disheartening to see your beacon of hope looking unseemly, wouldn't it?"

Natalie's eyes softened as she said that. She slipped her hand into the inner pocket of her uniform and pulled out a comb.

It was a high-class one at that. And then she held it out to Lisbeth.

"To start with, at least run a comb through your hair. I don't know what standards Lord Odin uses for his selection, but...with a little bit of effort, you could drastically improve your appearance."

She could have knocked away the comb, saying Natalie should mind her own business. And until right then, she had had an impulse to do just that.

But—

"You so pretty, Big Sis. Why don't you smile more?"

"——"

—a voice from long ago echoed faintly in the back of her mind.

It had been a long time. In the process of always forging ahead, she had neglected to even remember him.

"—Oh? I half expected you to swat it out of my hands."

"...That's harsh..."

Natalie was surprised to see Lisbeth slowly accepting the comb. It was still a rather rude reaction, but given how she had been feeling just moments ago, it was a reasonable point.

"I don't even remember the last time I used a comb."

"In that case, I'll brush out your hair for you next time. When you're sitting in front of the mirror, you'll have no choice but to hold still for at least a short while. I'm sure you'll be able to see something new once you do."

"I'll see something?"

"Yes, I'm sure of it."

Natalie nodded but didn't spell it out for her.

That pompous attitude still pissed Lisbeth off, but she didn't push it. At the same time, the anger swirling in the pit of her stomach had died down a lot. And as she wondered whether that was what Natalie had been after all along, she couldn't help being a little bit annoyed.

"—Natalie, Lisbeth, come back inside now."

As their exchange calmed down, a voice called out from the shelter. Looking over, she could see Rusalka from the darkness of the shelter, her beautiful silver hair swaying.

For a second, Lisbeth steeled herself for Rusalka having overheard their conversation, but—

"What is it, Major? Did something happen inside?" Natalie asked.

"Yes and no. Let's save the explanation for later. I'm not sure I totally believe it myself, but considering their unique abilities, it's best to assume it is true for the moment."

"—? What are you talking about? Quit talking in circles and just tell us."

Lisbeth latched on as Rusalka shook her head, evading the crux of the matter. With that, Rusalka's blue eyes looked down for a second before looking up at the sky.

Even though the trees blocked the view from the entrance to the shelter, almost entirely blocking the sky.

"A premonition of pillars appearing—if they are to be believed."

7

"My sister…Shiri has the ability to predict when pillars appear," Claudia calmly explained once Natalie and Lisbeth returned to the shelter.

Shirin was lying on a blanket laid out on the floor beside her. Ever since she had suddenly lost consciousness earlier, she hadn't woken up, though her eyes seemed to be fluttering.

"Narcolepsy?"

"Something like that at least. I'm not a doctor, so I don't really understand the specifics."

Claudia nodded at Rusalka's question, her expression unchanging.

Narcolepsy was a disorder where someone felt the sudden onset of sleepiness in the middle of everyday activity, uncontrollably falling asleep without warning. That sleepiness could occur in any situation or location, and it was not hard to see how that would cause significant problems in day-to-day life.

"It's a chronic condition she's had since birth. I've been with her so long I'm used to dealing with it, but..."

"But?"

"The rate it's been happening has been unnatural these past few years. It never happened this often before. And the reason is..."

"Pillars appearing? Is that what you're suggesting?"

There was more than a hint of disbelief in Natalie's question, but Claudia nodded solemnly. She looked down at her twin sister sleeping there and gently rested her hand on her forehead.

"You expect us to believe that? So, what? When a pillar is about to appear, your sister just falls asleep? That doesn't make any sense. What does that have to do with anything?"

Lisbeth scratched her head roughly. Her point was entirely reasonable and logical.

In truth, there was no logical explanation for what could possibly link Shirin's suddenly falling asleep with the appearance of pillars. This wasn't some fantasy where the pillars were a product of her dreams or anything like that.

But—

"Lord Odin has made clear that the Brafford sisters are special," Rusalka said.

Indeed, considering the origin of their mission, there was plenty of reason to believe what Claudia was saying for the time being.

Odin had said that the sisters would have a major impact on humanity's future and the outcome of Ragnarök.

"It's hard to believe. But it's also something I want to believe. Either way, we should save the arguments for later, though."

"That's rather like you to put it that way, Major." Natalie heaved an exasperated sigh. But deep down, she felt the same.

If Claudia's claim was true, then Shirin was capable of forecasting the appearance of pillars. That would allow a dramatic evolution in the strategy and tactics humanity could bring to bear against the pillars.

Odin's revelation also lent it a certain amount of credibility as well.

"So what should we do, Major?" Natalie asked.

"We'll save the debate for later, and for now we focus on achieving our initial goal—getting out of here. Apologies, but I must insist that you and your sister come with us. We can leave the question of whether you will help us or not for afterward."

"I suppose it would be pointless trying to resist. All right, I'll go along with you."

After calmly considering the difference in combat strength between her and the group of Valkyries, Claudia raised her hands in surrender.

Nodding at the wisdom of that decision, Rusalka glanced at Natalie and Lisbeth. All that was left was to carry Shirin, who was sleeping, and get out of the forest before nightfall.

"Then let's head outside—"

"No, I can't do that."

As Rusalka started to plot their next moves, Claudia, still with her hands raised, interrupted her.

"I said it, didn't I? Shiri predicts the appearance of pillars. Her falling asleep like that means a pillar has appeared. Not only that..."

"Not only that?"

"—It always means one nearby."

The moment she said that in a low voice, an explosion and sudden tremor occurred, rocking the whole shelter and the five of them inside it.

"—?!"

The blast destroyed her balance, but Rusalka managed to land safely on all fours. The shock had emanated from the entrance to the shelter—no, from out in the forest.

"Unless there is some unplanned artillery drill happening, that was..."

"Respond, Major Evereska. Evereska... Rusalka!"

The situation continued to change by the second, but this time it was something that gave her a flash of relief. The new voice she was hearing in the shelter was coming from Holm base through the satellite phone.

And the voice belonged to—

"Commander Ostley? Why are you sending a direct transmission?"

"Because you haven't made contact since the last perfunctory progress

report. Spare a thought for how it feels to be a parent who sent their kids out all alone. And to top it off, a pillar appeared right next to the forest you three are wandering around in. It's a relief the call actually went through."

"That's… My apologies, sir. I'll provide a brief status update."

Rusalka quickly gathered her wits about her as Alejandro complained about the lack of communication over the satellite phone. After briefly summarizing the relevant points in her head, she said, "The rest of the team and I are safe and uninjured. In addition, we have made contact with our targets and successfully taken them under our wing. Further, neither of them is injured."

"You found them? Got it. Judging from the GPS, you're in an underground bunker?"

"Yes, sir. The pillar's location is…"

"Right on top of you."

Natalie pulled a tablet out of her pack and was working on it while Rusalka was talking to Alejandro. A map of the area around the forest showed on the display as it synced with data from the base.

The next instant, the map was filled with red spots—pillar contacts.

"Th-this is…"

"*Bad* does not begin to describe it. For them to swarm up this much…"

Lisbeth's face turned pale, and Natalie's cheeks tensed as they both examined the screen.

As Valkyries, they were normally not scared of pillars. But that was when they had their Deus ex Machinas. Without those, a Valkyrie was just a normal human.

"They say pillars proactively target Valkyries."

Rusalka mentioned one of the rumors that floated around the military.

There was no way to tell if the pillars had any actual thoughts or sapient intent, but it was theorized that they did measure threat levels and tried to target the most dangerous enemies first. Because of that, their priority list was usually topped by Valkyries in Deus ex Machinas, then jet fighters, and then ground-based targets.

"In any case, it's safe to assume the pillars up there are either after us, or…" Rusalka left the rest unspoken.

"—It's us."

Claudia nodded calmly as Rusalka glanced over at her. She was packing a bag with practiced familiarity, and then she strapped it to her back before kneeling next to her sister.

"My sister and I are often chased by pillars. That is why we've changed locations so often and why we have been living out here: to prevent others from getting caught up in their hunt for us."

"So that was why you were here."

"However, the pillars' advance still caught up to us, as you can see. Naturally, we can't go to any towns or cities like other refugees, since we'd draw the pillars right to them."

Claudia easily lifted Shirin, fixing her sleeping sister to her body with a cinched belt to make sure she didn't fall.

"Escaping the pillars from a position like this will be incredibly difficult without support."

"There's at least a chance if I move from cover to cover. It's better than waiting here to be buried alive."

"Don't be stupid! You think I'll let you roll the dice on such a terrible gamble?!"

Lisbeth was the one to stop Claudia's resolute advance. She spread her arms, blocking the way out of the shelter as she stared Claudia down.

"I'm well aware that we are not going to be in agreement. However—"

"But nothing! I'm not movin'. This isn't a goddamn game!"

"Lisbeth, calm dow—"

"My family!"

Lisbeth was clearly getting emotional, but Natalie's hand stopped just as she was trying to calm her. Lisbeth's face was red with agitation and extreme emotion, and there was a faint tear welling at the corner of her eye. She seemed to be annoyed with herself for her reaction as she continued.

"My family couldn't all fit in the shelter. They said they'd go to the next one. He said he was confident in his legs…because my leg was hurt!"

"———"

"I always regretted not stopping them. I don't ever wanna feel that way again! That's why…"

Lisbeth had become a Valkyrie to get revenge for losing her family. It was just one more tragedy among a multitude after the pillars started attacking the human race. But even if it was happening everywhere all the time, the impact of personal tragedies couldn't be expressed by mere numbers on some cosmic scale.

Lisbeth had lost her family because she couldn't stop them from going back out in the middle of an attack by pillars.

That was why—

"...I'm not your family. Even if you stop me, your family won't come back."

"Obviously! I know that much! But..."

"...However, I understand your wanting to stop me."

Lisbeth's eyes widened, caught off guard by that response, having steeled herself to keep arguing as much as she had to. Seeing that, Claudia cocked her head.

"What? Would you prefer I swear that I'll respect your opinion?"

"That's not it! I—I was just surprised that you suddenly started listening! Seriously, who are you?!"

"Claudia Brafford, a pleasure to meet you."

"You know, there's supposed to be a flow to conversations... Argh, whatever, screw it!"

Their back-and-forth now a convoluted mess, Lisbeth gave up on trying to reason with Claudia.

And as their exchange started calming down, another tremor struck the shelter.

Dirt and gravel fell from the ceiling, and the simple light fixture went out. They didn't have much time for planning.

"Is your little argument finished over there? Have you grasped the situation?"

"Yes, sir. Are reinforcements...?" Rusalka started to ask about potential support.

"Of course, our cute little Sigrdrifa is taking off to deal with the pillars. I'm sending out Conturo, too, since she was sulking about being kept out of the loop. But..."

"But we don't have the luxury of sitting and waiting, right?"

Rusalka could hear a heavy sigh over the phone. Hearing that as she listened in, too, Natalie's courageous eyes clouded uneasily. But Rusalka just smiled at her.

"You don't have to worry. The colonel isn't so incapable of thinking ahead that he would contact us just to pointlessly stir anxiety. I'm sure he has a plan."

"What would you do after all that if I said I didn't have a plan?"

"If it came to that, I would write a last testament resentfully declaring how badly I had misjudged your character and then die."

"I raised a nasty subordinate..."

She could almost see Alejandro's exasperated grimace, even over the phone. But the task force commander who was the architect of Sigrdrifa rose to the challenge presented by his second-in-command's extreme expectations.

"Fine, I got it. I said it before, right? Making miracles happen is my job. I'll dangle a spider's thread down for anyone willing to do whatever it takes to survive."

"A spider's thread?" Rusalka didn't follow.

"It's a story from Japan. Your commander is quite erudite."

"Oooh, you're awfully young to be that well-read. I'm impressed."

Alejandro whistled at Claudia's answer before turning his attention to Natalie.

"Chase, do you have the tablet out? Heyman is sending you a map of that bunker. It's quite old, but there's no mistaking it's the same one."

"—I've received it. The floor plan is... Is this...a back door?"

Shock took hold of Natalie as she checked the tablet. Rusalka peered over her shoulder. There was a passage that was highlighted in a different color on the floor plan.

"A route aside from the standard entrance that passes underground and comes out on the other side of the forest?"

"There's the question of how well it's held up, given it's a bunker that's been abandoned for decades. But either way, it has to be better than just sitting under the bombardment where you are right now."

"—Understood. We'll use this route and escape the bunker."

Confirming the route Alejandro sent them, Rusalka immediately heeded the order. Finding where they were on the map, she soon found the hidden passage's entrance. After equipping only what she could easily carry, she turned to Natalie and Lisbeth.

"As you heard, we're going to escape the underground. We'll move in formation with the two of them at the center. I'll take point. You cover the rear, Lisbeth. Natalie, you stay in the center and watch our flanks."

"Yes, ma'am."

"Aye, ma'am."

Confirming their formation, neither Natalie nor Lisbeth had a complaint. Nodding at their responses, Rusalka walked over to Claudia, who had a dubious look on her face.

"As you heard, Claudia, our plan is to use the passage here to reach the other end of the forest. I know you may have reservations, but—"

"Right now, it is best to go along with what you say. I won't mistake my priorities. I'll be counting on you."

"…Thank you."

Rusalka silently adjusted her evaluation of Claudia with that response.

Claudia could be quite hardheaded when she wanted to be, but that did not really do her justice. Ultimately, it was clear from her reaction that she had undergone some sort of military education. And then there was the technique she had used to send Lisbeth flying. There were lots of little things about her that raised curious questions.

"We'll save those questions for once we are out of this."

"Rusalka, Sigrdrifa is going to engage soon. I'm sure you're lonely, but I can't just hang around chatting with you, either. And…"

"The passage goes even deeper belowground, meaning the satellite phone will lose signal and we won't be able to communicate at all soon. I understand. Good luck."

"You really don't know how to be cute at all. Get back here safe and sound."

With that, the call ended, and Rusalka put the phone back in her backpack. Then, looking at the others in the room, she spoke up again.

"We'll be entering the underground passage now. It's an old passage, so there is a danger of cave-ins… If it does collapse, though, at least we'll be saved the time and cost of a burial."

"Hey, that's not funny!"

Rusalka's dark joke was met by a loud shout from Lisbeth. Claudia's eyes widened, while Natalie clapped her hands.

"Yes, yes. I'm sure Claudia is shocked, too. You should be a bit more considerate of the time and place when you want to try and raise our spirits, Major… Have a bit more awareness of how you talk before trying something like that again."

"I thought that was a good one…"

She had been intending to soothe everyone's nerves some, but surprisingly, it had not gone quite as intended.

As she reflected on that, Rusalka broke down the dirt wall hiding the entrance to the passage. Shortly, a steel door appeared, and on the other side was a dark passage.

"No surprise that the electricity is kaput. Flashlights out. Watch your heads. And, Claudia, about your sister…"

"I'll carry her. I've always done this."

Hearing that confident response, Rusalka decided to trust in her supposed monstrous endurance.

"You focus on protectin' that sister of yours. As for you, well, we can cover your ass, at least."

"Yes, I'll be counting on you, Lisbeth."

With that, the group stepped into the passage.

——As they made their escape from the underground shelter, the battle in the sky began.

Chapter 3
The Cataclysmic Secondary Pillar

1

——Alma Conturo immediately reacted to the siren going off.

Bolting from her seat, she was out of the mess hall before anyone else. She was small and slender, but she never skipped out on training runs, and her speed was not to be trifled with.

She was running at full tilt to take down more enemies faster than anyone else—

It was often missed due to her childish appearance and usual flat tone, but Alma was particularly motivated to fight the pillars, even among all the Valkyries in Sigrdrifa.

In fact, Alma thought of her Deus ex Machina's overkill offensive power as a manifestation of her rage at the pillars.

The reason she had become a Valkyrie was the not-unusual desire for revenge. But in her case, unlike Lisbeth, what she had lost was not family or a homeland.

She wanted revenge for a friend from school.

A friend whom she had not spoken with much, whom she had never once hung out with outside of school. Just a friend from a school where she had studied abroad. A school filled with totally normal boys and girls who spent their days thinking about their studies and clubs and sports and first loves.

With the disastrous appearance of the pillars, those schoolmates had had their youth utterly and mercilessly shattered and ruined.

The only reason Alma had not died herself was because her small size had allowed her to fit snugly into the very back of the gymnasium's storage room, and that little corner of the building just so happened not to get squashed. It was nothing but random chance.

And that random chance had been the line separating life and death, leaving Alma Conturo as the only survivor.

At the time, she had been grateful to her friend, who had pushed her all the way to the back, since she was so small. But she was also bitter about being the only one to make it out alive.

She didn't fight out of gratitude to that friend, though. Nor was it because of a grudge at being the sole survivor. Alma fought because that precious time of her life had been stolen from her. She had chosen to keep her distance from her cheerful schoolmates, and she had chosen to not join in when they invited her into their circles.

Alma had liked her schoolmates. She liked watching them enjoy themselves. She had prayed from her little corner of the classroom that they would have a happy future.

But that simple little prayer had been shredded in the explosions and screams that split the air that day. She still remembered those sounds, along with the pain in her heart.

——That was why Alma Conturo fought.

"Alma!"

"You're late, Leili."

She was climbing into her flight suit by the time Leili finally reached the changing room. Alma grabbed her aviator hat and left the room as Leili panted.

"I'm going ahead—since Rusalka and Natalie aren't here."

Lisbeth was also gone on the mission, but that did not mean as much to Alma.

Alma struggled with how to interact with Leili, Lisbeth, and the newer Valkyries. It had been like that with her classmates, too, but Alma generally didn't like getting too close with anyone. It was less about her comfort level with any given person and more just outright evasion of intimacy.

In that sense, her relationship with Natalie was special.

Thinking back on it, Natalie had aggressively made a point of closing the gap between the two of them from the first time they met. And the way she went about shrinking that distance between her and Alma was unique and, put bluntly, unpleasant.

She would inconsiderately try to get close; she refused to listen at all when Alma tried to keep her at a distance; and she was always doing things for Alma whether she asked for it or not. For Alma, who preferred not to get pulled into a boisterous group and just keep people and their matters at a distance, Natalie's attitude was the ultimate annoyance. But—

"It's too late now."

She didn't have a reason to push her away, and not hearing her scolding voice anymore would feel wrong.

When Sigrdrifa was formed and Natalie was selected as the executive officer of the squadron, she worked earnestly day in and day out. And since arriving at Holm base, she had redoubled her efforts. And lately she had gotten even more annoying about telling off Alma and Shannon about their improper lifestyles. It made everything feel weird to not have her or Rusalka around—

"—You've got a pretty gentle look on your face, Alma."

"—Ngh."

Alma stopped, and her eyes widened at the unexpected voice and unexpected presence.

As she was going through the passage into the hangar, a person—no, a god—was standing there.

"O-Odin…?"

"You know there's no harm in being a little bit more respectful with the way you address me. If anything, I'd like you to call me Father… but there aren't really many of my daughters willing to do that."

Rattling off that comment, the handsome young boy in casual attire—Odin—shrugged.

From the way he suddenly appeared and the mysterious aura around him, it was immediately clear he was the real Odin.

What Alma didn't understand was why he was there and why he had called out to her.

"What? Ask me whatever you like. I'm happy to try to answer whatever questions my beloved daughter might have."

"…I don't have time now. Pillars just appeared…"

"Ahhh, that's right. Unfortunately, we're always stuck responding to them whenever they show up. I can't really say it's good to always be yielding the initiative to them, but…that will only be the case for a little while longer."

Odin slowly shook his head as he said something Alma couldn't even begin to comprehend. But she had no desire to press him on that point. Right now, she didn't want to waste a single second climbing into her plane and start fighting the pillars.

It was not just because she struggled to deal with Odin.

She had sort of instinctively realized it herself. The reason Rusalka and Natalie were both on a secret mission had something to do with the god standing before her.

"Without Rusalka and Natalie here now, you and Shannon are the most experienced girls. It's natural to get motivated in a situation like that. I'll be counting on you."

As if acknowledging that feeling, Odin smiled as he responded. Alma gulped at his gentle smile, forcing herself to respond.

"I understand… So may I…?"

"Of course, that's your job. I just wanted to give you a little encouragement. Your efforts have been spectacular. You might just become a very special girl."

"———"

She could not tell what Odin was trying to say with his dramatic euphemisms. But deciding to take that as permission to break off conversation, Alma bowed to Odin and was about to start running again when—

"—The decisive moment draws near. Do not make the wrong choice, Sveið. For the sake of your beloved friend."

There was an odd weight to his words, and Alma glanced back at Odin as she ran. But the god who had been there just moments before was there no more.

"Alma! Apologies for my delay!"

Alma frowned at seeing Odin had disappeared as Leili rushed up, having finally gotten changed. She would not deny feeling indignant that Odin had stolen so much time that Leili had managed to catch up to her, but—

"Alma?"

"...It's nothing. Let's go."

Alma shook her head as Leili responded with a hearty "yes, ma'am!" while following after her. As she led her junior into the hangar, Alma's lips moved softly.

"—Sveið..."

She murmured the word she had never heard before that Odin had left her with in his parting message. For some reason, it stuck in her ears, and she was filled with unanswerable questions as she ran.

"_____"

As they entered the hangar, she immediately raced to her trusty plane, which was already prepped and ready to fly. Slipping herself into the notably large plane, she took her place in the cockpit, which sat higher than a two-story building.

Leili and Shannon and the rest of the squadron all finished the preparations for their Deus ex Machinas, too.

All that was left was the men who would fly into the skies together with the Valkyries—

"*—Repeat! All non-Valkyrie pilots, immediately cease takeoff preparations!*"

"What...?"

There was a hint of unease in the operator's voice that came over the speakers. It was not just Alma—everyone in the hangar and the rest of the base stopped what they were doing at the sudden message.

What in the world had happened? The answer soon came from a different voice.

It was Alejandro Ostley, the commander of Holm base and the commander of the Sigrdrifa task force.

Alejandro was always brimming with confidence, but for once, his voice was stiff and tense.

And the reason was—

"*Warning—the enemy has been identified as the secondary pillar code-named Mistletoe.*"

"_____"

"*I repeat, the enemy is Mistletoe. No one other than Valkyries should enter its range. Even the briefest exposure* will *result in transformation.*"

2

"It's begun."

Rusalka murmured this as the ceiling of the narrow passage sprinkled bits of dirt and rubble down on them.

They were deep below a solid layer of ground as the battle with the pillars intensified. They could feel the tremors and hear the faint sounds of combat in the distance as they made their way through a dark underground passage that had lain abandoned for decades.

While staying vigilant against collapses originating from above or below, they carefully made their way forward. Perhaps because of their slow advance, Natalie looked up with a forlorn expression.

"Will Alma and Shannon be okay without me or you, Major…?"

"You shouldn't be overprotective. Neither of them is a rookie anymore. Shannon has a mentality well suited to leading a flight. As for Alma…well, her personality and her plane are not really suited for that."

Shannon had a knack for striking a good balance, so if she was flying, then there was not too much reason to worry about the squadron. And Alejandro's leadership could be relied on, too. The only question mark was—

"…What…?"

"No, I was just wondering whether Leili will be able to fight at her peak without you there, Lisbeth."

"What? What, without me? I'm sure she'll be glad not having me around."

"I wouldn't be so sure of that. When you spend so long worrying about someone, it can throw you off when they're suddenly not around. Speaking from personal experience."

Natalie touched her chest as if dwelling on something. In her case, it was probably Alma and Shannon whom she worried about most. Then again, she was constantly worrying about other people, so there were plenty of possibilities.

"You act like it has nothing to do with you, but you were on that list, too, until quite recently, Major."

"…I'm sorry for worrying you back then, Natalie."

Rusalka still couldn't begin to pay back Natalie and the others for all they had done for her before Sigrdrifa had been formed.

As they were talking, Claudia murmured in amazement as she watched from outside the circle of conversation.

"—You are quite composed, considering our situation…"

She was carrying her sleeping sister while wearing the safety helmet that Rusalka had brought with her. But there was no exhaustion in her eyes. Instead, there was a familiar emotion in her gaze—envy.

"The battle between your allies and the pillars is happening aboveground, right? And yet, the three of you are so calm. Is it because you simply trust them that much?"

"Ha! It's not anything that… Mrgh!"

"Yes, yes indeed! The Valkyries fighting out there are from our squadron. It's the strongest squadron in all of Europe—no, the entire world."

Natalie covered Lisbeth's mouth as she gave her appraisal of Sigrdrifa. The world's strongest was a bit of a heavy title to bear, but all things considered, it was correct.

Naturally, that was only true because Amy was no longer flying.

"The world's strongest…"

"Ummm, from your response, do you perchance have an interest in Valkyries?"

Claudia averted her eyes at Natalie's pointed question. A few moments of silence followed before she slowly started to respond.

"I do. I feel indignant, too. There hasn't been a night I haven't questioned whether it was right for me to keep running away when so many people were out there fighting."

"Huh? Whaddaya mean? In that case, why not just volunteer?"

"…Were it not for Father's last words, I'm sure I would have."

Lisbeth's cheeks twisted as Claudia responded quietly. The other Valkyries glanced at one another as they recalled the conversation from before Shirin fell asleep. Then Rusalka decided to speak up.

"You said the reason you refused our request was because of your father's final words, but…"

"As Shiri mentioned before… To the best of our ability, we are trying to live in accordance with his wishes. That's why." Claudia looked at the three of them. "I can't—"

"It's just 'to the best of our ability,' though, right? If you want to do something, why not just do it?"

As Claudia tried to reject them, Lisbeth interrupted. She looked away in annoyance, focusing her attention on the path they had come down.

"I can understand wanting to do what your dad asked. But you're the one living your life. You should be making your own choices."

"...You mentioned you lost your family, but..."

"What would they think if they knew I was fighting? No clue. Even in a dream, I doubt my parents or my brother would have been able to imagine me like this. But I'm the one who decided to fight. Me."

The intensity gradually increased as Lisbeth's words grew more forceful.

But her intense position wasn't simply due to the pure quest for revenge that had led many Valkyries to take up arms and fight back.

Lisbeth was not fighting for her family or because she hated the pillars. She was fighting to fill the gaping hole in her heart.

"You think I'll let those pillars sully my family's memory any more than they already have?"

Lives were lost. As far as Lisbeth was concerned, that was all there was to say. But she refused to let them steal anything else. Her revenge was keeping the pillars from being connected to her family any more than they already were.

——That was how Lisbeth Crown chose to live as a Valkyrie.

"...I should apologize."

"Huh?"

After hearing Lisbeth's story, Claudia gave an unexpected response. Lisbeth was left in shock as Claudia looked her in the eyes.

"I mistook you to be far more thoughtless than that."

"You call that an apology?!"

"I intended it as an apology..."

"Agh, fine. I got it. I'll just count the thought, then."

Lisbeth waved her hand, accepting Claudia's apology. She had finally learned how to deal with Claudia, who clearly bore her no malice.

"If it's not too rude, may I ask why it is you fight?"

Perhaps because Lisbeth's story had left a deep impression on her, Claudia turned her interest to Rusalka and Natalie.

Considering Odin's request, Rusalka thought about picking something that sounded good, but—

"I was a soldier before the war with the pillars began. This is just an extension of that for me..."

"Major...don't you think there's a little bit more you could share?"

"I'm not good at spinning tales or telling stories. It would be dishonest to why I serve."

And also because she didn't want to be even slightly insincere. It almost felt like Claudia was peering right into her heart with her straightforward gaze. It was eerily similar to what it had been like to be face-to-face with Amy—in that regard at least, the similarity extended beyond just appearances.

"If the major is going to be like that, then I suppose my situation would be the one most comparable to your concerns. My father and indeed my whole family were dead set against me becoming a Valkyrie."

Natalie sighed a little before picking up where Rusalka had trailed off. She lowered her green eyes as she twirled her finger in her red hair.

"I come from a distinguished family, and they were strongly against their only child becoming a Valkyrie. They were insistent that there were any number of other ways in which I could contribute to humanity."

"I think it's only natural your family would feel that way. So then, why?" Claudia asked.

"Shame."

"Shame..."

Claudia's brow arched at Natalie's simple answer. Natalie's gaze was focused forward, but her mind was elsewhere—on the other side of the ceiling, where her comrades were fighting.

"Shame is what led me to this place. A belief that merely averting one's eyes to an ability to fight out of personal concern is something wholly different from the agony experienced by those who are truly powerless and lack any means to fight."

"———"

"That is simply my opinion, however."

Natalie did not intend to force her values onto Claudia, who had fallen silent.

She would not berate someone who was in a different position from herself or label them a coward or shameless. She simply hadn't been able to endure the shame she had personally felt. That was all.

"But all three of you are of the same opinion."

"What? How the hell do you figure that…?" All Lisbeth had heard was totally different stories.

"—All of you decided for yourselves."

To kill enemies out of duty as a soldier, out of a sense of shame—they all had their own words to describe their motivation, but even so.

Claudia was right: They all had that one thing in common. In the most important sense, they had not become Valkyries—they had chosen to be Valkyries, and they continued to choose to fly and fight at every opportunity.

"Whatever the decision, we will respect your choice."

"You have my gratitude."

Claudia nodded deeply at Rusalka's words.

There was nothing else to say beyond that, at least not to the extent that Rusalka could bring herself to. The twins would have to talk among themselves and Alejandro and the IPO.

"—Hey! There's the exit!"

As Rusalka was thinking that, Lisbeth's triumphant shout reached her ears.

There was a door partially hidden by soil at the end of the passage, where she was pointing. Hidden from the outside and abandoned for so long, it was well within expectations that it might be blocked by collapsed dirt, but—

"—I'll break through."

With that, Rusalka stepped forward, and she unleashed a heavy kick against the door.

When she struck the steel door with the bottom of her heavy boots, the door warped from the impact. A ray of light shone in from the outside where the door had pulled away from the frame. For the first time in a long time, fresh air poured in from outside.

"Whoa… That's the major's gorilla kick for you…!"

"We can hear you, Lisbeth! Please stop treating the major like a gorilla! And do gorillas even kick?!"

"Calm down, both of you. You can save the debates for whether I'm a gorilla or not for afterward."

Rusalka put her subordinates' debate aside for the moment. The door had not fully given in from a single kick. Rusalka was steadying herself for a second kick when—

"No, please feel free to continue!"

Another pair of legs moved in front of Rusalka, and a long leg thrust into the warped door.

Claudia's kick delivered a monstrous amount of energy even as she stood there carrying her sister. With that single blow, the door that had stood vigil for all those decades finally gave up the ghost, earning an honorary double promotion for falling in the line of duty.

The door flew open from the kick, letting in sunlight and a breeze. Relishing their first taste of fresh air in quite a while, they started to leave the tunnel—

"—!"

The moment they stepped out into the light, they were greeted by a cool forest breeze and a thunderous explosion right overhead.

Looking up, they could see a familiar spectacle unfolding in the sky.

In the distance, on the other side of the forest, was a column of light and lots of small pillars flitting all around it. And dancing through the sky, taking those pillars on, was Sigrdrifa.

And facing them head-on was—

"—Major! You mustn't!"

The moment her eyes focused on the scene, Rusalka's body was forcefully pulled backward— No, it was not just Rusalka; it was Lisbeth and the Brafford sisters, too.

And the one who had pulled them was Natalie, who had been the first to grasp what was going on in the sky.

She had grabbed Rusalka and the rest by the arms and shoulders and forcibly dragged them back into the tunnel. Lisbeth started to complain about it just as a flash of light scorched the skies.

The blinding light washed out the entrance to the tunnel as well as the entire forest itself.

3

——The cataclysmic secondary pillar, Mistletoe.

Its existence was first confirmed immediately after the original Sigrdrifa, built around the First, was wiped out, when all humanity had faced their darkest hour.

Having lost their strongest weapon against the pillars, that secondary started rampaging across the lands, causing massive damage wherever it went, adding insult and further injury to an already grievous wound.

After that, the third generation of Valkyries was deployed after a basic crash course training, allowing humanity to just barely hold the line.

During that ensuing chaos, Mistletoe disappeared, and sightings of the infamous secondary had ceased for several months. But reports of sightings began again in the Schleswig region, and the newly formed Sigrdrifa had been ordered to relocate there to take it out.

And—

"—Major Evereska! Can you hear this, Major?!"

Light blinded her as the shock wave rattled her, almost wrenching her consciousness from her.

Rusalka blinked over and over, but the world was still white as she reached her hand to her back, groping for the satellite phone before finally getting ahold of it.

The voice she heard was different from the previous one, but it was a familiar voice—her personal operator.

"...This is Evereska. I can hear you, Michelle."

"—! Are you uninjured, Major?"

"That's probably a little debatable. It seems a stray shot landed near the underground bunker, considering the entrance was blown away."

She still couldn't see properly, but from the ringing in her ears, she could guess what had happened. If they hadn't managed to get the door open before the attack, it was likely the tunnel would have completely collapsed and they would have been buried alive. They had been lucky.

"I can guess what you are thinking, but I have a critical warning. Please do not leave the underground tunnel. Sigrdrifa is currently engaging an enemy."

"—Mistletoe, right?"

Because of the blinding flash of light, her vision still hadn't recovered. But from the whirling wind and the tremors she could feel from the ground, it was clear the battle was still ongoing. And it was also clear that Michelle gasped slightly at that response.

"If they are fighting Mistletoe, then that means the only ones who are flying..."

"Lieutenant Shannon Stewart is in command with a deployment consisting of only Valkyries. Deus ex Machinas with their divine blessing are the only things that can enter its area of effect... Anyone else would be transformed."

There was disgust in Michelle's voice, and Rusalka's expression tensed.

Mistletoe was known as a cataclysmic secondary. It was horrifically powerful in its fighting capabilities as well, but what really set it apart was its terrible ability.

Regions under the control of pillars had their very life force robbed by a draining effect. Both plants and animals would die, leaving only a barren wasteland.

But those under Mistletoe's influence had a different fate. That frightening effect was why it had been code-named after a parasitic plant.

"—Transformation."

In a barren wasteland, Mistletoe alone would grow trees.

In other words—

"Beings who come under the influence of its attack lose their human form and are transformed into trees."

That was the unique ability of the pillar known as Mistletoe.

In the past, when its existence was first confirmed, an entire town had fallen under its influence, and thousands of people had been helplessly transformed into trees. In the following days, a soldier sent to investigate confirmed the presence of trees wearing clothes, which led to them discovering Mistletoe's ability.

"But Lord Odin's blessing protects us even from that..."

"That's why it has just barely been possible to confront it with a force of only Valkyries. However, there is no data on what could happen to Valkyries lacking the protection of their Deus ex Machinas. If at all possible, Major, you should..."

"We can't afford to keep hiding down here, either. There's no telling when the tunnel might cave in, so we have to get ourselves to safety. And also..."

Her eyes were finally starting to adjust again, and her vision was returning.

She had been saved by Natalie's quick reaction. She looked around her gradually clearing field of view for Natalie as she thought to herself about how well she always kept track of her surroundings, when—

"...Natalie...?"

She couldn't see her inside the half-collapsed underground tunnel. There was only Lisbeth, leaning up against the wall, and Claudia, crouching down and cradling her sister.

"Major? I can't see yet. What did HQ want?"

"———"

"Major?"

Rusalka did not immediately respond to Lisbeth's question. She was quietly looking around, moving one foot after the other and putting her hand to the metal door, which had swung closed. It was easy to push open again after having broken through it once before. And on the other side—

"—Natalie."

Her voice was hoarse as she saw a single ring of white flowers swaying in the breeze outside the entrance to the tunnel.

They were dignified and in full bloom. Beautiful in the same noble way that—

"W-wait, no way..."

Looking out from behind Rusalka, Lisbeth was stunned by the same sight that had greeted Rusalka. And Claudia looked just as shocked when she spotted the white flowers, too.

The flowers were what remained of the beautiful and proud Natalie Ch—

"—Of course not! What are you thinking?!"

"Ugyaaaa?!"

There was a sound of foliage parting as the red-haired girl appeared from the overgrowth behind them. Hearing that, Lisbeth suddenly screamed.

"Wh-what...?" Natalie recoiled. "You don't have to let out such an adorable scream..."

"D-don't scare me like that! Makin' us think that—!"

"You mistook me for flowers because I jumped into the foliage for cover! I'm obviously the victim here!"

As Natalie and Lisbeth went at it, Claudia seemed unsure whether to be relieved or exasperated. And Rusalka was neither as she put her hand to Natalie's forehead.

"M-Major...?!"

"Are you okay, Natalie?"

"Y-yes, ma'am. Of course. That attack was nothing."

"—That's good."

Natalie's cheeks flushed slightly as she nodded. Rusalka breathed a sigh of relief. Then she turned her attention back to the phone she had left unattended.

"Apologies for the confusion. My subordinates and the targets are all safe as well. However, the underground tunnel can no longer serve as reliable shelter. Requesting instructions."

"—Roger. I'll plot an extraction route using your GPS signature. Just a moment."

Rusalka gestured for Natalie and the rest to crouch down as she received Michelle's forceful response. And then she saw Mistletoe and Sigrdrifa, who were still fighting overhead.

——An ominous amalgamation of enormous trees.

4

"The secondary pillar has begun moving again. The battlefield is shifting!"

Alma closed an eye and gripped the control stick in her cockpit as that report come over the radio.

As her plane flew along at high speed, the only things visible in the sky were black-shelled tertiary pillars that looked like flying ants and her fellow Valkyries from Sigrdrifa Squadron.

There were no other planes in the sky at all. And the reason was—

"Mistletoe..."

She kept the terrible, giant pillar in her sights wherever she flew. It was normal for a secondary pillar to be dozens of times larger than a tertiary, but even so, this one was massive. It was the largest of all confirmed pillars.

——The so-called cataclysmic secondary grated on her nerves even as it simply stood there, imposing and seemingly self-assured.

Mistletoe boasted an incomparable size, and the trees that apparently made up its body shared no sense of season or location. There were modern and ancient trees from species that grew all over the world. It was an amalgamation of giant trunks that had seemingly stood for millennia.

And befitting its overwhelming presence, its movements were ponderous, lacking even a hint of agility. It was almost always impossible to tell what pillars were thinking, but that was especially true for what seemed like a giant mass of plant life.

The other pillars at least mimicked one living creature or another, so their movement patterns could be somewhat predicted. But Mistletoe was different. There was no clear basis behind its attacks, making it impossible to read.

"Scatter!"

Shannon's voice called out over the radio. She was serving as the squadron leader, with both Rusalka and Natalie absent.

Alma immediately reacted and pulled into a climb.

"———"

Every Valkyrie had their own habits and quirks when it came to evasion.

For Alma, who was carrying the highest firepower and was often tasked with annihilating masses of pillars in a single strike, she naturally had a habit of climbing to gain an altitude advantage over her opponents.

Shannon tended to like having a bird's-eye view, looking out over everything, so she also favored climbing, while Leili circled to the right, smoothly adding to her plane's flight path.

Just as the other Valkyries all scattered in their own ways—Mistletoe unleashed a terrible ray of white light in all directions.

The world was scorched white by a fearsome high-energy attack. It was incomparably faster than the bullets of light that tertiary pillars normally shot. An actual beam of light that coalesced in the blink of an eye.

Mistletoe did not pay any heed to its allies as dozens of scorched flying ants dropped out of the sky. Pillar attacks were effective against one another. Rusalka often took advantage of friendly fire between pillars in order to take down enemies that would normally be beyond her lacking firepower. But none of the Valkyries was about to be grateful for what Mistletoe did.

Especially since not every Valkyrie had managed to evade successfully.

"Silva and Amanda are hit. We're withdrawing!"

"...All that's left is..."

"Just you and me. And Leili... This is a pretty heavy responsibility."

Two of their allies were beating a hasty retreat, trailing black smoke. While covering their retreat, their formation was finally down to just three Valkyries, and their odds were looking grimmer and grimmer.

"Is it not rather reckless to continue any further?! The number of enemies—"

"Why not just get rid of some of them?"

"Alma?!"

A hint of panic had crept into Leili's voice when Alma cut in, looking down on the battlefield from her new, higher perch. Leili couldn't believe her ears.

The ants that had avoided Mistletoe's attack were obnoxiously swarming again. Alma's big, round eyes, which often looked bored or sleepy, were currently scouring the battlefield on instinct.

——She had dropped dozens of Grand Slams on pillars already.

"I won't miss."

The bomb she released fell straight into the heart of the swarm.

They tried to scatter, but it was too late. And they had no business fighting her anyway.

"We're the reapers who will slaughter you."

And may the gods be with you.

—With that final ironic prayer, her bomb went off, consuming hundreds of pillars in the ensuing explosion.

It was a tactical munition that could change the flow of battle in one shot, no matter how much the enemy tried to concentrate their forces. Delivering that devastating strike was Alma Conturo's role and the duty she fulfilled without fail.

But—

"Even so, there's no end to them...!"

Leili was right. Even after blowing away hundreds of pillars, the enemy hadn't lost even half of its forces yet. As the flames faded, more black shadows piled in to fill the gap.

"Mistletoe was never going to be easy."

"...Wait, are you going in, Alma?"

Shannon noticed Alma was flying straight at Mistletoe's face, or back, or whatever it was while she was using her highly maneuverable plane to mop up the tertiaries in the vicinity.

"You realize there are only three of us and no ground support. And *we don't have Natalie or the major."*

"If the enemy is Mistletoe, then it was always going to be that way. Rusalka and Natalie don't have anything to do with it."

"Wellll, you're not wrong, but..."

Any non-Valkyries inside Mistletoe's area of effect would be unconditionally turned into trees, so it was impossible to create a battlefield that would be advantageous. It would be different if they could predict its appearance and amass Valkyries in preparation for its arrival, but—

"Things aren't that simple."

They had no choice but to create a chance to finish it in whatever battle it happened to appear. Even if that meant trading altitude for speed and ramming a Grand Slam down its throat right then and there.

"Even Mistletoe will—"

"—Friendlies to the southwest in the forest below where you are fighting! Requesting support to cover their withdrawal!"

Rising over the black wall of tertiaries, Alma hesitated for a second in her pursuit of Mistletoe. Heeding the transmission, she swung her head around, carefully scanning the terrain.

She saw a handful of figures barely larger than specks running out of the forest.

They were currently pulling back to friendly lines, but they were in a particularly nasty position.

She was confident she could keep them from getting caught up in the explosion, but she couldn't be sure that stray rounds from any dying pillars would not hit them. If she was going to support their retreat, it was more important to lure fire away from them than to make her attack run.

But—

"Mistletoe is..."

If she diverted to cover their retreat, she would lose her chance to conduct a follow-up attack on Mistletoe. Thinking of all the suffering it had already caused, Alma decided it was too painful to just let it go. And also, there was something new they had learned from the combat data.

To take down a pillar as large as Mistletoe, humanity had to rely on the greatest firepower at their disposal to even stand a chance. And one of the few weapons that fit the bill was Alma Conturo's Grand Slams.

Which meant she had a responsibility to defeat Mistletoe—

"Alma! The friendlies are the major, Natalie, and Lisbeth!"

What broke her out of her hesitation was Shannon, who had sharper eyes than she did.

If that's what she saw, then that had to be what it was. The ones running away from the pillars' fierce attacks were none other than Rusalka and Natalie, who were currently on a top secret mission.

Just that fact alone was enough to send the scale in Alma's mind slamming down on one side.

"Diverting to support the retreat."

Tilting her stick down, Alma picked up speed as she went into a dive, and then she pulled back up to level out, leaving the pillars chasing her out of position as Shannon and Leili peppered them with fire, like shooting fish in a barrel.

Then Alma left the pursuit to the two of them and picked the area with the highest concentration of enemies, finding a place where the ants were swarming just a short distance away.

It was far from Natalie and the others, the perfect location.

"______"

For just a second, her attention was drawn to Mistletoe, which was still visible in the corner of her peripheral vision.

She had only one more Grand Slam left. If she dropped it here, there would be no way to fight Mistletoe. But she had already made up her mind.

"—The decisive moment draws near. Do not make the wrong choice, Sveið. For the sake of your beloved friend."

For some reason, she heard Odin's warning again.

She was not even sure if it had really been directed at her, but those words weighed heavily in her heart. Biting down on the dull ache, Alma exhaled.

"—Releasing!"

The Grand Slam hit one of the flying ants trying to escape right in the head, easily crushing it just as the world around it erupted in a fiery inferno.

The brilliant burst of flames gleamed like the sunrise come to scorch away the night.

It swallowed the swarm of invaders seeking to turn the fertile earth into a barren wasteland, annihilating them to keep these lands safe.

And as the flames faded and the swarm of pillars turned into particles of light and faded—

"—The pillars have reached their activity limits. All units, return to base."

After Alma's firepower devastated the swarm, the pillars started disappearing from the sky after crossing a certain threshold of losses. And Mistletoe was no exception.

This was the third time Sigrdrifa had allowed it to escape.

"It won't happen again."

Alma pointed to the enormous pillar as she vowed that she would have her vengeance.

There was no way it could hear her declaration, but it quivered as the countless trees that made up its body started sprouting flowers.

Mistletoe disappeared in a swirl of scattering leaves and petals. Alma felt incredibly unsatisfied, as if that had been a direct challenge to her.

"Well done, Conturo. We've confirmed the friendlies' withdrawal. Time for you to come home."

"Roger."

Alma's expression was stiff as words of appreciation came directly from Commander Alejandro.

However, that was not enough to soothe the restlessness stewing in her heart. She would have to get back to the base quickly in order to vent that bitterness.

"Natalie and Rusalka are..."

It should start to fade some once she could meet up with the two of them again now that their mission was over.

Hearing that, Shannon whistled over the radio.

"...That's love."

"...I love you, too, Shannon."

Shannon burst into laughter at her reflexive response, trying to cover her embarrassment.

5

The sun was setting behind the mountains to the west, and the skies were growing dark behind the veil of night by the time the pillars were confirmed to be gone from the area and they had gotten back to Holm base in the car that had come to fetch them.

"Ugh, my head hurts..."

Shirin held her hand to her forehead and groaned.

She had lost consciousness when the pillars appeared, and she had been sleeping on her sister's back throughout the whole extraction, but when the battle was over and the pillars disappeared, she woke up, as if she had perfectly timed the whole thing.

"Hmph, must be nice. You have any idea what we had to go through?"

"Oh my. You might be surprised to hear it wasn't exactly all roses for me, either."

"Huh? What could be hard about sleeping through it all?"

"I have the worst dreams. Because of the pillars, I'm sure. Dreams of world destruction."

"That isn't just stupid—it's got literally nothing to do with anything!"

Lisbeth snorted in annoyance as Shirin woke up.

She had broken the ice to some extent with Claudia during the escape, but it would be an ongoing process to build relations with Shirin. Rusalka was just wondering how that would go…

"Shiri, they worked very hard to protect us. And were it not for Lisbeth, I would surely have lost my life as a result of my recklessness."

"O-oh…?"

"Haaah, you're always so trusting, Sister."

But none other than her sister came to their defense. Shirin sighed as Lisbeth looked shocked. The younger sister puffed out her cheeks in annoyance.

"Fine, then. Thank you very much for helping us. And the same goes for your friends who were fighting."

"*Friends* isn't really the word for it…but I'm sure they will appreciate the thanks."

As the conversation petered out, the car started to slow until they came to a stop right in front of the base. Rusalka was thinking about taking the Brafford sisters directly to Alejandro to report the results of the mission.

"—Natalie? Is something wrong?"

Rusalka suddenly turned back to the car, looking at Natalie, who was still inside.

On their return, she had been mostly quiet and leaning back in her seat, looking a little bit tired. But she roused herself at Rusalka's question.

"…Apologies… I suppose today has just worn on me a bit."

"That's only natural, having traveled through a forest for so long without being used to it. How are you, Lisbeth?"

"Of course I'm tired. Unlike a certain gorilla, who returned to her natural habi— Arghhh!"

"Then let's increase how many laps you run so you won't be tired next time."

Grabbing Lisbeth by the head, Rusalka urged her to reflect on her response for a moment before releasing her and holding out the same hand to Natalie. Seeing that, Natalie looked a little surprised.

"It's an odd feeling, being escorted by you like this, Major."

"I'm happy to do this much anytime. Assuming you aren't scared to take my hand after seeing what happened to Lisbeth."

"Heh-heh."

Natalie laughed softly and took Rusalka's hand without hesitation. Rusalka's expression softened slightly as she helped Natalie out of the car.

And just as all five of them safely arrived—

"—You made it back, Rusalka."

"...Commander?"

It was a familiar voice, and sure enough, the handsome, dirty-blond-haired Alejandro appeared at the entrance to the base. Rusalka was taken aback to be greeted at the door by the task force commander himself.

"Hey, now, what's with that face? Is it that strange I would come out to welcome back my trusty right hand?"

"...When you put it that way, I suppose not, but you just finished overseeing an entire operation, sir. It's hard to imagine you have much time to spare with all the briefings and reports, since you are the task force commander."

"I can leave that to my top-tier subordinates. A proper division of labor is the mark of a great officer."

"A smooth talker, as per usual..."

Alejandro did not hesitate to puff out his chest in pride as he brazenly made that declaration, and Rusalka made no effort to hide her exasperation as her eyes narrowed. She was almost certain he had ditched his work and left his aides with all sorts of shirked responsibilities.

But even so—

"It isn't such a bad feeling to be greeted at the door."

"You've gotten a lot more comfortable with the witty repartee... Good work on the mission."

"—? Yes, sir. It was all thanks to the help of my subordinates."

She looked askance at him when his voice stiffened slightly. But Alejandro looked to Natalie and Lisbeth, who were standing at attention behind her.

"Well done carrying out a mission that came straight from God, you two. It's like a story straight out of legend."

"I must agree with the major—hearing that does not feel so bad."

"It was just running some errands, though."

Natalie added her two cents and smiled as Lisbeth offered a cheeky reply. Alejandro smiled wryly at the two extremes before turning his attention to the pair they had brought home with them.

Claudia was standing straight up, and Shirin was half hiding behind her sister.

"You have my thanks for taking the trouble to come all the way out here. I am the commander of Holm base, Lieutenant Colonel Alejandro Ostley of the International Peacekeeping Organization..."

Fully identifying himself, he was in the process of according the two girls every courtesy he could, but partway through, he trailed off.

"Sir?"

Alejandro had caught his breath, and his eyes were wide in surprise. Rusalka was shocked. This was her first time seeing such an extreme reaction coming from him, but she quickly realized the reason.

It made perfect sense. She had had the exact same reaction herself, after all.

"...Well, this is a nasty twist..."

He murmured it to himself, so only Rusalka, who was right beside him, had been able to hear it.

Alejandro had known Amy. The Miracle at Lamia, his greatest accomplishment, had been possible only with her help.

But he hid the shock that had rocked him with a single blink of the eye.

"I guarantee your safety while you're under our care. I hope none of my subordinates were rude in the process of bringing you here."

"No, their hospitality was faultless. My sister and I are quite in their debt...," Claudia responded as Alejandro feigned calm. "Ah." Claudia adjusted herself elegantly. "I haven't introduced myself. I am Claudia Brafford, and behind me is my twin sister, Shirin Brafford. We are grateful for all that you did for us today."

"So polite. Still..."

Alejandro nodded deeply as he looked at the girl behind her. Shirin was glancing at Alejandro with a cold stare.

"Eep." She pulled her head back when her eyes met his.

"I guess she doesn't like me."

"Apologies, my sister takes time to get used to people. In particular, she has little experience interacting with men."

"S-Sister! Don't go saying stuff like that! And I bathed with Father without any problems!"

"I'm pretty sure that was more than five years ago at this point…"

Shirin was blushing as Claudia cocked her head. For Rusalka, who had experienced Shirin's courage down in the underground bunker, seeing her reaction now was utterly unexpected.

Perhaps she had just been putting up a brave front to stave off their approaches.

"Sir, I'm sure they must be tired. Perhaps we should change locations?" Rusalka suggested.

"Yes, of course. A great escape out of an underground bunker, only to make a forced march beneath a major shoot-out in the sky. I'm sure you must be fairly tired, t— Actually, you seem a little *too* sprightly."

"I'm well trained."

Rusalka had said many times before that being a soldier was a battle of endurance, and she stood by that.

Claudia, with her nigh-infinite stamina, and Shirin, who had been sleeping the whole time her sister carried her, were complete outliers. The only ones worn out were Natalie and Lisbeth.

Of course, both of them were not happy to be in the minority in that regard. As they were all talking—

"—Rusalka, Natalie."

—Alma called out to them as she and Shannon appeared, waving as they came from the direction of the hangar.

They had seemingly finished giving their after-action reports, and Rusalka was relieved that they had held down the fort without too much trouble while she was gone.

"Well now, the whole gang's here."

"Yes, sir. But it is fortunate that everyone made it back without issue."

Rusalka put her hand to her chest in relief. Alejandro nodded as well.

"—Without issue? Are you sure about that?"

"Shiri...?"

As everyone else was sharing sighs of relief, the Braffords, or more specifically Shirin, raised some doubts.

When Claudia called Shirin's name and everyone turned their attention to her, she waved her hand and said, "Ah, ummm, maybe I said something I shouldn't have?"

"What do you mean...?"

Shirin looked uneasy at Rusalka's question. She quickly remembered Shirin's special ability—the mind reading one, not the pillar prediction one.

"What did you hear?" Rusalka wasn't about to let this go without comment.

"*Hear* is... Look, keeping these sorts of secrets just leads to both parties being hurt, so you should probably stop it."

Shirin's voice weakened as she glanced over at the red-haired girl—Natalie Chase.

"______"

Natalie was silent. But her lips were pursed.

"Natalie?"

"...I really can't hide it any longer, can I?"

Natalie looked almost resigned as she murmured that in response to Rusalka.

She turned to the rest of her comrades, who all had confused looks on their faces.

"Mistletoe's transformation process has begun—there's no saving me anymore."

Chapter 4
Gjallarhorn

1

It was almost translucent, with just a faint bit of color to indicate life as it moved.

It was clad in a pale-green light. A tree of life that numbed the hearts of those who saw it. It was like a gentle illusion that warmed the heart and resembled a sapling beginning to sprout.

——Or at least it would have been, were it not for the fact that it was growing out from the center of Natalie Chase's chest.

She was lying in a bed in the infirmary of Holm base with her top opened. Everyone in the room gasped when they saw the plant protruding from her skin.

"...How rude. You shouldn't stare so openly at a pure maiden's skin."

"Natalie..."

Natalie smiled weakly as she closed her top. But there was no one there who could laugh at her joke. They were unable to hide their shock and gloomy expressions—there were just two exceptions to this.

One was Shirin, who had revealed Natalie's secret with her mind reading. And the other was—

"How is your condition, Chase? Has there been any change from before you went on the mission?"

It was Alejandro who asked that question.

Only a look of quiet observation appeared on his handsome face. There was no sense of surprise at all. Natalie shook her head.

"No, fortunately I haven't noticed any overt changes. But I don't believe I'll be able to exert myself like before."

"...I see... In that case, like we promised, this is it."

"—Yes, sir."

Natalie nodded, averting her eyes as her long eyelashes drooped. Alejandro accepted it naturally. But they were the only two who understood what was going on.

Everyone else, Rusalka included, was entirely lost by their exchange.

"Could you please explain yourselves? Colonel, Natalie...what are you talking about?!"

"Nothing of any importance, Major. I had merely reported it to Colonel Ostley before. That as the process progressed, there would come a point where I would be unable to fly."

"What do you mean...? Before...?" Alma's lips trembled as she knelt next to Natalie's bed. She was normally expressionless, never really showing the highs or the lows of her moods, but it was clear how pale she was right now, even with her swarthy skin. "I-it's not because of this mission...?"

"No, it's not. This plant started growing during our first encounter with Mistletoe."

"B-but that was more than two months ago! You're saying..." Lisbeth could not hide her shock at Natalie's stunning confession.

But hearing that, there was someone for whom it all clicked—Natalie's wingmate ever since her first mission, Shannon Stewart.

"So...you really were hiding something... That's so cold, Natalie..."

"I'm sorry... When it first appeared, I never told anyone other than the commander and the physician."

"Why...?"

Alma's voice was quivering as she clung to Natalie on the bed. It was the first time Natalie had seen Alma so emotional, leaving her motionless with surprise for a short while before she started gently patting Alma's head.

"I never would have expected you to react like that for me."

"Ugh, kh..."

"...Alma's not the only one. It feels like I just had a hole ripped out of my heart."

Rusalka shook her head as Natalie kept a smile even while consumed by such a cruel situation. There was something familiar about her expression and the look in her eyes.

That was the gaze of someone who had made her peace with her fate.

Why hadn't she noticed it sooner? It was impossible to not notice how similar her eyes were to Amy's, the object of Rusalka's greatest regret.

"—Don't blame Natalie. I was the one who ordered her to keep it quiet."

"—!"

The Valkyries turned around at the sudden interruption from a sweet, high-pitched voice.

Though there was no indication the door had been opened, standing at the entrance of the room with his back against the wall and his arms folded was a boy—the unmistakable figure of God.

"Lord Odin..."

"That kid...?"

Claudia and Shirin gasped at Odin's sudden appearance.

They were not Valkyries, or even members of the military, so it should have been their first time seeing a real god in person. It was only natural they would be surprised.

But no one had the wherewithal to worry about their reactions at the moment.

"What do you mean you ordered Natalie to keep quiet, Odin?" Rusalka demanded.

"...There is no saving those infected by Mistletoe. Even if it touches the most beloved incarnation of light in this world. From the moment that Natalie was afflicted, there was no salvation possible for her. My blessing has slowed the progression. But it cannot stop it, nor can it excise it. I could not just abandon my child to such unease and fear. And..."

"I couldn't bear to make the major and everyone else suffer... No..."

Natalie picked up from Odin, but partway through, she shook her head. Her gentle eyes turned to Alma, who was clinging to her.

"That's not it. I was scared of this moment that's happening right now."

She had been terrified of hurting her comrades when they finally found out about her fate. And she was afraid of seeing the grief in their eyes.

Rusalka could understand that. If her fate was decided, she wouldn't want to cry or have others crying for her for months until her time came.

"—I'm aware I'm an outsider, but may I ask a question?"

As grief spread, Claudia fearlessly raised her hand slightly. Her gaze turned to Odin, who was standing at the door.

The immature-looking god's eye narrowed.

"What is it?"

"I do not have much knowledge, so this might be misdirected, but..."

"Speak. I'll hear my child out to the end, whatever she might have to say."

"—? I'm not your child, but...this transformation, was it? Would it not clear up even if the pillar that was the source of it was defeated?"

Rusalka caught her breath at that question.

Alma and the others all had shocked looks on their faces. If they defeated the calamitous Mistletoe, the source of the ability that had changed so many people and was even now changing Natalie—

"It would be difficult is all I can say."

However, Odin's response was heartless, refusing to grant even an inch to the small bud of hope that had sprung up.

As everyone turned their gaze to him to ask why, Odin sighed slightly.

"I have seen with my own eye those who have been transformed into trees. They were reconstituted into different beings at a fundamental level by Mistletoe's power. They are already a piece of the world tree. That fact cannot be changed by killing the being that transformed them."

There was frustration and disappointment at God's confirmation of where things stood.

Rusalka had heard the IPO was still preserving those trees that might have been transformed humans just in case there was any chance they could ever be restored.

So for that possibility to be rejected outright was—

"—You said those who have been transformed... Are you sure about that?"

"...Sir?"

Rusalka arched her brow at Alejandro's stiff response.

There was a serious gleam in his blue eyes as he looked to the god. Odin nodded.

"...I cannot be sure. My eyes are not omniscient, much to my chagrin."

"But still, there's a big difference between no chance and some chance." Alejandro clenched his fist at Odin's response.

Meanwhile Lisbeth looked anxious as she watched their exchange. "What?! Quit acting like you've got it all figured out! What are you talking about?!"

"It might be possible to save Chase if we defeat Mistletoe."

Everyone gulped at that response.

In the silence that followed, the desire to hear more outweighed both the confusion and the shock many of them felt. But not merely because they had their hopes up now. It was because it was Alejandro saying it. The miracle maker who stood at the front lines of humanity's war himself. If he said there was a chance, it might just be the one ploy that could overcome the depths of despair and transform it into victory.

Hounded by anticipatory gazes, Alejandro resolutely crossed his arms.

"When someone has been transformed by Mistletoe's attack, there is no changing them back. That's because they've become something entirely different. But what about Chase? She's still herself."

"Ah..."

Alejandro continued, saying, "Her situation is an anomaly caused by Odin's blessing counteracting Mistletoe's ability. In which case, it might be possible to change her fate."

"Only Natalie can..." A heat ignited deep in Rusalka's chest when she heard Alejandro's theory.

Her blood started to boil at the thought it might be possible to save Natalie. Even knowing that it wouldn't help any of the multitude of other victims, it meant there was at least a chance of saving her comrade.

"Natalie, that means... Ngh."

"I deeply appreciate the thought, sir, but..."

Alma was looking at Natalie with wide eyes as the seed of hope sprouted. But before she could finish, Natalie had put her finger to Alma's lips, not letting her finish. She was calm as she slowly shook her head.

"Please don't get everyone's hopes up over nothing. I was able to keep fighting through today thanks to Lord Odin's blessing. That's quite enough for me."

"Wh-why…? You can't be sure yet…"

"I already know how this ends. How exactly are we going to find Mistletoe? We still don't know what triggers its appearance. It's a pipe dream… No one can do that."

Natalie tried to end the conversation, not wanting to prolong everyone's suffering even though it was her life that was at the heart of this debate. It was a clean conclusion that was brought about by her unwavering virtue.

—But if humanity could just accept such a high-minded decision, they would have been destroyed long ago.

Alejandro had said it already. If they defeated Mistletoe, there was a chance of saving Natalie. Meanwhile, as Natalie said, without a means of finding Mistletoe, the idea of defeating it was a pipe dream.

So—

"—You sisters are capable of summoning pillars."

Rusalka turned to look at Claudia and Shirin.

Those who had not been on the mission were naturally taken aback by Rusalka's statement. But Lisbeth, who had been on the mission, also gasped in shock.

Attention turned to the girls as the elder sister stepped forward to shield her sister.

"Yes. That is true. The pillars have been chasing after Shiri and myself."

"And Shirin has the ability to sense the approach of pillars… Is this why you had us protect these two, Lord Odin?"

When Claudia did not hesitate to confirm her statement, Rusalka turned her gaze to Odin. The god shrugged.

"Do not misunderstand. The true reason was because of the great value that sensing the appearance of pillars would provide. But if at all possible, I would want the chance to save my beloved daughter from her encroaching affliction."

"You are a far more compassionate deity than I thought."

"Well now, I'm not sure if I should be upset or pleased by your revelation."

Odin smiled slightly at Rusalka's appraisal. However—

"Please don't go talking about other people like they don't exist just because they happened to stay quiet for a little while."

—a young girl's sullen voice resounded through the room, interrupting Rusalka and Odin's exchange. It was Shirin, who was hiding behind Claudia's back. She was still hiding as her cute face twisted into a mask of disgust.

"It's true that the pillars are drawn to us. But do I really have to explain to you that we're not exactly fans of that fact? I would have hoped you could understand that much without me having to explain it."

"I apologize for my inconsideration in discussing this. Even though I knew that you were hiding in the woods to avoid causing problems for the people around you—"

"That's not it. Argh, that's not it at all. Don't get the wrong idea."

"Wrong idea?"

Shirin continued her emotional rejection when Rusalka tried to soothe her. Rusalka didn't get what Shirin was claiming that she misunderstood.

And seeing that she still didn't comprehend even slightly, Shirin covered her face with her hand.

"I wasn't avoiding people to not cause them any problems. It's because of how they looked at us when problems *did* happen. I would collapse, and Sister would be leaping all over to protect me…and when it was all done, how do you think they felt about us? I could hear it all!"

"——"

"'*Creepy.*' '*Is this their fault?*' '*Scary, scary, scary.*' '*Why did this happen?*' '*Why me and not someone else?*' '*She ran across the roofs carrying her sister.*' '*She's not human.*' '*They're monsters.*'—I'm sick of it all!"

Lowering her arm, Shirin screamed, her breathing ragged.

Knowing about her ability—her mind reading—Rusalka's heart hurt as Shirin exposed her harrowing experience.

Shirin could hear it all: people's goodwill and their malice, their doubts and hatred and blame-shifting and everything else. That was why they had kept running away. And yet—

"—Those eyes, too, Major. I don't need your pity."

"Shirin..."

"As long as I have my sister, I don't need anything else. She doesn't hide anything. The voice in her heart is the only thing that can soothe me. So please, Sister..."

She clung to Claudia's back, pleading with her older sister.

The gifts one was born with did not always bring happiness. Shirin was a perfect example of that. She had been forced to give up a great deal in exchange for being special.

And there was no way her sister, who had always been by her side, didn't know about her distress.

So having heard that pained plea, Claudia would surely reject the hope that they had been clinging to—

"—Even so, I still want to help them, Shiri."

But Claudia's response was resolute even as her sister pleaded with her.

"Sister..."

There was a disagreement between the sisters as the older one looked at her younger sister with an intent gaze.

Claudia stood straight, looking Shirin in the eyes as she tried to make herself smaller.

"Father... If we want to honor Father's wishes, then I should take you away from here. I've always been at your side, watching you suffer from others' heartless words. That's why..."

"Then just run away together with me, Sister."

"...I'm sorry, Shiri."

For several seconds, Claudia tried to find the words to explain herself to her sister, but she bit her lip when she saw Shirin's teary eyes. But even so, she would not heed her sister's request.

Claudia pursed her lips as she pointed to Rusalka and Alma, who was still clinging to Natalie.

"My family is precious to me. There isn't anything in this world that means more to me than you do, Shiri. But family is precious to everyone. They want to help their family, too."

"Then they can do it... They can do it themselves! Leave me out of it!"

"Shiri..."

Shirin refused to accept Claudia's explanation. Claudia was at a loss for how to continue in the face of her younger sister's stubbornness.

So the next person to act was Rusalka, who moved to stand beside Claudia.

She could have explained the logic of the situation, or promised some kind of fitting reward in exchange for their cooperation, or even fallen back on the authority of the military. She had several options at her disposal, but—

"—Please, Shirin Brafford."

"...Ngh."

"Please help us. I want to do whatever I can to help her."

—she chose to just lower her head and convey her simple, honest plea.

Seeing her, words failed Shirin as her eyes opened wide. But her reaction quickly changed as she got ready to reject Rusalka's request.

"Please! I want to help my friend!"

"—Ah."

But before she could reject Rusalka, Shannon also came forward and bowed her head.

It was something that anyone who knew Shannon would have been shocked to see. She was always going at her own pace, never letting anything disrupt her way of life, and it was always impossible to tell how serious she was in any given moment. That was Shannon Stewart in a nutshell.

So for her to be so fervently lowering her head to someone was almost beyond imagination.

"Me too! Please help us! We have to do something!"

"Please! Natalie isn't someone who should die like this!"

Lisbeth and Leili followed suit. They were always like oil and water, never agreeing on anything, but on this one point, they wanted the same thing.

And—

"...Please...help Natalie..."

Alma's eyes were filled with tears. Her cry for help was the one that finally broke through the last of Shirin's defenses.

Shirin's lips trembled as she gritted her teeth.

"Not…fair…"

"______"

"This isn't fair at all! This is dirty! How selfish can you be?! You're all older than us, aren't you?! So…!"

Shirin yelled in a rage as the Valkyries made their case. They made no effort to disagree with the young girl, resigning themselves to her censure. It was only natural.

After all, Shirin was not wrong in the slightest. Rusalka and the Valkyries were being unfair. It was cowardly and despicable.

"…I knew it would end up like this…"

The extreme emotion in her voice faded as she murmured that. The Valkyries looked up when they heard the change in her tone. They were greeted by the scene of Shirin covering her face with her hand as she sank to the floor.

As she sat on the floor, her voice was tearful like a child's.

"…Fine, fine! I'll be your bait or whatever." She finally managed to force the words out.

"Shiri…"

Claudia knelt and hugged her sister as Shirin continued to hide her face. Leaning into her older sister's embrace, Shirin's breathing became ragged, like she was sobbing.

Shirin's resigned acceptance tortured the conscience of everyone who heard it. There was nothing crueler they could have done to a civilian, and one who had been constantly fleeing for her life for so long, at that.

But even so—

"You have my gratitude, Shirin Brafford."

Rusalka had not been able to ignore the expectations they had for her, and so she wanted to at least say her thanks. Even though she knew that it would only be a knife that stabbed into Shirin's heart.

"Major… Everyone… I…"

Natalie's eyes were clouded as she watched the scene unfold. But what was probably going to be a noble declaration of her desire to maintain her humanity was stopped by Alma's embrace.

Alma tearfully peered into Natalie's eyes.

"Please…Natalie…"

She pleaded with her not to reject a chance at being saved.

Natalie averted her eyes, caving to Alma's tearful request.

In a way, it was the same as with Shirin. Both of their opinions were pushed aside by the egos of those around them. And—

"Shirin, Claudia, you have my thanks for your cooperation… Odin, with this—"

"Yes, with this, we have the minimum required pieces to carry out your proposal."

Odin responded in the affirmative to Alejandro's question.

The god touched the patch covering his right eye as he focused his one remaining eye on the two sisters, who seemed to be holding on to each other for dear life. To Rusalka, it looked almost like she could see a lonely hint of nostalgia in his eye.

That said, it was unclear why he would look at the Brafford sisters like that.

Before she could ask him about it, Odin spread his crossed arms.

"Here we have gathered all my daughters who have sworn to help! Out there lies the pillar of light, Mistletoe, a monster that would kill even a child of light! By slaying it, you may gain the chance to save your sister! Then there is no choice but to face it in battle! Naught now but to lay it low! I shall lend my strength to my daughters who wish to take up the sword!"

As Odin spoke sonorously, he exuded an overpowering aura that could only come from a true god. As the people in the room stiffened under the swelling tension, he continued.

"The time has come to restore the horn of battle possessed by the Shining God—Gjallarhorn!"

2

"What is Gjallarhorn?"

They had left Alma with Natalie in the hospital room and moved to the base commander's office to continue the conversation before Rusalka asked that question. In the room were her; Odin, who was standing with arms crossed; the Brafford sisters, whose presence Odin had requested; and the room's owner, Alejandro.

Shannon and the other Valkyries were on standby for the time being, while also being sworn to secrecy about everything that had been said in the hospital room. And—

"I would like an explanation that actually makes sense. Both in regard to them and in regard to Mistletoe."

"You've quite the scary look on your face, Rusalka. It's almost like you're staring down an enemy."

"In my experience, allies who cause problems by hiding things can be far more dangerous than any enemy."

It was a truly arrogant way to address a god, but Rusalka was intentionally choosing an aggressive tone. Hearing that, Odin flashed a smile at her.

"Admirable. Concerned for others even if it means provoking my displeasure? You've grown into the role of squadron leader quite well. I suppose this could also be considered the fruits of your training, Alejandro?"

"Give me a break. That's just how she is naturally. The credit for her growth is all hers. All I've done for her is just keep being my same great self."

"I was on the verge of having a change of heart about you, but you dashed my hopes in the second half, sir."

Alejandro could only scratch his head in response to Rusalka's stiff comment. But then his expression turned serious as he shifted his blue eyes to the Brafford sisters.

"I didn't have a chance to confirm with you, Odin, but these two..."

"Your guess is correct. It's easy enough to tell at a glance, I imagine. They are my daughters."

"...Again?"

Odin shrugged as Alejandro sighed in equal parts exasperation and frustration. However, the one who felt that most was Rusalka, who found herself out of the loop yet once more.

"Please explain yourself, Commander. What sort of tricks are you and Lord Odin plotting?"

"Tricks? What a terrible way to put it. And the one plotting things is the god over there. I'm a victim here, too... Particularly when it comes to them."

Alejandro jerked his chin in the direction of the Brafford sisters. Seeing that, Claudia, who was still holding her sister, spoke up.

"Apologies, but Shiri…my sister…has already agreed to help you. And I plan to support her as well. However, there is something I would like to confirm."

"What?" Odin asked.

"What exactly is it that you would have us do? We naturally draw pillars to us. So are you planning to just have us stand around outside?"

"Stand around? Not at all! And you seem to be suffering a slight misunderstanding, Claudia."

Odin ostentatiously clapped his hands at her question. His eye opened wide with a hint of excitement as he took a step toward Claudia, who instinctively pulled back ever so slightly. And as she struggled to decide on how she should respond, Odin put his slender finger under her chin, tilting her head up.

"My lovely daughter, you have beautiful eyes."

"…I'm honored by your praise, but I am not your daughter."

"So cold. But as I said, you are misunderstanding something. You seem to be under the impression that the pillars are drawn to you and your sister, but that is mistaken."

"What?"

Claudia's eyes widened at the totally unexpected response even as Odin maintained his grip on her chin. Odin turned his gaze to Shirin. She trembled and shrank back as the god's eye focused on her.

"—Ah."

"You've been a bad child. Have you been deceiving Claudia all this time? The sister who has always protected you and to whose love you cling?"

"N-no… I—I…"

Shirin's eyes widened as she shook her head violently in denial.

Ever since she had met Odin, Shirin had been shrinking back in fear, constantly betraying the impression she had made when Rusalka and the other Valkyries first met her out in the woods.

Which was the real her? No, regardless of which one might be real, it was clear to see which was the least painful for her to live as.

"Odin, please don't pointlessly torture her. What are you trying to say?" Rusalka was curt.

"It's simple. The pillars are not after the two of them. They are only after Shirin. And she has known that all along. The only one who didn't know was Claudia."

Shirin's expression froze at Odin's sudden reveal. Alejandro and Rusalka were both shocked. And naturally Claudia, who had had the truth hidden from her all along, was no different.

"Shiri? Is that true?"

"Ah… N-no… I…"

"…So it is true."

From Shirin's reaction, Claudia could tell immediately. Then she closed her eyes and exhaled slightly.

"I finally understand what Father meant. He told me to protect you."

Their father seemingly knew something about their unusual situation, and remembering his words, Claudia came to an acceptance in her heart.

And having reached that acceptance, she opened her eyes and looked directly at Odin.

"Lord Odin, I've heard that you choose Valkyries and grant them your divine blessing. Is that true?"

"Yes, that's true. I welcome those who have the natural disposition as one of my daughters and grant them my blessing along with wings with which to fight."

"Do I have what it takes to become a Valkyrie?"

"—!"

She held a hand to her chest as she posed that question to Odin. Shirin was aghast when she heard it, but Claudia ignored her sister's reaction as she pressed on.

"My family…my father and grandfather were both pilots. I don't know how much of that runs through my veins, but I believe I may at least have some aptitude for flying. I may even be able to make use of my experience riding with Father in a small plane long ago. And I have always loved looking up at the sky."

"The contents of your sales pitch aside…your determination is clear. And you need not worry, Claudia. I've known all along that you have the potential to be a Valkyrie."

"Then…"

"W-wait!"

Claudia leaned in as Odin nodded, but Shirin broke into the

conversation. She grabbed her sister's sleeve, clawing Claudia back as she resolutely started forward.

"I'm fine, Sister! I'm fine! So you don't have to..."

"I said it before, Shiri. Everyone wants to fight for their family. I'm no different."

"—Ah."

"I want to fight for the sake of my precious family—even if I'm a pathetic older sister with whom you couldn't share the pain you felt in your heart."

She had always thought that they were both saddled with the fate of being chased by pillars. But that wasn't the truth of the matter. And discovering that was like a heavy barb buried deep in Claudia's heart.

As long as the pain of that thorn remained, there was no way Claudia's resolve would ever break.

"———"

Perhaps realizing that, Shirin slumped. She looked even more brokenhearted than when she had accepted serving as a lure for the pillars.

Almost as if she had had her only wish shattered—

"What beautiful sibling love. An older sister determined to fight for the sake of her younger sister. Truly, a moving scene."

Watching the two of them, Odin nodded in satisfaction. Feeling an imprudent irritation at his reaction, Rusalka glared at the god reproachfully.

"Odin, to show such contempt—"

"Contempt? Spare me your distrustful suspicions. I meant nothing more than what I said. And Claudia will become a powerful asset in the battles to come—she has the potential to come close to Amy's level of strength."

"—! Close to Amy...?"

Odin's endorsement was connected directly to Rusalka's weak point.

Hearing that Claudia was comparable to Amy, Rusalka reflexively turned to examine Claudia. She was holding her sister's shoulder while meeting Rusalka's gaze straight on.

She resembled Amy, but she was more dignified and wore a tenser expression.

"Odin, can you get around to explaining this Gjallarhorn already?

Rusalka and I have a lot of work to do with all the reports from the last battle."

Not pleased with seeing the conversation stall out, Alejandro pressed Odin to continue.

"It's rude to rush a god. But I'm in a good mood, so I'll allow it. Gjallarhorn is a sacred treasure, something you desperately want more than you can possibly know."

"A sacred treasure that we want… Do you mean—?" Rusalka didn't dare to hope.

"That's right. A treasure capable of foretelling the coming of pillars."

Rusalka's and Alejandro's expressions stiffened in shock at his answer.

The ability to predict the appearance of pillars. That was exactly what humanity had been wishing for. Until now, humanity had had no choice but to yield the initiative to the pillars. Their attacks were random and unpredictable, leaving humanity to fight an opponent that came on like a natural disaster. With Valkyries bolstering the front lines, they had managed to fight back to a certain extent, but even so, humanity was gradually being worn down.

Those Valkyries were still only human after all. They could not avoid fatigue and attrition. No matter how hard they tried, it was impossible to effectively protect civilians from the first strike of a pillar attack, and faced with that unchanging situation, their will to fight gradually broke down.

"This whole war will change dramatically. If Shirin is willing to help."

The vast majority of Valkyries were suffering that gradual erosion of their spirits, and Rusalka was no different. She gulped as Odin's words toyed with that raw layer of her emotions. Her next words were halting and tentative.

"With Shirin Brafford's help… Is it somehow related to the way pillars are drawn to her and how she falls asleep when they appear?"

"More precisely, the pillars are being drawn to her as a side effect of her ability to sense their presence. They don't want to end up at a disadvantage. So…"

"They are preemptively attacking in order to crush any possible advantage we might get."

Odin smiled as Rusalka reached the correct conclusion. If his explanation was true, then it would certainly explain why the pillars had chased after Shirin so tenaciously. And also—

"It means there was something gained by your long and difficult flight," Odin said.

"If we...no, if Shiri was to die, then this sacred treasure would become irretrievable."

"Yes. As painful as it is to say, that is the truth of the matter."

Whether that made up for their suffering was another story, but it meant that there had been more gained by their flight than their mere survival.

"If you seek a greater meaning than that, then there is no choice but to save all of humanity."

Claudia looked to Odin as he said that.

"And thus, Gjallarhorn?"

"And thus, Gjallarhorn."

Odin confirmed Claudia's question. Then he shrugged his slender shoulders and glanced around the room.

"If Gjallarhorn is restored, the tides of war will shift dramatically. However, there is not much time left for Natalie. Your subordinates should focus their efforts on preparing to defeat Mistletoe."

"However, even with Shirin, there's no guarantee Mistletoe will actually appear..." Rusalka didn't see a clear way forward.

"No, you needn't worry about that. Mistletoe will surely appear in the not-too-distant future. For no other reason than"—Odin's eye narrowed as he looked to Shirin, examining the limp, lifeless girl from top to bottom with a hint of nostalgia in his eye—"Mistletoe rushes to the light that illuminates the world. Whether that be Shirin Brafford, who holds the key to restoring Gjallarhorn, or whether it be the first Valkyrie, who shouldered the hopes of all humanity, Amy Ostley."

"...Huh?"

There was an immense loneliness to Odin's words that quietly rocked Rusalka to the core.

Ignoring Rusalka, who struggled to figure out why in her confusion, Odin stepped toward the Brafford sisters and held out his hands to them, one for each of the sisters.

"Take my hand, Claudia, and I shall give you the wings to fight."

"...Yes..."

Claudia took Odin's outstretched left hand. And Shirin looked at his right hand.

"Take my hand, Shirin. I will grant your wish."

"...My wish is..."

"I know what it is. Who do you take me for?"

Odin smiled as Shirin audibly gulped. And then, exhaling slightly, she firmly grasped his hand.

Holding both of their hands, Odin nodded.

"I shall take these two to Mimir's well. I shall see you later, Alejandro."

"...Got it. I'll leave it to you, then."

Alejandro nodded, and then Odin lightly tapped his toes against the floor. The next instant, light appeared on the wall of the office, and in the blink of an eye, a door appeared.

It led to Odin's room, Hlidskjalf. Every Valkyrie had passed through it and been taken to the mystical Mímisbrunnr—Mimir's well—where they underwent the ritual to gain their blessing and become a Valkyrie.

It was something Rusalka had experienced, and having made her decision, Claudia would surely receive her blessing in the same way.

However, right now—

"Give Rusalka an explanation, Alejandro. It's painful to have my daughter looking at me with eyes like that."

"...You reap what you sow. Don't go shifting responsibility to me."

"You're the one who sowed this seed. Quite a long time ago in fact."

With that parting remark, Odin led the sisters through the door.

As they passed, Claudia's and Shirin's determined expressions were both striking, but Rusalka's focus had already turned away from them, focusing squarely on the familiar man standing across from her in his office.

There was something she could not let pass in what Odin had just said.

"Odin said Amy *Ostley*... Care to explain?"

"______"

"If that is the Amy I know, then it would be strange. She said that she had given her family name to God. The moment she became a child of God, she had become just Amy."

Stoically hiding her true feelings, the First, Amy, had given Rusalka that explanation. At the time, she hadn't given it too much thought.

But that wasn't true now. Now she wanted to know everything she could about Amy.

"As always, your instincts are impressive. You're right. Amy was actually my younger sister."

Now that quest included the similarity between Alejandro's troubled expression and Amy's mischievous grin.

3

"It was out of the blue when Odin suddenly appeared in our house. He had apparently appeared in her...in Amy's dreams several times before, but she didn't believe those dreams at all. The first time I met him was right around the time he started getting impatient and came to meet her directly."

Alejandro gradually started to talk at Rusalka's urging. Telling the story of the time he and his sister, Amy, first met the god Odin.

"We had lost our parents long ago in an accident, so it was just the two of us. That pain-in-the-ass god came barging in, telling me to give him my sister for the sake of humanity. Of course there was no way I was going to accept that."

"So then what? Don't tell me you actually tried to punch a god?"

"Whether he was a god or not, I wasn't going to be beating up on someone who looked like that... I did try to throw him out, though, but that obviously didn't work."

Odin had appeared in their home and suddenly launched into his explanation about saving humanity and how he needed Amy, ignoring their confusion and bewilderment.

Naturally, this was all to make her the First Valkyrie and bestow his blessing upon her.

"At the time, it was about a year after the pillars had appeared... I was an officer, and I could tell just how badly things were going for the human race. But I wanted to do everything in my power to keep my sister as far from the battlefield as possible."

"...That's rather ironic. You wanted to keep her away, and yet, she had to become the tip of the spear in the war."

"Right... And the worst part of all is that when it mattered the most, I couldn't do anything to help her. Not as a soldier and not as her brother."

Biting down on the shame he assuredly felt, Alejandro clenched his fist. His face was filled with an intense anguish that he would never ordinarily show anyone. And the object of the pent-up rage he kept hidden away was none other than himself.

"Let me ask you something, Rusalka: How did Amy look to you?"

"How...?"

"Was she the kind of girl who flew carrying the weight of the world, bound by a sense of duty?"

Rusalka was at a loss for a second as she considered his question. But she quickly found her answer. Amy was not a warrior driven by a sense of duty.

"She was just a normal girl you could find anywhere. I'm sure the reason she was flying was not for anything as grand as the fate of the human race..."

"It was to protect her friends and the people she knew...and her powerless brother."

Rusalka averted her eyes as she let her silence speak for her.

If Amy had been thinking of anything when she flew, it wouldn't have been the heavy responsibility she bore for the world or the future—it would have been her loved ones, whom she treasured most. And Rusalka had learned from none other than Alejandro that she herself was included in that list.

She finally understood why Amy had left Alejandro that message, too.

"So it was because you were her brother."

"...Or so I'm told."

"What? That's a rather evasive response."

Alejandro averted his eyes and almost seemed like he was in agony as he responded. Rusalka was confused and lost as to what was causing that. He rustled his blond hair before lobbing another explosive revelation at Rusalka.

"It's a pathetic story, but I didn't know it at the time. When Amy told me about you, I didn't recognize Amy as my sister."

"...Huh?"

"She told you, right? Amy offered up her family name to God. That wasn't just some symbolic thing. It was the very fact that she was Amy Ostley. In other words..."

"The fact that you were family disappeared?"

Rusalka was stunned as she realized the tragedy that had befallen Alejandro and Amy. Two siblings who no longer knew each other, crossing paths on the battlefield—

"I'm sure she remembered still. At the time, I had thought it was odd for a celebrity like the First to be so friendly with me..."

"...I'm sure she was glad to be able to meet you again."

"...And I realized how pathetic a brother I was when Amy died while I was in the middle of that hellish retreat that they arbitrarily decided to call a miracle."

Alejandro scoffed, his words barely hiding the anger he felt at himself for his carefree survival while his sister was dying on the same battlefield.

Or perhaps that anger had been the source of power that had allowed him to pull off his miracle.

"—I couldn't stop. I had to keep moving forward."

An awkward silence was on the verge of forming after he had finished his story, until he murmured that.

Rusalka looked up to see Alejandro clenching his fist again. An intense resolve now inhabited his imposing, lionlike expression.

"That time, Amy put her life on the line to grant humanity the means to fight the pillars. And this time, I'm determined to be ready to lead the counterattack against the pillars. I've gathered the pieces that have become the foundation of Sigrdrifa, and now...what comes next is crucial."

"Sir..."

"Rusalka, the person I wanted to protect the most in this world is gone. I'm a worthless man who even forgot what it was he was fighting for. But even so..."

Alejandro looked Rusalka straight in the eyes. She was entranced by his blue eyes, unable to speak.

"There's still something in this world that Amy wanted to protect."

"———"

"That's why I fight. Why I kept fighting. Why I'm still fighting."

As that empathic statement became ever so slightly gentler by the end, Alejandro smiled.

It was an almost childlike, carefree smile. Rusalka's eyes narrowed as she felt deeply moved. Seeing that smile, she knew beyond a doubt that Alejandro and Amy were siblings.

"We're both comrades who failed to fight together with Amy. So—"

"—This time, let's be sure not to mistake who and what we are fighting for."

Alejandro looked just a little bit surprised as Rusalka finished his thought.

He smiled again with a bashful mix of gratitude and embarrassment, nodding. But the smile soon slipped away, and he became serious once more.

"If Odin's prophecy is to be believed, this Gjallarhorn is going to change the war. Mistletoe is going to come calling to keep it from falling into our hands. When that time comes..."

"We will have one final chance to challenge it."

Alejandro nodded.

That moment was their chance to defeat Mistletoe. Their only hope to save Natalie.

"You're going to be busy, Rusalka. Odin said Claudia's latent potential might rival Amy's, but she's not even a fledgling Valkyrie yet. We can't count on her to fight so soon. This is going to come down to your Sigrdrifa."

"Yes, sir. I know. I will ensure everyone is prepared for the decisive battle. Myself included, of course."

Rusalka saluted, and Alejandro returned it.

"I'll be counting on you. I'll be using my authority as a frontline commander, though I'm not looking forward to duking it out with the hardheaded bigwigs upstairs."

"That's the job of the commander, sir. Do your best," Rusalka responded. "And also, it's not my Sigrdrifa. It's your Sigrdrifa, sir. The Valkyries, me, all of it. It's your Sigrdrifa."

4

After exchanging promises to prepare for the coming battle, Rusalka left the commander's office and returned to the infirmary.

The planning would be important, true, but even more important was to not overlook anything. As she focused on that, she went to see Natalie.

"...Ah, Rusalka..."

She was greeted in front of the door by Alma, who was leaning against the wall.

Alma looked down awkwardly. Rusalka made every effort to not let the heartbreak she felt at seeing Alma so weak and frail show on her face.

"Alma? Why are you in the hall? Are you not going in?"

"...Shannon is inside right now. I don't want to get in the way."

"I see. Shannon..."

Rusalka's eyes narrowed as she studied Alma waiting at the door.

Ordinarily, she was not the sort of person to stand around in the hall with nothing to do. The fact that she wouldn't leave was because she couldn't bear to be any farther away from Natalie for even a single second.

Remembering how Alma and Natalie interacted when they first met, Rusalka was surprised to see how deeply Alma cared about Natalie.

She had thought they got along well, but Natalie was the only one who outwardly made any effort to interact.

"Rusalka...those sisters...?"

Looking up at Rusalka, who had stopped next to her, Alma worked up the nerve to ask about the Braffords.

It's rare for her to show an interest in others was something Rusalka might have said if the circumstances were different. As things currently stood, Claudia's and Shirin's decisions would potentially decide Natalie's fate. Her question was perfectly understandable. It sounded nice to call it a keen interest, but it was really more pitiful than that.

"For now, the two of them have agreed to help, just like was discussed in the room. Claudia will become a Valkyrie, and Shirin will be helping to bring Gjallarhorn to completion. Lord Odin has taken the both of them to Hlidskjalf for that sake."

"...Odin did..."

Hearing that, Alma's throat clenched slightly. Rusalka furrowed her brow, sensing a hang-up when she said Odin's name.

Alma bit her lip as Rusalka looked questioningly at her.

"—It might be my fault."

"Alma...?"

"Because I didn't follow through, Natalie is... Gh."

Alma's emotions suddenly cracked in the middle of her explanation. Seeing big tears start to fall from her round eyes, Rusalka frantically pulled her into a hug.

Nestling into Rusalka's chest, Alma sobbed uncontrollably.

"Odin told me... Before the battle today, in the hall..."

"Odin? What did he...?"

"'*Do not make the wrong choice.*'"

Alma slowly, falteringly explained what had happened through her tears.

While Rusalka's team was on their mission and Sigrdrifa was deploying to attack Mistletoe, Odin had left Alma with a prophetic warning right before she departed.

With the battle over now and having found out about Natalie's progressing transformation, Alma was dwelling on those words.

What had the right choice been?

"I didn't attack Mistletoe."

"———"

"You were just barely in range of the explosion, so..."

"You held back to prioritize covering our retreat."

Rusalka inhaled sharply, realizing the source of Alma's tears and her regrets. She wanted to grab the small girl's slender shoulders and tell her she was wrong. But she wasn't sure her words would actually reach her.

—Letting a precious person die because of a mistake in your judgment.

Rusalka knew both the pain of that regret and the self-reproach that accompanied it better than most.

"______"

She couldn't think of anything to say as Alma continued sobbing. As both an adult and a superior officer, her powerlessness hurt more than she could begin to describe.

"Huh, Major, Alma? What are you doing?"

"Shannon..."

Shannon's eyes widened when she saw the two of them holding each other after she emerged from the room. But her surprise lasted only a moment.

"Oh, I see." She nodded to herself in understanding. "You have business with Natalie, right, Major? I'll take Alma off your hands."

"But..."

"It's fine, Major. I already got to see the flight leader today."

Shannon flashed a lazy smile as she gently pulled Alma from Rusalka's arms. Alma didn't resist, still unable to stop crying.

Rusalka felt insincere leaving Alma in that state to go see Natalie, but—

"All you were doing is hugging her anyway, right? I mean, I can't provide as much padding, but I can still lend Alma a shoulder to cry on, too."

"You... No, never mind. Please take care of Alma."

"Aye, aye. But me being flight leader is a one-day-only thing. Seriously, count me out..."

Shannon thoughtfully acted laid-back as she gave Rusalka some much-needed help. She would be far more capable of comforting Alma.

Still feeling a little bit reluctant, Rusalka left the two of them outside and knocked on the door to Natalie's room. After getting permission to enter—

"...Oh, now it's the major. I suppose this must be what it feels like to be popular."

Natalie was lying on the bed, smiling, as Rusalka walked over to her. Her expression was normal, and Rusalka was awestruck by the depths of Natalie's mental fortitude.

Would she be able to stay as composed if she were put in the same situation?

"I'm not sure how I should take it when you don't even react to my joke."

"...Ah, sorry about that. You've always been popular, Natalie."

"That's...not exactly the reaction I was hoping for."

Natalie's cheeks reddened slightly as she ran a finger through her hair. Seeing the beautiful streaks of red hanging loosely down her back made Rusalka almost painfully conscious that this wasn't how she usually wore it.

Forgetting herself, Rusalka couldn't tear her eyes away.

"What?" Natalie narrowed her eyes. "Please don't stare... Is my weakened state really so intriguing?"

"No, it was just surprising to see you with your hair down. I don't really look closely when we're showering..."

"If I noticed someone looking that closely in the shower, I would have been quite a bit more proactive in addressing it than I was just now!"

That energetic response and everything about her reaction was so incredibly *normal*. It was hard to believe that an inescapable affliction was eating away at her from the inside of her chest.

"...What did you talk about with Shannon?"

Not wanting to let grief seep into her gaze, Rusalka switched to a different topic. But as if seeing right through her, Natalie smiled faintly.

"Just pleasant nothings. Memories from training together, her future work... I'm sure Shannon will become second-in-command, so I have to make sure she is up to snuff."

"...I see. At least until you return, Shannon will be the most likely candidate to fill in for you. It would be a problem if the handoff didn't go smoothly."

"Yes. After all, this squadron is filled with problem children, from Alma on down... Lisbeth and Leili still have quite a bit to learn as well."

As she went down the list of what she covered with Shannon, it was clear Natalie had been paying attention to each and every member of the squadron. That only drove it home even harder—she really was Sigrdrifa's executive officer.

"What about me? From your perspective, do you have any advice for me on flying?"

"You, Major? From me? Nothing at all."

Rusalka grimaced slightly, feeling almost like she had been told she had no more room for growth. But Natalie dashed those thoughts with her next words.

"Your flying is beautiful, Major… If I was to say anything, it would be to tell you that you were always the one I looked to for guidance."

"——"

"I'm only sorry I couldn't fly with you to the very end."

Rusalka couldn't muster a response as Natalie lowered her head apologetically.

How long had she kept that grief-stricken thought hidden? How many times had she been forced to dwell on her fate as she concealed the plant growing in her breast from everyone? And how many times had she dreamed of being saved when she heard that her death might be prevented by defeating Mistletoe?

——It must have been a living hell…

"…It is love."

"Eh?"

Rusalka was blindsided by the seemingly out-of-place statement. Looking into Rusalka's widened eyes, Natalie smiled like an adoring mother.

"Love is why I can feel so at peace with everyone."

She had denied it with a bright-red face before, but now to hearten Rusalka, or perhaps to buoy her own spirits, she confidently declared it without any shame.

Hearing that, Rusalka felt humbled and ashamed of her own fainthearted nature. Those words, those thoughts—they were inappropriate for the situation.

Instead, she smiled.

"I love you, too, Natalie."

"——"

For an instant, a difficult-to-describe emotion filled Natalie's eyes when she heard that. But after the briefest of moments, she hid what she was feeling behind a veil.

"Then that makes it mutual."

A breeze from the open window played with her hair a bit as she responded jokingly. Letting the breeze run through her hair, she half closed her eyes.

"Please take care of Alma and Shannon and everyone else, Major."

Rusalka did her best to match Natalie's courageous smile.

She cursed the fact that she hadn't practiced smiling enough to be sure she was doing it properly—

5

"—A pint of ale."

With a brusque order, Rusalka grabbed the glass that was placed in front of her with a death grip. She downed the foaming ale in one go, trying to drink away her shame.

She hadn't been able to say anything meaningful to Alma or Natalie. All she had done was force the Brafford sisters' decision. And she was supposed to be the oldest of the group.

"You're drinking too much, Major."

"Yeah, that sort of drinking is bad for your health and for your heart."

Michelle and Roger, who were sitting there with her, both warned her about self-destructive drinking.

Rusalka could only open up about what she was feeling to some extent with these two, whom she had known for so long and were in similar positions—especially when it came to her feeble complaints that she could never say in front of the other Valkyries.

"Even when my subordinate's facing such a tragic fate, I couldn't say a single thing. And pathetic as I am, she ended up worrying about me instead. When will I ever start being like all the people who guided me?"

It almost seemed like simply being in the bar had summoned the images of a number of people in the back of Rusalka's mind.

So many people she had met. Her family and the people living in her hometown, the officers who had trained her when she joined up, all the comrades with whom she had flown through the valley of death.

To Rusalka, all of them loomed so large in her memories. Though she had managed to cobble together a fairly respectable service record, the people she looked up to still seemed so far away.

"When did you two become such adults?" Rusalka demanded to know.

"That's a question just brimming with the passion of youth. Well,

I suppose it's not that strange to ask that in your situation," Roger remarked.

"…Are you saying I have the mentality of a little girl? That seems like an exaggeration."

"If you think that was rude of me, then you might want to consider taking back your question."

Rusalka bit her lip at not-so-subtly being told that she wasn't behaving very maturely.

Roger and Michelle glanced at each other with wry smiles as they continued to watch over the young squadron leader.

"People grow up by dealing with their worries… Don't worry, honey. I won't leave you hanging with a cliché like that. Obviously, not having to worry about anything is ideal."

"——"

"You and the other Valkyrie girls have been forced into a position where you have to act like adults, so it's only natural to have doubts."

"I…volunteered for this myself. And so did the other Valkyries." Rusalka rejected Roger's sympathy.

Valkyries decided for themselves to join the fight. No one forced them into it.

But could she really say the same for the Braffords? How could she claim that Claudia had freely chosen to become a Valkyrie and Shirin had agreed to help with Gjallarhorn after the emotional blackmail she had perpetrated?

"What a cruel thing we are doing."

Without the pride of saying she had chosen her wings for herself, her self-consciousness had nowhere to go. If someone else were responsible for her making the choice to put everything on the line every time she took to the skies, then…

"I wouldn't be able to fly… I'm just not that strong."

"Rusalka…," Roger murmured.

"If I can't say anything to help them down here on the ground and I can't give them even the bare minimum of support up there, then what am I good for?"

She wouldn't be able to pay back the many friends she had lost or aid the Valkyries still fighting, nor would she become a cornerstone for building a new future for humanity.

Those were all the reasons why she was afraid to fold up her wings.

"The girls who are stronger than me—the ones who have a bright future ahead of them—they're constantly being exposed to terrible peril, so why am I still clinging to the sky so desperately?"

It didn't make any sense. If it were at all possible for her to trade places with them, she would do it in a heartbeat.

Amy's death, Natalie's transformation, the Brafford sisters being pressed into service—how much easier would it have been if she could have taken any or all of their places?

"I don't believe in fate or destinies and the like. If you say that you've chosen this path for yourself, then you shouldn't be hiding behind fatalism."

As Rusalka's thoughts unraveled from the effects of the alcohol starting to set in, Michelle broke in with her personal take. It was a logical philosophy that was fitting, given how she always gave her all within the confines of what she knew she could accomplish.

Michelle had chosen to continue fighting through everything, even though she couldn't become a Valkyrie.

"Major, you have certainly watched many people go. There are few active second-generation Valkyries left, and there is no Valkyrie who has flown longer than you."

"———"

"I hate the idea of determinism. However, if there was any reason for you to serve as a Valkyrie longer than anyone else, it assuredly wasn't to subject you to excessive grief."

Michelle's words held a hidden intensity the likes of which she never showed. Rusalka blinked over and over as she digested that thought.

"...I was well aware that I am an old Valkyrie, bu— Owww."

"Whoa there. Don't get ahead of yourself. You're still just a girl in her twenties."

Roger flicked Rusalka in the forehead as she struggled to respond to Michelle. Ignoring their horseplay, Michelle raised her glass and wet her lips.

"I can't afford to stay long and drink too much. Let's get back to the base."

"Yes, I'm sure tomorrow will be busy, too... Come on, Rusalka. That means you, too."

Standing up to follow Michelle, Roger made sure to grab Rusalka by the collar and hoist her up as well. Easily holding her aloft, almost like a cat, he poked her sullen cheek.

"You got to say all the complaints that you've just been bottling up inside, so you're feeling a bit better now, right?"

"Thank you for your concerns… Did the colonel put you up to this?"

"'*Help her vent a bit,*' he said. Though I suspect he meant for me and Chief Technician Reever to take a load off as well."

Michelle shrugged, having realized what Alejandro had been after all along. As someone who spent a lot of time in the command post, she was yet another person who had been run around in circles by Alejandro many times before.

Because of that, she knew deep down that for all his appearances, he was sharp and capable and didn't make a habit of giving out pointless orders.

"Regardless of what the colonel intended, next time, let's raise a glass to victory," Michelle suggested.

"Oooh, well said. I'm all for it, of course. Let's have a toast to celebrate once we make it through the battle for humanity's sunrise!"

Michelle and Roger smiled as Rusalka followed behind them silently, deep in thought.

She had flown longer than any other Valkyrie, but what meaning or purpose did that have…?

6

——From there, time became a blur, passing in the blink of an eye.

Not wanting to waste even a single second, they prepared everything possible for the impending clash.

But they were not restless as the moment drew near.

"I will perform the ritual for restoring Gjallarhorn at noon five days from today—Mistletoe will undoubtedly appear to stop the ritual. That will be the start of our battle."

Odin had left them with that prophecy the day after whisking away the Brafford sisters.

Holm base, and really all of humanity, had little choice but to believe Odin's revelation, given the connection between the Braffords and Mistletoe, which had become clear.

Because of that, the base was completely focused on increasing their readiness.

That didn't just apply to equipment or their Deus ex Machinas, either. The soldiers who would be participating were also busy hardening their resolve.

"—As you are aware, this base will become the battleground for the decisive battle against Mistletoe in the coming days. You know full well the horror of its abilities. On top of that, if a certain god is to be believed, it's not going to be in the mood to retreat this time. This battle won't end until one side or the other is completely wiped out."

The morning Odin's revelation had arrived, Alejandro gathered everyone on base and explained from the podium what position they had been placed in and the mission they had been given.

Even the Valkyries, protected by Odin's blessing, could not avoid being weakened by Mistletoe's ability, and every other person who faced it would be entirely transformed within a few hours' time.

In previous encounters, Mistletoe had chosen to withdraw after sustaining a minor amount of damage. Because of that, humanity had been able to fend it off. But this time, things would be different.

"As we expect Mistletoe will not be willing to retreat, the people at this base will inevitably be affected by its incomprehensible ability. There might be individual differences in how quickly the symptoms present, but every single person here will undergo transformation, guaranteed."

Once the tree began to sprout from someone's body, they were already living on borrowed time.

"I'll be clear with you up front. If we win this battle, humanity will gain a powerful new tool. In the battles to come, having that tool will no doubt make a huge difference. But I will not order you to die here so that humanity can gain some advantage."

Alejandro held up his right palm so that everyone could see.

"—Five minutes. Starting now, I will give you five minutes to think it through. The battle with Mistletoe will be dogged and intense. I'm going to win this fight, no matter the sacrifice required. So make up your mind. I won't blame anyone who wants to leave. There won't be any punishment, either. You are free to choose. However—"

"——"

"Once these next five minutes are over, know that there won't be a single moment's rest from now until we win. I'll grind each and every one of you down to dust if I have to in order to win. Your time starts now!"

Speaking with great force and immense gravity, Alejandro gave the soldiers five minutes to make their choice.

If many people left, it would obviously make things more difficult leading up to the decisive battle. Alejandro likely had some contingency plan lined up, but even so, it would still hurt their efforts.

Silently praying for as few quitters as possible, they waited out the five minutes and soon realized—

"Your time is up. You goddamn fools."

As he made that announcement at the podium, not a single soldier left their position.

No one had chosen to leave. It was a far more impressive feat than could be done justice on paper.

It signified their refusal to take even one step backward and a determination to use up their lives to the very last dregs in the coming battle. There was no greater unison possible than for every member on the base to be united in a singular goal.

"—Let's do this. I'll provide the miracle we need to win!"

"Oraaaaaa!"

The roar that swelled in their throats almost seemed to shake the ground as the personnel of Holm base became one.

And at that same time—

"—Claudia Brafford, reporting for duty."

Wearing the IPO uniform, Claudia saluted Rusalka.

It was a proper air force salute, proof of the pride she had for her father's and grandfather's service records. However, if she was going to be a Valkyrie, she would have to learn a different salute.

And to teach her that, Rusalka and the rest of Sigrdrifa touched their right hand to their closed right eye as one.

"—Mine eye for thee."

A sign of respect to the one-eyed god, Odin. That was the Valkyrie salute.

——Having completed the ceremony at Mimir's well, Claudia was officially a Valkyrie.

However, with the crucial battle only days away, there was some concern about having a rookie join the fray. Even while dealing with that preconception from those around her, Claudia passed her flight test with flying colors.

"Ooooh, wow. She's sure something."

The jet-black Deus ex Machina—Claudia's Gladiator—danced through the skies like it owned them. Even Rusalka couldn't help being surprised by how Claudia handled her plane with utter ease.

It was nothing short of astonishing. Proof that common sense held no meaning at all in the face of true innate talent.

Shannon, who was peering up from beside Rusalka, also seemed to be more exasperated than astounded. Odin had said it before that Claudia had talent with the potential to rival Amy. No one dared laugh that statement off as hyperbole anymore.

Of course, Claudia wasn't only exceptional in the sky. Back on the ground, she exhibited a well-ordered, soldierly behavior that Rusalka would have loved to instill in Lisbeth.

"As a child, I pestered my father to tell me all about various rules and customs in the military. Shiri never had any interest, but I was always curious about Father's work."

"...So when you sent me flying, that was something your dad taught you?"

"You sent Lisbeth flying?"

As Lisbeth grimaced at the memory, Leili's eyes sparkled in curiosity. Her expression a little bitter at Lisbeth having said something she would have preferred not having come up, Claudia nodded.

"Yes, Lisbeth's movements are direct and easy to read. Are you like that in the air as well?"

"Just gotta *whoosh* right up to 'em and make sure they can't get away while you keep going *wham* until you take them down! You don't need anything more than that!"

"That's a lot of sound effects, but it is clear you fight using instinctive tactics."

Leili responded with a pained laugh, while Claudia seemed to react with a sense of astonishment. Lisbeth's face turned red as she exploded in annoyance at their exchange. Meanwhile, watching from a distance—

"Do you really need me anymore with the three of them, Major?"

Shannon flashed her trademark easygoing smile.

"That again...," Rusalka said, rejecting the suggestion that Shannon was obsolete.

"All joking aside, though, Lisbeth and Leili, and Claudia, too...those girls are the real deal. I'm sure you realize that, too, Major." Shannon cocked her head.

Her analysis was correct as usual. Of the young Valkyries in Sigrdrifa, those three were head and shoulders above the rest in terms of latent potential. Lisbeth was rough around the edges, Leili was a little too cautious, and Claudia was lacking in experience, but—

"They will surely become the strongest Valkyries since Amy," Rusalka declared with confidence.

"In that case, I wonder if God will give them some kind of nice name or something."

"Yes. Something appropriately fitting... Fitting..."

As she watched the three of them talking, Rusalka put her hands together, almost as if in prayer.

The battle that was brewing was not something that could be resolved by praying to God. They would have to fight using the information their patron god had given them. That was the only way out they could hope for.

It was the least she could wish for. When the dust finally settled, she hoped those three would be able to smile and laugh together like this again. She hoped they could enjoy a similar moment as the people on the base smiled and watched over them from a distance.

And—

7

"—How goes it, Rusalka? Not getting too tense the day before the all-important battle, are you?"

Rusalka's eyes widened in surprise at the greeting that awaited her in her room.

It was the second trespass she had endured, but it would be pointless to ask how. Locks did not mean anything. Nothing and no one could stop a god.

"Lord Odin..."

"Don't look so bitter. It is only natural to dislike a father who enters his daughter's room without permission, but your room has no cuteness to it at all. It's almost like a fugitive lives here."

"I have to move around quite often, so I have a limited number of personal effects... Why are you here? Shouldn't you be...?"

"Preparing a ritual to restore Gjallarhorn?"

Rusalka was silent as he finished her thought.

It had been five days since Odin's prophecy. The fateful day had arrived. The hour of battle that God had foretold—noon—was just sixty minutes away.

The base had heatedly prepared for the battle, and a solemn aura had fallen over it. Rusalka was no exception, harboring an intense anticipation of the fighting to come. She had returned to her room to retrieve the aviator cap she had gotten repaired when she ran into Odin, who was lying in wait.

"———"

Last time she had stood face-to-face with a god in her room like that, she had been tasked with safeguarding Claudia and Shirin. She wanted to believe Odin wouldn't burden her with an unreasonable demand with the important battle less than an hour away, but—

"Worry not. It would be misleading to say this was one part of the ritual, but it is absolutely necessary. Shirin has requested your presence for the ritual that is about to begin. That is why I am here."

"My presence? And Shirin requested it...?"

Rusalka was unsure how to respond to that bolt from the blue.

The actual ritual to be performed for the restoration of Gjallarhorn was unknown, and it was a mystery why she was being asked to participate, but the oddest part was that Shirin had specifically chosen Rusalka.

"I haven't seen her in five days, and it isn't as if I had spoken with her much before. So why me?"

"Well now, you would be better served posing such questions to her, rather than me. Of course, if you refuse, I won't force you…"

"…No, I'll come."

She hesitated for a moment, but she didn't reject the request from Odin—no, from Shirin.

Hearing that, Odin smiled slightly as he waved his hand. Another door appeared in the wall in a flash of light. Opening it, he invited Rusalka inside.

She wasted no time passing through the mysterious door.

"—Welcome. Ummm, it's Major, right? Sorry about the sudden invitation."

On the other side, Shirin was spreading her hands wide in greeting as an enormous movie screen extended behind her.

"———"

Rusalka needed a moment to process what was happening.

There were many seats lined up around them in the dimly lit space, all facing the giant screen right in front of her. She had not been many times, but even with her minimal experience, she could recognize it was a movie theater.

It was certainly an odd one, though—the room where Odin normally passed his time, Hlidskjalf, which was capable of looking out at every place in the world.

Rusalka had set foot there once before, for the ritual where she became a Valkyrie. Shirin was standing there in a sheer white silk dress, like she was perfectly at home in that divine space.

"What do you think? I look like a proper shrine maiden, right? *'Start by looking the part,'* he said. God's surprisingly lowbrow."

"You've got a mouth to you. It is true I said that, though. This appearance is befitting the values of the time. You need not be ashamed."

"Rather than cheeky little boys, I'm more into the sort who's obedient and overly serious, like my beloved sister…"

Shirin's exchange with Odin was going over Rusalka's head as she struggled to respond. Shirin had her fill of banter with the god before turning her blue eyes on Rusalka.

"—I requested your presence, Major Rusalka Evereska."

"…So I've been told. May I ask why?"

Seeing Shirin's mischievous expression, Rusalka cut straight to the point without any playfulness. Shirin arched her brows slightly, putting her finger to her mouth.

"Hmmmm."

For a moment, her gestures and the similarity of her face almost made it seem like Amy had been brought back to life.

Both Claudia and Shirin looked incredibly similar to Amy, but in terms of their behavior, Shirin was far more similar to Amy, which made it all the more painful.

"Because of that. Because you are the one who seemed the most likely to be hurt."

"—Ngh, reading my mind?"

"Just a little bit. But I would bet basically anyone could have realized that much just now without any special powers."

Shirin smiled slightly as she looked at Rusalka. There was no malice in her smile at all, which did nothing to explain what she had just said.

What did she mean by "*the one who seemed most likely to be hurt*"?

"All you soldiers weren't the only ones who had a difficult time these past five days, you know. Purification ritual this and taking in some divine spirit that, and having to fast, and being forced to smell and drink some super-odd things."

"What do you mean '*odd*'? It was a product from the time of gods."

"Honestly, I'm about to collapse from hunger even now… Sister's cooking leaves a lot to be desired, so I always had to prepare meals."

Pressing her stomach, Shirin stuck out her tongue. Her each and every gesture seemed to project an odd fragility, and Rusalka was struck by an illogical unease.

She still didn't understand why and for what reason Shirin had wanted to see her—

"Major, I'm choosing you to be my witness."

"———"

"If I chose my sister, she would probably be upset, and I wouldn't want that to happen. So sorry, but that leaves you as the best choice by process of elimination."

"W-wait a second, please! I don't understand what you mean. I recognize it's a manifestation of your determination in the face of what you are attempting, but it almost sounds like…"

Her throat clenched in dread as she desperately searched for the words to stop Shirin.

Scared. She was scared. Not Shirin but Rusalka. Because Shirin looked just like Amy had that night when Rusalka had revealed the terrible thoughts hidden deep in her heart.

Shirin looked like a person who possessed a very particular kind of resolve.

"To complete Gjallarhorn, my existence is necessary. I have to give up the container that is Shirin Brafford and plant my foot firmly in the world of myths. In other words…"

"—Your existence is going to disappear, consumed by a god?"

Shirin smiled weakly, not denying Rusalka's conclusion.

Her smile was so frail and delicate—the smile of someone who had fully made up her mind. Rusalka remembered the pain of forgetting family that Alejandro had shared with her.

Shirin's resolve was the same as Amy's. The only difference was—

"The appointed person serves as the connection between the participant and humanity. And my child Shirin has chosen you for that role."

"I'm not your child. Quit making me repeat myself."

Shirin immediately grumbled about Odin's explanation as Rusalka tried to process what she had heard. From that exchange, she had a bad feeling about the word *connection*—

"What do you mean by that, exactly? What does it mean for me to serve as a connection like that…?"

"Basically, me being offered up to God means everyone will forget about me, right? And that's just sad. I want at least one person to remember me. And I've decided that one person should be you, Major."

"Why?! That doesn't make any sense at all! Claudia is the person who cares most about you! The person you should want to always remember you is…"

"Of course I want my sister to always remember me. But even more than that, I don't want her to be sad and suffer because of me."

There was nothing but affection for Claudia in Shirin's eyes as she held her hands to her chest. A loving warmth and tenderness for her other half, who had been by her side through her entire life.

However—

"I…can understand that logic… But then, why me?"

"Because, Major…no, Rusalka…you are a witness."

Addressed by name and then told something she was not remotely expecting, Rusalka inhaled sharply. Seeing that reaction, Shirin narrowed her eyes, and for the first time, there was a loneliness to her gaze.

"As the crazy girl about to be consumed by God, I'll let you in on something. You are a person who sees things through to the end, Rusalka. You will see off a great many people after this."

"——"

"And I'm sure you've seen off more than your fair share as is. But instead of growing used to the loss, you just keep accepting ever greater pain. That's why. I want to become one of your scars."

"——"

"I mean, I'm a cute little girl, after all. If I'm going to go, I want someone to really feel it, to really be hung up over me."

In the end, she slipped back into her teasing tone with a wink. Hearing her charming, painful, selfish wish, Rusalka exhaled slowly and deeply.

It was a difficult thing to believe. Was she really just venting, hoping to enact a small revenge? Did she really just want—?

"By any chance, do you hold a grudge against me for putting an end to the fugitive lifestyle you and Claudia pursued?"

"Absolutely! Our lovey-dovey life on the run was all ruined thanks to you."

Shirin stuck out her tongue as Rusalka's shoulders slumped.

Rusalka had her own thoughts on the matter, of course. A feeling of wanting to grieve and a wish to make everything bend to some kind of logic, too. But she had long, long ago run out of ways to try to make that happen.

And it was a bit strange, but being called a witness…after hearing that, a certain part of her could accept everything that was happening. She was a bystander who watched things unfold, forever unable to react to them herself.

In a sense, that was a fitting role for her—

"—I didn't mean it that way, though."

"Huh?"

"No, never mind. Just think of it as a final bit of harassment from me."

Putting her finger to her lip, Shirin refused to clear up Rusalka's confusion. Then she extended her back in an exaggerated stretch.

"Well then, I suppose we should get this show on the road. I don't want to let it get gloomy with this depressing mood hanging over everything."

Breaking into a laugh, Shirin glanced over at Odin. The god shrugged and slowly stood up.

"Is this sufficient for you?"

"Not at all. Don't get me wrong—I'm being forced to be a sacrifice to a god here."

"It's not as if… No, I suppose being forgotten bears little difference from a true death. I should acknowledge as much myself."

"Oh, looks like you get it. Not that that's enough for me to forgive you, though…"

Shirin closed an eye in acknowledgment of Odin's humble response. Just then—

At some point, an onlooker, someone besides Rusalka or Shirin, who were standing in front of the screen, opened the great door behind the seats and set foot into the room.

"…Commander…?"

Raising a hand in greeting at Rusalka's hoarse question, Alejandro slowly stepped down the stairs. As he descended, he gradually made his way to the front of the theater.

"Wait a minute," Shirin said sharply. "Why is he here? Rusalka was the only one I chose…"

"Sorry for dropping in uninvited. However, I'm sure it won't be a problem for me to be here, right, Odin?"

Standing next to Rusalka, Alejandro placed a hand on her slender shoulder. When he touched her, she finally noticed that she had been trembling.

Odin looked down slightly.

"Forgive me, Shirin. This man is special. He has my permission to enter here freely."

"Even if you say that, do you really expect me to just accept that and meekly say, *Oh, I see…?*"

Shirin was uninterested in this selfish conclusion contrived by those two men. However, she decided to give up on her argument just as she finished her thought. Turning her gaze to Alejandro, she said, "Colonel, is there any chance that you're also…?"

"Well now, I just came to check in during a brief lull in preparing for the battle… Apparently, my family has a distant connection with the Brafford family. I don't suppose that might be reason enough for me to be here?"

"—Ah."

Rusalka subconsciously reacted to that.

It was entirely reasonable to suspect their families were somehow connected, given how similar Amy and the Brafford sisters looked.

However, Rusalka was the only one surprised by that fact. Alejandro, who had shared that revelation, was calm, as was Odin. Shirin too, naturally.

Taking a step forward, Shirin drew closer to Alejandro and struck her pale fist against his chest.

"I'm not some replacement for your little sister. Please don't say such selfish things, big brother."

"I wouldn't dream of it. Amy was much more ladylike and refined."

That was a lie. Shirin's mischievous smile was like a mirror image of Amy's. Shirin stuck out her tongue at that obvious lie.

"Liar… Bye-bye."

"Yeah, take care."

Putting his hand on her head, Alejandro caressed her blond hair. Feeling ticklish, Shirin pulled back and spun around.

With that, she went toward the screen—no, beyond the screen. That was where Mimir's well lay. That was where the ritual would be performed.

"———"

Rusalka could not think of anything to say as Shirin's dignified figure receded. Accompanied by Odin, Shirin walked forward, marking her farewell with the human realm.

"Is there anything? Anything you want to tell Claudia?"

What suddenly spilled out were words that she knew touched a tender spot for Shirin. Hearing that, she stopped. But she did not turn back.

"Don't tell Sister anything… That's exactly why I'm doing this."

That decisive statement was what made Rusalka finally realize the shape of her resolve.

Shirin started walking again, and watching her grow more distant, Rusalka gritted her teeth.

It was strange to see something other than resignation in her when she had finally given in after having struggled against the fate she had been shouldered with for so long.

Rusalka finally understood the reason why—Shirin was going in order to save her sister.

Claudia did not balk at becoming a Valkyrie for the sake of her younger sister, who was targeted by pillars. And this was the best thing Shirin could do for her older sister, who would have to fly in dangerous skies countless times going forward.

She was becoming the foundation of Gjallarhorn in the hopes of making those future battles even just a little bit less dangerous for the Valkyries fighting the pillars. But the loss of Claudia's reason for fighting in the first place was getting things so badly out of order—

"I won't forget you!" Rusalka suddenly cried out.

"———"

"No matter what may happen, I will remember you and your determination. I will never forget how much you sacrificed to achieve your wish."

That much was absolute. Even if it came at the cost of her life, she would never allow herself to forget that.

Even if Shirin was forgotten by everyone, left behind by the person she so desperately wanted to save, never known to the world that she protected—

"I will remember. Because I am a witness."

Putting her hands to her breast, Rusalka swore that to Shirin, who never stopped walking. And then the young girl was standing in front of the white screen.

Stretching her hand out to the screen that would allow her to pass with a single touch, right before she crossed over to the other side—

"Thank you, Rusalka."

With those final words, Shirin disappeared. Even in the end, she hadn't turned back. But Rusalka would never forget the damp glimmer on her downturned cheek.

Rusalka Evereska alone would remember the crime humanity had committed in forcing a girl barely even fifteen years old to make such a cruel and painful choice.

"I will start the ritual now. Once it begins, Mistletoe will surely notice and come immediately to interrupt. I cannot move during the ritual. Don't expect any help," Odin announced as he stood partway through the screen.

It would not be accurate to say Rusalka had been eagerly awaiting it, but this meant the decisive battle would finally begin.

"Fight with all you have, humans. Odin's blessing is with you."

Leaving that final message, Odin also disappeared into the screen. Having watched all that happen, Rusalka's shoulders relaxed, and a hand gently settled on top of her head.

"...Why is your hand there?"

"You did well not to cry there, Rusalka."

"I won't cry. I'm a full-grown woman. And please stop patting my head."

Knocking away his arm, Rusalka glared at Alejandro. He scratched his unshaven cheek beneath her sharp stare.

"Sorry, sorry. First impressions leave a powerful mark is all."

"If you like, I can re-create the brawl at the pub with you."

"Ha-ha-ha, please spare me. After all..."

Alejandro looked up, and just then a broadcast echoed in the theater. Through some kind of mechanism, the announcement that could be heard in Holm base was also piped into the theater.

"—A pillar of light has appeared fifty kilometers northwest of the base! Visual confirmation of the target Mistletoe! Prepare for combat!"

Hearing Michelle's voice coming from the command post, Rusalka and Alejandro looked at each other. And then they both started sprinting at the same instant, kicking open the great doors to the theater and returning to the base. They leaped out into a hallway. To the right was the command post and to the left the hangar—that was where they parted ways.

"Go kick their asses, Rusalka. Show them what you've got."

His strong, resolute hand pushed her forward as she accelerated down the hall. She didn't look back, keeping her eyes straight ahead, still seeing the image of that brave girl.

"It's not what I've got. I'll show them the strength of your Sigrdrifa."

With that, she ran straight ahead to get up into the sky as soon as possible.

Chapter 5
Total War

1

"Should you really be here, Alma?"

Alma stopped cutting the apple in her hand at that question and glanced over at Natalie, who was sitting beside her.

They were currently in Natalie's room on the base. Alma had come to check on her as she lay in bed.

Natalie's condition wouldn't improve even if she stayed in the infirmary, so she mostly chose to rest in her room to avoid troubling the people around her more than strictly necessary.

And because Alma was almost always with her, the amount of time she spent there had grown significantly, too.

"Everyone else has gone to the hangar. You should be going soon, too."

"...Mmm..."

Natalie winced slightly at that half-hearted response.

Alma had stayed by her side almost constantly after finding out about her condition. Honestly, that had been the biggest surprise. And a blessing that she could not begin to express.

Shannon and Lisbeth had both been there as well until just a little while earlier. While waiting at the ready for the decisive battle to begin, they had sworn to do everything in their power, and Natalie had shared her own words of encouragement.

For an outsider, it might have been a bit of an odd sight, since they would all be risking their lives in a deadly sky just for a chance to save Natalie.

"It's all mixed up...," Natalie murmured quietly.

She was, of course, grateful that they cared so much about her. However, she had secretly resolved herself to her fate back when the sapling first appeared in her chest, and the idea that she might possibly be saved by defeating Mistletoe was a hope that had appeared out of nowhere.

"This battle is to blaze a new path for humanity...to ensure Gjallarhorn is completed. You should not—"

"No."

"Still adamant, I see."

Alma shook her head, refusing to acknowledge Natalie's position.

They had had the same exchange several times during the past five days. In the end, Alma's stubbornness did not subside on the day of the battle. Even with the fight mere minutes away, that didn't change.

"This is where I can focus best."

"———"

"I'm going to fight... I won't make the wrong choice this time."

Everyone had their own way of maintaining peak condition, so Natalie didn't think Alma was lying.

The small Valkyrie before her flew by storing up the rage inside her heart. Natalie understood that, and so she did not try to quell that anger.

But at least—

"Then at least promise me this, Alma. If you get a chance to defeat Mistletoe, don't let it slip away."

"Of course."

Natalie held out her pinkie. Alma did not hesitate, nodding as she intertwined her own with Natalie's. The next moment after they exchanged their promise, the siren began ringing.

The sound signaled the appearance of Mistletoe and the beginning of an unavoidable battle.

"Eat your apple and wait for me."

"Yes, I understand... Best of luck to you, Alma."

"You too, Natalie."

Picking up one of the apple slices, Alma put it into her mouth. Biting into the bittersweet fruit, she started running.

——Just this once, she would take flight not out of wrath but to save someone.

2

The mechanism by which pillars appeared was still unclear to humanity.

A point of light would appear in the sky without any advance warning. Then it would extend vertically, bringing forth a blinding column that seemingly connected the sky and the ground. And then invaders would begin pouring out from inside the light.

That same process had just occurred fifty kilometers northwest of Holm base.

The only difference was that this time, there were ten different columns of light that came in varying sizes, and the number of pillars they spawned was far greater than usual.

Tens of thousands of enemies surged forth in all kinds of forms, from flying ants and fireflies to snakes and frogs. And the being controlling all of them was the cataclysmic secondary, Mistletoe.

With an enormous column of light at its back, an amalgamation of giant trees leisurely floated in the air. A great host raised to bring about Armageddon filled the skies behind it.

It was a scene so daunting that it threatened to break the spirits of the brave soldiers shouldering the fate of humanity as they watched their enemies assemble.

"———"

In truth, even the radio operators in the command post were speechless at the sight.

The monitors tracking the battleground were covered by unbroken streaks of red from the mass of radar contacts. Everyone in the command post was taken aback by the overwhelming lack of space left unfilled by enemies—

"—It looks like they're really worried."

——save a single man who refused to let the hopelessness of the scene consume him.

A well-trained body, dirty-blond hair, and a ferocious, feline grin on his face, it was the commander of Holm base, the hero standing at the forefront of humanity's defense.

——Alejandro Ostley, the man synonymous with miracles, who did not falter even with the weight of the world bearing down on his shoulders.

"I suppose the little fledgling we've got incubating here at the base must be really problematic for them. They could have just come at us like normal, but they've decided to throw everything they've got at us. That's proof enough they don't understand war. Bunch of cowards!"

Alejandro slapped his knee as he roared with fangs bared.

The commander's indomitable voice carried over the radio to everyone at the base. Every soldier whose hands had frozen, who had forgotten to breathe, whose spirit had faltered—they all regained their senses when they heard his voice.

That's our commander. Humanity's savior. Who else could say something so bold as their instinctive first response upon seeing such a hopeless scene? But faced with that overwhelming difference in numbers, even as their heartless enemies cornered humanity's forces, he, Alejandro, would make all of that a weapon to wrench victory from the jaws of defeat.

Everyone looked up to the sky. There was an uncountable horde of invaders filling the skies. As they processed that sight, they dug in and all shared the same thought:

——*Same as always.*

"Let's do this! All of you are ready, right?! This is the day we've been waiting for!"

"———"

Alejandro's voice resounded, a manifestation of the shared dream that everyone there held.

It was a thought everyone on the battlefield had. If they were going to risk their lives in combat, then they at least wanted a commanding officer who understood the value of their lives and knew how to actually claim victory if he was going to hurl them into the meat grinder.

And the man who embodied all of those hopes was Alejandro Ostley—

"The skies are filled with enemies, but we're going to take them back!"

"Uraaaaaaaa!!!"

The soldiers' cheers and their footsteps shook the earth.

As the entire base's morale reached a fever pitch, Alejandro grabbed the radio.

When faced with your greatest foe, send in your greatest firepower. There was only one choice for the first strike.

"—Do it, Rusalka! Show 'em the power of Sigrdrifa!"

3

"—Do it, Rusalka! Show 'em the power of Sigrdrifa!"

A passionate, rough, entirely-lacking-in-solemnity order came flying in over the radio.

Hearing that, Rusalka clenched the stick as she cut through a gap in the clouds. Seeing her reckless advance, a group of pillars that was deployed in the air swarmed toward her craft.

The ants with their stout jaws, the fireflies and their projectiles made of light, the frogs and their bullet-like tongues, and the poison rain spewed by the snakes all rushed in to make the overeager Valkyrie regret her rashness.

"Sorry, but..."

Her pink lips moved, though the words would never reach the pillars. But the deadly intent embedded in her voice would surely bridge the gap, even though they were so incapable of mutual understanding.

An instant later, the pillars swarming her were all shredded in a storm of gunfire.

Machine guns roared, and the pillars rattled beneath the impacts before shattering and disappearing in fragments of light. In their place, tree after tree erupted into being and fell to earth. No matter many times she saw the phenomenon unfold, she was always moved by how strange it was for that beauty to come from the deaths of the hideous pillars.

"As if they're making the case that death itself is beautiful. It makes me sick."

As the glimmering fragments of light scattered, Rusalka's plane cut across right in front of the enemies' noses as she turned. Many of them tried to keep clinging to her tail, but they were shredded by the same hail of lead before shattering just the same.

This was Rusalka's attack—no, the full force of Sigrdrifa's attack.

"Raaaaaaaaaaaagh! You better not be lookin' away from me!"

The pillars were shot down by a destructive force on par with a hurricane. And the ones who had achieved that feat were the Valkyrie formation following closely behind Rusalka.

Flying point, shouting boldly as she shot down the most enemies, was Lisbeth Crown. And adroitly mowing down all the pillars that slipped through her initial attacks was Leili Haltija.

"Lisbeth! You're pushing too far ahead! Watch your surroundings m—"

"I am already! You're always such a pain in the ass about it, it turned into an annoying habit! That's why I'm expectin' you to cover my ass, Lily."

Leili was speechless for a moment at hearing the nickname, but she quickly changed gears in the face of that brusque tone and implicit faith.

"Could you please refrain from such unladylike phrases, Liz?"

"Ha! So posh! But I still can't stand that kind of crap!"

Lisbeth and Leili dove into the enemy formation after that exchange.

Lisbeth's Messerschmitt BF109 was superior in acceleration and maneuverability, while Leili's Spitfire was superior in terms of firepower and ability to climb. Despite the differences in their personalities and their machines, they tore through the enemies with refined movement and coordination, like wingmates who had flown together for years.

Rusalka flew lead, and the twin stars Lisbeth and Leili trailed behind her. But that was not the end of the trials the pillars faced.

"Put them through the grinder! Attack, attack, attack!"

Sigrdrifa's executive officer for the battle, Shannon Stewart, shot off an order, and in response, the Valkyries began an all-out assault that continued without rest.

And amid that fusillade of concentrated fire, there was one plane that particularly stood out for the way it flew.

The suspect was—

"A Gladiator, Claudia Brafford."

As the enemies pressed down on them in a swarm that blotted out the sun, she was easily evading the rain of glowing projectiles, a black meteor that held Rusalka's eye when she glanced back to check the status of the Valkyries behind her.

A split second after the black flash passed, the light of pillars dying erupted in its wake. Her attacks were not just limited to bullets clad in divine light, either. She even relied on her wings to slice through the air and sever the pillars that lingered in her path too long.

"——"

Claudia's Deus ex Machina, a Gladiator, did not merely crush the pillars with precise gunfire. Nor did she only slash them with her wings. She was even leading them to crash into each other with her nimble maneuvers. No one who saw her performance would have believed it was her first combat mission.

She was like an embodiment of death, shooting enemies down one after the other and reaping any enemies her wings could reach.

——The title goddess of death suited her well.

"Talent is a dreadful thing."

Seeing the death that Claudia was mass-producing, Rusalka could only express abject wonder.

It was a talent she would have been jealous of in the past. But now she could think only about how awful it was. But at the same time, it was incredibly reliable.

Odin had said that Claudia had a potential that approached Amy's.

As someone who had actually flown with Amy several times, Rusalka could feel that in her bones. Though that was not why she was flying, flying together with Claudia like that was a view into what could have been to walk the path Rusalka had not chosen that fateful day.

A what-if where she had chosen to fly with Amy—

"Not that I have time to be getting sentimental like that!"

Casting aside the emotions welling inside her, she suddenly shot up into a steep climb right in front of the enemy formation charging at her from straight ahead. Entering a somersault, she edged her wings around slightly to evade the flurry of light rounds coming at her as she changed paths. Escaping the swarm of pillars, she withdrew from the front line in one burst.

And she was not the only one, either. All of Sigrdrifa pulled back as one.

The reason was—

"Alma!"

The moment she called out, the focus shifted to far above the battlefield. Incredibly high up, at an altitude that even the pillars could not reach, there was a single plane flying that was larger than all the other Deus ex Machinas.

——Alma Conturo unleashed her most powerful strike, a Grand Slam.

"——"

Their momentum stalled by the Valkyries' preemptive strike, the pillars were slow to spread out, and a vast swarm of them was engulfed by the massive ensuing explosion. The erupting flames easily broke through the pillars' defenses, scorching the hideous creatures.

Hundreds or even thousands of pillars were turned to ash by that one bomb.

It was surely the deadliest single strike the pillars had suffered in the entire war. The sort of attack destined for the record books and the stuff of meritorious decorations.

"All that's left is to open a path to Mistletoe..."

The explosion dyed the sky red as the pillars caught in the blast scattered in fragments of light.

Faced with such a vast number of enemies, their plan to take down their target was exceedingly simple.

It was a two-part scheme, with one team to break through the swarm of smaller enemies protecting the target and buy time for the second team, which would attack the target itself using the path that had been cleared for them.

Alma's massive firepower could thin out the enemy formation, while the breakthrough team centered around Rusalka, with its superior maneuverability, opened a path. From there Lisbeth and Claudia and the other heavy hitters would leap into the gap and crash down on Mistletoe, using that chance to deliver a painful blow.

As the fireball cleared, it became apparent that Alma's strike had torn a massive hole in the enemy formation.

The moment she saw that, Rusalka was sure they had cleared the first phase of the operation. Gripping her stick, she started to surge forward, moving on to the next phase—

"Warning! Do not close with the target!"

"Wh…?"

Hearing the difficult-to-believe order fly in over the radio, Rusalka inhaled sharply. She was just about to query what command was thinking, but she didn't manage to get the question out.

Because the reason for the order leaped into her field of view.

"———"

In the sky beyond where the fireball had been, the gigantic Mistletoe was floating.

And centered around it were new pillars that had not been there moments ago. And they were far too large to be tertiaries.

In other words—

"Multiple secondary pillars have appeared! This is an unprecedented situation!"

4

The appearance of multiple secondary pillars.

The shock of that report landed heavily at every major base around the world, and indeed, it was a powerful blow to all of humanity.

A secondary pillar was such a powerful foe that challenging it with a fully equipped base large enough to have a flight of Valkyries was considered an even fight. More and more third-generation Valkyries were completing their accelerated training and being sent out so that every base could maintain the bare minimum deployment, but before that, the army had been helpless to do anything other than buy time for evacuating any region attacked by a secondary.

And three more of those enemies had just appeared, bringing the grand total to four, after counting Mistletoe itself. Mistletoe was already a pillar so dangerous that it had become almost synonymous with cataclysm, so to add such an absurd force alongside it—

"I take it back… You damn pillars are nasty strategists."

Grasping the situation from his command post, Alejandro gritted his teeth at the outrageous tactic the enemy had unveiled.

Just like Odin had predicted, they must have been terrified of Gjallarhorn. Their all-out attack was proof of that, and the clash currently unfolding was proof that humanity would not go down without a fight.

The pillars were fully utilizing every bit of fighting power they could mobilize to stop the completion of Gjallarhorn.

Alejandro was genuinely impressed with their thorough and overwhelming deployment. It was a heartfelt bravo out of respect for whatever tactician was behind the enemy's moves.

Since—

"This is exactly what I would've done."

"——"

"Come on, you're supposed to laugh there."

As he sung his own praises, the rest of the command post's staff continued holding their silence. Alejandro chuckled as he glanced over at Michelle. The leader of the operators, she alone understood the meaning of that look, and she nodded.

"The secondary pillars that have appeared do not match any past records."

Returning to their senses at her report, the rest of the command staff began moving again all at once.

Analyzing the new combatants to begin to understand their unique abilities, calculating the potential activity time limit based on the enemy's draining effect, and preparing an antiair artillery fusillade with conventional rounds to distract the tertiaries—there was plenty that needed doing.

Seeing life blown back into the command post, Alejandro crossed his arms.

Operators had to be tough. Their transmissions were heard by all the soldiers on the battlefield. If there was obvious despair in their voices, the whole army would start to lose its will to fight.

That was why the operators and the commanding officer had to maintain their confidence all the way to the end.

"Send the order, Heyman! It's a little early, but let's put our cards on the table, too."

5

"Lisbeth! Leili! Claudia! You three take one of them! Alma, maintain altitude! The rest of Sigrdrifa, on me!"

"—Roger!"

Faced with the never-before-seen situation of multiple secondaries deployed to the same part of the front simultaneously, every Valkyrie flying was dumbfounded. The first to return to her senses was Rusalka.

Not out of some pride as the squadron leader of Sigrdrifa or the rebellious spirit of a Valkyrie who could not keep up. But because her preparations in advance were finally paying off.

"I had considered it before. What to do if two or more secondaries appeared on the same battlefield."

It had been a thought more firmly rooted in extreme pessimism than a simple abundance of caution. Most Valkyries subconsciously prayed that such a hopeless situation would never come about, but in her pessimism, Rusalka had fully considered what to do if it came to pass.

Humanity's greatest enemy, the pillars, would surely go beyond whatever worst thing they could imagine.

However—

"Takin' care of a rookie while fighting a secondary?! Gimme a break here, Major!"

"But we don't have a choice. We have to do it."

"Allow me to learn at your back…or your tail, I suppose."

"Is this really the time for that shit?! —Argh, don't get left behind!"

With a clamorous din, Lisbeth, Leili, and Claudia headed for the secondary to the west—to the pillar with a body constructed from an amalgamation of spheres that gave off a blue light.

The three new pillars were deployed in a defensive formation with one in the west, one in the east, and one right in front of Mistletoe. Rusalka was leaving one of them to Lisbeth's group.

"We're taking the one to the east! Don't slow down! Stay on my tail!"

"Major! What about the third one…?"

"Don't worry. The enemy always surpasses our expectations in the worst way, but…"

Hearing the almost-scream over the radio, Rusalka broke into a smile. Not realizing she had a tranquil smile even in the midst of such an intense battle, Rusalka exhaled, and then she grinned ferociously, the spitting image of her commanding officer.

"—Our commander is even nastier than the pillars."

The loving, trusting, heartfelt trash talk that crossed the airwaves left the other Valkyries stunned.

Immediately afterward, a new transmission proved just how true her reaction was.

"______"

A thunderous boom resounded, like the world ending, as another massive bomb exploded in the air. A crimson flame bloomed like a flower, ripping another massive hole in the pillar formation. And the ones who gave their enemies that bloody nose were—

"Ah-ha-ha-ha-ha! What even is this?! This is crazy! Pillars, pillars, pillars, pillars everywhere you look! Ah-ha-ha-ha! This is awesome!"

"Shut up already. Maybe be a little more concerned about why we were sent in ahead of schedule."

"Commencing operations nineteen minutes before planned. Considering th—"

"—Hakuna matata, girls! It'll work out somehow, so let's just do this!"

A noisy clamor filled the airwaves as Deus ex Machinas appeared out of the clouds one after the other. There was no coordination to their formation, each with their own unique personality and style that did not mesh into a coherent whole at all.

But they were all Valkyries who dreamed of the same future and flew in the same sky—and they had come to Sigrdrifa's aid for the decisive battle with Mistletoe.

"We knew Mistletoe would be coming to destroy Gjallarhorn, so I used that as leverage to borrow the aces from every base I could. I had to bow and scrape so much, I'm sure my stock value is at an all-time low."

"Don't worry, Colonel. Even if your head is at an all-time low, you are still our greatest commander."

"You're supposed to reassure me that the all-time-low part isn't true!"

Having envisioned the worst-possible situation, she was impressed by his skill in preparing a response to overcome it. She felt a deep respect in fact, and her heart had even skipped a beat just a little bit there, to her everlasting shame, though she would never tell anyone that.

In the grips of that shame, Rusalka led her group to the secondary that was divided into countless partitions with a single enormous flower.

They would take the east, Lisbeth's group the west, and the reinforcements would handle the center, methodically breaking through the newly arrived secondaries one by one.

And once they wrenched open the path—

"—There won't be any escape this time, Mistletoe."

Rusalka glared at the secondary watching the battle from safety, gritting her teeth.

She could not—*would not*—let it escape. Humanity could not afford to lose this battle. The die was cast, and the ships at port had been fired.

"_____"

Putting a hand to her chest, Rusalka reached for a small plant giving off a faint light.

Mistletoe's ability was affecting Rusalka—no, every Valkyrie in the sky. Indeed, its effect might even be reaching the base now.

She had known it from the start. The battle with Mistletoe would be on a time limit.

"But we won't lose. This time, we will win…!"

Moving her hand away from the plant she could not feel, she gripped the control stick tightly and danced through the sky.

——The battle to decide which side of the war would have the upper hand intensified.

6

There were many things the IPO still did not know about the Deus ex Machinas they relied on.

In the first place, they were not machines developed by humans but sacred treasures bequeathed to Valkyries by Odin. When the ritual was performed in Mimir's well and qualified girls awakened as Valkyries, they were given their Deus ex Machinas as well.

At the same time they were granted their divine blessing, their wings appeared as well.

There was no uniformity in the planes that Valkyries flew. According to Odin, each Deus ex Machina was a manifestation of its Valkyrie's essence. Thus, Rusalka, who had yearned to fly from such a young age, received a Spitfire that gracefully danced through the blue skies. And thus Alma, who hid such an enormous rage in her small frame, received the Lancaster, with its massive, overwhelming firepower.

There was no overarching consistency to Deus ex Machinas—save one. The only thing they seemed to have in common was that they all took the form of propeller planes of some sort that had seen use during the interwar period and World War II.

Normally, those ancient planes could not begin to compare to modern jets equipped with the most up-to-date technology. However, Deus ex Machinas did not follow human logic.

By appearances, they were almost identical to those antiques from an age long past, but their abilities did not pale at all in comparison to modern jets. In fact, they even surpassed modern fighters in certain respects, when it came to their specialties.

That illogical fact was, according to Odin, due to a gap in faith.

——*Faith*. It was a term that encompassed a rough approximation of whether people would believe in something with absolute unwavering confidence.

And apparently, the propeller craft from the World Wars had garnered far more of that faith than the most modern fighters.

It was difficult to judge on such vague reasoning, and so the mystery of how Deus ex Machinas worked was still largely unexplained.

While being a sacred treasure granted by God, they could still be repaired by human hands, and they were powered not by some mysterious energy source but by aviation fuel. They could run out of bullets and did not have any special shielding. Those inconveniences had not been hand waved, and there was no end to the list of complaints when it came to keeping these machines in good working order.

But even so, they were humanity's fangs, the one power available to them that they could use to reach the pillars.

And using them to their fullest to take down all the invaders trying to drain the earth of its life force was Alejandro Ostley, the most gifted commanding officer in the world, who had established a record for getting the best results.

There was no human better than him at making sure pillars died.

Because of that, he was engaged in a battle to decide the fate of humanity with the cataclysmic Mistletoe.

——However…

"Registering more tertiary pillar contacts! Combat time has exceeded ninety minutes!"

The hole in the wall of tertiaries that had been opened was filled by more reinforcements, and the monitor was painted by a solid swathe of red again.

The operators and analysts were frantically evaluating the ever-changing battle state, reporting the results, and scanning for new developments. Hearing their fervent voices, Alejandro's thoughts accelerated, constantly looking for the next best move.

——The battle had already gone on far longer than he had expected.

Ordinarily, battles with pillars were almost always settled within an hour, due to the pillars' draining effect, which absorbed the life force from the surrounding landforms.

Bluntly, the pillars were quick to run out of gas. Their lack of endurance was one of the main reasons humanity had been able to contest their dominance at all. But Mistletoe had apparently overcome that limitation.

By transforming everything around it into trees, creating life force rather than stealing it, the pillars were able to extend the relatively short amount of time they could stay fighting. That was why the battle was becoming drawn out.

Deus ex Machinas were capable of active combat operations in the air for between two and three hours. In that sense, they were similar to standard planes. That limit came down to the amount of fuel it was possible for them to carry as well as the physical and mental limits of the Valkyries piloting them.

It was easy enough to imagine how exhausting it was to keep fighting in the skies with danger all around. On top of that, the Valkyries were young, almost all of them girls who had not fully grown into their bodies. They could not compare to a fully trained veteran soldier.

The limit on their endurance was approaching far sooner than they realized.

On top of that, it was generally believed that humans were not really capable of maintaining their full focus for more than ninety minutes at a time. There were individual differences, but it was exceedingly rare for someone to be able to last for hours longer than that.

If their endurance or mental focus gave out, they would be far more likely to misjudge situations, and just a single moment of hesitation could make the difference between life and death when fighting the pillars in the skies.

"Milene's and Etta's performances are dropping! They're taking more hits!"

"They can't maintain formation! At this rate—"

"C team, pull back! Crown, fill the gap!"

As the operators' voices crisscrossed, Alejandro ordered a change to the deployment. He immediately pulled the Valkyries who had sustained damage, calling them back to base for repairs and a brief break.

But he had filled the gap in the formation with just a single Deus ex Machina—

"That's impossible! Even for Lieutenant Crown..."

"She's just going to have to do the impossible, then. Haltija isn't suited for this, and Brafford doesn't have the experience. Crown is the best... No, she's better at least."

"—Ngh."

It was a decision that Alejandro, who was always sure of himself, could only call *better*, rather than the *best*. Hearing that, Lisbeth broke off from her team and charged into the enemy alone.

And mowing down tertiary after tertiary along the way, she evaded the attacks of the secondary, shifting to disruption. Her forte: dogfighting.

But even after taking the fight on her own terms so she could fight as she pleased, Lisbeth couldn't hope to defeat a secondary all by herself. That was something no one except Amy had ever achieved.

"———"

Clutching his chest, Alejandro clamped down on the idle thought of his lost sister.

He didn't have time to be dwelling in the past. He had already grieved, cursed, and lamented her fate more than enough. The version of him who had forgotten who she was and fought free of care was already long dead.

So—

"Sir, requesting permission to attack."

As he gritted his teeth, the monitor in front of him displayed a man in a flight suit—no, more than one of them. All of them were air force pilots.

Anyone other than a Valkyrie who confronted Mistletoe would be transformed within a short time, so Alejandro had been cautious about letting the regular pilots take to the skies. With the right timing, they could support the Valkyries' advance or cover their withdrawal, but it was an incredibly cruel trade-off—in exchange for the Valkyries coming back, the pilots would be sent on a one-way flight guaranteed to end in their deaths.

But even knowing that, they had contacted the command post after having made all the preparations to take off.

"You…"

"The girls are doing great out there. But they're reaching their limits. Pull those amateurs back, and let's show them how professionals fly."

The pilot at the front jerked his scarred chin skyward.

He was an old hand who had been with Alejandro since Lamia. A veteran who had survived that hell and rushed to join the battle with Sigrdrifa as well.

"Are you willing to die like that?"

"That's a cheap price to pay to safekeep girls with bright futures ahead of them, particularly beauties like them. And, sir…no, Colonel—"

"——"

"We should have died that day with that cute little girl who saved the world. The only reason we lived this long was all for this moment."

As someone who had experienced the same hell, the same despair, and the same regret, he didn't need to hear any more to know who the pilot meant. And he also realized that their resolve was not something he could hold back.

"Then get out there, you damned fools. You better at least buy us some time."

"Tell Major Evereska to visit my grave. Her rack's one of the seven wonders of the world."

"If I told her that, she'd bury me alongside you."

With that last, foolish schoolboy exchange, Alejandro gave his men the coldhearted order. And there was no one in the command post who reproached him for it.

There was no one in all of the IPO who could say a word about it.

"Pull back Sigrdrifa as the regulars reach the pillars! Get them to resupply and let them rest for as long as we can. And hurry up with the repairs on any planes that have been hit! You're up, Chief Technician Reever!"

"I don't need you to tell me. I've been on standby this whole time. If anything, it's been so boring, I've been working on my skin care."

"You're most beautiful when you're smeared in engine grease, so go get spruced up."

"You know just the right way to get me going, playboy."

Catching Roger's blown kiss through the radio, Alejandro regained just a little bit of his energy.

Everyone around him was grinning, even in the face of such a hopeless situation.

It was almost as if they were absolutely confident that he would find the narrow exit to the valley of death and wrest victory from such a hopeless battle.

Argh, it pisses me off, but it's just like Odin said.

It was just like the Deus ex Machinas—their faith was like a curse that granted Alejandro strength.

"A curse or magic, whatever's fine with me. I've got a reservation in hell to keep once this is all over."

Glaring at the screen, his eyes were locked on Mistletoe, which was still standing there without so much as a scratch. Then he turned his attention to the three guardians protecting it. They had accumulated their fair share of damage.

All that was left was to see which would be the first to fall and how to push forward—

"—If we're going to get past them, it has to be all three at once."

7

Rusalka's bloodshot eyes were wide-open, and she felt like she was flying in a dream or maybe an illusion.

She had been in the air from the very start of the battle, holding her perch on the front lines for over a hundred minutes already. She had lost count of the times her plane had taken a hit and wobbled or when she had started streaming a trail of smoke. She had long since run out of ammunition and had no means left to take enemies down other than maneuvering to induce friendly fire and collisions.

But even so, her focus was exactly the same, unchanged from the very beginning of the battle—no, if anything she was even more focused now.

"I could fly through the eye of a needle—!"

Even if that was an exaggeration, she had refined her technique down to an art, weaving between the pillars with just a dozen of centimeters to spare on either side until they crashed into each other.

Rusalka Evereska had accepted her lack of talent and knew it was her fate to be overtaken by those who had started flying long after her. And ironically, on that most desperate of battlefields, the world's most famous Second Valkyrie discovered the talent that lay sleeping within her.

In other words, it symbolized the limits of her growth, but—

"Haaaaaaaaaaaah!"

Howling like a beast, she maneuvered wildly, surrounded on all sides by pillars but somehow managing to escape their grasp nonetheless. The enemies before her, or beside her, or behind her all crashed into one another and crumpled from the impacts.

But did a victory await at the end of all that—?

"Rusalka, return to base!"

"Please don't stop me, sir! I still have plenty of endurance! I—"

"Even if you're fine, your plane isn't! You need fuel and ammo! Listen to me, you idiot!"

"But—"

That was when Michelle suddenly broke in.

"But nothing. That was an order, Major Evereska!"

As she was arguing with Alejandro, Michelle's cool voice brought her to her senses like a douse of cool water.

Inhaling sharply, she realized just how pathetic her Spitfire must look. The paint was flaking, and parts of the innards were peeking out here and there. The reason the wind had become oddly annoying was because the windshield shattered, and she realized long after the fact that a stray shard of it had cut her neck.

Somewhere along the way, her plane had become covered in wounds. And it was not just her. All of the Valkyries, the reinforcements included, were badly beaten up. They were certainly dealing damage to the secondaries protecting Mistletoe, but they couldn't quite seem to reach the tipping point.

"Sorry, but we'll be stealing the show here."

As she realized the situation, a spirited voice reached her ears. Looking out, she saw it was not just a single person, either. Arrow-like jets were leaping into the line of fire against the pillars to cover the fatigued Valkyries—state-of-the-art Typhoon jets were joining the fray.

They were steady allies when it came to fighting pillars, and their reliability paled only in comparison to the sorrow they embodied.

"Against Mistletoe..."

"Yep. He's our mortal enemy! Which makes this hero time."

There was no one in the skies who would laugh his words off as mere bravado.

It wasn't just the air force pilots, either. She could see the ground forces departing from the base as well. All of them lacked any divine blessing to protect them against Mistletoe's power.

None of them really believed they could defeat the secondary. They were all laying down their lives to buy just a second of breathing room for the Valkyries.

And by adding up all those seconds they sacrificed themselves for, they believed the Valkyries would reach the enemy's throat for them.

"Go take a breather, Valk. And maybe bring us an ale when you get back."

There was an unshakable faith in his confident voice that caused Rusalka to exhale slowly.

Something about it triggered a memory, a memory from when she had folded up her wings and served for a brief time as an operator. The exchange she had had with that infantry officer.

Just like then, the only words she had for the men charging to their deaths was—

"—I love you."

"______"

There was a moment of silence—

"Bwa-ha-ha-ha-ha!"

—followed by a boisterous laugh.

Listening closely, it was not just the pilot she had been speaking to who was guffawing; it was all the men listening on the radio.

And their response was—

"Ahhh, we've got the blessing of the goddess with us. Forget God, men. We've got a goddess's love!"

The pilot howled in high spirits as the others cheered.

Talk of love and being called a goddess were a heavy burden, but if that could help them in any way, if that could give them the strength to fight on just a little bit longer, then she would accept it with pride.

——Seconds later, the blue sky was filled with explosive fireworks.

Conventional weapons were largely ineffective against the pillars. But humanity had not just been twiddling their thumbs, waiting to die before Odin revealed himself. They had developed several different meaningful, effective tactics. One of which was saturation fire—overwhelming the enemies' abilities to keep up with a wave of constant attacks to buy time.

There was a heroic tank officer who once said that it wasn't explosives that would take down the pillars; it was guts. And he had been right.

The tertiaries were assaulted by waves of antiair missiles and shells launched by self-propelled artillery. Even if they couldn't crack the pillars' stout defenses, the explosions and the shock waves that accompanied the flames were enough to momentarily stall the pillars' advance and delay humanity's destruction by a tiny amount.

And as humanity embarked on that desperate tightrope walk of resistance, the pillars mercilessly bathed the soldiers in their destructive light, sending one brave man after the next to his death—

"—Gh."

Gritting her teeth, Rusalka wheeled around, setting a course back to the base's runway.

Seeing her battered Spitfire land, the crews rushed out of the hangar and immediately got to work. Crawling out of the cockpit as that went on all around her, Rusalka looked for a place to get a moment of rest. Her legs were wobbling, and there was a decent chance she would have just sunk to the ground right then and there.

"—Get ahold of yourself, cutie. It'd set a bad example if you plopped down here."

"Chief Reever…"

She looked up as Roger grabbed her arm before she could collapse. The tall technician was covered in oil and grease, a smile on his chiseled face as he flashed her a wink.

"At the very least, you've got to keep up appearances. I'll get her ready for you to fly again in a jiffy."

Saying that, Roger pressed a towel and a bottle of water into her hands before quickly joining the crews working on the plane.

Having come back for a brief respite at Alejandro's orders, the Valkyries went to get what little rest they could as the emergency repairs, refueling, and reloading continued at a fever pitch.

Watching the frantic rush, Rusalka leaned back against a wall and sat down on the ground.

Considering her rank, it would have been preferable not to look feeble or slovenly, but the exhaustion she felt was all-consuming. The fatigue that hadn't bothered her one bit while flying suddenly came crashing down all at once the moment she landed.

And she had not had any time to worry about it while flying, but—

"…Transformation…"

Opening her flight jacket slightly, she could see the faint light emanating from her chest. The barely perceptible tiny sapling was making its presence known.

When she tried to touch it, her fingers mysteriously passed right through it, but there was still obviously something there.

——And just like what Natalie experienced, there was a feeling that accompanied it of having her life force gradually sucked away.

Closing the jacket, she pushed the transformation from her mind.

But she could not just ignore Mistletoe's intrusions entirely, either, since she was not the only one being affected.

The pillars had begun their attack two hours ago, and Mistletoe itself had not moved even a centimeter from where it had first appeared. However, its terrible influence over the surroundings was slowly spreading.

The ultimate proof of that was the repair crews going about their work—it was clear the same sort of saplings were already sprouting from their shoulders and backs.

They had always known that what made Mistletoe so terrible was its indiscriminate encroachment.

All the soldiers gathered at the base, the ones who were even now fighting outside, knew what would happen when they made their decisions, and they had long since accepted their fates. The aviators, infantry, and gunners, the repair crews and signal officers, and even the medical officers. Every last one of them knew.

In other words, the scene before her was—

"—All of humanity is truly united in this fight."

Rusalka looked up as someone said exactly what she had been thinking. Glancing in the direction of the voice, she saw a girl walking toward her, her flight cap off and her long blond hair swaying behind her.

"Claudia..."

"It's quite the intense battle, Major... I knew that going in, but even so."

Wiping the sweat from her brow, Claudia took a deep breath. Even she could not hide her exhaustion, but there was a distress apart from fatigue in her blue eyes.

Recognizing that the true source of that emotion was a sense of guilt, Rusalka narrowed her eyes.

"...I'm sure you have your own thoughts on the matter, but you don't need to worry that this is the fault of you or Shirin. Don't get the wrong idea."

"...That's surprising... Can you read people's minds, Major?"

"Your sister's the only one with a special ability like that... No..."

Shaking her head, Rusalka remembered there was one other person who seemed to have an ability like that. Amy. Thinking back on it, she had often seemed to have an oddly good instinct. Rusalka had assumed it was just the First's top-class observation skills, but it would make a lot of sense if she could read minds.

If she had been able to see into Rusalka's heart, then what had she been thinking when she had wanted to talk that last night?

"Major?"

"Sorry, I got a little distracted... I cannot read minds. If I had such an ability, I suspect I would have been able to get through life with many fewer problems."

"I'm not so sure. From my perspective, it would be hard to say that Shiri has lived her life adroitly. And I was never able to understand the worries and pains that she bore through it all."

Seeing the look of shame in Claudia's gallant figure, Rusalka felt a pain in her chest unrelated to the sapling that had taken root there. The cause was unmistakably what had happened in Hlidskjalf.

Claudia wasn't aware. She didn't know the feelings her sister held deep in her heart, the resolve she carried as she offered herself up to restore Gjallarhorn in the ritual happening behind the scenes of this battle.

Shirin had not told her sister the truth that she was the one being targeted by the pillars. Odin had said it was a lie to protect herself, to keep her elder sister from abandoning her, and Claudia had believed him. Believed that it was a lie she had been forced to tell out of a desire to remain with her beloved sister.

But Rusalka knew that interpretation was false. Shirin's goal in lying was to protect Claudia, who in turn was trying to protect her. The two sisters cared deeply for each other, and as a result, their bond had been offered up to God, only to disappear from the world.

Rusalka would be the only one to know the truth. Once the ritual was complete, Claudia would forget the reason why she had chosen to take to the skies. Rusalka was unsure whether that was really okay—

"—Major, I am fighting alongside you and everyone else here."

Having slipped into thought for a moment, her focus was pulled back to reality by that powerful statement.

There was a fortitude in Claudia's voice as she stood in front of Rusalka, looking out at the repair crews working on their Deus ex Machinas and, beyond them, to their comrades still fighting in the sky.

She had the shortest time of service of anyone fighting that day, the least combat experience, and the weakest foundation as a Valkyrie. And yet, it almost looked as if her back bore wings clad in a radiant light.

Seeing that, the thought that immediately crossed Rusalka's mind slipped past her lips before she even realized what had happened.

"Amy..."

"Major? Is there...? Ah."

Claudia turned around, only for her eyes to widen in surprise when she saw Rusalka. Rusalka was going to ask what had caught her so off guard when—

"Ahhh?! Th-the major's crying! This ain't funny!"

All of a sudden, there was a loud shout that cut through the din of the hangar. The source was Lisbeth, who looked absolutely indignant. Having returned to the ground, she was pointing to Rusalka as she continued in a loud voice.

"The fight's not even over yet, so why are you crying?! Is this your fault, Claudia?!"

"Stop it, Liz! I'm sure the major has her own thoughts concerning her..."

"I-I'm not sure what I did, but if it is my fault, I apologize..."

Leili was holding Lisbeth back as she started to reach for Claudia, who nervously raised her hands in a show of innocence.

"———"

Watching them, Rusalka put her hand to her cheek. Just like Lisbeth said, her cheek was wet with tears.

It had been a long time since she had last cried. And the last time had been—

"—From my experience, you're surprisingly prone to waterworks."

"—Ngh."

Rusalka suddenly turned around at the unexpected voice.

Someone who had no business being down in the hangar was standing at the entrance—Alejandro. Why was the commanding officer, who should have been holed up in the command post, tracking the flow of the battle down there?

"Obviously to light a fire under any crybabies. But looks like that won't be necessary."

Rusalka frantically wiped her tears as the blond lion chuckled at her expense.

It was likely he hadn't been lying. He was probably worried about a drop in morale among the Valkyries who had come back and wanted to encourage them personally.

And he surely understood the reason behind Rusalka's tears.

They were not a sign of morale breaking, let alone her will to fight collapsing—they were tears of joy at finally being able to fight alongside the wings she should have joined once before.

"Colonel! Should you really be here? Aren't you kinda busy?" Lisbeth wondered aloud.

"Yeah, it's pretty bad up there. I forced Heyman to handle things for a bit, so I'm sure I'll get an earful when I get back. But seeing your faces has been a relief."

"Our faces?" Leili asked.

"That's right. No broken spirits here. You're all still as beautiful as ever."

Lisbeth and Leili, not used to dealing with Alejandro, were slightly taken aback by his playboy-like joke and wink. But Claudia, who was unshakable to begin with, and Rusalka, who had long ago grown used to dealing with him, were different.

"Depending on how we looked, would you not have been relieved, sir?" asked Claudia.

"That's right. The fate of humanity is on the line here. I can't rely on someone who has lost their will in the key moment. If your spirits had been broken, I would have to start thinking about how to organize a retreat."

If it started to look like defeat was inevitable, Alejandro would have to consider the best way to manage the loss as the commander leading the battle. If it became clear they were going to suffer irrecoverable damage, he could not afford to just order his subordinates out on a suicide charge. He had come down to the hangar resolved to potentially make that final choice.

"But all that has gone out the window. So all that remains is to win," Rusalka concluded.

"...Sheesh, just when you show a few tears for once, you're back to being as uncute as ever."

"...Are you sure you weren't just imagining things, sir?"

Not interested in giving in to his teasing, Rusalka tried to brush off her tears. Alejandro just smiled without saying anything, and Leili covered Lisbeth's mouth before she could say anything, either.

And then Alejandro looked around at the faces of all the Valkyries there.

"As you know, those bodyguard secondaries are in the way of us beating Mistletoe. But seeing how the tertiaries seem to be getting revived, we can't assume that doesn't apply to those secondaries, too. So if we're going to take them out, we have to do all three at once."

Unease swept over the gathered Valkyries at that concerning statement. These were powerful enemies that had not fallen in almost two hours of fighting. Most of those listening could hardly think it anything more than an absurd pipe dream.

The first one to raise her hand was the fearless Claudia.

"Sir, forgive my insolence in speaking out of turn during my first time seeing combat, but is it not reckless to aim to defeat all three at the same time? They have suffered significant damage, so it's probably not impossible, but..."

"Don't worry—it's our job to be the tailwind that helps you carry out such a reckless plan."

"Do you have a method in mind?"

"We haven't just been twiddling our thumbs in the command center these past two hours. We've finished analyzing the enemy secondaries' attack patterns. But we're only going to get one shot at this plan."

Alejandro held up three fingers in response to Claudia's earnest concern. But he did not mean three plans. He meant three Valkyries.

——Claudia, Lisbeth, and Leili.

"Forget about combat experience. Right now, you three are the most powerful single fighters Sigrdrifa has. That's why I'm giving you the job. One-on-one. You three need to take down one of the secondaries protecting Mistletoe each."

"——"

"And here I was all ready to break out the 'it's not a question of can or can't' line."

Seeing the three of them digest his order in their own ways, Alejandro closed an eye.

"I mean, there's nothing else to say, right?" Lisbeth said as she rustled her short hair. "We're way the hell past the point of *We can't* or *It's impossible.* If you're sayin' we're the only ones who can do it, then we'll do it—we'll save the world."

"I agree with Liz… Though I would have put it more elegantly."

"Come again?!"

As Lisbeth and Leili finally managed to find some sort of balance on the ground, too, Claudia snapped to attention and saluted.

"You do me a great honor, sir. I will do my best to live up to the faith you've put in me."

"…Who would believe she's a newly minted Valkyrie? I guess she takes after Rusalka?"

"Sir, this isn't the time for jok—"

Rusalka started to rebuke Alejandro's response to Claudia's earnestness, but before she could finish—

"—I would like to think so at least, sir."

"Eh…"

That was all Rusalka could muster in response. Claudia stood tall, maintaining her earnest gaze as she turned to Rusalka.

"It is perhaps presumptuous, but I have relied heavily on your records as my model for how to be a Valkyrie, Major. Your wings in the air. The way you carry yourself on the ground. I would say that I have learned much from you, ma'am. The colonel is correct. It is just self-proclaimed, but I consider myself your student, Major."

"——"

"And I think the same can be said for everyone who has learned from the Second Valkyrie."

Claudia then looked to the rest of the Valkyries for agreement. Her gaze moved from Lisbeth and Leili to Shannon and everyone else who had also come over to join them. Faced with her straightforward gaze utterly lacking in malice, they glanced at one another.

"I've respected the major for a long time. It's not any different now."

The first to respond was Shannon, whom Rusalka had known since Hamburg.

"A student of the major… If it is not too presumptuous, I would be honored to call myself that. I consider it the greatest fortune to have been able to fly with you and learn from you."

Leili was the type who never had to try to achieve the top marks at whatever she studied, but there was a certain passion in her response.

"I'm the opposite from Lily. I'm always suffering 'cause of you. If I hadn't met you, I never would have endured any of that... But if I hadn't met you, I would have been dead a long time ago, too. So I guess I'm grateful."

Lisbeth linked her hands behind her head, an aggrieved sullenness seeping into her begrudging tone.

And the other Valkyries all looking to Rusalka had the same trust and faith in their gazes. Even as they turned to the one among them who was surely the weakest there, turning their gazes onto the weak, foolish Valkyrie who had done nothing more than fly longer than anyone else.

"Amy talked about it, how Valkyries are all sisters flying together to achieve the same goal."

Rusalka inhaled sharply at Alejandro's words.

"Valkyries are sisters." Amy had told her that, too. At the time, she had not really agreed or disagreed. And she had not really thought about it again until today—

"In that sense, that would make you, the one who's flown as a Valkyrie longer than anyone else, the eldest sister of all the Valkyries here."

Alejandro set his hand lightly on her head. Rusalka could not make herself reject the warmth of his palm. A far greater shock had pierced her breast.

The feeling was entirely different from when she had first heard it from Amy. Or perhaps that had been the same sort of feeling Amy had carried, trying to be everyone's elder sister with that small frame of hers.

A loving affection for the Valkyries, her fellow sisters, who were all flying with the same future in mind.

"It's a big burden being the oldest, ya know?" Lisbeth spoke from experience.

"...I grew up the youngest with two older brothers, so I always wanted to have younger siblings."

Looking back, meeting the gazes of all the Valkyries looking to her, Rusalka exhaled. All the Valkyries there, and all those not assembled there as well—they were sisters who shared the same wings.

What a large family.

"I never would have thought I would end up with so many younger sisters."

"—Ha-ha-ha! That's the spirit."

Alejandro moved his hand from her head and laughed at her response. Then his face hardened as he firmly planted his feet. The Valkyries snapped to attention as one.

"Once the preparations are in order, prepare for a simultaneous attack on Mistletoe. Crown, Haltija, and Brafford will take down the three secondaries. Rusalka, you pry open the route to Mistletoe."

"Yes, sir."

"And once it's open—"

Alejandro turned his gaze to the back of the group. At the tail end of the line stood a girl who had been watching in silence throughout. The decisive weapon against Mistletoe—Alma Conturo.

Her angelic face bore the expression of a warrior as she nodded.

"I will take Mistletoe down. I won't mess up this time."

She pressed her hand against her chest, as if crushing the sapling that had started to sprout there. Her powerful resolve was undoubtedly the will of all Sigrdrifa.

Hearing that and seeing the Valkyries burning with a renewed determination, Alejandro nodded.

"—I'm proud to serve with you all."

8

The battle intensified. He could see an explosion to his right and then to his left.

The bullets from his growling machine guns bounced off the enemy's outer shell right as he just barely managed to twist his jet to avoid the return fire of light rounds.

Slipping past an enemy's lifeless gleam, he pulled off yet another miracle in a long list of close calls that he had already lost count of.

"Anyone else would've kicked the bucket a long time ago…"

In awe of the skills he had awakened to in such a dire fight, the man looked down at his hands. Gripping the stick were the godlike hands that had pulled off the miracle of surviving the last dozen minutes—though they had already lost most of their original shape.

The transformation—the cataclysmic pillar's green death, which looked almost tranquil in its aftermath. He had noticed the early signs of it even before taking off, but it had accelerated dramatically once he was in the air.

The same effect was afflicting the other pilots, too. Where it started and what parts of their body it violated next came down to pure chance. There had been many jets that had already dropped out of the sky because the process started at the pilot's head. On that point, he was one of the lucky ones, since it had started at his legs, and he could still feel his fingers.

"...That said... I'm reaching...my limit..."

The difficulty in speaking was because the transformation had reached his torso and upper body. His lungs and other organs were already being changed, and he couldn't explain how he was still breathing. Or what was keeping his body moving after his heart had become wooden.

"Ob...vious...ly..."

What was it that was driving this brave aviator—and all the people at the base—fighting for the fate of humanity?

It couldn't be anything but the dauntless, gallant figures of the girls who conquered the same terror and flew in the same skies as them. The Valkyries were what buoyed the spirits of the men going out to fight alongside those brave girls.

——Fighting for the sake of the Valkyrie who said that she loved them.

"Gotta...show...off...for..."

Struggling to speak, the man relied on the ingrained reflexes he had harnessed in battle after battle to evade the incoming attacks as he turned his fighter's nose straight at the pillar's body, charging straight at it. He could not make any progress with smaller calibers, so the only choice was to smash it with something even larger—

"—Gh."

Just before his final display of obstinate will, he heard a voice over the radio. His ears were apparently still unchanged. Somehow, he managed to focus on the sounds—

"—Sigrdrifa is returning to the battle!"

He heard the rousing voice of a Valkyrie.

The same voice that had said she loved them was calling out loud and clear over the radio, signaling their return to keep hope alive.

"...Ahhh...she's...really a...great woman..."

He smiled in pure admiration.

And the next moment his jet crashed straight into the center of a tertiary, explo—

There was an explosion as another fighter jet crashed straight into a tertiary.

As the transformation progressed and they stopped being able to take evasion actions, they resorted to the final measure, at least trying to take the enemy with them when they went. They couldn't penetrate the pillars' shells with their weapons, so they resorted to a kamikaze attack, using their own jets as their greatest firepower.

And that was how the men who had taken to the skies to buy just a few minutes for the Valkyries met their ends.

The vast majority of jets that had taken off from the base had already gone down, and the few pilots remaining would join them soon. They had taken to the skies knowing that was what would happen.

So at the very least—

"I won't let your sacrifices go to waste...!"

Rusalka roared as she led Sigrdrifa back into the air.

Getting refueled and reloaded had been a rush job, and most of their Deus ex Machinas couldn't truthfully be said to be in perfect working order, either. But they would just have to make up for it with however much explosives, bullets, and a sense of duty they could pack into their planes.

"Scatter! Stick to the plan!"

"—Roger!"

With a reliable response from her squadron, the battle continued anew.

Weaving through the gaps in the hail of light rounds, Rusalka used herself to draw the enemies in and lead them to the slaughter at the hands of the Valkyries following behind her. She used the cracks in the pillars' shells, opened by the men's valiant sacrifices, to slip her own shots into the enemies' cores, shattering the hated pillars.

Meanwhile, the three strongest Valkyries flew through explosions of light that came from dying tertiaries as they turned to face the three secondary pillars.

"I'm gettin' really tired of that crap!!!"

Lisbeth Crown turned into a barrel roll, acrobatically evading the incoming fire pouring down on her. In contrast to her violent personality, her plane's movements were delicate and subtle, practically composing a dance routine as she flew through the skies.

She was staring down the blue pillar that looked like an amalgamation of countless spheres. When she closed in tight to it, they exploded from the inside out, catching the surrounding tertiaries in the overwhelming force of the attack before regrouping to a different location to repeat the move and fend off the tenacious Valkyrie once more.

Lisbeth had been foiled countless times because of that idiosyncratic attack—

"You think you can get away from meeeeee?!"

Closely following the sphere that was splitting and trying to get away, she pushed her Deus ex Machina past its limits. Her wings creaked, her fuselage cracked, and fragments started streaming away, but it did not break, and the wings held. The machine was a reflection of its pilot's unyielding, indomitable spirit.

Silencing the wails of her plane, Lisbeth transformed into a demonic bullet launched straight at the enemy's heart. Dogfighting was Lisbeth's specialty—there was no one in the world who could best her.

Twisting her body and launching into a turn, Lisbeth aimed for the main body of the pillar that was trying to escape. Because it split into clones to hide, its main body's defenses were not as strong as it could be. That was her target.

The spheres all took aim at her as she closely followed the main body, but she had no intention of getting knocked out of the sky by some flailing. She just tore into them, cutting down on the total number of spheres even as she maintained her pursuit—

"Go and apologize to my family and everyone else who's died…!"

Tears ran down her cheeks as she nailed the secondary's main body with a blast from her guns.

* * *

At the same moment, Leili Haltija was approaching her target secondary.

She could hear Lisbeth's passionate shout over the radio. In contrast to her, Leili's heart was quiet as she threaded the needle through the enemy's hurricane-like attacks.

Less so calm and collected, her stance was one of almost detachment. She was aware that she was lacking in strength compared to the other two who had been assigned the same mission.

On talent alone, she had been able to accomplish anything without trouble or effort since long ago, but that was her limit.

She could be top-class, but she would never stand at the very top. It had been the same for everything she had practiced, from piano to dance to schoolwork. And it had been the same when she became a Valkyrie as well.

Fate had chosen for Leili to be a jack-of-all-trades.

"I've cursed my lot before, but..."

She had also scorned herself for not being serious enough, for being unable to overcome the walls she encountered, for not being desperate enough to break out of her shell.

But—

"I'm glad I'm like this."

Able to accomplish anything without trouble, never becoming obsessed with anything, never getting too attached, reaching her current position by merely going with the flow and simply reacting to things that happened around her. But because she had been like that, she had been able to take part in such an important battle.

She had never been best in anything—but she was able to protect the people she loved most.

"______"

As Leili closed in, the silver secondary came spinning at high speed. The snakelike pillar that was coiled around a single support column was moving at a blistering speed in order to hide its weak point.

Apparently, we're both fond of keeping up appearances. But in that case, I can guess where your weak point is.

Homing in on the weak spot that was twisting in a spiral around the column, Leili's Deus ex Machina became one with the wind. As a sonic boom cracked in the air, the pillar's long torso was split in half. And after she flew out of the torso, which had been severed by the sheer force of the wind, the enemy's weak point, the vandrande, came into view.

"Unfortunately, I am just a tad bit better at keeping up appearances."

And then Leili unflinchingly launched the final strike—

The thoughts left to her, the hope placed in her—they all gave Claudia Brafford strength.

This was her first battle. She was utterly lacking in experience. She hadn't even been counted as a comrade of the people of the base for long, and this battle had begun because of her and her sister.

Yes, not just her sister. She and Shirin both shared responsibility.

Even if a god said otherwise, that did not change how she felt about the matter. That was because she and her sister had shared everything from the moment they had been born.

"—Stop trying to carry everything all by yourself and rely on your elder sister a little, Shiri."

At that very moment, Shirin was with Odin, embarking on the ritual to reform a sacred treasure. She did not know the details of what that involved, and Shirin had refused to tell her.

She said it was because it was embarrassing, but that was surely a lie. Shirin was masterful with her words, worldly wise, and skilled at acting like a spoiled child, but she was terrible at lying when it really counted.

Bad enough that even Claudia, as terrible as she was at deciphering the subtleties of others' emotions, could see through her lies.

"Don't worry about me, Sister. Go on now. Get out there and protect me already."

Those were the last words she had said before Claudia left for battle.

She had been beautiful in the sheer white silk gown she was wearing for the ritual. It evoked a scene out of ancient legend, and it caused Claudia's chest to tighten.

There was something about it that made the sister she had known from birth feel distant and fragile.

Once the fighting was over and she was sure Shirin was safe, she would have to force her to explain exactly what it was she was hiding. Even if a god had sworn her to secrecy.

It was only natural for an elder sister to be desperate to protect her younger sister. She would even fight a god if she had to.

So—

"—I'm afraid I must insist such a vulgar enemy leave the stage!"

Claudia shouted as the soft and flabby, mucus-like torso of the secondary pillar before her eyes quivered. It scattered the liquid that formed its body not at Claudia but at the tertiaries surrounding it, swallowing them up and fusing with them.

The tertiaries it consumed started glowing red and swelled. Each grew to a size that practically made them pseudo-secondaries, and they were all blocking Claudia's way.

"———"

The enemy was a single secondary and around thirty ersatz secondaries. Unbeknownst to Claudia, her blood started racing, and she licked her lips.

Her black Gladiator tore through the blue sky. The sun was still high. In a sky too bright for stars to be seen, her jet-black fuselage became like a shooting star. She drilled into her marks, shattering those before her—

Following the arc her plane drew, one imitation secondary after another exploded in her wake. She kept her machine-gun bursts to the minimum, but her aim had a deadly precision, perfectly hitting the weak point that afflicted every pillar, their cores—the vandrande, which was the source of the absorption that granted them power.

"If you hit the weak point, it won't matter how large or small the enemy might be. I've grown tired of your tricks!"

While the theory was nothing new, there were few Valkyries who could even hope to pull it off with any consistency.

Wielding a natural talent that could not be held back by a lack of experience, Claudia closed in on the secondary that was still trying to resist. Sensing danger, it spread its body thin, almost as if it had exploded, sending its red core swimming swiftly through the flowing body—

"Too late."

But she had already foreseen that it would try that. That it would attempt to flee as fast as it could once the tide of battle had turned against it. That was only natural.

She and her sister had always been fleeing their fate in just the same way.

But—

"There is no escaping fate."

With that cruel pronouncement, her wing, clad in wind, bore down on the red core—

9

Three enormous flashes of light illuminated the battlefield at the same time.

In the blink of an eye, massive trees blinked into existence, imbued with all the life force contained within the secondary pillars that had been there just a split second earlier. Those trees falling to the earth were proof of an incredibly difficult mission having been accomplished—

"The three secondary pillars have all been annihilated! Only Mistletoe remains!"

Rusalka could sense even Michelle's iron mask cracking slightly over the radio as she reported the unprecedented feat. However, it was not just limited to her. Everyone who heard the report and everyone who saw the scene clenched their fists at the miracles those three had pulled off.

With the three bodyguards peeled away, Mistletoe's defenses had been neutralized. There were still several thousand tertiaries left, but compared to the secondaries, the difference was like night and day.

This was their chance.

"—Rusalka!"

"I know! Converge on Mistletoe!"

Rusalka aimed her wings straight toward the enemy at Alejandro's encouragement.

She needed to open a path to Mistletoe so Alma could get through. With her firepower, they could incinerate the enemy whole. If they could just manage that, they would—

"———"

—win. But just as Rusalka thought that, she sensed the sapling in her chest pulsing.

She didn't know what it meant, but it wasn't something she could ignore.

"Evasive maneu— Gh!"

She immediately shouted, pulling her Deus ex Machina into a loop—just as an intense ray of white light filled the sky, just barely grazing her wings and fuselage.

——It was an attack from Mistletoe just when they were about to bombard it with concentrated fire.

Ordinarily, Mistletoe tended to watch over the battlefields it appeared on, but on a few rare occasions it had displayed an omnidirectional, wide-ranging suppression attack.

"Gh..."

The premonition she had felt from the sapling's pulse had saved Rusalka's life by the skin of her teeth.

But it had also completely robbed her of her momentum. She immediately maneuvered to take up position again. She needed to continue the attack run as soon as possible.

As she was thinking that, she prepared to order the Valkyries to form back up and execute their plan. But then she realized that the only one who had fully evaded it was her.

"Wha...?"

Other Valkyries had managed to react to her shout. Many had succeeded in avoiding a direct hit from the light ray. But most had lost a wing or engine function and were belching black smoke as they bled altitude. That was not the worst of it, though.

The Valkyries in the air were not the only ones subjected to the ray. It had reached Holm base, too, and there were tendrils of flames rising from all the facilities. Just like at Hamburg before, the command post had taken a direct hit. The damage was almost as bad.

"Command! Come in, command!"

She desperately called for a response, but there was only static. Imagining the worst, she called out again, determined to continue the attack in the air at the very least.

"—Gh! Alma?!"

"...I'm okay. I went high. But..."

The lynchpin of their attack was still safe and operational, but that wasn't reason enough to breathe easily.

Her half-finished thought was proof of the fatal position they were in. Looking around, well over a thousand tertiaries had also been scorched by Mistletoe's attack, but there were several times that number still in the air. Meanwhile—

"Lisbeth! Leili! Claudia!"

The three who had each taken down a secondary solo had been caught off guard by Mistletoe's attack in the immediate aftermath of their hard-won battles. She could see their three planes trailing smoke badly in the distance. But it did not end there. No matter how she counted it, the only ones who could continue fighting on their side were her and Alma.

"Rusalka..."

"—Gh. Maintain altitude! I'll open a path for you!"

"...Got it..."

Nodding at Rusalka's instructions, Alma nosed her Lancaster up, gaining altitude.

With her flying far above the heads of the swarming tertiaries, they still had a chance of winning if she could just drop her Grand Slam on target. The problem was that they had just lost the fighting strength necessary to open that path for her.

"———"

Retreat was not an option. The enemy wouldn't retreat, either. Pulling back would only mean getting overwhelmed. But even if Rusalka resolved herself to a suicidal charge, she knew she wouldn't achieve much.

If at least one of those three were still able to fight—

"—Rusalka, can you hear me?"

The next instant, Rusalka almost cried when she heard a man's voice over the radio. She turned her face to the radio, clinging to that voice.

"I can hear you! Are you uninjured, Colonel?! Alma and I are the only ones still capable of continuing combat operations! I am going to open the route to Mistletoe myself so that she can—"

"Even you can't do that alone."

When he rejected the only answer that she had been able to find as she struggled to think of any answer, her mind went blank. But before despair could overwhelm her, Alejandro continued:

"So I'm sending you one more Valkyrie. Make a miracle happen, Rusalka."

"...Another? Who could...?"

Every Valkyrie who could be mustered should have been sent up long ago. But they had all suffered hits from Mistletoe's attack and were unable to keep fighting.

So what Valkyrie had he—?

"You can't mean—"

"—Indeed, Major."

The only possibility that suddenly came to mind was confirmed by none other than the Valkyrie herself.

Rusalka gasped as a silver Spitfire leaped into the fray, taking the place of the Valkyries who were rapidly approaching the ground—

"Natalie?!"

"Yes, ma'am. I couldn't just stand by and watch from the sidelines, so I took to the skies as well."

Natalie Chase, who should have been in her sickbed, had taken flight.

—With just three Valkyries left, Sigrdrifa entered the endgame.

10

When she was asked why she became a Valkyrie, Natalie Chase's answer came down to pride.

A sort of noblesse oblige. Natalie had a strong belief in the duty of those who were born to high standing and thought they should always behave in a manner befitting that privileged position.

Because of that, when she was judged to have the aptitude to become a Valkyrie, she had rejected her parents' objections and not hesitated to receive Odin's divine blessing. Even as the exhaustion caused by the encroaching transformation intensified and she struggled to even breathe, she never allowed it to show on her face.

She knew she was an unfilial daughter. But she hoped her parents would understand. She had been born a daughter of the Chase family, and she was proud to fulfill her duty.

* * *

——The silver and red Spitfires danced as one, smashing through the enemy formation.

By some twist of fate, Natalie had been granted the same model of Deus ex Machina as Rusalka.

However, their planes' images were like mirror reflections of each other. Natalie, with her red hair, flew a silver Spitfire, while Rusalka, with her silver hair, flew a crimson Spitfire.

Natalie secretly believed it was destiny. Deus ex Machinas were reflections of the disposition of the Valkyrie to whom they were granted. In Natalie's case, it was aspiration.

Before she had become a Valkyrie, she had encountered a disaster caused by pillars. She had been a volunteer doing disaster relief when the pillars attacked the refugee camp she was working at.

She had called out frantically, doing her best to help the people around her as much as she could. But in the terrible panic, she had been powerless. It was the first true failure she had ever experienced in her life—and it might well have been the last in a life cut short.

——It was in that moment of hopelessness that a flight led by a crimson Spitfire had clashed with the pillars and drawn them away from the refugee camp.

The instant those red wings cut through the despair that filled the skies had been seared into Natalie's mind ever since.

That image was always there, always asserting itself. That yearning more than anything else was why Natalie Chase had become a Valkyrie—

"With how poorly you value yourself, I'm sure you never understood just how much of an honor I considered it to be able to fly in the same squadron as you."

Having received a matching set of wings, and having been assigned to the same base and later the same squadron, she had seen Rusalka at her worst as well as her resurrection. She could not count how many times she had felt grateful to be able to fly side by side with those reborn red wings, striving toward the same bright future.

How many times she had struggled to hold in the swell of emotions that threated to overrun her defenses.

How many times she had wanted to come clean, to convey just how grateful she was for that day.

"Natalie! The left!"

"Understood!"

Natalie's soul trembled as Rusalka's instructions streamed in over the radio.

Her gleaming silver fuselage swinging wide, Natalie let loose with her machine guns at the tertiaries pressing in from the side. Several of them were caught up in the explosion, and she forcibly twisted her plane to dive through the opening that created.

The tertiaries had crafted a complex multilayered defense, but Natalie and Rusalka managed to slice through those barriers with just their two planes, pushing forward to create an opening for Alma's lethal shot to pass.

"………"

Alma's unease came through in the silence on the line as she maintained altitude.

As ever, the changes in her expression were minor, but she had begun to show a wealth of emotions. Though perhaps it was just that Natalie had gotten better at reading the minute changes after getting closer to her.

She had thought for the longest time that Alma had disliked her. But she had been surprised by how devoted Alma had been in coming to see her after finding out about her condition.

And she also regretted that there was still so much she didn't know about Alma, who was so kindhearted and compassionate.

And she had stumbled upon several other realizations, too.

She had been run around in circles so many times by Shannon since their days in training, but that was just a manifestation of how wide her perspective was and how considerate she was of those around her. And while she had been concerned about how Lisbeth and Leili would turn out at first, she had been able to see the signs of their growth already.

And the newest member, Claudia. There were so many things she had wanted to talk about with her.

What she liked, what she didn't. What she hoped to do now that she was a Valkyrie. Natalie had wanted to talk with her, to understand each other. They would surely have been able to get along well.

"Since we are all Valkyrie sisters."

"Natalie?"

"Do you know, Major? *Sigrdrifa* is apparently a word that refers to the very first Valkyrie."

Spreading her wings as the enemies filled the skies, Natalie's heart was mysteriously at peace.

Perhaps that was just because Mistletoe's encroachment had expanded and was starting to reach her heart and lungs. Not that she was in the mood to crack a joke about being in a vegetative state.

——She had heard the origin of the word *Sigrdrifa* from Odin.

It was what the very first Valkyrie, the beloved eldest daughter who had received God's divine blessing, had been called. In that sense, it assuredly referred to the First, Amy.

However, having lost her, the eldest of the Valkyrie sisters still flying through the war-torn skies even now was the Valkyrie who had once been called the Crushed Crimson, someone utterly lacking in self-confidence.

However, that is exactly why Natalie believed she was most deserving of that name. Rusalka Evereska, the one who had become the eldest of so many Valkyries, was—

"Sigrdrifa, the wings of victory."

"——"

"Major, *you* are the manifestation of our hope. *You* are the guiding light of the Valkyries. *You* are my ideal. You are Sigrdrifa, the Valkyrie who brings victory."

She could feel Rusalka's speechlessness over the radio when she said that. Smiling faintly at that reaction, Natalie nudged her nose through a gap in the tertiaries toward Mistletoe.

Her body was in terrible condition. But she had only just started flying. Unlike Rusalka, who had been fighting for hours, she had focus to spare. In fact, she felt more focused than she ever had before.

Weaving through the onrushing enemies, she clipped their wings with her machine guns. Slapping down the jaws trying to tear at her fuselage with her blessed wings, she misdirected the enemies to crash into each other before slipping through the openings they left behind. And then—

"I can see it!"

As she burst through the explosions of light, she saw the path to Mistletoe open before her. Accelerating, Natalie pressed in on the enormous amalgamation of giant trees.

——The next instant, Mistletoe unleashed the power it had been building, letting loose another omnidirectional blast of light.

It also closed in on Natalie, unerring in its aim, but—

"Aaaaaaaaaaaaagh!"

With a roar, fighter jets charged out in front of Natalie, intercepting the ray of light. A small handful of brave pilots who had managed to keep flying even when so many Valkyries had been grounded.

There were only six of them, but in that moment, without any signal or planning among them, they had thrown themselves between Natalie and the devastating beam of light, giving her just a split second longer to react. She didn't let that moment go to waste.

The six jets disappeared into the light in an explosion, but Natalie's silver Spitfire escaped, bearing down unerringly on Mistletoe.

"Aaaaaaaaaah!!!"

The moment she reached Mistletoe, which never allowed any enemy to approach it, Natalie subconsciously broke into a ragged bellow.

Controlling the stick subconsciously, she twisted through the innumerable tree trunks composing its body, dodging, evading, and eluding the branches stretching out to her that seemed to be guided by a consciousness.

Her movements were superhuman, like a work of art.

Having gotten that close, Natalie's aim was a single point on the floating island.

The vandrande, the weak point of all pillars and the point that needed to be hit or else they would not fall. Mistletoe was no different in that regard. Even if Alma landed her Grand Slam, if the vandrande somehow managed to escape the blast, Mistletoe would not be defeated.

And with such a vast body to hide it in, Natalie and Natalie alone could tell instinctively where it was hiding. Because—

"Right now, you and I are almost one and the same."

With her transformation progressing at a steady clip, Natalie was standing firmly with one foot on either side of the line. Looking down at her chest, where her heart had already ceased to beat, the pulsing green life growing there was celebrating the return to its mother.

It was seeking the loving warmth of its mother.

Then allow me to oblige you.

The heartwarming family reunion was guiding Natalie Chase to Mistletoe's weak spot.

As if rejecting its child's return, it flung vines and sap at her with abandon. With an acrobatic flight befitting a fighter actually flying at ground level through a forest, Natalie made her way to the enemy's heart.

—Before her stood a fortress of vegetation made of countless interwoven vines.

At a glance, it seemed impossible to break through, but inside it lay Mistletoe's fatal weakness. The red, pulsing vandrande, containing a single coin. Sensing Natalie's approach, it extended more vines and took flight, trying to flee together with its fortress.

I won't let you go. I can't. If I did, that would be the end of everything.

"—Ngh."

That instant, Natalie let go of everything controlling her and laid herself bare.

Her ragged breathing, the dozens of damaged and flaming Deus ex Machinas, the sapling's joy at being reunited with its mother—she turned it all into fuel to propel her forward as she homed in on the fleeing vandrande, refusing to let it escape.

Her machine gun tore into the vines, roaring fire until she finally ran out of bullets. The shredded plants were blown away as her Spitfire charged forward like a shooting star.

There was a shock wave and a tremendous crash as Natalie's plane was half crushed. That was the natural consequence of charging headlong into the enemy. It was a miracle her plane had not exploded. But she didn't have time to be grateful as she hauled herself out of the shattered canopy and left the plane behind.

Her legs hurt. Her vision was shaky. But—

"Checkmate."

It was the catchphrase of her commanding officer, whom Natalie could not help but love and respect.

—Having taken her plane's charge head-on, the vandrande was pinned. If that could just be broken, humanity would win. Natalie pulled a gun from her jacket and steadied herself.

Sensing danger, Mistletoe immediately formed a defensive wall of vines over the vandrande. However, Natalie merely smiled.

Smiled and pointed the gun—a flare gun—skyward.

With a distinct pop, the flare flew up and exploded in a burst of colored light, indicating her position.

The position of the enemy's weak point. And Natalie Chase's final resting place.

"Alma!"

Natalie shouted, still pointing the flare gun upward. She called out to the girl flying far above where the flare exploded. To her comrade. Her friend.

Alma Conturo's heart was stuck by a heartrending pain as she saw the flare burst below her, and again as she saw Natalie standing right atop the enemy's heart.

"........."

She couldn't summon a single word because she perfectly understood what Natalie was after, what she wanted.

In under a second, a slew of thoughts flashed through her mind.

It was nothing short of a miracle that had brought Natalie to this point. And now Alma had been shouldered with the burden of deciding this battle, which so many people had sacrificed their lives for and might very well decide the ultimate fate of humanity.

Miracle after miracle had led them to this moment, giving Alma her first and last chance—in exchange for the one person Alma most wanted to save.

A second passed. The tertiaries quickly moved as one to protect Mistletoe in its exposed position.

The path that Alma's comrades had wrenched open for her was closing. And she could only watch helplessly—

"I won't let youuuuu!!!"

With a furious shout, Rusalka charged into the swarm of tertiaries trying to plug the hole in their defenses. Supporting Natalie's charge, her Deus ex Machina had surpassed its limits, too. Rushing into the enemies beginning to swarm, she stole back the second that had been lost.

"—Alma!!!"

In that moment Rusalka had gained with her desperation, she shouted to Alma.

Alma realized this was her final opportunity to choose.

She had only two options—one could live, or both could die.

"Why...?"

Why was she never given another choice? Why could she not find a route where they both survived? She didn't want to die and didn't want her friend to die. That was all she wanted, so why was that so impossible?

If living, if the future she so badly wanted, meant going through hell, then what was she fighting for? Would it not be easier to just let it all end there?

She would rather die there, together with the people she had let into her heart—

"Alma."

It was a voice she could not possibly have heard.

Her plane was over five thousand meters above the ground. There was easily more than a thousand meters between her and Natalie. She should not have been able to hear her voice.

But even if she couldn't hear her voice, she could *see* her.

——Having awakened as a Valkyrie and receiving a Lancaster for her Deus ex Machina, Alma had also acquired a certain ability—divine eyesight. In order to avoid hitting her allies with her Grand Slam, she was capable of seeing an extraordinary distance if she focused.

Her divine eyes could see Natalie with the flare gun still pointed over her head. She could see her lips moving, murmuring something, and she could hear the voice she knew so well in her head.

Natalie had called her name and then let go of the gun. With her now empty hand, she was holding out a finger. Her pinkie. Alma understood immediately what she meant by that.

"Keep your promise."

The promise she had made before leaving to fight, that she would not let a chance to defeat Mistletoe slip away.

This was that moment.

"______"

The blood boiled in Alma's small body.

Her heart pounded like it was about to explode, pumping hot blood throughout her entire body, scorching her frozen fingertips as they finally moved.

Her hands moved on instinct. It was a practiced motion she had done hundreds of times before to put a final exclamation mark on countless battles.

Alma's hell would surely continue, but that was what she had chosen.

She promised to join Natalie in hell.

"...I loved you, Natalie..."

"Yes, I loved you, too, Alma."

Tears that should not have been possible to see streamed down their cheeks as they exchanged final words of parting that should have been impossible to hear. And just as the tears ran down their cheeks, the Grand Slam dropped.

"____"

The ten-ton bomb fell straight down. Its aim was true, falling straight toward Alma's closest friend.

As death approached, Mistletoe howled. The secondary pillar known to the human race as a cataclysm flailed in a final attempt to avoid its impending doom, desperate to escape.

An enormous tree swung upward to smash the Grand Slam falling toward it—

"—I won't allow it."

The tree was hit by machine-gun fire from a crimson Spitfire, shattering it into splinters. As the hideous tree broke into fragments, humanity's greatest attack slipped through and went straight for Mistletoe.

An instant later, there was a massive explosion as a fireball consumed Mistletoe's heart and incinerated it. And with it, the noble girl who had served as the marker for that heart.

"______"

The floating island and the horrific amalgamation of trees hovering in the sky plummeted to the earth.

The supernatural, mystical forest was consumed in flames, turning to ash and then changing into many motes of lights as the cataclysmic pillar failed to maintain its form, and it collapsed, scattering in its final moments.

The tertiaries that were not consumed by the Grand Slam's blast began to fray as Mistletoe underwent annihilation, disappearing along with it.

Having brought that much destruction, that much death, that much barbarity, the pillars, in their dying moments, disappeared with a fragility that almost seemed to evoke a sense of beauty by design.

"______"

Looking down on the pillars scattering below her, Alma bit her lip.

She thought that if she didn't do that, she wouldn't be able to hold on. Exactly what she wouldn't be able to hold on to, she couldn't say.

She could not hide it anymore. There was no stopping it. The tears were welling up and overflowing from her eyes.

If this pain in her heart was the price of victory, then she would rather rip it out and be done with it. The terrible sapling that had been pulsing in her breast had disappeared without a trace.

Natalie had taken it away. But she had not taken Alma with her.

It was because she understood that now that she was weeping so terribly.

But no matter how much she cried, the tears would not stop.

"______"

Rusalka could hear it over the speaker: Alma's sobbing voice.

She understood painfully well that there was no joy for victory in those tears. She had been there to follow Natalie, ensuring she reached Mistletoe. And she had been there to support Alma, ensuring her Grand Slam would reach its intended target. And she had been there, providing assistance so that humanity would gain the chance to live for another day.

"______"

Guiding her battered and broken Deus ex Machina, she gradually descended for an emergency landing as she looked up in the sky.

Even though she was in the air herself, she was looking up to the sky high, high above her. To a place far beyond, where she could not reach no matter how far she stretched her hands, to the other side, where so many of her comrades had gone before her.

Rusalka quietly stretched out her hand.

Reaching out without heed to the tears running down her cheeks. Her fingers unable to grasp anything.

But there was one undeniable truth: Humanity had defeated Mistletoe.

That was the end of the battle that would in later days come to be known as the Battle of Weihnachten.

Chapter 6
Rusalka Evereska

1

——At a terrible cost of life, the battle with Mistletoe finally drew to a close.

Having failed to fully evade the pillar's omnidirectional attack, most Valkyries had taken damage that made it impossible to continue flying, but few had died—they had not all survived, though.

The Valkyries who had been called in for the decisive battle were all top-tier, and while their craft had been badly damaged, they managed to safely make emergency landings. The ones who picked them up where they fell on the battlefield were friendly forces from another base that had been stationed at the very edge of the combat zone as a precaution.

Rusalka was picked up by them as well, leaving her plane behind for the moment and returning to Holm base.

Along the way, she confirmed the safety of Lisbeth, Leili, Claudia, Shannon, and the rest of her squadron, and she managed a sigh of relief. And of course she confirmed that Alma was safe as well.

The soldiers giving them a ride all praised Sigrdrifa's spirited efforts in battle and congratulated them on finally defeating Mistletoe. Rusalka quietly accepted their words while consumed by a terrible swirl of conflicting emotions.

She suspected Alejandro was feeling the same thing back at the base.

Thinking of him struggling to deal with the aftermath of the battle, she felt just a little bit relieved.

Right then, all she wanted was a short respite. A brief moment where she could forget about the counting of those who had been lost.

But—

"——"

As she rode in the military transport, Rusalka was speechless when she finally made it back to Holm base.

Soldiers were already hard at work repairing the damage caused by Mistletoe's attack, the clearing of rubble and putting out fires.

But she did not recognize any of the faces of the people working.

They were not from Holm base. They were all allies who had heeded the request for support that had gone out before the battle.

And at the base, her comrades, the people who had faced Mistletoe together with her and the rest of the Valkyries, were—

"...This...is..."

She stepped forward falteringly, her hand outstretched. For a second, she hesitated to touch it, but when her fingers brushed the coarse surface, the reality of the situation hit home.

It was real, not a figment of her imagination or some dream.

"Michelle..."

In the command post, at Major Michelle Heyman's designated post, stood a tree the size of a human, wearing her uniform.

She wasn't alone in that bizarre scene, either. It was the same no matter where she looked in the command post. Every seat of all the operators and analysts were filled by human-size trees wearing uniforms.

And it wasn't just the command post. It had happened everywhere, all around the base.

Mistletoe's ability had swallowed every last one of the brave fighters who had stayed at their posts until the very end, transforming all of them.

Michelle Heyman, Roger Reever, and every other soldier on the base.

The only ones who survived were the Valkyries who had defeated Mistletoe and from whom the saplings had been expunged.

——Twenty-one survivors.

That was the final tally for the Battle of Weihnachten.

"—! Gjallarhorn."

Rusalka shuddered, turning on her heels as the worst thought crossed her mind.

Every human on the base had fallen victim to Mistletoe's ability. That meant it was entirely possible that the person they had needed to protect above all else—Mistletoe's target, Shirin—had suffered the same fate.

If she had fallen before completing the ritual, the battle could not even be called a Pyrrhic victory. It would render everything meaningless.

Rusalka desperately sprinted through the base—

"Where are you going, Rusalka?"

Inhaling sharply, Rusalka spun around at that question.

The figure she was searching for was standing in a random hall in the base.

Odin stood there, his visible red eye trained on Rusalka while a patch covered the other.

"Odin...I was looking for you."

"I see. What a coincidence. I was looking for you, too. I guess we were brought together by mutual affection."

"What are...?"

Rusalka stepped forward, latching on to Odin's terribly out-of-place response. But she stopped when he tossed something to her.

"——"

Catching it reflexively, Rusalka gazed in wonder.

It was something that she had seen in pictures and books but had never held before. A blowing horn. It was slick to the touch and made of some mysterious material.

Rusalka gasped.

"This is Gjallarhorn," Odin stated simply.

"This..."

"At first glance, it just looks like an ancient horn, but there is no mistaking it. That is a true sacred treasure. It will sound a loud note when it senses the appearance of a pillar... Make replicas. I won't ask how."

Pointing to the horn in Rusalka's hands, to Gjallarhorn, Odin gave her that command. The replication of a sacred treasure. It was unclear whether that was even possible to do by human hands, but Odin would not have ordered it without some reason to believe it possible. There was almost certainly a way.

And by the fact that Gjallarhorn had been completed…

"…What happened to Shirin?"

"…You already know. I said before that her existence was necessary for the restoration of Gjallarhorn. That was neither hyperbole nor a lie. The fruits of Shirin's existence rest there in your hands."

"———"

"…I'll be going back to Hlidskjalf. Even I am weary after all this."

Odin turned his back on Rusalka with an explanation that sounded almost detached. Something about his dearth of emotions nagged at Rusalka.

"Please wait. There's still more. We defeated Mistletoe like you said. There are still many things to… Ah."

"Forgive me, Rusalka."

Rusalka was speechless when Odin stopped and turned around to face her head-on. As she stood frozen, he apologized to her.

A single tear trailed from his one eye—

"You and I have both lost too much today. Look at yourself in a mirror. You look terrible."

"———"

"And I can hardly say I look very godlike reflected in your sky-blue eyes."

His expression softening, Odin started to leave again. This time, Rusalka could not find it in herself to stop the god walking away from her.

But he had shed a tear. His breast was pained by the thought of what had been lost.

That was enough for her. She didn't need to know anything else.

"Major! So this is where you were!"

A voice called out as someone approached Rusalka. Looking up, she saw Claudia running toward her from the other end of the hall, her golden hair swaying behind her. Like Rusalka, she was still wearing her flight suit, a slight sense of relief visible in her gallant expression.

"I was concerned when I heard you had run off alone, ma'am… If something had happened to you as well…"

"…Apologies, I didn't consider that."

"No, it's understandable… Really…"

Getting close enough to touch Rusalka, Claudia's voice dropped softly in tone.

No one could rejoice unreservedly at their victory in the battle. Too much had been lost to achieve it. Far too much. There were too many things—too many people who could never be brought back.

"I didn't have many chances to speak with Natalie. I can't claim to understand how you and Lieutenant Alma must feel. But it is truly a shame."

"…Yes, it is. I'm sure you and she would have been able to get along well."

Rusalka nodded as Claudia mourned Natalie.

It wasn't a lie. Natalie was the sort of person who could become close with anyone. Or rather, she simply wouldn't give up until she had become close with them. There was surely a future where she and Claudia would have become fast friends as well.

Rusalka closed her eyes as the thoughts of all that had been lost tormented her heart.

"…Major…what is that?"

Claudia furrowed her brow as she looked down at the thing in Rusalka's hands. At an ancient-looking horn that seemed terribly out of place—

"Gjallarhorn. I received it from Odin just now."

"That's…! I see. So at the very least, we managed to achieve our goal."

"Yes, Claudia. I'm grateful to you. Though words cannot adequately express it."

"—? Not at all, ma'am. I'm glad I was able to help, whatever little help I may have provided."

Claudia shook her head as she looked at the completed Gjallarhorn, responding with a polite confusion.

"Whatever little help" did not remotely begin to describe it. She had been critical in defeating Mistletoe. And more than anything, Shirin had been the sine qua non for the completion of Gjallarhorn.

Claudia didn't know the specifics of the ritual, but Rusalka did, and it was her role to convey that to Claudia, to let her know what had been lost.

"I swear on the many lives that were sacrificed to complete this, especially for your precious Shirin—"

"—Shirin?"

"———"

Rusalka stopped in the middle of her vow. It was because Claudia's reaction to hearing her sister's name was nothing like what she expected. It was a confusion akin to hearing a word she had never encountered before.

And with Rusalka unable to say anything, Claudia cocked her head slightly—

"Who is Shirin?"

2

——The cleanup after the battle continued at a hectic pace.

The vast majority of trees around Holm base were identified by the rank insignia and uniforms they were wearing.

With Mistletoe confirmed to have been destroyed, the fact that there was no change in their conditions made it impossible to argue with Odin's theory.

Those who had been transformed could not be changed back. What had been lost could not be brought back.

And even aside from those who had been transformed, there had been many soldiers who had simply died in the fighting. There were many even in the base who had been lost to Mistletoe's omnidirectional attack. It was perhaps a more fortunate fate that they had died without being transformed and their still-human bodies could at least be recovered.

It was difficult for many people to find closure when the bodies of their loved ones could not be found. It was the same for those connected to the several hundred people whose bodies had been transformed.

No one could blame them for holding out hope beyond hope for some impossible miracle.

Even if the man synonymous with miracles was among those who had been lost.

* * *

"______"

A memorial was held to commemorate the victory as well as to mourn those lost in the line of duty.

Lined up for the ceremony were the allied forces that aided the cleanup in the aftermath of the battle as well as the twenty-one Valkyries who had made it back alive after participating in the operation—Rusalka was there, too, of course.

In exchange for almost complete losses, they had achieved an incredible result. The generals from the IPO in attendance for the ceremony praised Holm base's incredible bravery and dedication.

They also declared that, with the help of Odin, the mass-production of Gjallarhorn had made it possible to have advance warning of pillar attacks, and this development was hailed as a massive step forward in humanity's counterattack against the invaders.

Every Valkyrie involved in the operation was given awards and promotions.

And from Rusalka on down, it was a thorough ceremony that did not bring any shame to the name of Sigrdrifa. It had been a beautiful commemoration, and no one would deny that the greatest Valkyries in the world had gathered there.

The cenotaph was buried with flowers, and the names of every last one of the heroes who died in the battle were inscribed on the large memorial. Natalie's name was there of course. And Michelle's and Roger's, too.

And the name inscribed at the very top of the memorial—

3

"______"

When she opened the door to her room, she half expected to see the sight that greeted her.

Whenever an important conversation happened, it always seemed to take place in her room. She had changed rooms often with all the times she had moved around, but the people bearing important things to discuss always seemed to find her.

And that day as well, an uninvited guest had helped himself to a seat on her bed when she came back after a full day's work.

And to top it off—

"...Why are you reading someone else's journal without permission?"

"I had time on my hands, so I just gave in to temptation on a whim."

"I'm quite sure you had to have gone out of your way to unlock the drawer of my desk to be able to do that."

He held up the bent paperclip in his hands without any sense of guilt. A desk drawer lock was a simple enough thing. Even a paperclip would be enough to open it with a little effort...

"But even if it was possible, to actually act on that potential is ethically problematic."

"Hey now, this is a necessary measure in the course of professional duties. I'm your commanding officer. I have to understand the sorts of concerns my subordinates are dealing with in their day-to-day work."

"And do you think you can understand those concerns now?"

"Unfortunately, your journal reads too much like a daily log of business reports, so I can't get a read on the emotional level. There's hardly anything to profile in here."

"My thanks for the compliment, sir."

She saluted ironically as he snorted.

Still, though, it had been a long time since she had shared this kind of exchange. They had both been too busy in the lead-up to the battle, so it had been difficult to have a conversation like that.

And if she was forced to say it—

"Also, regarding your previous comments, unfortunately you are no longer my commanding officer. There have already been several staffing adjustments. And more than anything..."

"More than anything?"

"—You died during the fight, sir."

"———"

Hearing that, the man sitting on her bed, Alejandro Ostley, playfully shut one eye. Closing her journal, he set it down next to him.

"Well, that's how it goes. There's no helping it."

"No helping it? I find that hard to believe. Since you are..."

"Here now? That's true... But that's all it is. I'm sure you understand, Rusalka."

Alejandro slowly stood up, looking directly at Rusalka. She couldn't help averting her eyes to avoid his straightforward gaze.

She could not manage to muster the courage to face Alejandro head-on.

"Rusalka."

"...I'm not sure what you are trying to say, sir. Please explain yourself."

"Rusalka."

"You were always like this. Perhaps because all your subordinates were so skilled. You never explain yourself enough. You mistake it for everyone being able to understand you even if you don't finish your thoughts."

"Rusalka."

"Have some consideration for those of us who have to figure it out. Michelle, Lieutenant Colonel Hammond, me...we all had to deal with your... And yet you always...!"

"Yes, I'm sorry for always being so selfish. All the way to the very end."

Rusalka's voice trembled as she voiced her complaints even now. Hearing that, Alejandro slowly stepped toward her, a meek look on his face that was out of character with how he usually behaved.

They were inside a room. There was not much distance between them. With only three steps, they were close enough that he could hug her.

But that didn't happen. Because—

"It's true; I'm a failure of a commanding officer... I can't even wipe away my subordinate's tears anymore."

Alejandro's fingers tried to brush away the tear running down Rusalka's cheek, but he couldn't. His fingers passed through her.

Having it confirmed for her with her own body, Rusalka exhaled slightly.

"It doesn't make sense. Why could you read my journal?"

"It looks like animate and inanimate objects are treated differently. I can touch memories but not make them... God is awfully cruel."

"...God..."

Rusalka's lips trembled slightly as Alejandro shrugged.

It was a mysterious scene that should have been impossible. It was only natural that God had had something to do with it. The problem was that she still could not begin to guess what his intent was.

She didn't understand anything at all.

"Can you just stay here like this...?"

"...It would be nice if I could. But it's not that sweet of a deal. And it's already a pretty good deal as is."

"What do you—?"

"—Rusalka, I'm dead. I died in battle long ago."

Alejandro interrupted her as she tried to ask for some sort of explanation.

Her eyes widened as a hoarse gasp escaped her throat. But there was no trace of playfulness in Alejandro's expression. It certainly didn't look like he was trying to trick or mislead her.

He touched his chest as a self-deprecating smile crossed his lips.

"My heart stopped long ago. Even before I met you."

"...More than six months before then, right?"

"That's right. Since I died in the middle of the Miracle at Lamia... More precisely, I achieved the Miracle at Lamia after dying and being resurrected."

The feat that had made him synonymous with miracles. Pandora's Calamity, where Amy had died to defeat a secondary pillar. The continuation of that battle, the Miracle at Lamia, had actually been achieved with the intervention of a god.

"Though, to be clear, the actual situation on the ground and the fact that so many people were saved was still due to my quick wits. That part wasn't some god. Your precious commander wasn't just a paper tiger."

"I wasn't worried about that at all... Actually, I am a little bit relieved."

"Ha-ha-ha. If you're going to be like that, then why not act a little cuter?"

Alejandro laughed wryly as he tried to put his hand on Rusalka's head in what had become a habit. He looked a little sad as his hand slipped through her, though.

"Like I said before, I died once in Greece. The pathetic brother who had forgotten who his little sister was when Amy fell met his death there. But someone grabbed that dead man by the scruff of the neck."

"Odin?"

"That's right. That god said he had hopes for me. So he revived me in exchange for giving me a certain mission. On a limited time basis."

"A limited time..."

"That's right. Until I achieved my mission of defeating Mistletoe."

Odin had been watching Mistletoe from long before.

In order to protect the Brafford sisters and complete Gjallarhorn, it had been necessary to stop Mistletoe's obstructions. And the one he had chosen to see that through to the end was Alejandro.

"Einherjar is the name for it supposedly."

"Einherjar..."

"Basically, it's like being a soldier of God. Personally, I didn't ever really feel like considering Odin my superior officer, though. He's more like a chess partner."

That was far too disrespectful when discussing a real god, but Rusalka didn't comment on it.

She didn't really feel much at hearing the term *Einherjar.* The part that most concerned her was Alejandro himself.

His time limit was until his mission was completed. In that case, he—

"—I'll disappear. This right now is a reward from Odin for having fulfilled my duty. Letting me say my last good-bye to the person I most wanted to tell it to."

"...Why...why?"

"——"

"You too... Why does everyone choose me as their last...?"

Alejandro scratched his cheek as Rusalka looked him in the eyes and quietly questioned him.

At the very least, she had intended for it to be quiet. But she didn't have the composure to be sure that her voice wasn't quivering, that there wasn't an undertone of grief creeping into her tone.

She just wanted to know the answer. Why was it always her—?

"I'm always left behind. By Amy, by Natalie... It was a little different, but Shirin was the same. And now it's you."

"I'm sorry for always burdening you. But this one thing is something I can't leave to anyone else. I can't imagine leaving it to anyone other than you."

"——"

"A witness—that's what you called yourself."

She had said it in Hlidskjalf when she saw Shirin off. Shirin had described her that way, and she had confirmed it bitterly.

Did Alejandro expect the same thing of her?

To see him off, to not forget him—

"You can forget about me if you want, Rusalka. But there is one thing I want you to remember."

"—Ah."

"Sigrdrifa is in your hands now. Teach them, guide them, and do what you can to make sure that as many of them make it through alive as you can. And that applies to yourself, too. There's nothing great about dying."

"——"

"Survive, Rusalka. Stay alive and make it out. And once you've exterminated all those damn pillars, find yourself someone nice, get married, have some kids, live a nice life, and then you can die."

"——"

"That's my final order for you."

Alejandro took a step back, opening up enough space so they could properly see each other's faces.

Rusalka looked at him, her eyes pleading, asking how she should take that final order.

"...You really are siblings. Always running me about with your whims."

"Yeah, I guess so. Seems like our family really loves you. And Claudia's a distant relation, too, so you should watch out for her."

"She won't become like that... She will surely become a splendid Valkyrie. And I will live through the end of this war, find a good partner, have a child, and die peacefully."

"Heh, sounds like a nice life. Think you can do it?"

"Were you not aware? I'm quite used to following absurd orders. And an order from a superior officer is absolute in the army."

And among all the remaining active Valkyries, Rusalka was the only veteran who had worked her way up the chain of command capable of saying that. A true believer in the myth that orders were absolute.

Rusalka saluted as she looked at Alejandro. Not the Valkyrie salute covering her eye but the first one she had learned—the army salute.

"Yes, sir, Brigadier General Ostley. Lieutenant Colonel Rusalka Evereska hereby acknowledges your order and will comply."

Hearing that, he nodded in satisfaction.

"Still, though, me a general and you a colonel? Personnel has been busy."

"It was simply that large of an operation. It was splendid work, sir. Were it not for your direction, we wouldn't have won. I will surely think of you with pride for the rest of my life."

"You don't say. In that case, pass down my story to the next generation and tell them about how great I was."

"I'm not sure about telling my grandchildren about the troublesome boss I had to deal with..."

"I'm sure you can find a better way to put it!"

Rusalka and Alejandro both burst into laughter at the same time. And after laughing, and laughing, and laughing—

"It's in your hands now, Rusalka. You were the best subordinate and a great woman."

"The latter aside, the former is an honor, Alejandro."

She put her hand over his outstretched hand. They could not touch, but it was a handshake in form at least. A trifling exchange that proved the connection that could not possibly be shared between the living and dead.

But even so, even if it was a hackneyed line, as long as they saw the same thing...

"———"

They both pulled their hands back as Alejandro moved away from Rusalka, a smile still on his face.

Mysteriously, just like with her journal, his hand gripped the doorknob and managed to turn it. And just like that, he stepped leisurely out through the open door.

But while the door should have led back into the hall, the other side was a place she couldn't reach—

"Thank you so much!"

Turning around, Rusalka shouted to the back that was receding into

the light. Hearing that, Alejandro stopped and then raised his hand, a wild, lionlike smile on his face.

"Yeah, I love you, too."

And with those last words, he disappeared beyond the door.

——With that, Alejandro Ostley truly vanished from the world.

The name engraved on the memorial became reality, and the man who gave so much for the world even after having already died once was finally able to venture into what lay beyond.

Would she be there? Would she be waiting for him?

Would the siblings whose bond had been severed for a time be able to meet again?

"—That was a nice good-bye."

Having seen Alejandro off, another voice called out to her.

She did not have to wonder whose voice it was. The closed door opened again as Odin appeared. Rusalka was no longer surprised by the visit of a god who no longer seemed to have any reservation about seeing her on a whim.

She just wiped the tears from her cheeks as she looked at him.

"Thank you, Odin."

"That's surprising. I was prepared to be berated, honestly."

Odin arched his eyebrow. Rusalka shook her head.

"Not at all. Alejandro had accepted his fate. And the world would not be what it is now without him. You were right to choose him as the man to orchestrate Mistletoe's defeat."

"It is an odd feeling to have my daughter bragging about her man to me… Still, there were other candidates besides him. But fate chose him."

"Fate…? Not you?"

"—? Fate is what you call the decisions made by a god. Do you not agree?"

It was a haughty and proud belief, but there was a logic to it. In a sense, it was natural to think of God's will as fate.

"Then again, you feel too human to believe that."

"I know Alejandro entrusted you with taking up his cause, but you don't have to copy his lack of respect for me, too."

"I shall bear that in mind."

Rusalka looked at Odin as she addressed him with a formal salute.

And then as she fell silent, the god's eye narrowed. She cocked her head.

"What is it?"

"If you have anything you want to ask, you should do so now. Right now, I will answer most things. Even about such topics as how this world came to be."

"That's a rather grand theme, but unfortunately it holds little interest for me. But if I may impose on you and ask…?"

"Yes."

Crossing his short arms, Odin nodded.

"You chose myself, Lisbeth, and Natalie to bring Claudia and Shirin under our protection."

"That's right."

"Was that because we were the three Valkyries who were most disposable?"

"——"

Odin fell silent at Rusalka's question. Rusalka had always been thinking about why they had been chosen that night. And when she found out that Natalie had been afflicted by Mistletoe's ability for weeks before that, she had finally come to an answer.

"I have little in the way of abilities, Natalie didn't have a future ahead of her, and Lisbeth was…"

"Utterly lacking in any sense of cohesion. If left like that, it would surely have led to many of her allies dying. But Natalie appears to have broadened her perspective. There is no longer any fear of that."

Odin did not show any shame as he affirmed Rusalka's guess. And she was not shocked by his response. She was a little surprised that she was not shocked by it, but that was all.

"Schwertleite, Roßweiße, Sigrún, Ortlinde, Helmwige, Geirskögul, Randgríðr, Reginleif, Sveið."

"—?" Those are?"

"The names granted to those among my daughters who wield a special power. Think of it like a title. In time, Claudia and those three will surely gain them as well."

Rusalka remembered a conversation she had had with Shannon before. Valkyries like Lisbeth, young and with great power, would someday be granted a name or rank befitting their abilities by Odin.

That had been true. And—

"—Sigrdrifa. Do you know the meaning of that name?"

"…I heard it from Natalie. It is a name that refers to the eldest of the Valkyries."

"That's right. Brynhildr…the name of my first daughter. I had always imagined I would someday call Amy that, but that chance was lost. Brynhildr will never be used. Instead, Rusalka, you are Sigrdrifa."

"———"

She had been told something similar by Claudia and by Natalie as well.

Even God himself had acknowledged that she was befitting the role of eldest of the Valkyrie sisters.

"There is no special blessing inherent to it. It is simply a name. I have no intention of spreading it around. It is simply a vow from me to you. You are befitting that name, my daughter."

"…I've come a long way from someone who wouldn't be missed if she died."

"Don't joke like that. I would much rather you not die in any operation." With that, Odin looked at Rusalka closely. "My child, you are splendid. Fate has put you on a cruel path. But you have chosen to continue to struggle against the hardships placed before you instead of turning back. Allow me to grant you a reward."

"A reward…"

"Ask whatever you like. To the extent I am able, I will grant your wish. As I am now, I lack the ability to grant something absurd, but…"

"Ah, in that case, I do have a request."

Rusalka immediately had a wish, speaking up without hesitation.

"Oh," Odin remarked. "Very well, then. What is it you desire?"

"Please make it so that noises from inside this room cannot be heard outside for a little while."

Odin's eyes widened a bit at the terribly uninteresting request. Rusalka put her hand to her chest.

"I'm going to cry very loudly now. I don't want anyone to be able to hear it."

"—I understand. I shall honor your wish, my daughter."

Treating her request with earnestness and not making a joke of it, Odin solemnly snapped his fingers. And then he quietly turned around and departed through the portal he had entered.

The door clicked shut. Grateful for his consideration, Rusalka sucked in a deep breath.

"—Gh."

And then everything she had been holding in finally erupted.

Tears poured from her eyes as thoughts of everyone who had been lost overwhelmed her.

Rusalka wept. For her friends, her subordinates, her comrades.

She wept and wept and wept. Crying like a child.

She cried how she had been blessed to have met them. About how devastated she was having lost them.

About what a large part of her life they had been to her.

——And she kept crying.

4

She didn't feel like she would grow used to her new chair anytime soon.

But she didn't have the time to gradually grow accustomed to it. Even if it had been a great leap forward, humanity didn't have the luxury to wait for their officers to gradually grow into their positions.

Humanity needed them to break out of their shells as soon as possible. All the more so when it came to a commander charged with safekeeping the lives of every person on a base.

"—Captain Shannon Stewart, you are hereby ordered to take command of Sigrdrifa Squadron. Henceforth, you will be in charge of leading them."

There were two Valkyries lined up in front of the base commander's desk.

They were both familiar faces, but their attitudes were different. Given how all their positions had changed, they couldn't interact the way they used to.

At the very least, that was what Rusalka cautioned herself as she sat in the base commander's chair.

"Yes, ma'am… It's a heavy burden you just saddled me with, though."

"I believe you can handle this. Do your best."

It was a response befitting Shannon, but after Rusalka gave her a few words of encouragement, she turned her gaze to the second Valkyrie. To Alma Conturo, who was standing next to Shannon, looking terribly apathetic.

"I also have something to tell you, Alma."

"...Me?"

Alma responded with an emotionless voice.

Ever since the battle, Alma's heart had frozen over, and she avoided all contact with those around her. It was clear for all to see that it was rooted in the fear of losing anything else.

She alone didn't seem to realize the cause. Rusalka wasn't sure if what she was about to say was the right thing to do for Alma, but—

"Lord Odin has bestowed a reward on you for your defeat of Mistletoe—think of it like a title that is granted only to special Valkyries."

"——"

"Sveið. That is the name Odin has granted you."

Alma's brow twitched when she heard that name.

Perhaps she had heard it before, as indicated by her minute reaction. Having confirmed that, Rusalka took a short breath before continuing.

"Also, I was the one who ordered Natalie to fly that day."

"—?!"

"Major?!"

Alma's expression changed dramatically when she heard that. And Shannon reflexively addressed her by the rank she had grown accustomed to. Two very different kinds of shock filled the room.

"...What do you mean?" Alma demanded.

"There is nothing to explain. I merely wanted to face Mistletoe with the greatest force possible. Commander Ostley gathered Valkyries from bases all over the front, but I wanted to be prepared in the event of unforeseen circumstances. That was why I ordered Natalie's last flight."

"—Ngh."

Rusalka deliberately kept her tone cold, and Alma's reaction was immediate. Emotion was visibly returning to her frozen eyes. A terrible rage. Rage at Rusalka for sending Natalie to her death—

"I want to be clear on that, for Commander Ostley's sake."

"Is that all?"

"...What do you mean?"

"—Whatever..."

Rusalka clearly narrowed her eyes as Alma averted her gaze in abject disappointment. She gave a perfunctory salute and then turned away from Rusalka and left the room.

And once the door closed, separating them—

"I understand what you're trying to do, but that's a little too tactless, Major."

"...I'm not a major anymore. I was promoted to lieutenant colonel in order to assume command of the base. You should begin to adjust yourself accordingly. And also..."

"Also?"

"Take care of Alma. You don't have to worry about me."

Shannon exhaled in exasperation as Rusalka shook her head. And then she shrugged.

"You know you don't have to twist yourself up worrying about others just because you're the oldest sister, right?"

"———"

"If you'll excuse me, ma'am—mine eye for thee."

Performing a Valkyrie salute, Shannon hurriedly left the room.

She really was incredibly perceptive. Even if she was several years younger, Shannon saw through Rusalka's clumsy thought process with ease.

—People were much more likely to throw away their lives when they lost their attachment to everything around them and fell into despair.

Emotions were necessary to continue living. Sometimes hatred could be a great teacher and grant the necessary motivation to carry on.

Even if it was a lie, if that lie could be the kindling that kept Alma alive, then...

"Even if you hate me, I will never hate you."

Even if Alma hated Rusalka, despised her more than anyone else, as long as that hatred was what kept her alive, then Rusalka was fine with that.

Even if she had taken a step back from the front lines as a Valkyrie and assumed the position of base commander, Rusalka Evereska's vigil was not over.

It had only just begun.

She had never gotten a chance to tell him directly. Rusalka had a lot to learn as she tried to fill the shoes of the great man who had been her predecessor.

As she turned her thoughts to something else—

—an unfamiliar horn echoed, almost seeming to shake the whole base to its foundations.

A girl heard it as she walked through the hall, her shoulders squared as she swore vengeance for her friend.

A girl heard it as she struggled with what to do next, worried about both her friend and her clumsy commanding officer.

A girl heard it as she tried to brush her hair while thinking of a promise that she had not been able to keep.

A girl heard it as she smiled awkwardly at that terrible brushing and took the comb from her friend to brush out her hair for her.

And a girl heard it as she felt a mysterious twinge in her heart, unsure what to do with a room for two that she had to herself.

"—Gjallarhorn."

The resounding horn of legend. Hearing it go off, Rusalka stood up.

It was the tool humanity had newly acquired, signaling the opening of the next stage in their war against the invading pillars of light. The step forward that humanity had won at such a great cost—

She hurriedly headed for the command post. But just before she left the room, her hand resting on the door, she glanced back at the desk. And for just a second, she saw the image of a man smiling that smile that was always so full of confidence.

"I'm going now."

With that, she leaped out of the room and ran boldly through the hall as she saw everyone around the base frantically rushing to their posts.

As she burst into the command post—

"Status report!"

"Confirmed precursor signal from a pillar! From Gjallarhorn's response, it will appear twenty kilometers to the northwest."

"The enemy is expected to be a type-C secondary, accompanied by multiple tertiaries!"

Rusalka inhaled sharply as she received the report from the operator who had already begun an analysis.

Previously, they had never been able to get information like that before a pillar had appeared. Gjallarhorn would surely have a dramatic impact on the war going forward.

It would make it more likely for Valkyries to survive—just like the younger sister had wished for her older sister.

"Commander, the Valkyries have completed preparations to take off!"

As a deep emotion gripped her heart for just a second, she received another report. On the monitor right in front of her, she saw several Deus ex Machinas lined up at the ready on the runway.

Gathered by Alejandro and broken in by Rusalka, they were the world's strongest fighting force.

The squadron that would carry on the fight going forward. To win a future for humanity and so that they would live to see another day as well.

"—Sigrdrifa, launch!"

"*—Roger!*"

The Valkyries responded to her order and began to leap into the air.

Spreading their wings, the Valkyries took to the skies.

The sky was clear and blue as far as the eye could see. The same sky that Rusalka loved and had longed to soar through from a young age.

The same sky that humanity had looked up to in wonder from before the beginning of written history. That unchanging expanse that brought with it the promise of a new tomorrow.

Though they had lost much, they were still bound together in pursuit of their common future. That was humanity's unrefined, desperate way of fighting.

"Let's fight, to claim the tomorrow we all wish for."

Rusalka—the woman called Sigrdrifa by God—had made up her mind. No matter what it took, she would bring a tomorrow to every last person she could.

Because that was the wish of the selfish, pitiful girl who had chosen Rusalka as her witness.

She would push onward for the sake of that hope, that singular wish, so as not to bring shame to the people who had gone before her.

"To find our way through the Ragnarök that lies before us."

* * *

Because that was all Rusalka Evereska could do. This was her awkward attempt at repaying the people most precious to her.

5

——It was a white, white space.

He walked through a vast white emptiness with no sign of any notable landmarks. Just walking forward aimlessly. But his footsteps were light. He had left everything to the person he trusted most in the world.

If his footsteps weren't light after that, then that would make his final statement a lie—

"—Isn't that reeeeally selfish, Big Brother?"

All of a sudden, he heard a sweet voice. Right in front of him, there was someone standing at the end of his white path.

It was a girl. She had her hands on her hips and long golden hair swaying around her childish face.

"Don't force such unreasonable demands on my Rusalka."

"...You waited for me?"

"Don't be silly. I'm not that inconsiderate. If anything, I'm an angel."

Pouting, she stuck out her tongue adorably. And then she smiled at her brother, Alejandro, who had fulfilled his duty even after death.

"But knowing you, I was sure you wouldn't go to Valhalla. That's all!"

"Yeah, I love you, too."

"Grrr! I know you pulled the same thing with Rusalka!"

She puffed out her cheeks as Alejandro grinned and rested his big hand on her head. And then he kept patting her head until her mood improved.

"They said I was synonymous with miracles, but..."

If this was the miraculous reward awaiting him in death for all his hard work, then it wasn't all so bad.

Even though so much had slipped through his fingers, and he had been forced to leave so much more for his capable and trusty right hand to clean up...

"—Thanks for all your hard work, Big Brother."
"...Ahhh, yeah..."

...that one line from his beloved younger sister made it feel like it might have all been worth it.

The End.

Afterword

Hello, everyone, this is Tappei Nagatsuki!

Last time, the afterword got a little muddled as I struggled with how I should introduce myself, but you don't have to worry this time! I can't imagine there are that many people who would pick up the second half of a two-part story. And if there are, I'm sorry!

Also, for those for whom this is just your second book by Nagatsuki, this all may be coming off as overly familiar, but if you don't mind letting that slide, I would appreciate it. Let's build a comfortable relationship with a bit of give-and-take from both sides!

Anyway, that was *Warlords of Sigrdrifa Rusalka*. Thank you very much for reading along. For those of you who like to read the afterword first, consider this a thank-you in advance. And if you are one of the people in a bookstore reading this, allow me to cut off your line of retreat by saying, "If you're reading this, I'm right behind you. Thank you for your purchase."

Whichever group you happen to fall into, I hope you enjoyed this book.

As I discussed in the last volume, this is a spin-off of the original anime *Warlords of Sigrdrifa*, a prequel to the events of that story.

As you can tell from the anime's official site, it features one of the characters who appears in this book. In the anime, she is one of the main protagonists, and her feats are covered in great detail. Of course, please keep an eye out for the appearance and performances of several of the other characters who have appeared in these short stories as well. I'm the type of person who likes to lick their plate clean. Metaphorically speaking of course!

I am extraordinarily relieved to have gotten both parts of this story to publication without any delays, but this is not actually the end of the prelude to *Sigrdrifa*. True to its name, this covered Rusalka's story. It's an episode on the European front from before the anime, but the anime takes place in Japan! Which means, naturally, there must be a prelude touching on the story there as well.

Because of that, the next story will be on the Japanese side—*Warlords of Sigrdrifa Sakura*.

As the war with the pillars heats up all around the world, the second phase of the prelude stars one of Japan's Valkyries, Sakura Okita, a classic Japanese beauty!

There is a possibility the title will be changed, so please don't take it as written in stone! The general contents should not be changed, though, so please look forward to the next installment without any reservations about this being a fake preview!

I digress, but while a certain virus has been proliferating around the world, it has not really had any major effect on my personal workload as an author. As ever, I've been hounded to keep writing. But my work efficiency has gone down, since I can't just sit and work at my local family restaurant anymore! Curse you, virus. Not only delaying the anime's broadcast but even intruding upon my sanctuary?! How much must you make me suffer…?!

Anyway, while I have been dwelling on my hopes for the future and those resentful complaints, my daily page count has been limited.

Allow me to borrow this platform and shift to the usual thanks and acknowledgments.

To my editor Kida, thank you for allowing me to proceed with such high performance despite the novel making everything a mess. I am in awe at how implacably you withstood being sent a draft that had even fewer survivors than discussed at the plot stages! I will do my best next time as well!

To the illustrator, Takuya Fujima, thank you for all your support in this book as well! The cover with the Brafford sisters was particularly beautiful, and the scenes depicting Alma and Natalie were truly a delight. To see such an unexpected synergy deepening the characters' bonds is one of the joys of being an author. Let's keep pushing each other to greater heights in the next book as well!

I of course received help from Takaaki Suzuki with the military setting and research. I'm utterly out of the loop with military things in general, so Suzuki provided a great amount of assistance with this volume as well. The anime is also a product of our tag team, so please look forward to that as well!

And also to all the people in the editorial offices of Sneaker Bunko and to the proofreaders and the people at various bookstores, without whom this book would not have been published. It is thanks to you that this book made it to publication.

And with the anime premiere to look forward to, thank you to all the people involved with the anime who have been plugging away at the production. Unlike the individual work of a novelist, an anime needs the efforts of so many people working at the production, so having worked together to get past such a difficult situation, I hope *Sigrdrifa* will be a hit. I can't wait to continue our work together!

And finally, my greatest thanks to you readers who have picked up this book. With this, the curtain will fall on Rusalka's story for now, but the story of this world will continue on in the form of the anime and even more light novels. It is because of all of you that I am able to work as a creator in such a fortunate position. I hope you will enjoy the future stories of *Sigrdrifa* as well.

I hope we will meet again in the next book! Thank you so much!

May 2020 (Hoping for the sun during the long rains)

Read the light novel that inspired the hit anime series!
Re:ZeRo
-Starting Life in Another World-
Re:ZeRo
-Starting Life in Another World-
TAPPEI NAGATSUKI
SHINICHIROU OTSUKA
Re:ZeRo
-Starting Life in Another World-
TAPPEI NAGATSUKI
SHINICHIROU OTSUKA
ART: DAICHI MATSUSE
Re:ZeRo
-Starting Life in Another World-
Chapter 1: A Day in the Capital
ART: DAICHI MATSUSE
Re:ZeRo
-Starting Life in Another World-
Chapter 1: A Day in the Capital
Also be sure to check out the manga series!
AVAILABLE NOW!